Three Weddings
and a
Scandal

Wendy
HOLDEN

HEAD
of ZEUS

First published in the UK in 2017 by Head of Zeus, Ltd
as *Laura Lake and the Hipster Weddings*
This paperback edition first published in 2017 by Head of Zeus, Ltd

9 7 5 3 1 2 4 6 8

A catalogue record for this book is available from
the British Library.

ISBN (PB): 9781784977566
ISBN (E): 9781784977535

Typeset by Adrian McLaughlin

Printed and bound in Great Britain by
CPI Group (UK) Ltd, Croydon CR0 4YY

Head of Zeus Ltd
First Floor East
5–8 Hardwick Street
London EC1R 4RG

WWW.HEADOFZEUS.COM

To Red Dog and Bluepistol

Three Weddings and a Scandal

Chapter One

Laura Lake sat on the bed, staring into space. She did not move. Amy Bender had told her not to. To move, she had said, would compromise the integrity of the piece.

Amy Bender was a British contemporary artist. The piece was an installation named *Call This Art?* It consisted of a dirty mattress on the floor surrounded by rubbish.

The floor on which the mattress lay was in Paris, in an ex-morgue turned exhibition space. Amy had chosen the site because it was Paris Fashion Week. A number of edgy designer shows were taking place at a nearby abattoir. It was the intention of the newly graduated, drivingly ambitious Amy that the fashion crowd leaving the slaughterhouse would be tempted into the morgue. Her career would then be launched.

Laura's own career was some distance from launching. She was currently earning a pittance working for a firm that rented flats in Paris to rich holidaying Americans. The business was owned by a pugnacious New Yorker called Ulrika Burgwinkle who directed operations from Brooklyn. Laura was the Paris face of the business: meeter-and-greeter, blog-writer, concierge and general dogsbody.

As Ulrika was still building up the business and most clients arrived at night, sometimes right in the middle of it, Laura had little to do during the day. She filled her time writing articles for the rentals company blog, which Ulrika said should cover current trends. 'There's always some crazy new fashion in Paris,' she instructed from New York. 'Cat-racing, naked restaurants, yadda yadda.'

Laura was yet to come across cat-racing and was not actively seeking naked dining. But yesterday she had found a salon where face-shaving for women was all the rage. Removing the tiny fuzzy hairs gave one a whole new glow, apparently.

Afterwards, Laura had been sitting outside a cafe, rubbing her stinging cheeks and worrying about five o'clock shadow when Amy Bender loomed over her. Laura stared at the strange woman in red patent eighteen-hole Dr Marten boots, black leggings and a Pussy Riot T-shirt. She had musty blonde dreadlocks that sat on her head like a heap of old rope and she was clutching an iPhone with a neon green cover.

'Are you French?' Amy Bender demanded in English.

'Half-French,' Laura replied. 'My dad was English and I went to school there. But now I live here with my grand-mother.'

'Well, you look Parisian,' Amy Bender declared, 'which is all I care about. You've got that whole Jane Birkin thing going on.'

Laura let pass the fact that Jane Birkin was English as well. As for the thing going on, she had hit on her uniform of ankle boots, skinny black jeans and navy shirts years ago. She had stuck to it because it was cheap, easy and suited her. A big scarf and a trenchcoat were the only variations.

She listened to Amy Bender explain her artistic concept. It sounded silly, but no sillier than the tour of Parisian sewers or the man who kept chickens in his flat that she had recently covered for the blog.

'There's a day of rehearsing tomorrow and then the show opens. After that, we'll see how it goes.'

Amy Bender was not paying much. But any money was welcome. The only potential problem was Ulrika ringing and demanding she rush to the Marais to show some Californians how to use the toilet. Parisian loos had semi-human qualities and required very careful handling. But she'd cross that U-bend when she came to it.

And so she said yes. Unwisely, as she had come to realise. The mattress had a horrid, musty odour which the dirty fast-food cartons surrounding it, smeared with ketchup and congealed *frites*, only made worse. And Laura's back was killing her. Amy had specified that she sit with her legs twisted to the side, Little Mermaid-style, rather than with her arms round her knees, which might have been more comfortable.

Sensory deprivation was another issue. Beyond the retina-frazzling spotlight, all was as black as the blackest hole. This was deliberate and emphasised the theme of alienation, which was, Amy Bender claimed, central to *Call This Art?* The work's other alleged themes were life and death, being and nothingness, belief and scepticism, hope and despair, and knowledge and ignorance.

But the main theme, it seemed to Laura, was money. There was obviously plenty behind Amy Bender. Someone had paid to hire this space in the up-and-coming rue Morgue. Someone had flown Amy over and was bankrolling her stay at La Morticienne, a nearby boutique hotel. Someone was paying for Jamie Dodger, the London-based PR professional coordinating the guest list for the private view of *Call This Art?* tomorrow night. Today was the dress rehearsal.

Laura felt sorry for Jamie. Amy was hardly ever off the phone to him, barking that she didn't just want the fashion crowd who were in Paris for the shows, she wanted the celebrities and artists invited by the designers as well. Her voice bounced off the morgue walls as she strode up and down.

'Have we heard from Will and Kate? Kate Winslet? Ned Rocknroll?'

Her mockney tones mingled strangely with the echoing voiceover which completed the installation's alienating effect. This was a loop tape on which a loud and expressionless male voice endlessly repeated four words with a two-second pause between each.

'There had better be a good crowd!'

'HATE!' went the voiceover.

'Did you ask Damien and Tracey? The Beckhams?'

'BEANS!'

'Have you heard from Anna Wintour yet?'

'FEAR!'

'And Bono?'

'CHEESEBURGER!'

'This tape's doing my crust in,' groaned Caspar, who sat beside Laura on the mattress. He was the other person in the installation, a resting actor from London. He was not especially tall and not especially bright, but made up for this by being extremely handsome. He had floppy dark hair, big melting eyes and huge white teeth.

4

Caspar, who was two years older than Laura, had been sitting outside Coffin and Son, one of rue Morgue's fashionable craft coffee bars, when Amy Bender swooped.

'She thought I was Parisian because I was wearing a T-shirt that said Paris on it,' he told Laura. His surname was Honeyman and at university he'd been part of a successful double-act called Cheese and Onion. The other half was someone called Orlando Chease.

'I think I've heard of him,' Laura said. 'He's quite famous, isn't he?'

A pained expression crossed Caspar's face. His own acting career was a lot less successful than his erstwhile partner's. Having failed to get in to drama school, he had spent eight months demonstrating toys in Hamleys, working in call centres and re-enacting the Battle of Hastings at English Heritage properties. There was, Caspar said, no fury quite like that of children forced to visit historic buildings at the expense of an afternoon on the Xbox. Especially when they were armed with wooden swords.

Though he was amusing about his lack of acting success, it was obvious Caspar was frustrated at his failure. Laura could see that he had genuine talent; he was, for instance, a surprisingly good ventriloquist. 'But no one wants ventriloquists now,' he lamented. 'If only it was 1912. I'd have gone down a storm at the Hackney Empire between Vesta Tilley and The Dancing Dogs of Dagenham.'

His ability to speak without moving his lips did, however, come in handy on *Call This Art?* It meant that he could still talk despite the Bender embargo on movement or conversation. As could Laura, once Caspar had taught her. It was quite fun, she found, and helped pass the time.

Caspar was impressed with her ability. 'You're a natural,'

he told her, without moving his lips. 'Which is amazing, given how big your mouth is.' He then glanced around to check Amy's whereabouts before moving his face in close and planting it on hers.

'Get off!' Laura gasped, pushing him away. She was shocked at his audacity but even more at the bolt of pleasure he had sent through her.

'Spoilsport.' Caspar pouted from under his long lashes.

'All you ever think about is sex,' accused Laura.

'Your point? I'm sitting on a mattress all day next to a gorgeous bird. What else am I supposed to think about?'

'I'm not interested.'

'Yes you are,' Caspar teased. 'Why resist the irresistible? You're young, free, single and gorgeous. And so am I.'

Caspar was sleeping on a friend's floor in Montparnasse. It sounded as if the friend was getting fed up with the arrangement. He would be going back to London as soon as the Bender installation was over. 'Come with me,' he said, as if it really was as easy as that.

Laura shook her head. 'Thanks, but I can't. I've got to stay here. I've got my grandmother to look after.'

'Can't she look after herself?'

'She's ninety-three,' Laura pointed out.

'Well, mine's eighty and runs every committee in the village. She also plays bridge and gardens like a maniac. Only ever sits down to sentence juvenile delinquents.'

She sounded terrifying, Laura thought. It was impossible to imagine her own grandmother doing anything of the sort – the sentencing in particular. Mimi loved young people, especially naughty ones. She was quite naughty herself, invariably starting the day in the downstairs bar reading the newspapers with a glass of champagne.

'You're joking,' Caspar said when Laura found herself mentioning this.

'She says the news looks better that way. She thinks everyone should do it.'

Caspar cackled. 'Sounds like quite a dame. What else does she say?'

Laura grinned. 'Loads of things. How long have you got?'

Caspar's dark eyes twinkled in the piercing spotlight. 'Till the end of this rehearsal, and as long as you like after that.'

'Okay then, you asked for it. Put tights on with wet hands so you don't get holes in them.'

'I'm definitely trying out that one.'

'Always rub the soles of new shoes with cut potatoes.'

'Why?'

'Stops them being slippy. Oh, and be wary of labels. Double Cs, D & G, YSL. You are not a billboard. Letters are for the optician's chart.'

'I'm throwing out my Chanel now!'

'No leather or stretch denim after forty! No furs after fifty! Put perfume behind your knees!'

'Blimey, how did she think up all this stuff?'

Laura smiled. She wasn't entirely sure herself and perhaps there wasn't a straight answer. Mimi's style philosophy, like the wonderful soups she regularly made, was the product of many different ingredients. It was part natural flair, part *joie de vivre* and part wit, along with an observant eye and a big dollop of experience. Other elements were common sense and the need to economise, all forged in the crucible of wartime Paris.

'Ever thought of writing all this down?'

Laura had, in fact. 'Parisienne' style guides were popular at the moment and a collection of her grandmother's hints and tips would be the best of the lot. Mimi, however, had not been keen. 'She thinks writing a style guide would be boring,' Laura told Caspar.

'And I'm guessing boring isn't stylish.'

'Exactly!'

'I can see why you want to look after her. I'd quite like to myself.'

'Hands off!' Laura chuckled. 'But yes, I can't leave her. She's looked after me ever since...' She stopped, her smile fading.

'Ever since what?' Caspar ventriloquised, as Amy Bender came past.

Laura wanted to tell him to mind his own business. Instead she found herself replying, 'Ever since my father died and Odette moved back to France and remarried.'

'Odette's your stepmother?'

'My mother, actually.' Not that it had ever felt like it. 'I'm on my third stepfather now. He's a perma-tanned hairdresser called Leon with teeth you can see from space.'

'Big, you mean?'

'Kind of blindingly white. And he's got huge bouffant hair.' Laura stopped. Caspar's own teeth were of a preternatural brilliance and his hair, while floppy, had a front that was high and full. Thankfully, he seemed not to have made this connection.

This latest wedding had been last winter, in Monaco. Odette's once taut jawline had been buried in the collar of a squashy blonde fur coat. Her pale blonde hair, which had been brown on Laura's rare childhood sightings of it, was set off by a matching fur hat. Leon too was resplendent in furs, along with a bright pink tie that matched his gums. Mimi had not been present, claiming the journey from Paris was too long. Odette had made no secret of her relief. The two of them had never got on.

Odette had not seemed especially pleased to see Laura either, but there was nothing new in that. 'Really, Laura. Jeans for a wedding!'

'And that hair!' shuddered Leon. 'Just let me get my hands on it!'

Laura would rather have died. She hated Leon's gloopy serums, sprays and mousses, all bearing his signature lion logo and encased in his signature pink bottles. Laura did her hair herself at home, chopping the fringe and ends with kitchen scissors whenever it needed it.

'You're still wearing that old coat!' Odette scoffed, adjusting her glossy sables and pursing her thickly lipsticked mouth.

Her mother really didn't have the first idea, Laura thought. Had Mimi never told her that if a Parisienne could wear just a Burberry trench with nothing underneath, she would be in heaven? Her grandmother's personal brand of elegance had skipped a generation. A cornerstone of her beauty philosophy was not to be scared of ageing, but that Odette was terrified of it was obvious. Her brow was entirely smooth, her trout pout enormous. Leon, too, was doing his Canute-like best to turn back the tide of time. His eyes were strangely hooded and his brows permanently raised in an expression of surprise that Laura was sure he never felt. Curiosity was not one of her stepfather's traits.

Caspar was asking her something.

'What?'

'You don't live with them?' he repeated.

She suppressed a shudder. Her mother and Leon lived in a flat whose view of Monaco harbour was permanently obstructed by superyachts the size of shopping centres. It was from here that Leon danced attendance on his clientele of thin-haired elderly duchesses and oligarchs' wives of the old school who wanted bouffants of a Kremlin solidity. He was often flown out to their yachts; arriving, in the case of one wife, in the same helicopter as the Fortnum & Mason sausages she was particularly partial to. Laura did not explain all this to Caspar, preferring merely to shake her head. Hopefully he would take the hint and stop the questions.

She had hoped in vain, however. 'What did your father do?' he asked next.

'Journalist,' Laura said shortly. 'A foreign correspondent.'

Caspar's eyes widened. 'Shot in action?'

'Yes, actually.'

There was an awkward pause, then Caspar changed the subject to university. 'I'm guessing Oxford.'

'Never went to any. After A levels I just came here and got a job.'

'Didn't go to uni?' Caspar was so amazed, he forgot to ventriloquise. 'Got a *job*?'

'No talking!' barked Amy Bender, coming past again and using the toe of her boot to adjust the position of a hamburger carton.

'What job?' Caspar hissed, poker-faced, after Amy had stomped off into the darkness. 'Can't be a very good one or you wouldn't be doing this.'

'It isn't. I work for a company called Paradise in Paris.'

'Is that an escort agency?'

Laura couldn't resist teasing him. 'Kind of. I do meet clients late at night. I've got to meet one tonight, in fact.'

Once Amy Bender had gone for lunch, to which they were not invited, Laura switched off the alienating voiceover tape. Blessed silence descended. Caspar lay on his back practising his Alexander Technique. He sat up immediately when Laura handed him his phone, having called up the Paradise in Paris site.

'Holiday rentals?' Caspar sounded pained, which he was. In his eagerness to see he had raised himself too quickly and had pulled a muscle in his back. 'Thought you were a posh whore.'

The expensive apartments on the Paradise in Paris site were supported by evocative shots of the city. Most were very up close, such as the shot of a macaroon as seen by the macaroon next to it, or the one showing how a rose might appear to a fly about to land.

'The prices are amazing,' said Caspar, examining images of snowy bedsheets and roll-top bathtubs. 'So people let their places when they're out of Paris for a few weeks?'

'People let their places out whenever anyone wants them. They just move in to the local Novotel and wait for the rent cheque.'

Caspar was opening the blog tab. He started to laugh. 'A bloke who keeps chickens in his flat? Why?'

'He sells the eggs at the trendy farmers' markets.'

'He's called Jacques Oeuf? You're not serious.'

Laura sighed. Jacques Oeuf had been all too serious. And seemingly without a sense of smell. He lived in unimaginable squalor three floors above the rue de Belleville.

'You write really well,' Caspar said. 'Seriously, you're wasted on this. Don't you want to write for a paper? Be a derring-do reporter like Pops?'

Laura shrugged. Of course she did. But she had no intention of admitting as much to Caspar. It was her dearest, wildest and most private dream, though it was hardly likely to happen. She had no connections (her father had been dead for fifteen years) or idea how to go about it. She wasn't even in the right country. London was the capital of journalism and here she was in Paris.

Far away in the darkness, a door banged. 'Quick,' she hissed. 'Get into position. Amy's coming back.'

Chapter Two

Later, Laura went to meet Ulrika's client in the place Dauphine. It was Paris's priciest square and the apartment here was Laura's favourite. It occupied the entire second floor of one of the *place*'s lovely seventeenth-century buildings and was a hymn to wealthy good taste.

Just walking across the lobby made you feel elegant. Laura loved the tap of her boot-heels on the marble floor and up the curving stone staircase that led to the apartment's polished door. A polished door that, Laura now saw, a woman was standing outside. She seemed to be trying the door handle.

'Miss Gold?' Laura called, scampering up the last few stairs. But it was already obvious that the woman now turning round was not the client. Carinthia Gold was a glamorous senior blonde with pale skin and a restrained personal style. This woman had tousled long black hair and wore a short ruched red dress with silver high heels. The parts of her not caked in make-up looked dipped in Ronseal.

'Can I help you?' Laura called, as the woman clattered rapidly up the staircase in the direction of the apartments above. She was relieved when answer came there none. Something and nothing, no doubt.

What had been demonstrated beyond all doubt, however, was that Carinthia Gold was not at home. Typical, Laura thought. Few Paradise in Paris clients credited her with a life of her own or the desire to do anything other than sit around waiting for them. The reverse also applied; clients were supposed to be checked out by Laura but frequently failed to stick to the rules. It was more than possible that Carinthia Gold had already gone.

Laura let herself into the flat. The hall's shining floorboards looked emptily back up at her. No key had been pushed through the letterbox. Had Carinthia taken that with her too?

The sound of footsteps now sounded on the stairs outside. Laura opened the door just in time to see the mysterious black-haired woman clack across the lobby in her silver heels and disappear through the front door. She seemed to be in a great hurry.

Laura did not dwell on the episode. Parisian apartment blocks were full of strange people doing odd things. The Montmartre one where her grandmother had lived for the last fifty years was especially rich in idiosyncratic residents. Perhaps the woman upstairs had had a message for Carinthia, a note maybe, although, looking around, Laura could see nothing on the floor.

She started her check-round. Soft grey panelling hung with gold-framed paintings lined the walls of the sitting room.

The moonlight looked so lovely that Laura paused before switching on the lamps. It shone in through the stately windows, its silver beams shimmering on the chandelier, glancing off the varnished lid of the harpsichord and gleaming on the Venetian mirror. Had Carinthia Gold appreciated any of this?

Laura doubted it. She hadn't seemed the appreciative type. She had arrived very late in the evening some days before. Waiting for her in the apartment, Laura had felt the mobile in her pocket buzz with a text.

Miss Gold is at the front door. My best, Xanthe Vernon, PA to Carinthia Gold

She had gone downstairs to find Miss Gold standing beside a people carrier in the lamplit street. Despite its being near midnight she was wearing enormous, intensely black sunglasses and tapping into a phone screen with thin gold-ringed fingers. Her extreme slenderness was accentuated by narrow black trousers, accessorised with gleaming patent pumps and a snakeskin handbag dangling with gold trinkets. She did not look at Laura.

Three large, wheeled suitcases of gleaming black ribbed metal stood expectantly on the pavement. The taxi driver, grumbling audibly, was extracting another from the back of the people carrier.

A second text from Xanthe Vernon had shuddered into Laura's mobile. *Miss Gold would like you to take her luggage upstairs. My best, Xanthe Vernon, PA to Carinthia Gold*

Ping. *Miss Gold is wondering why you are just standing there. My best, Xanthe Vernon, PA to Carinthia Gold*

Laura went to check the kitchen. The period elegance which informed the other rooms here gave way to uncompromising modernity. Harpsichords and chandeliers were all very well elsewhere, but no one wanted an eighteenth-century kitchen.

This one, accordingly, was all polished steel and the latest appliances. There were machines for grinding your coffee and slicing your truffles. There was an 'intelligent' wine rack which chilled your Pol Roger whilst maintaining at room temperature your Pétrus.

It didn't look as if Carinthia Gold had used any of this, but Laura had been warned that she wouldn't. Xanthe Vernon had sent messages to that effect as well.

The front door banged open. Laura dashed into the hall and almost collided with Carinthia, who glared at her. 'What are you doing here?'

Laura explained about the check-out. 'I thought you'd gone. I wouldn't have let myself in otherwise. I'm sorry.'

'I've been at a meeting,' the other woman snapped.

One that hadn't gone well, Laura guessed. She wondered what Miss Gold did. The existence of Xanthe, the PA, suggested she was a high-powered company director of some sort. She had that plain-clothes-with-fabulous-jewellery look that Laura associated with mistresses of the universe. Today she was wearing an elegantly simple, biscuit-coloured dress that ended bang on her bony knees. The lobes of both ears glittered with what looked like enormous diamonds, but they couldn't be real, surely. A gold cuff gleamed on one thin arm and a status-symbol watch on the other – the type you never actually owned but looked after for the next generation.

Ping! *Miss Gold will be leaving now. Her luggage is in the bedroom. Kindly call a taxi for her and arrange for the bags to be taken downstairs. My best, Xanthe Vernon, PA to Carinthia Gold*

Laura texted the usual cab firm and continued her check-round of the flat. She was distracted by a muttered curse from Carinthia, who had pushed up her vast shades to scan the contents of her bag. Her hooded, snake-like green eyes were narrowed in irritation. 'Where the *hell* did I leave it?'

'You've lost something?'

'No shit, Sherlock,' Carinthia snapped, nastily.

'What was it?' Laura politely persevered.

'My wallet. Must have left it in the cab just now. *Bugger.*'

'Do you remember the name of the cab company?'

'No!'

'Might Xanthe?'

'*Who?*'

'Your PA,' Laura prompted.

'Is that what she's called? God, you must be joking. Hardly knows what day it is.'

As there was little else she could do, Laura pulled a sympathetic face and continued checking round. In the master bedroom, where the enormous metal cases were lined up against the wall, she glanced under the sleigh bed. You often found hairbrushes and pairs of knickers there. Nothing today, though.

Wait...

Was there a shape under there, something small? Right in the middle of the floor? Yes. Definitely. With her arm fully extended, she could just about touch it.

The something was cool and slippery. She walked it towards her under her fingers and finally pulled it out. It was a long wallet of beautifully soft black leather, sealed with a circular gold clasp.

Laura rubbed it on her jeans to get rid of under-bed dust and hurried back into the hall. Carinthia was standing with her back turned, tapping into her phone. She did not look up.

'Is this your wallet?'

Carinthia's head flew up. 'Where...?'

'Under the bed.'

Something strange was happening to Carinthia's face. Something strained. Something strained, painful and possibly unaccustomed. It was, Laura eventually realised, a smile. 'That's actually quite honest of you,' she said. 'You knew that I thought I'd lost it. There's money in it, you could easily have kept it. You obviously need it.'

Was it that evident? Laura felt even more messy and scruffy next to this polished and elegant woman. Carinthia gave an airy wave. 'Oh, you don't look it. Your hair's actually not too bad. That blunt, slightly uneven look can be hard to get right. Who does it?' She raised a hand and ruffled her own brass-coloured bob.

'*Ciseaux de cuisine,*' Laura said, quick as a flash. Kitchen scissors.

'Caesar de who? Never heard of him. Where's his salon?' Laura smiled. 'In Montmartre.'

'Quite a nice shine.' Carinthia walked around her, studying it. 'I'm guessing Caesar's using bee venom serum?'

Actually it was plain old white-wine vinegar diluted with warm water. Her grandmother swore by it; swore by beer too. 'Better on your hair than your hips,' she would say with the Frenchwoman's distaste for the Englishman's notoriously calorific tipple.

'Caesar de Cuisine,' Carinthia mused, tapping into her screen. 'Nothing's coming up. He's obviously one of those very cool, off-grid ones.' She looked up. 'Now, where were we? Oh yes. Money. I'm guessing you need it, because you let me in the other night. It was late, past midnight. Anyone prepared to hang around like that must be pretty hard up.'

Laura was surprised she had noticed. She hadn't seemed to, at the time.

'Not much of a job, is it?' Carinthia went on. Laura reluctantly admitted that it wasn't. Carinthia tapped her elegant foot. 'Can't you get anything better? You're obviously an intelligent girl.'

Warmed by the unexpected compliment, Laura found herself confessing her journalistic ambitions. What was there to lose? Carinthia was about to leave and they would clearly not meet again.

She was half-expecting Miss Gold to look scornful, but she seemed interested. 'I can see that. Your father was a foreign correspondent, so you want to be a reporter too.'

Laura nodded. 'But I can't see how.'

'Got any writing experience?'

She explained about the blog. Carinthia tapped her screen and peered thoughtfully into it for a while. Then she looked up. 'Ever considered magazines?' she asked, narrowing her snake-like eyes at Laura.

'Magazines?' Laura repeated stupidly.

'It's a way in. You report for the glossies. There's a great track record of magazine journalists going on to newspapers. And vice versa, actually.'

Laura had never thought of this. It didn't quite make sense to her. Magazines were all about fashion and make-up. Neither was her particular area of expertise.

'Magazines are about all sorts of things,' Carinthia stated once Laura had stuttered this out. 'There's beauty and fashion, as you say, but also proper reporting. And of course the papers follow us. Quite slavishly, actually. Lots of stories you see in newspapers were in magazines first.'

Us? 'You work on a glossy magazine?'

Of course, this was Paris Fashion Week. Magazine editors came from all over. And that one was standing in front of her was obvious now. The sunglasses. The PA. *The Devil Wears Prada* manner.

'I am the editor of *Society*,' Carinthia said grandly. 'And the newspapers have followed my stories lots of times. Get me a Unicorn!' Laura was startled. It wasn't a service Ulrika offered.

'I'm not sure...' she began.

'No, no,' Carinthia looked irritated. 'Get me a Unicorn! was the headline for one of my exposés. An investigation into top concierge companies.' She paused, before adding proudly, 'I got Editor of the Year for that.'

'Wow,' said Laura, impressed. She hadn't seen the piece, but she had seen *Society*. She had read it at boarding school.

Many of the girls had magazine subscriptions, so there were always piles of them in the day room. *Society* was the most unashamedly glamorous of all the glossies, full of fabulous parties and beautiful people living perfect lives in wonderful houses. It was a dazzling, ditsy, dashing world light years from anything Laura knew.

'And I might be able to offer you a job, if you want it,' Carinthia added, even more grandly.

'A job?' Laura gasped. Was she hearing right? A job on *Society*? She had never even imagined working somewhere like that.

'As an intern of course. You work your way up. But it's a start. And who knows? Come up with the right idea, get asked to write the story, make the headlines, you can see how it works.'

Laura could hardly speak, so dazzled was she by this fabulous vision. Yes, she could see exactly how it worked. She had always been good at ideas; she had come up with hundreds for Ulrika. She would come up with hundreds more for Carinthia, and they would become huge features stretching over endless pages illustrated lavishly with photographs and flagged up on the cover. Newspapers would pick up these stories and start giving her work too; she would become a famous reporter. It was all so easy, so obvious. The future rolled out before her like a sparkling carpet, glittering with possibility. 'Thank you,' she managed at last.

Carinthia waved her wallet. 'One good turn deserves another. Come to the office, we'll get it set up.'

The editor wasn't just waving her purse now. She was getting something out of it and handing it to Laura. A card with the *Society* logo on it: elegant interlinking black capitals. Below it were the words 'Carinthia Gold, Editor in Chief'. The address was Society House, Winchester Square, London W1.

London. Panic surged through Laura. She hadn't thought of that. She had vaguely imagined filing her headline-grabbing stories from Paris.

'I can't,' she stammered lamely.

Carinthia was bending to pick up some glossy designer carrier bags. She paused to stare. 'Can't?' she echoed acidly. 'Why ever not? Have you nowhere to stay in London?' She made it sound like a personal failing.

'It's not that.' There was Caspar's offer, for what that was worth.

'So what is it then?'

'I've got my grandmother to look after.'

'Your *grandmother*?' The editor's face was a picture of disbelief.

'She's ninety-three. There's only me to look after her.'

'Do you quite realise what you are turning down? There

are girls in London who'd do anything for an internship on *Society*.' The snake eyes were boring into Laura. 'And believe me, when I say *anything*, I mean *anything*.'

Laura was almost weeping. 'I'm sure. And I would so love to do it. But I can't.'

Her phone now chose this moment to burst into a cheery computer-generated pop salute. Carinthia's cab was here.

Carinthia pulled down her shades; the subject was closed. Dejectedly, Laura went to open the apartment door to start wheeling the heavy suitcases out.

Carinthia sailed past and down the stairs. When Laura finally got outside with the cases, she was already enthroned in the people carrier. The windows were tinted, but Laura, struggling with the luggage alongside the taxi driver, could see the glow of her phone screen. She was forgotten. Carinthia was back in her own glossy world.

The driver started up the engine. Laura turned away to begin her heavy-hearted trudge to the Métro.

'Laura Lake!' It was Carinthia's voice. The editor had wound down her window. Her expression, behind the big dark glasses, could not be guessed at.

'If circumstances change, get in touch.'

Laura eagerly assured her that she would. But as the cab rounded the corner her shoulders slumped with guilt. There was only one event that would change her circumstances. And that did not bear thinking about.

Laura arrived back home to find the tiny, white-painted apartment silent. Her grandmother had gone to bed.

She took off her beige trench and hung it on a hook by the door. Then she prised off her ankle boots and tiptoed in striped-socked feet over the polished floorboards. The door of the one bedroom was ajar. She stuck her head in.

The night being warm, the bedroom's French windows were open on to the sliver of balcony and its wrought-iron railings. The sound of voices, the snarl of a motorbike, drifted up from the street. The long white curtains, lifted by the breeze, billowed softly back into the room, touching the edge of the bed.

In it her grandmother lay sleeping under a coverlet massy with pink roses. As usual she wore men's pyjamas – small-sized and made of soft white cotton edged in piping of palest blue. 'Better made, better value and infinitely more elegant than nightdresses.'

Laura regarded her fondly. Mimi looked nothing like her incredible age. While she believed that a woman should not fear growing old, this didn't mean that age shouldn't be argued with. Her hair was a case in point. Mimi did not go to Caesar de Cuisine but to a lady round the corner who cut it into a perfectly smooth side-parted bob. 'The messier the face gets, the neater the hair should be,' Mimi would quip, pointing to her wrinkles.

The same moonlight that had shone on the splendours of the Dauphine flat now turned Mimi's white hair to silver. Laura bent and dropped a soft kiss on her grandmother's unconscious, very clean cheek. 'Never go to bed without taking off your make-up' was what Mimi claimed she wanted on her gravestone.

Her grandmother's faint but distinctive perfume still in her nostrils ('a woman should pick her scent by thirty, then stick with it'), Laura looked out of the open window. Before her, brilliant white against the dark night sky, the illuminated tops of the Sacré-Coeur domes rose above grey mansard roofs.

It was, Laura often thought, like a scene from *An American in Paris*. Or the set of *La Bohème*.

She went into the tiny kitchen. Mimi's apartment was five floors up in a nineteenth-century building perched high on the Butte Montmartre. From this height, one could see the whole of Paris.

It was a view whose every millimetre Laura knew by heart. She had seen it in all weathers, all seasons and at all hours, yet she never tired of it. Its drama and beauty always struck her afresh. She could never decide whether she liked it better by day or, as now, at night. She preferred Notre-Dame at night, its great carved façade glowing with light. But Les Invalides was best on the type of bright, blue-skied winter's day which set the gold dome decorations blazing. The Eiffel Tower was wonderful all the time, rising from the jumble of buildings like a strange, vast, metal flower. By day its lacy ironwork stood black against the white Paris sky, its top often lost in cloud. By night, every hour on the hour, it danced with thousands of glittering lights. Laura loved seeing the great solid construction dissolve into quivering illuminations and now, as if on cue, it did just that. Eight minutes later the magic would stop and the tower would be dark again. But for those eight minutes there was nothing like it, and nowhere in Paris had a better view of it. Not even the palatial place Dauphine apartment.

Laura thought with a pang of Carinthia Gold, now rattling towards London in her first-class Eurostar compartment. But there was no point crying over spilt champagne.

She was staying put in Paris. And now she was going to have supper.

Mimi had promised to make *soupe de poisson* today. On the little hob stood an aluminium pot, and beneath its lid a thick terracotta liquid gave off a rich scent. Laura got a spoon from the drawer and slipped it in, closing her eyes as the flavours exploded on her tongue. Garlic, tomatoes, thyme. The aniseedy tang of dill. Marjoram and the best olive oil they could afford. 'Never stint on the basics,' Mimi would say. 'For the best taste you must build from the bottom.'

Many of the soup's building blocks would have come from Raquin on rue Lepic, a long-established family-run fishmonger whose big tiled windows, six days out of seven, were heaped with sea-fresh wares. Men in blue caps, white overalls and big yellow Wellingtons sold thick-shelled oysters, clams from barrels, pink piles of prawns, and silver fish beached on jagged shores of broken ice. Mimi had been shopping there for half a century and her loyalty earned her as many shells, bones and other flavour-rich scraps as she cared to ask for. Simmered and strained, it was this stock that made the soup so delicious.

Laura switched on the kitchen lights: a row of four suspended over the wooden counter. The soft, rosy glow that now filled the kitchen was another of her grandmother's beauty tricks. Mimi bulk-bought pink bulbs and put them in every lamp in the flat. This made it impossible to read anything, but, she insisted, cast a flattering glow on the face. 'So much cheaper than plastic surgery!'

La vie en rose, Laura thought fondly. The soup was hot now and she ladled some out. She took the bowl to the window, raised the spoon to her lips and savoured the wonderful flavour while looking out at the glittering lights below. How could she even think of leaving?

Chapter Three

The next evening, at the private view for *Call This Art?*, Amy Bender paced about agitatedly in her big red boots. She had painted a row of black dots on her eyelids and stuck a bright red bindi between her brows. Knives and forks had been inserted at irregular intervals in the dreadlocks and rattled as she walked. The Pussy Riot T-shirt had been replaced by a top which looked as if Amy had cut a hole in the crotch of some fishnet tights and stuck her arms down the legs.

This was exactly what had happened, although Amy had not wielded the scissors. That had been done by Irina Pushamoff, a Knightsbridge designer in town for Fashion Week and keen to count artistic geniuses among her clients. Or so she had told Amy when she'd dropped in to the morgue earlier and handed over the top as a gift. Wildly flattered and unable to resist a freebie, Amy had put her straight on the list for the party.

When not courting admirers, Amy had spent the afternoon putting the finishing touches to the installation. She had circled the bed, altering the positions of polystyrene cartons by centimetres and adding wrinkles to the sheets with pinched fingers covered in skull rings. She had also snapped at Caspar to stop playing Angry Birds. When he had switched to Candy Crush, she made him turn off his phone altogether.

Phones had been a source of irritation from the off. Amy's original idea had been that Laura and Caspar should sit side by side, a couple staring into their smartphones and symbolising urban disconnectedness. She had been amazed to discover that Laura didn't have one.

'You don't have a *smartphone*?'

'Just a brick.'

'But why the hell not?'

Laura reddened. The reason was that she could not afford one, but she was reluctant to admit this to Amy, whose artistic imagination did not extend to the idea that not everyone was as rich as she was.

'This is all about urban disconnectedness!' stormed the artist.

Caspar had leant forward. 'But isn't not having a smartphone the ultimate urban disconnectedness?'

The guests were arriving. At the far end of the former morgue, voices could be heard in the gloom. They sounded excited at first and then alarmed, once it became obvious just how dark it was. There were a couple of screams and some shouts.

'Amy? Ames, babe, turn the fucking lights on, can't you?'

A woman in gold trousers covered with zips and a gold

quilted jacket with enormous shoulderpads was the first to appear. She had skilfully streaked blonde hair, a face that had clearly been lifted several times and, daringly given the lighting conditions, towering heels flashing Christian Louboutin's signature red soles.

'Darling!' she shrieked when she saw Amy.

'That's quite an outfit, Ma,' Amy remarked, as if she herself were sporting twinset and pearls rather than dreadlocks with forks sprouting out of them. 'You look like Flash Gordon.'

'Fabulous, isn't it?' Mrs Bender stretched out her quilted arms to expose fingers on which several large diamonds glittered. 'I've discovered this marvellous new designer, Irina Pushamoff. She gave me an enormous discount, which pleased your father no end.'

Mr Bender did not appear pleased at all, let alone to the infinite levels suggested. He looked as furtive as his wife looked exuberant. But unlike her, he had not just downed two champagne cocktails in the Georges V bar for Dutch courage.

The diamonds on Mrs Bender's fingers had confirmed Laura's suspicions that Amy came from a very wealthy background. It was equally evident that Mr Bender was the fount from which all this money flowed. He radiated the stuff, from his designer horn-rimmed spectacles via his perfectly cut grey suit to the soles of his hand-built leather shoes. His look was understated, but this just reinforced the effect.

Laura suppressed the urge to giggle. Amy had given the distinct impression that she'd grown up somewhere edgy: the Bronx, say, or Huddersfield. But it was now easy to guess where her formative years had actually been spent. She could picture the tall white house on the exclusive Notting Hill street where Amy's artistic flame had been fanned once the parent Benders reluctantly accepted she was no good at anything else.

'Irina gave me this top for free, actually,' Amy boasted, stretching out her arms in the fishnet tights. 'Said she wanted my artistic genius on her client list.'

'She said she wanted my taste and discernment!' hit back Mrs Bender.

Laura, overhearing, was impressed. Irina Pushamoff was clearly a mistress of persuasion. She was due to attend the party and judging by her creations so far could be relied on to cut quite a figure.

Amy's mother was looking askance at the glass of white wine being offered. The waiter was from one of the morgue's approved caterers, Le Boeuf sur le Toit, who were also providing the clean-up service afterwards. There had been ructions earlier when they had tried to tidy the mess around the bed.

'Don't you have any Krug?' Mrs Bender enquired.

Mr Bender stood at the edge of the pool of light by the bed. He was frowning at the catalogue and patently wishing for it all to be over. He stood so still and frowned so hard that he could have been part of *Call This Art?* Possibly the person asking the question.

Other people were arriving now, compromising Amy's artistic integrity by using their phones to light the way through the alienating darkness and find out where the bar was.

Laura watched with interest as they emerged into the spotlight. Would one of them be the famous Irina? Or the famous anyone? So far as she knew, Jamie Dodger hadn't produced any definite celebrity acceptances, although he had done a sterling job of covering up the fact. She had heard him earlier reassuring Amy that everyone from Theresa May to Coleen Rooney was 'a ninety-nine point nine nine nine per cent definite yes'.

Laura did not recognise any of the guests now drifting in, and nor did they especially look like the fashion crowd. Most of them were old, male and paunchy. They seemed to be there mainly for the free wine, which they were downing with alacrity in between saying open-ended things to Amy like, 'What a statement!'

Amy was receiving these somewhat equivocal blandishments with a tense expression. In between greeting people she could be heard snarling at Jamie Dodger, who was young with cropped and gelled hair and a rather too tight shiny suit. He looked panicked, as well he might.

'You promised me Victoria Beckham!' Amy accused.

'CHEESEBURGER!'

'And Carole Middleton.'

'FEAR!'

Laura's eye was now caught by a pair of young men standing some distance from one another just within the spotlight's penumbra. Their slim builds and good looks marked them out from the surrounding paunches. But in other regards, they were polar opposites: one wore a grey suit and had dark hair, while the other, whose black suit was of a more fashionable cut, had spiky hair of a startling peroxide white, which contrasted with his dark brows. His large eyes switched constantly about, giving him an excitable air that differed from the other's apparent calm. The dark-haired man's eyes did not move, Laura noticed. They were watching the blonde man closely. She guessed that they were artistic rivals and the man in grey was the less successful one.

'Not even Chu Ginsberg has turned up!' Amy was ranting. 'The fashion blogger?'

'HATE!'

'But Irina Pushamoff is here,' Jamie protested, sending a frisson of anticipation through Laura.

'Amy!' a throaty voice now declared, and a woman emerged from the dark. She had wild black hair and was wearing a bodice of tightly laced black rubber. Her long silver skirt was split down the middle to reveal a pair of cobalt-blue thigh boots with thick platform soles. She seemed vaguely familiar, Laura thought. And yet, how could she be?

'Why's she staring at you?' muttered Caspar.

'My clothes?' Laura guessed, as, from between false lashes of astonishing thickness, Irina Pushamoff continued to look her up and down. 'Probably thinks they're a bit understated.'

'Your show is perfect, darling,' the designer assured Amy in husky tones with only a trace of an accent. 'Truly, you are a genius! A genius!'

'Look! His screen is blank.' A woman with bubblegum-pink hair and pale blue glasses was peering at Caspar as if he were an animal in a zoo. 'I guess that's saying something really deep about alienation.'

'BEANS!'

Mrs Bender seemed resigned to the lack of vintage champagne now and was clutching her wine glass in one hand and Mr Bender in the other.

'CHEESEBURGER!'

'What is that man shouting about?' Mrs Bender asked her daughter.

'FEAR!'

Laura glanced about for the young men she had noticed earlier. She could not see either of them. Irina Pushamoff appeared to have gone, too. A few local tramps had arrived, though. They too were enjoying the free drinks and were discussing their chances of using the bed once the installation had closed for the night.

'So nice to meet you!' Mrs Bender exclaimed to one of them. 'Are you an artist as well?'

Laura's lips began to twitch. A feeling of hysterical mirth began to build inside her.

Jamie Dodger, meanwhile, had gone into crisis mode. He was now striding about in his smart shiny suit, a smartphone to each ear. 'Tell me it's not true, Daniel, mate,' he lamented loudly as he passed Amy. 'You *promised* me. I've told them *all* that James Bond is coming. Man, you have let me down. You have let me down *so bad*. You have let me down *big time*. Okay. Okay. I hear you. It can't be helped. But you owe me one, Daniel, yeah?'

'He's quite good, isn't he?' Caspar ventriloquised to Laura. 'I'd almost be convinced, were it not for the fact that the chances of Daniel Craig coming to *Call This Art?* are slightly south of hell freezing over a squadron of flying pigs.'

'Amy believes him though,' Laura replied, shaking with suppressed laughter. So far Amy had received, straight-faced, the regretful can't-comes of Mick Jagger, Angela Merkel, Lady Gaga and Ban Ki-moon.

'Such a shame,' Mrs Bender was exclaiming. 'I'd have tried to persuade Daniel to stay as 007. There's all this talk about Orlando Chease doing it now...'

'Who?' Amy butted in rudely.

'That actor with the nice bum. That was so good in *The Head Concierge*.' Whether it was actor or bum that was meant was not clear.

'Is he on the list?' Amy roared at Jamie Dodger, who was now loudly receiving the apologies of Queen Elizabeth II.

'Okay, Your Majesty, well, if you can't, you can't... Is who on the list?' Jamie Dodger looked like a rabbit in the headlights.

'Orlando... whatsisname?' Amy glared at her mother. 'Toast, is it?'

'Wish it were,' ventriloquised Caspar, with feeling. 'I didn't realise he was up for Bond as well as everything else. *Asshole.*'

'Asshole?' repeated Amy disbelievingly to Mrs Bender. 'His name is Orlando Asshole?'

Mrs Bender looked affronted. 'I never said that. His name is Chease.'

'Well, someone near you said asshole and if it wasn't you, who was it?' Amy shook her dreadlocks accusingly and one of the forks fell out and rolled away into the dark.

There was a scream, a scraping sound and a mighty crash.

'I'm dying for a poo,' Caspar muttered. 'How much longer do you think we have to sit here?'

Laura snorted loudly.

Her shoulders were heaving, her eyes were brimming and her nose was running. Her lips ached with the effort of keeping them still and she felt she might explode. Beside her, Caspar was shuddering with laughter and emitting little squeaks.

The woman with blue glasses was back again. 'Wow. They're laughing.' She sounded awed. 'After alienation, redemption. Amy, you're a genius.'

From this point on, the evening was a success. The laughter, it seemed, had clinched it. The paunchy freeloaders came down off the fence and started to praise Amy for her boldness and vision. Phone calls were made and more guests turned up. Mr Bender sent out for cases of champagne, much to his wife's satisfaction. Reviews started coming in from online arts forums that had watched the live streaming of the launch.

Amy paced about excitedly, broadcasting the comments in a voice magnified by alcohol. 'A slap in the face for algorithmic culture!'

Caspar had switched his phone back on and was following events as well. 'Bender raises the question of aesthetic relativism. Is the spectator less free to laugh than the artist? *Toilet Attendant.*'

'There's an art forum called Toilet Attendant?' Laura asked. Admittedly, it seemed highly likely.

'No, I think it actually is a toilet attendant. It's one of those sites where anyone can join the conversation.'

'Bender is all about appropriation!' yelled Amy, coming past again. 'Oh wowsers, another great review. Bender has popped the poached egg on the shared pizza of life. *Rapist.*'

'Oh my God. Where?' wittered Amy's mother, clinging on to her husband in alarm.

'*Rapist* is an online art magazine, Ma. Each issue is launched from somewhere really amazing like a tent in India or a former condemned cell. This one comes from a horse butcher in Saigon.'

Laura and Caspar watched as a small, barrel-shaped Asian woman approached. She was dressed in a pair of green tweed breeches, a man's tartan dressing gown and unlaced white ice-skating boots on which she tottered with obvious difficulty. The effect was completed by a transparent shower cap over dark hair twisted up into a bun.

Amy leapt into her path. 'Ah, Chu!'

'Here!' Mrs Bender's diamonds glittered as she passed her daughter a tissue.

Amy glared at her. 'Ma, this is Chu Ginsberg. She's a lifestyle blogger. Her reach is incredible.'

'I have ten million Instagram followers and six million on Twitter.' Chu held up her phone. 'I vlog as well. I have five million hits on YouTube.'

Laura could feel Caspar straining every muscle to stop himself leaping in front of her camera.

A man with large glasses and Bill Nighy hair accosted Amy. 'Miss Bender? Will Gompertz, BBC. Can I ask you about the laughing? Is it a question of predetermined spontaneity, or is that an oxymoron?'

Amy rolled contemptuous eyes. '*Oxymoron* was my graduation show. It had a talking bottom.'

The journalist scribbled feverishly. 'And what was your inspiration for the piece?'

Amy clutched her dreadlocks and yelped as she impaled her palm on a fork. 'Sometimes the fabric of who you are, the artist and the woman, merge too much and you can't find your way out,' she said.

'I'm glad you brought that up,' said the respected arts correspondent. 'Has something gone wrong with the lighting? I couldn't see a thing, coming in.'

Chapter Four

Afterwards, as Amy Bender's parents conveyed their daughter and her guests to a lavish afterparty at their expensive hotel, Laura and Caspar were left standing on the rue Morgue pavement.

'Drink?' suggested Caspar.

'Okay, but not round here,' Laura said. 'I'm sick of bars with start-up entrepreneurs playing Scrabble and men in tweed waistcoats taking forty-five minutes to make coffee with blowtorches.'

'But I like all that,' Caspar objected as a barefoot waiter in dungarees and a man-bun shoved past with a tray of Guinness. 'It's so Parisian.'

Laura rolled her eyes. 'I'll show you what a real Parisian bar looks like.'

Caspar was excited. 'You mean the one where your granny drinks champagne for breakfast and reads the papers?'

'The very same. But don't get the wrong idea, it's pretty basic.'

As they left the rue Morgue they discussed the amazing success of the private view and the equally amazing speed of it all. 'It's a social media sensation,' Caspar marvelled.

This was no less than the truth. It was the exposure on Chu Ginsberg's blog that had transformed Amy Bender's fortunes. She had gone viral, was trending and had a phenomenal hit rate.

They were now walking through the place du Tertre, Montmartre's cobbled village square and home of La Mère Catherine, supposedly the world's first bistro.

A tour guide had halted his legion of yellow-baseball-capped Chinese troops. 'It's called a bistro because some Russian soldiers banged the tables and yelled "Bistro!"' he was explaining. 'It means "hurry up" in Russian.'

Laura had never believed this story. Parisian waiters did not like being shouted at to hurry up. Least of all by foreigners.

An unending stream of people pushed through the square, drawn by the brightly lit tat shops and the thuggish cartoonists touting supposedly humorous pencil drawings of largely unrecognisable celebrities.

'Fucking hell,' she heard Caspar exclaim from behind.

She turned. He was staring at a caricature of a young man with floppy blonde hair and enormous teeth spread in a persuasive smile.

'Who's that?' she asked, as the thickset creator of the masterpiece approached, grinning with threatening expectancy, huge thumbs stuck into his money belt.

'Nice picture, yes? Great actor. Very big star. I give you good price, yes?'

Caspar was raking a hand despairingly through his hair. 'It's just so bloody crap. Just so...' He searched for the epithet. '... shit.'

The heavy brow of the hovering artist darkened angrily. 'You say my work is crap?' he shouted, lifting a large fist. 'Sheet?'

'I wasn't saying his *cartoon* was crap,' Caspar lamented as they hurried away past staring tourists.

'But it was,' Laura pointed out.

'Yes, but that's not what I meant.' Caspar stopped. 'It was Chease!' he wailed. 'He's now so famous, people are doing rubbish cartoons of him in Montmartre!'

Not this again. Groaning inwardly, Laura hastened to reassure him. 'You're famous too, don't forget. You're part of a celebrated art installation. One that's trending and gone viral.'

'So I am,' Caspar agreed, looking gratified. 'Now all that needs to happen is for a Hollywood casting agent to see it.'

A message pinged into his phone. He seized it hopefully, but then his face fell.

'What's the matter?'

His puzzled eyes met hers. 'Amy's closing the show.'

'But it's a success!' Laura exclaimed.

'Yes, so she's making hay while the sun shines. Going on tour. First stop Kazakhstan, apparently.'

'But I can't go to Kazakhstan.'

Caspar was scrolling down. 'You don't have to, we're not wanted on voyage. La Bender's going to audition a new couple in every city. She says it's all about local relevance and resonance, but it's obviously about not having to pay our travel and hotel bills. You know how bloody stingy she is.'

Laura shook her head at the rank ingratitude. 'Honestly. When it's us that made it a success.'

'You, actually. You're the one who laughed.'

'But you're the one who needed the loo.'

'Started a whole new movement, you could say.'

'Ha ha.'

They walked on. The place du Tertre was behind them now and the street they headed down was quiet and dark.

'I'll have to go back to Blighty now,' Caspar said mournfully. 'Back to the smoking ruins of my career.'

'It won't be that bad.'

'No, it'll be worse. A crowdfunded tour of *Puppetry of the Penis* if I'm lucky. While bloody Orlando Chease gets to play Bond.'

Laura wished he would shut up about Orlando Chease. But Caspar was clearly a man obsessed. 'He's really made it. His masterstroke was to do all that BBC Shakespeare stuff. So now he's respected as well as famous and rich. Talk about King Learjet.'

Laura giggled. Caspar glared at her. 'It's not funny! Orlando always had better contacts than me. His father runs about a million West End theatres and his mother does the Walberswold panto.'

Laura had never heard of the Walberswold panto but now learnt that it was a production in a small Sussex seaside town where the greatest acting, writing and producing talent on the entire planet met, networked and cross-fertilised to the exclusion of everything and everyone else over the course of a few weeks in the summer.

'When will I get a break?' Caspar fretted. They had picked up speed as he had become more agitated. 'When will I get my Honeywomen?'

'Your what?'

'My fans. Benedict Cumberbatch has his Cumberbitches and Eddie Redmayne has his Redmayniacs. Tom Hiddleston has his Hiddlestoners. And I'm Caspar Honeyman, so mine would be Honeywomen.'

'I'm a Honeywoman,' Laura said loyally.

Caspar, soliloquising his frustration, took no notice. 'I could always change my surname to Dench. I might get auditions then, at least. Or I might go to a refugee camp.'

'Oh, Caspar! Things aren't *that* desperate.'

'Not to *live* there. I mean for the opportunities. Those places are the new RSC. A-list luvvies everywhere you look. Plus hot teenage girls recruited on Facebook to hand out toothpaste and underpants.'

Laura shook her head. 'You're appalling. Anyway,' she added, as a familiar doorway loomed, 'here's the bar.'

Chez Ginette's decor hadn't changed for forty years and maybe not even before that. Football pennants so faded one could no longer see what the teams were hung from a ceiling brown with nicotine and age. Its *propriétaire* sported a tea-towel on her shoulder, a pair of clacking white mules and a plain blue dress accessorised with glasses which swung on a chain of orange plastic links. She greeted Laura effusively, kissing her hard on both cheeks, but ignored Caspar, to his chagrin.

'I'm guessing you have to know Ginette for twenty years before she smiles at you?'

'Something like that.' Laura pulled out two battered wooden chairs.

The bar owner brought the Kirs. Laura smiled at her. '*Merci*, Ginette.'

'*Merci*, Ginette,' echoed Caspar, crinkling his eyes

charmingly. Ginette scowled at him and stomped off in her mules, flicking her teatowel over her shoulder.

'She's definitely warming to me,' said Caspar.

Laura sipped her wine. As usual, Ginette had been a bit overgenerous with the crème de cassis. It was like alcoholic Ribena but none the worse for that.

Caspar was looking more cheerful, certainly. He was even able to think of someone other than himself. 'What will you do now, anyway?' he asked her. 'Back to your escort agency?'

Laura had been too busy comforting Caspar to think about what the show closing might mean for her. Now she did, she found the prospect of not being in *Call This Art?* depressing. She had not enjoyed working for Amy Bender, but she had enjoyed being with Caspar. Learning ventriloquism had been fun. He had been fun. She might be unable to go with him to London, but that didn't mean she was ready to part ways. She would miss his flirtatiousness. The way he made her laugh. His appalling flattery. The fact that he so obviously fancied her. Perhaps she fancied him a little bit too. Perhaps more than a little bit.

Laura stared at the Kir and swallowed hard. She wasn't normally like this, all sad and needy. She tried to pull herself together.

'Something's up,' Caspar said, crinkling his eyes persuasively. 'You can tell me. It'll go no further, I promise.'

Laura shook her head. 'It's nothing.'

'Aw, come on, Laur. Don't be so buttoned up. Do you good to unburden yourself. Come on, darling. I'm your friend. I love you,' Caspar added, easily.

The buttoned-up bit stung as much as the love bit soothed. Laura felt herself melting under the heat lamp of his attention. Soon she was telling him about Carinthia and the offer she had been unable to accept. She found she was close to tears by the end. It was so frustrating to be so close to her dream and yet still so far away.

'You've got to do it!' Caspar exclaimed. He reached for her hand over the table. 'Like I said, you could live with me.' He put his lips to her fingers, sending warm waves of pleasure through her.

'*Ma petite* Laure!' someone now called from the door. Someone with dyed blonde hair, a moth-eaten fur coat, bright pink blusher and outsized high heels.

Caspar snorted. 'It's Grayson Perry.'

'Actually,' said Laura, smiling, 'it's Ernest.'

'And who's Earnest?'

'Our friendly neighbourhood transvestite prostitute.' Laura hurried to embrace the new arrival.

'And how is your grandmother, *chérie*?' Ernest's voice was part falsetto, part growl. He pulled up a chair and sat down, legs spread wide, huge hands clamped on enormous knees in tan tights.

'Fine, thanks.'

Ernest shook his frizzy yellow head. 'Well, I'm exhausted.'

'Tell me about it,' chipped in Caspar.

Ernest looked at Caspar as if seeing him for the first time. Laura waited. Ernest was a shrewd judge of character. In his line of work, you had to be.

'No, literally, tell me about it,' Caspar urged him brightly. 'I'm considering a film role as a transvestite prostitute.'

Ernest's much-mascaraed eyes lit up. Five minutes later he and Caspar were deep in discussion. 'I love it when he calls me his little *chou-fleur*,' Ernest was saying of one of his regulars, 'but when he calls me sugar-face, it really gets on my nerves.'

When Ernest tottered off to the loo, Laura rounded on

Caspar. 'Are you really considering a film role as a transvestite prostitute?'

'No, but I would if someone offered me one. It worked for Eddie Redmayne. But I can't complain.' Caspar waved his phone. 'I've just been asked to do *The King and I* opposite Elizabeth Hurley.'

Laura gasped. 'Fantastic!'

'But it's not happening.'

'Why not?'

'She won't shave her head.'

Laura shoved him, hard, as Ernest came back to the table. 'What are you talking about? *Mon film?*'

'No,' said Caspar, quick as a whip. 'I'm trying to persuade Laura to come to London. She's been offered a job there on a glossy magazine.'

Laura looked at him in amazed fury. How dare he? It was none of his business.

'*Mais c'est formidable!*' Ernest was almost erupting with excitement. 'Ginette, Ginette!' He waved at the bar owner. 'Come over here! *La petite* Laure, she has been offered a job in London. On a magazine!'

As Ginette hurried over, and other people in the bar screeched their wooden chairs round to smile encouragingly, Laura had the sense that events were running away with her.

Ginette stood there excitedly waving her Ricard bottle. Her eyebrows, perfect semicircles in orange pencil, rose into her firmly dyed black hairline. '*Mais c'est parfait*, Laure! Just what you always wanted!'

'A glossy magazine in London!' Ernest exclaimed. 'You can go there with your *savoir-vivre à la Parisienne*. Tell them all you know about Paris style! Your grandmother has taught you well.'

'All those Parisienne rules of elegance!' Ginette egged him on. 'Remind me, what are they again?'

'Let me think.' Ernest accepted a refill of pastis. 'Never waste good money on expensive face cream. A week-old Camembert, massaged in last thing at night, will do just as well.'

Caspar's brow was furrowed as he pondered the results of this. Ginette cackled. 'And don't forget that cigarette ash makes the best mascara. Simply add water to the ashtray, dip in the brush, *et voilà*!'

Caspar was looking amazed. Laura's shoulders began to shake. Ernest and Ginette were a formidable double-act when in the mood.

'The canny Parisienne,' Ernest went on, his face still perfectly straight, 'never wastes money on expensive teeth-whitening. She gets the guy painting her apartment to run over them with his brush.'

Ginette slapped the table. 'If you snore and you're worried your lover might leave you, two *cornichons* shoved in the nostrils work wonders.'

'Washing your hair in *bouillabaisse* gives it a marvellous shine. The trick is to not rinse it off.'

'Always rub garlic under your armpits to increase your... allure.'

Laura held up her hand. 'Stop it, Ernest! *Arrêtes!*'

Ginette put an arm round Laura. '*Ma petite*, we are only teasing. Your new job sounds wonderful.'

'But I can't do it,' Laura said, part annoyed, part defiant, part desperate.

There was a silence. Then Ernest cleared his throat, a sound like a motorbike blasting into life. 'We know you are worried about Mimi, Laure. About leaving her.'

'But you can leave her with us.' Ginette gently shook Laura's shoulders. 'We will look after her. You can trust us.'

'We will check on her all the time,' Ernest added, taking Laura's hand in his enormous fist and squeezing it so her eyes watered.

They were watering anyway. Laura's annoyance and defiance now gave way to a great rush of affection. She had known Ginette and Ernest all her life and loved them dearly. She knew that she could trust them and that they meant what they said.

She took a deep breath. So why not go to London? She could feel her previously immoveable position begin to move. She had a job. And if Caspar was really inviting her to live with him, she had a place to stay too.

'We can take it in turns to have dinner with her, so she is not alone,' Ernest was saying.

Laura smiled at him. 'That would be really kind.'

'Kind?' Ernest interrupted with a snort. 'Enlightened self-interest, ma petite. Mimi is the best cook in Paris, bar none.'

Ginette glanced at the zinc-topped bar. 'Oop!' she exclaimed. 'Customers waiting.'

'Me too.' Ernest grunted and rose to his feet. 'No, don't get up.' He planted a kiss on Laura's cheek and ceremoniously shook Caspar's hand.

'What amazing people,' Caspar said wonderingly, as they moved off.

'They're the best,' Laura said simply.

'You've known them a long time?'

'I practically grew up in this bar. I used to play under the tables and build houses out of ashtrays.'

'Ah. That's how you learnt how to use ashes as mascara,'

Caspar said sagely. He had clearly swallowed the performance whole.

His phone pinged. As he read the text message, his soppy expression disappeared.

'Oh fuck. Dave's thrown me out.'

'Dave?'

'Guy whose floor I was sleeping on. Turns out it wasn't his floor after all.' Caspar reached for her hand. 'Darling Laura. You couldn't put me up for the night?'

'You'll have to sleep in the kitchen,' Laura warned as she let him in to the silent flat. There was no way he was sharing the fold-down sitting-room bed with her.

'How about the bath, like "Norwegian Wood"?'

Laura shook her dark hair. No chance. Mimi's door was shut and she was presumably sleeping. But if she needed the bathroom in the night, the shock would kill her.

Caspar was at the window. 'Wow, what a *ridiculously* Parisian view.'

'Quite good, isn't it?' Laura concurred, proudly.

'Yes, she's taking her bra off now.' His eyes were fixed firmly on the third-floor window of the next block down.

Laura was at the stove, lifting the lid off a pan. Tonight's dish was *soupe au pistou*, another of her favourites. The sweet basil scent of freshly made pesto rose from the hearty mixture of beans, vegetables, pasta and home-made chicken stock. 'Hungry?'

'Completely Hank,' Caspar replied.

'What?'

'Hank Marvin, starving. Cockney rhyming slang. You'd better get used to it, we speak it in London all the time.'

'Really?' Laura eyed him uncertainly.

'I'll give you a crash course. Nice daisy roots on your plates of meat,' Caspar began in a cockney accent.

'Nice what?'

'Daisy roots, boots. Plates of meat, feet. Here's another. I was Brahms and Liszt in me whistle and flute.'

'I don't understand.' But Laura was laughing.

'Brahms and Liszt, pissed. As in drunk. Whistle and flute is suit. Er, why's everything pink?' Caspar was staring at the light fittings.

Laura explained about Mimi's lightbulbs, and Caspar nodded. 'Oh yeah. Those beauty tips. Camembert on your face.'

'Ernest was joking. Mimi never said any of those things.'

'Well, they all work. You're very beautiful.'

'I'm not beautiful.'

'Well, you're not perfect, it's true.' Caspar gazed at her appraisingly.

'You're too kind.'

'There's that scar on your face – how did you get it, by the way?'

'An accident when I was little.'

'And you've got what they call a strong nose.'

'Thanks.'

'But you've got something else, too. Depth, I guess. Style. Mystery.'

'Oh please. Do me a—'

'No, hear me out.' He pulled her to him with a suddenness that made her gasp. 'I know you think I'm a bit trivial...'

'A *bit*?'

She could see, in the window's reflection, Caspar standing over her, his cheek against her head. They looked surprisingly good together. The expression on his handsome face was one of transforming tenderness. Then again, he was looking at himself.

'… but I think I love you.' He kissed her hair and she felt a bolt go straight down through her body and out through the soles of her feet.

She made herself wriggle free, deliberately breaking the spell. 'Don't be ridiculous.'

'I'm not. Won't you sleep with me?'

She folded her arms. 'So that's what this is about. No.'

He looked at her beseechingly. 'Really no? Oh well. Don't ask, don't get. But you'll still come to London with me, if I promise to keep my hands off you?'

'If you promise to keep your hands off me.' Laura kept her voice low to prevent Mimi overhearing. She would break the news to her grandmother in the morning, choosing her time carefully.

Caspar sighed theatrically. 'I promise. The future of British magazine journalism hangs in the balance, after all.'

Laura ladled out the soup, grinning. 'Shall we eat?'

Later, while Caspar brushed his 'Hampsteads' (Hampstead Heath – teeth), she heaped a pile of coats on the kitchen floor and made sure he was comfortable before closing the door dividing the kitchen from the sitting room and folding down her sofa bed. Sleep proved evasive, however. Was she really going to London? Would she really be okay without Mimi, without the little flat and her favourite view? And – the biggest question of all – what was she going to say to her grandmother?

The windows were open, but the air seemed still and hot. Laura was burning and restless. She thought of Caspar sleeping next door – Caspar with his ridiculously long eyelashes, his melting gaze, his wide, full mouth capable of

48

saying so many filthy things without moving at all. And, no doubt, capable of much else besides.

She took off her pyjamas and threw off the duvet. Then she pulled it back on again. She had lain awake for what seemed like hours, when the kitchen door creaked and pushed open.

A male figure stood silhouetted in the doorway, the light from the bathroom licking the muscles of his chest. Caspar said nothing, and neither did she when he lifted the duvet and slid in beside her. He pressed against her, warm and firm, and put his mouth to hers. She didn't resist.

Chapter Five

Laura awoke the next morning to the scent of coffee. She sat up and her head pounded; Ginette's Kir had a lot to answer for.

Caspar's side of the bed was empty. He had left?

The memories from last night had loaded up now. Laura lay back and examined them. Caspar was an extremely physical lover, as was she. 'Uninhibited' was the word he had used as he had persuaded her into some incredibly uncomfortable positions, all with very strange names. *Tethered Rams*, *Rearing Stag* and *Rough Dogs* were, Caspar explained, all titles of paintings in the National Gallery's Victorian wildlife section. He had once spent a few weeks there as a security guard and imagining the titles as sex positions had been one way of staying awake. It was, Laura thought, an unexpected insight into the minds of gallery workers.

Staying awake had certainly not been a problem last night. She had not realised Victorian paintings could be so much fun and she, for one, would never look at *The Monarch of the Glen* in quite the same way again. All the same, it was just one night, and it didn't mean anything. Really, it was just as well Caspar had gone. She didn't need a man complicating things and Caspar, for all his skills beneath the duvet, wasn't really her type. He was dim, vain and utterly self-absorbed. He was an actor, with all the depth of a saucer. He was friend, not lover, material. But he would certainly be fun to share a flat with.

Given that her pyjamas seemed to have disappeared, Laura wrapped the sheet round her and opened the door into the kitchen. As she entered, Mimi was wiping her eyes. '*Comme il est original*, your boyfriend!'

'Good morning!' Caspar, resplendent in flowered cotton, raised a cup of espresso and gave her a sunny beam.

'He's not my boyfriend,' Laura said, shooting Caspar a sharp look. Just because they'd spent the night together, he needn't get ideas.

'He is wearing your pyjamas, *chérie*,' Mimi rather mercilessly pointed out.

Her grandmother had fallen for Caspar hook, line and sinker, Laura saw. Her old eyes were sparkling and her perfect skin glowing. Otherwise she looked her usual dapper self in a neat white shirt, smart wool trousers and pearls gleaming in her ears. Like Laura, she had her uniform.

'And he tells me that you are going with him to London!'

Laura glared at Caspar again. How dare he jump the gun like this? It was her news, not his.

'*Mais oui, chérie*. We have it all planned, Gaspard and I. You have been offered a job on a magazine. It is perfect!'

'Isn't it?' put in Caspar.

'Go and get in the shower,' Laura ordered him.

With an ironic salute, he obeyed, and now Laura turned to face her grandmother. Mimi got there first, however.

'You must go to London. I insist. It is a great opportunity.'

'But are you sure, Mimi?' Laura searched the bright old eyes with her own.

'What is stopping you, Laure? Ginette and Ernest will look after me. You have a wonderful job. And your boyfriend is offering you a house!'

'He's not my boyfriend,' Laura repeated. 'And I shouldn't think it's a house.' Actually, she didn't know where or in what Caspar lived. All would be revealed once she got to London.

'Gaspard is charming. He adores you.'

'But I don't adore him. I can't take him seriously.'

Mimi snorted. 'Who cares? He's funny. As Sacha Guitry used to say, you can pretend to be serious. But you cannot pretend to be witty.'

Laura sighed. It was a mutual admiration society.

'Your granny's amazing,' Caspar raved as, later, they walked down the spiral stairs from the flat. 'She's been teaching me some great Parisian sayings.'

'Like what?' Laura asked apprehensively. This could mean anything.

'That one when you wish you'd said something and didn't. The wit of the staircase.'

'*L'esprit d'escalier*, yes. That brilliant line you remember, but only on the way out of the party.' Laura felt relieved. Mimi evidently hadn't been too outrageous.

'And *l'auberge du cul tourné*. The inn of the turned back-side. When a woman is sulking in bed.'

Laura glared upwards towards the hall ceiling. *Mimi!*

'And apparently those really massive pepper grinders are called Rubirosas, after some Dominican playboy who was hung like a donkey. Remind you of anyone?' He nudged her.

In the entrance hall, a glass door requiring a code stood in her way. As Laura tapped it in, the street door opened and a woman came in, pulling her shopping trolley behind her. It was Evelyne, the sixtysomething widow who occupied the block's *chambre de bonne*, the tiny, top-floor room that would once have been the maid's quarters.

Evelyne was incurably nosy, knew everything about everyone and was happy to share her information. She cut a distinctive figure with her perm, thick glasses, bright blue cream eyeshadow and white plastic boots. Like most Parisian women, Evelyne had kept her slim shape, her *ligne*. But she seemed also to have kept her entire 1970s wardrobe.

'She looks like something out of a sitcom,' Caspar muttered, without moving his lips.

'*Bonjour*, Laure!' Evelyne sang in her reedy voice, eyes darting wildly between Laura and Caspar. 'And this must be your *petit ami*! Ginette has just been telling me all about it! You are going to London! To work on a glossy magazine!'

'Er...'

'But, Laure, how *wonderful*.' Evelyne looked so thrilled for her that Laura felt guilty. She leant conspiratorially forward. 'And of course, Laure, you must not worry about Mimi. Ernest and Ginette and I, we will look after her.'

Laura's eyes were now definitely pricking. While undoubtedly nosy and strangely dressed, Evelyne was also kind hearted and well meaning. Moreover, she was an acquaintance of many years' standing. Along with Ernest and Ginette, she would now form Team Mimi, the group that would watch over her grandmother. There was nothing stopping her from leaving now.

Carinthia Gold had not been in the *Society* office to receive Laura's news that circumstances had changed after all. Neither, to her disappointment, had Xanthe. The person who answered knew nothing about an internship and Laura had faced the ghastly possibility that the whole offer had never been intended as serious.

But then, one anxious hour later, she had received an email telling her to report to the British Magazine Company's HR department at Society House. It was official! Only one thing remained to be decided.

'What shall I wear?' she asked her grandmother.

'What you always do, *chérie*.'

Laura looked down at her usual dark jeans, navy shirt and boots. 'Do I really look my best though?'

Mimi gave her a wise look. 'One should never look one's best. That way, people imagine the best is so much better. *Attends, chérie*. I have something for you.'

Mimi disappeared into her bedroom and reappeared with something Laura had never seen before. It was a small brown leather bag, part case, part handbag. It was superbly elegant, a beautiful shape and the perfect size, neither too big nor too small, with neat leather handles and a zip running across the front.

'It's wonderful, Mimi!'

'It's old. But you know what they say, *chérie*. Old is always new!'

★

When Laura waved Caspar off at Gare du Nord, she had only intended to give him a peck on the cheek. But he had pulled her into a passionate clinch on the platform. People had held up smartphones and Caspar had snogged her even harder, milking the attention.

'Text me when you get to London, baby,' he called huskily from the carriage entrance. But as the train slid away, he was already deep in conversation with the pretty blonde in the next seat.

Now about to make the same journey herself, Laura sat on the train and felt a pang as she saw the distant white domes of Sacré-Coeur glide past the window. She felt suddenly like a schoolgirl again, waving goodbye to Paris as she made the seemingly endless journey back to England each term.

Why was she remembering this now? She had not thought about St Margaret's for years. She had suppressed the memories of the hated Dorset institution where Clemency Makepeace with her horrible red hair and her horrible gang of bullies had seemed to lurk round every corner. That was all over. It belonged to the past. She would never see Clemency Makepeace again.

She thought of her grandmother instead. How would Mimi be feeling, alone in the little flat? But, actually, she wouldn't be alone. Ernest, Ginette and Evelyne were taking her out to her favourite bistro for lunch. The glorious prospect of oysters and Chablis seemed almost to have driven the ghastly parting from her mind. Their goodbyes had been cheery, although Laura had expected nothing less. However sad she was really feeling, Mimi regarded a smiling outlook as a moral imperative.

Gradually, Laura allowed herself to relax. There seemed no reason not to. Her life, which had been on hold for so long, was finally about to begin. She was on her way to a magazine internship in London. Her first step towards being a newspaper journalist like her father. An investigative reporter, even. Perhaps a foreign correspondent. Why not? Now she had a foot on the ladder, anything was possible.

As the last of Paris slipped past the window, Laura smiled, a big, huge beam of relief. There was no one to see it. The seats immediately around her were empty, although she could see the top of a dark head a couple of rows back.

A newspaper lay on the table. Laura pulled it towards her. To her surprise there was a photograph of Mrs Bender on the front page. Resplendent in her gold quilted jacket and zip-festooned trousers, Amy's mother was beaming at the camera and clamping a champagne glass in fingers blazing with diamonds.

Laura's initial assumption, that the piece was about Amy's party, gave way to amazement as she realised it was about something else altogether.

'DIAMOND HEIST,' read the headline. 'Artist's Mother in Top Hotel Jewel Break-In.'

Laura gasped and read on. It appeared that Mrs Bender had been relieved of her rings following a daring break-in at the luxury hotel apartment rented for their stay in Paris. It was not, Laura was relieved to note, one of Ulrika Burgwinkle's flats; she would not have welcomed this extra trouble on top of the inconvenience of finding a replacement meeter-and-greeter. She and Laura had parted cordially, even so; Ulrika, ever the businesswoman, had spotted an opportunity in Laura's move to London. 'Now the pound's crashed and burned, we can launch a Brit arm of the business,' she said. 'We'll call it Luxury in London. I can see the website now – guardsmen, taxis, red phone boxes, punks, yadda yadda. Look out for flats, willya? Maybe that guy you're gonna stay with wants to rent out his.'

Laura read how the luxury apartment's concierge had been bound and gagged, as had the Benders. They had been package-taped naked to chairs on the balcony and one reason it had taken so long for the alarm to be raised was that people assumed their unmoving seated forms were state-of-the-art statues. The hotel had additionally assumed that the Benders had gone, abandoning their possessions behind them in the suite – 'Our wealthier guests frequently leave everything,' the hotel manager laconically remarked. 'For people at this level, their time is too precious to waste on packing.' It was only when the apartment's subsequent occupiers saw Mrs Bender's eyes move that the truth came out.

Laura felt sorry for the Benders, but there was a definite element of farce to all this. Especially given that the gang had apparently escaped on Segway machines.

'You think it's funny?'

The voice was low, male and English. Glancing up, Laura saw that the owner of the dark head whose top she had spotted down the carriage was now looking down at her. He was young, tall, and good-looking, but not in a blatant, grinning Caspar-ish way. His gaze was unsmiling, disapproving almost.

'You're laughing about the robbery,' he said.

'Well, there is a funny side,' returned Laura. According to the paper, one school of online thought held that the whole episode had been a stunt to draw attention to Amy's exhibition. 'Call This a Robbery?' uncharitable souls had tweeted. 'What's it to you, anyway?' she challenged. It was up to her what she laughed at in the papers.

He had installed himself opposite without waiting for permission. The bright light flooding through the train windows meant that she could really see him now. His eyes were deep set, which gave him an inscrutable air. He had a straight nose and a long mouth with a cryptic sort of twist to it. It was a face she felt she had seen before, and now she realised where. At the *Call This Art?* private view. He was one of the young men in suits, the rival artists. The dark-haired one, not the blonde one. Though she could see now that the hair that had looked black at the party was in fact mid-brown, with reddish glints to it.

'You're a friend of Amy's?' she asked.

'Not as such. I wouldn't aspire to move in such elevated circles.'

His eyes gave nothing away, but there was something about his mouth that suggested humour. 'I should introduce myself,' he said. 'Harry Scott. Investigative reporter.'

Laura took the hand extended to her. It was big, strong, dry. 'Investigative reporter!' She tried not to sound too impressed.

'You sound impressed,' he said. 'Most people are either suspicious or disgusted.'

'Disgusted? Why?'

He shrugged. 'Because journalism's one of the least trusted professions. Right down there with bankers and politicians.'

Laura was taking in more details. He wore jeans and a dark blue shirt, same as her. Maybe all journalists dressed this way. The thought was encouraging. A black leather jacket was stuffed through the shoulder straps of his navy rucksack. 'You're investigating the robbery?' she asked, as everything now began to make sense.

'That's the idea.'

Laura licked her lips and tucked a strand of hair behind one ear. This was a nervous tic; she only ever revealed her ears by accident. They stuck out slightly, as Clemency Makepeace and her gang of bullies had always delighted in pointing out. 'Wingnuts! Wingnuts!' She could hear them now.

'How do you get to be an investigative reporter?' she asked eagerly.

'Why do you want to know?'

'Because I want to be one too.' She sounded, she knew, naïve. But this was no time to try and be cool. She might learn something important.

'Really?' His laconic tone lightened with surprise. 'Thought you were Amy Bender's muse.'

'What? Oh, because of the installation.' Laura rolled her eyes. 'Hardly. If Amy has a muse, it's kept in vaults in banks.'

'You surprise me. I thought she was pushing the envelope of aesthetic relativism and slapping algorithmic culture in the face.'

Their eyes met and it seemed to Laura that suddenly something happened between them. A sort of flash, a rush of excitement and heat. Perhaps she had imagined it though, as his expression gave nothing away. She sought a businesslike tone. 'It was just temporary. Until something better came up.'

'And has it?' He was looking at her closely.

She nodded. 'I've got a job on a magazine now.'

'Which one? *The Economist*? *Newsweek*?'

'*Society*.'

Harry's brow creased as if he were trying to recall something unimaginably distant. Then it smoothed and he looked amused. 'Not that posh glossy? Full of toffs in tartan trousers?'

Laura recoiled at his mocking tone. How dare he laugh at her? 'There's more to it than that,' she said, recalling Get Me A Unicorn! and Carinthia's claims to have set the newspaper agenda.

He looked unconvinced however, and irritation swept through her. Easy for him to be superior.

'You've got to start somewhere,' she snapped.

'True.'

'So where did you start?'

'On a local paper. My first front-page story was a scoop about litter in the park. The photographs sent shockwaves through the entire community.'

'Really?'

'Yes, two empty plastic water bottles and a fag packet. People where I grew up are easily alarmed.'

Laura laughed in spite of herself. 'So how did you get from there to investigative journalism?' He still hadn't said what paper he worked for. 'Contacts?'

He raised his eyebrows ruefully. 'You must be joking. I didn't know anyone.'

'No-one?' This was unexpected. No contacts, like her. A kindred spirit.

'Well, apart from one person. Proper old-school journalist. Taught me all I needed to know about reporting.'

'Lucky you.' Carinthia's vague encouragement didn't really compare. 'I'd love to have a mentor.'

'Oh, I never met him,' Harry said quickly. 'He died a long time ago. I just read his stuff. All of it, over and over. Learnt to do it that way.'

'He was a news reporter?'

Harry shook his head. 'A foreign correspondent. The best.'

The pulsing sound of her heartbeat filled Laura's ears. 'My father was a foreign correspondent.'

Harry threw her a doubtful glance. 'Yeah? What was his name?'

'Peter Lake.'

Harry stared at the table. He did not speak and Laura reddened. The name meant nothing, obviously. But then he raised his head. 'That's amazing,' he said quietly. 'That's the guy I was talking about.'

Laura met his eye steadily. That would teach him to be rude about her job.

'You're Peter Lake's daughter?'

'Laura, yes.'

He gazed at her for what seemed a long time. She waited for him to make some remark about her following in her father's footsteps. Instead he said, as if he couldn't quite believe it, 'And you're working for that toff magazine?'

Laura was stung. 'Well, obviously I'd love to do what he did. But like I said, you have to start somewhere. I don't have any other contacts in London. I haven't even been living there.' Briefly, she explained about Mimi, Amy Bender, Carinthia and Caspar.

'You're staying with him in London?'

Harry sounded appalled and Laura was secretly flattered. Was he jealous? 'Do you think I shouldn't?'

'You're sure you trust him?'

'What do you mean?' He was watching closely, she realised.

Harry shrugged. 'You don't think he might have been involved in the robbery?'

Sheer disbelief made Laura almost splutter. 'Caspar? He's completely chaotic. He's absolutely incapable of something like that.'

Harry shrugged his broad, blue shoulders. 'It's just a theory.'

'Well it's way off the mark. Caspar's not that sort of person.'

'If you say so. You'd be surprised at the people who are that sort of person, though.'

'Well, Caspar isn't.'

'Know him well, do you?'

Laura raised her chin and eyed him challengingly. Then she remembered the Rutting Stag, and coloured violently.

The ping of a message being received inserted itself into the ensuing uncomfortable pause. Harry felt in his pocket and produced a distinctly battered smartphone. His dark brows drew together. 'Sorry. Got to go.' His phone pinged again, and again. He was scrolling through the messages, his face serious, his attention clearly elsewhere. He was getting to his feet.

'But,' Laura began, feeling that she didn't really want him to leave. He'd annoyed and confused her, but that wasn't what mattered. The point was that here was someone who, in stark contrast to her mother, unlike Mimi even, she could talk to about her father. Someone who admired him. Who might, unlike Laura, actually know something about him.

He had exited the carriage before she had a chance to act. If only she had asked which paper he worked for! Her frustration now gave way to the realisation that he had left his card on the table. She picked it up. It was thin, creased and much less expensively produced than the once Carinthia had given her. There was no logo to give a clue as to where he worked. 'Harry Scott' was all it said, along with his mobile number. Smiling, Laura put it in her jeans back pocket. Her father was not lost to her after all.

Now to contact Caspar, make sure he was at St Pancras to meet her. He would be surprised to discover he was suspected of being a jewel thief. But there was no signal, as least not on a cheap brick like hers and, putting it away, Laura wondered whether, actually, she shouldn't keep Harry's remarks to herself. Her new acquaintance might be hopelessly off target, but he was both an investigative journalist and a fan of her father. She should give him the benefit of the doubt, at least for now.

Laura went to the buffet and returned with a mini bottle of red and a glossy magazine she had found at the carriage end. It had been one of many piled on the racks beside the loo and was presumably free for passengers.

Laura examined it with professional interest. Whatever Harry Scott might think, she would be working on something like this still seemed amazing. Her heart rose at the sheer glamour of it, its thick, shiny weight in her hands, the scent of the perfume wafting up from the glossy pages. This was to be her new world!

The cover model, a beaming blonde, lay sprawled on a sea of designer handbags. As she was naked, some had been judiciously positioned to half-conceal her modesty. Laura recognised her: Lulu, a well-known London socialite. She often appeared on the website of one of Laura's favourite British newspapers, a mid-market tabloid with a lively interest in the rich and famous.

'THE PAMPERED LIFE OF A PARTY PRINCESS,' read the coverline.

Laura knew little about Lulu apart from her being rich, blonde and going to lots of parties. And being famous enough to have only one name. Time to find out more, she decided.

There was a small paragraph on the magazine contents page about the interview, accompanied by a photograph of the writer. Jemima Baker was a pinch-faced brunette whose summary of her subject went as follows:

Lulu has long evaded questions about her birthplace and background, preferring blithely to declare herself a 'citizen of the world'. Her accent is international and amazing, the distilled essence of the carpets of first-class lounges all over the globe combined with malapropistic manglings and grammatical catastrophe.

Charming, Laura thought, turning to the interview.
'PRIVATE JETS ARE CHEAPER THAN SCHEDULED, HMMM?' read the headline.
Had Lulu *really* said that? It seemed so. Jemima Baker lost no time in getting stuck in.

We meet in a central London hotel, where Lulu seems surprised that the suite, into which you could fit my flat twice over, has only three bathrooms. But perhaps this isn't out of character for someone with homes all round the globe, including the huge house in Knightsbridge where Lulu currently bases herself.

I ask her if it's true she's never taken a scheduled flight. Lulu looks up from the *Dora the Explorer* game she is playing on her iPhone. 'Am always in my PJs,' she reveals laconically.

Pyjamas?

'PJ is private jet, hmm?'

'You go everywhere by private jet?'

'Is cheaper than EasyJet when you have twenty suitcases and two dogs and there are five of you including chef, hmmm?'

Once I have recovered from this, I ask her if, as the girl who has everything, there is one thing she wants more than anything else. Lulu raises thickly mascaraed eyes from *Dora the Explorer* and says, 'A penis.'

'A penis?' I gasp.

Lulu nods. 'Everyone want a penis, hmm?'

A discreet cough, and somebody steps forward. It is Lulu's

female butler, who has accompanied her to the interview. 'Madam, here it is pronounced "happiness".'

Laura chortled. Lulu was absolutely brilliant. She loved the idea of a female butler, too.

The announcer now interrupted her. '*Mesdames et messieurs, nous sommes arrivés à London St Pancras International...*'

Excitement leapt within Laura. The amused smile begun by Lulu now spread to a beam of joy caused by London. She was here at last!

'I'm working on a glossy magazine!' she wanted to shout. 'And after that I'll work on a newspaper! How lucky am I? *La vie est belle!*'

Chapter Six

Laura walked through passport control with a spring in her step, swinging Mimi's leather bag in excitement. She loved everything, instantly. The St Pancras station shopping hall heaving with people. The great soaring Victorian roof.

She pulled out her phone and called Caspar, smiling as she dialled. He was going to love the story about Harry Scott. But again there was no answer, which was unexpected. Laura checked the number, frowning. No, she had the right one. Where was he?

She took a deep breath. There was nothing to worry about. He might be at an audition or something; he needed the work. He would be in later. He knew she was coming.

But it was strange, even so. Might it be possible...? But no. Caspar was not a jewel thief on the run. It was out of the question that he had anything to do with the missing

Bender bling. He would be at an audition, that was all. And later on he'd give her a wry account of it, and she would tell him off for not answering when she called. And then they would make up, which would be a lot of fun. She felt a frisson of lust. A *lot* of fun.

But that was all later. For now she would go to *Society* and check in with the HR department. She had investigated the location; the Tubes were either Oxford Circus or Bond Street. But it was only early afternoon and she had two hours before her appointment. Should she walk? Or take the bus? Yes – the famous, iconic, red London bus?

Outside, on the Euston Road, a stream of double-deckers was passing. Laura studied the timetable and caught the 73. She clambered upstairs; the seats at the front were empty. Perfect.

Off the bus chugged. Laura stared out at thronged pavements and choked crossings. It all seemed much busier than Paris. When, eventually, the bus reached Bond Street, she got out and walked down, examining the tableaux in the smart shop windows.

Mannequins in Bond Street were living the dream. In one display, top-hatted male and fascinatored female dummies were enjoying a champagne party. They stood about convivially on green fake grass studded with bright fake flowers.

In the windows of an expensive lingerie store a group of mannequins in underwear were getting ready for a night out. One sat on the loo applying lipstick while another stood before the mirror. The third lay in the bath, one high-heeled mule swinging from the end of her foot.

It made Laura suddenly long for the banter and freedom of living in a flat full of girls. She had never shared a place with anyone but Mimi, and whenever she had made female friends at school, they had always been scared away by Clemency Makepeace. In the end she had given up trying. But hopefully London would bring opportunities to form new bonds. It might have to. She had just checked her mobile again and there was still nothing from Caspar.

Had he really robbed Mrs Bender? Was that why he'd gone AWOL? The jewellers' shops had now begun: Cartier upon Bulgari upon Harry Winston upon Boucheron upon Van Cleef & Arpels. Pausing to look at pear-shaped emeralds, sapphires the size of Scrabble letters and diamonds strobing like disco lights, Laura could see how a penniless actor might be tempted. They were hypnotically beautiful, as well as worth a fortune.

Did Caspar have the ruthlessness that one associated with jewel thieves? Laura was beginning to wonder. She may have spent hours on end sitting just inches away from him and, yes, she had slept with him. But she didn't really know him. She knew the funny, seductive, outrageous exterior, but had she ever glimpsed the inner man? How Caspar really felt about anything? Only when he'd been complaining about Orlando Chease. And he'd sounded pretty ruthless then. Positively murderous.

Passing Tiffany's, she remembered her grandmother's advice on acquiring a radiant complexion. 'A stroll with the right man round Tiffany's! The air there is excellent – very good for the skin.'

Laura smiled and felt better. She must focus on the fact that her professional future was as bright and brilliant as a jeweller's window. Soon she was cheerfully entering an imposing garden square. Rising before her was a building of pale stone with letters cut above the entrance. 'SOCIETY HOUSE'.

It was all she could do not to run towards the revolving silver door set in the large glass frontage. Beside it, mounted on the cream stone wall, was a highly polished brass plaque on which was engraved 'The British Magazine Company'.

A pair of thin young blondes passed her as she entered. One wore a clear plastic cloak over a green neon tutu, the other a tweed boilersuit and pink jelly shoes. 'Body chains with prehistoric teeth,' she was saying.

'Vengeful ballet pumps with punky buckles,' replied the other.

Laura grinned. How wonderfully glossy!

A woman with red glasses carrying an open MacBook swept past. She was barking into a phone. 'The new interiors colours are Penis, Pigeon and Pout.'

Laura was delighted. She was going to absolutely love working here!

On the door was a sign reading 'Suzanne Silver, Director of Human Resources'.

'Laura Lake for you, Miss Silver,' said the girl who had met Laura at the lift.

'Thank you, Antigone...'

A plump, groomed blonde in a black dress looked up, unsmilingly, from a desk. On the desk were some enormously thick books, *Who's Who* and *Debrett's* among them, as well as a framed page from a newspaper, 'London's Most Powerful', as well as a big red number 5 beside a photograph of Suzanne.

Laura realised she was in the presence of a media potentate.

'I've got lots of features ideas,' she began, reaching for her bag with her notebook in it.

'Ideas?' Suzanne looked startled.

'For the magazine.'

Suzanne gave a dismissive chuckle. 'I don't need to know about that sort of thing. I do the background checks.'

Laura had previously filled in a form online, but that was incomplete anyway; her London address was yet to be added. Perhaps that was what Suzanne meant. But she had her passport, which she now put on the table.

Suzanne did not pick it up, however. She was consulting a huge red book with 'Burke's Peerage' in gold on the spine. 'Lake,' she was murmuring to herself, flipping through the pages. 'Hinton St Magna?'

'Sorry?'

Suzanne looked up irritably. She had very hard blue eyes, Laura noticed. 'Are you one of the Lakes of Hinton St Magna? A cadet branch of the Codde-Chitterling family?'

Laura sensed that Suzanne would quite like her to be. Ambition urged her to say yes. 'I'm not sure,' she hedged.

The personnel director had now turned to consult an enormous poster on the wall which was covered in coats of arms. 'Mole rampant on a background of azure with gules and half suzerain. Motto: "I toil in the dark"?'

'What?'

The hard blue eyes had swung back and were boring into Laura. 'Isn't that your heraldic achievement?'

Laura decided to err on the side of caution, as well as truth. She took a deep breath. 'I'm sorry, but I've got absolutely no idea.'

The irritation went from Suzanne's face, and she smiled. 'Congratulations, you've passed the first test. I always invite people to claim they're related to bogus families. Just to see whether they're truthful or not.'

Laura felt light-headed with relief at not having succumbed to temptation.

'The last girl I had in here said she was one of the Prawn-Sandwiches.' Suzanne was shaking her head and beaming fondly. 'And I've had plenty of fun with Lew-Rolles and Jolly-Silleys in the past.'

Laura chuckled obediently.

Suzanne gave a happy sigh, then looked hard at Laura again. 'So who *are* you related to, then?'

'Er…'

The blue eyes froze. 'We only want well-connected girls here.'

'My father died when I was little. I've been living with my grandmother in Paris.'

'Can you name some of your friends?'

Laura's mind was blank. Thanks largely to Clemency Makepeace, she didn't have many friends, as such. Apart from Ernest and Ginette. But a transvestite prostitute and an elderly bar owner were not what was being asked for here.

She sat silently, heart sinking, before the chill azure stare. Would her lack of grand contacts cost her the job?

It seemed not. Suzanne now leant forward with a conspiratorial smile. 'Absolutely,' she whispered. 'The truly well connected never talk about the people they know. Quite right. Not at all the done thing. Just as long as you open your address book when Carinthia needs it, eh?'

Realising that, most unexpectedly, she seemed to have passed another of Suzanne's tests, Laura nodded fervently. And she meant it. The minute Carinthia wanted to do a feature on Ernest, Laura would lay all his contact details at her feet.

'Well, that's it,' Suzanne said brightly. 'You can start tomorrow. Antigone will have an ID card ready, and your exes. £20 a week to cover travel. We don't pay interns, as I expect Carinthia explained.'

Laura didn't think Carinthia had, but decided it didn't matter. It couldn't matter. She would manage, and she had a roof over her head with Caspar. The main thing was, she was in!

Too excited to wait for the lift, she ran down the back stairs and almost danced across the lobby. The revolving door whizzed in her wake.

Outside, the sun beat down happily on the well-swept pavement. Laura felt for her mobile and called Caspar again. She was desperate to share her good news, as well as check in about the flat. But his end remained unanswered. Again, no answerphone clicked in.

Her joy faded. Worry clawed at her, as well as annoyance. This really was ridiculous. She was now definitely beginning to think he was a jewel thief on the run. Or had he simply forgotten all about her, gone off with the blonde from the train? She'd almost prefer him to be a jewel thief.

Well, she had to be practical. Wherever he was, whatever was going on, it left her homeless. She must find a hotel if she was not to sleep on the streets. She had enough in her account for a few days if necessary. Caspar was bound to have emerged by then.

And when he did, she would tell him what she thought of him.

The Euston Road seemed her best bet. It had three mainline stations on it; there would be cheap chain hotels offering a decent level of cleanliness and comfort. She set off towards the Tube.

It was horribly crowded; this was rush hour. At Euston she lost her way among the escalators and tunnels but eventually made it to the train station concourse. This too was heaving with people, shoving in the opposite direction and dragging after them suitcases whose wheels bashed her ankles and feet. Laura skipped out of their way as best she could. London was a battleground!

Spotting the logo of a bargain hotel chain, she hurried gratefully towards it. Saved!

In the purple, deskless foyer, a lank-haired woman in a trouser suit and corporate neckscarf stood behind a touch-screen console. A badge on her lapel read, 'Kayleigh, Guest Welcome Operative'. She tapped the greasy screen. Yes, there was a room, and within Laura's budget. 'If you could just hand over your card,' said Kayleigh in a nasal drone.

Laura reached for the purse in her bag. Strangely, the bag was not in her hand. She realised that she couldn't remember the last time it had been. She glanced at the floor; had it fallen? It was not anywhere on the grey and purple carpet.

Panic closed in, but she forced herself to think rationally. Remember. Had she left it on the Tube? No, she'd had it at the exit, she had shoved her ticket in the zip front. She had had it on the concourse at Euston; she had put it down to put her coat back on. Was it then that someone had snatched it?

The hideous possibility clanged through her just as the nasal drone cut in. 'Your card?'

Laura stared at Kayleigh. 'My bag... I... someone's taken it.' Her mind reeled. Not only had her purse gone, her phone had too. She couldn't even call Caspar now. His number was in its memory.

'Someone's taken your bag?' The Visitor Welcome Operative sounded sceptical. She had clearly heard all this before.

Laura fought not to lose control. She spoke slowly, clearly.

'Yes, it's gone. And so I don't have a card.' God, and her *passport* had been in there as well. Her passport!

'Can't give you a room if you can't pay for it.'

'Yes, I see that, but it's not my fault. Someone's taken my bag.'

Kayleigh was tapping impassively into her console. 'Reported it to the police, haveya?'

'Well... no.'

'Better do that then.'

Laura stumbled away. She was penniless, passportless and roofless, with the strange London night coming on. How on earth had this happened? Not long ago, she had felt on the edge of something big. But it was an abyss. A huge black nothing.

Oh God. What now?

Chapter Seven

Laura found a policeman outside St Pancras Station.

'Lost yer passport, eh?' He looked less convinced even than Kayleigh.

'Yes, and my credit card. My bag was stolen.'

The policeman sighed under his hi-vis jacket. 'Taken copies, have yer?'

'Copies?' She recognised his Cockney accent. But now was not the time to try out whistles and flutes and Hampstead Heaths.

'Of yer passport. We recommend that anyone travelling takes copies of all their cards and documents, and emails them to themself. So, in the case of a situation like this, they can call 'em all up on their smartphone.'

Laura forced herself to be polite. She needed this man on her side. 'Well, I can see that's a good idea, but the thing is I haven't.'

'Haven't taken copies?'

'No, or got a smartphone. And even if I had, it would have been in my bag and got stolen with all the other stuff.'

'We recommend that people keep their smartphones separate,' the policeman informed her, before asking her, with a stunning lack of logic, if she had called to report her stolen cards.

'My phone's been stolen,' shouted poor Laura.

The policeman told her that there was no need for that attitude, and that she needed to fill in an online Home Office form reporting the passport theft and applying for a new one.

'But I don't have any internet access,' Laura began before realising she was just going round in circles. 'I haven't got anywhere to stay tonight,' she said, switching the topic to the most pressing one.

'There's hostels,' the policeman said. 'Got any ID?'

'No, I just told you. It's all been stolen.'

The policeman's walkie-talkie crackled urgently. 'Sorry, miss, I've got to go. You can always go down the station.'

Laura's heart leapt. 'I can stay there?' A night in the cells would be better than outside.

The large helmeted head shook. 'No, but you can report the theft.' He strode off, his radio blaring agitatedly.

Laura took a deep breath and glanced up at the façade of St Pancras. Its graceful Victorian Gothic had looked like a fairy palace before. But now it looked like Castle Dracula, sharp spikes and steeples stabbing the sky.

She felt despairing. Her place to stay had vanished into thin air. And now her money, cards and passport had been stolen. It was tempting just to give in, fling herself on the floor, and weep.

But what good would that do? People would just step over her. She'd have to think of something better.

Had she left any money in her jeans pockets? Rummaging, she felt her fingers touch something. A piece of card. The memory of Harry Scott rushed back.

An idea struck her. What about the jewel robbery? Caspar had disappeared, but was that really significant? In her heart of hearts she still couldn't quite believe it. But it was an excuse to contact Harry. And the mess she was now in was mostly Caspar's fault.

It was now that Laura remembered her phone had gone with her bag. She had nothing to make the call with. She clenched her fists and groaned.

There had to be a way out of this though. Somewhere, in this vast station, there had to be a phone that she could borrow. She must screw her courage to the sticking place. Use her wits, and her charm. Everyone had a phone; she only needed to ask somebody. Had she been in their position, she would happily have helped out.

Unfortunately, none of the people Laura now stopped shared her attitude. They ranged from a grim-faced old lady who walked away without speaking to a spotty teenager who told her to fuck off. It was all most discouraging.

Laura forced herself to remain cheerful. Being positive was her only weapon.

She had by now walked into the station. The lights of the concourse shops and cafes shone. Perhaps she could just stay here? It was only a few hours between now and when her new job started. In the offices of *Society* she could sort herself out, call the banks, fill in the online passport form.

She realised now that she was terribly hungry. Her stomach seemed to be cleaving to her backbone. Quite suddenly, food was all she could think about. Everywhere she looked there were tables full of people eating and drinking.

She sat down on a bench and reached for a magazine supplement someone had left. She would ignore the hunger pangs through sheer willpower.

She turned the magazine's creased pages. A familiar face grinned up at her, surrounded by cascades of shining blonde hair. Lulu was being interviewed again.

'I FED-EX MY LAUNDRY TO NEW YORK, DOESN'T EVERYONE?' was the headline.

In the main photograph, seemingly taken on a building site, Lulu's buxom form had been shoved into a silver bodycon dress. She was being lifted up by men in hi-vis jackets and was waving a sign proclaiming 'I'll Do Anything for Diamonds'.

'I'm super-normal,' Lulu told the writer, Shona Sowerby.

And it's true she's a big fan of recycling. Reader, she wears some of her vast wardrobe of designer items as often as twice a year! And she loves nothing more than a night in with a takeout in front of the telly. But forget Curry in a Hurry on the Seven Sisters Road. This takeout's from Nobu and picked up by the chauffeur. And the telly is a state-of-the-art private cinema in the multi-million-pound mansion's mega-basement.

We move on to relationships. Lulu's name has been linked most famously with *Frat Guys Go Large* star Ryan Small, who was photographed with his hand on her bottom at last year's Golden Globes. The shot went viral and resulted in Small's wife, *Balls Out* actress Findlay McGroot, temporarily moving out of their $50m Beverley Hills mansion (the couple have since patched things up).

Other exes include playboy Jay Phillips, for whom home is

a megayacht in Monte Carlo harbour. The relationship ended
when a tape showing him pleasuring a wombat went viral...

Laura wondered what Lulu would do in her situation. She
doubted she would sit about on the concourse feeling sorry
for herself. She would probably head straight to the hotel,
the luxurious five-star number whose glass-doored entrance
she had passed on the way in.

And so why not do the same? Laura raised her chin,
straightened her back, shook back her hair and smiled. Then
she strode confidently forward, maintaining a measured,
unhurried pace.

The hotel lobby was separated from the outside by great
shining sheets of glass. They leapt apart as Laura approached.
She walked between silver tubs of topiary twisting up like
shaggy green screws. Doormen in green tailcoats and black
top hats stood on hand to help guests in and out of the
succession of taxis and gleaming limos that drew up.

Laura fully expected that these doormen would stop her,
but, amazingly, they did not. They beamed, 'Good evening,
madam,' and on she passed into an enormous light-filled
lobby. The first hurdle was over.

Her confidence rising, Laura appraised the scene. Placed at
regular intervals about the thick, pale carpet were supersized
sofas adjoined by winged armchairs. Couples or small groups
of people sat before silver cakestands or lifted polished
champagne flutes to smiling lips. In contrast with the frantic
concourse outside, the atmosphere was all decorous luxury.
Lamps glowed softly, waiters moved quietly, people talked in
low voices. All was calm and comfortable.

Laura's fear had almost gone now. In a tense sort of way,
she was even starting to enjoy herself. If she played her cards

right, she could buy herself a few hours here in which to gather her wits. Perhaps even turn her luck round altogether. All she had to do was avoid looking suspicious. And find someone to lend her a phone, of course.

Keeping on the move seemed the best idea. Sitting down in the lobby would attract the attention of the waiters, from whom she could order nothing. Smiling a confident smile and not slackening her pace in the least, Laura sailed blithely past the bar and found herself in a corridor lined with luxurious Victorian Gothic wallpaper on which brass plates with room numbers were screwed.

She was now in the hotel proper. She had passed out of the public area and away from general scrutiny. While she was still looking for a phone, her new plan was to move as far up the building as possible. The higher she went, the further she would be from the ground floor where she might invite suspicion. She was a woman alone in a luxury hotel, in an area of London whose reputation, as even Paris-based Laura knew, was somewhat colourful. Her presence would be open to misinterpretation.

The corridor had now become a huge stairwell which rose the entire height of the building. A shallow flight of steps split in two and climbed like fantastical stone foliage to a distant ceiling curved, ribbed and gloriously painted in the style of a medieval cathedral. Set in a red wall painted with gold fleur-de-lys, graceful pointed windows let in the flooding light. It was so breathtaking that Laura forgot for a second her predicament and just stood lost in admiration.

This was a mistake. A tall thin young man in a dark suit slightly too big for him now appeared. 'Can I help you, madam?' A hotel badge glinted on his lapel. He looked her up and down suspiciously.

Laura could imagine the figure she presented with her train-creased jeans and rumpled shirt. She willed her suddenly blank brain to come up with something. If it didn't, she'd be thrown out and back on the concourse.

She noticed his name, Nicolas, and put it together with the slight accent she had detected. She remembered that the Channel Tunnel meant this station and its environs employed a great many workers from France.

'I'm so glad to see you,' Laura exclaimed in French. 'I'm looking for housekeeping and I'm completely lost.'

Nicolas's suspicious expression disappeared. 'Ah! You are here for a job?'

Beaming, Laura assured him she was.

'So housekeeping is on the top floor. You are French?'

'Parisienne.'

He looked her up and down. 'Yes, I can see that now.'

Nicolas was from the Auvergne. Laura, who had never been and knew only that it was mountainous and famous for cheese and a strange aperitif brewed from gentian root, did her best.

'I love the Auvergne!' she declared immediately.

'Marvellous, isn't it?' Nicolas puffed out his skinny chest.

'So romantic. All those, erm, mountains.'

Nicolas looked thrilled.

'And all that... cheese!'

'Yes! The cheese!'

'And that fantastic aperitif they make there, from that plant...'

'You like it? Great stuff, isn't it?' There was something rather simple and touching about him. Laura sensed he had not been long in London.

He was looking at her expectantly with misty eyes, but she

had run out of Auvergne facts now. One of Mimi's pieces of advice now floated back to her. *If in doubt, flirt.*

She grinned at him. 'And I can see it's true what they say about Auvergne men!'

He grinned back. The mist in his eyes had been replaced by something rather more wolfish. 'My shift finishes at four. I could take you for a drink. Give me your mobile number?' He was getting his out. For a country bumpkin, he was a faster worker than she had expected. On the other hand, he was French.

Her heart leapt at the sight of the longed-for instrument. At last! This was too good a chance to miss. But would it look suspicious if she asked him to lend it to her?

Just then a portly couple appeared in the stairwell. Their large faces were creased with irritation. Spotting Nicolas and his hotel badge, they bore down on him. 'We have a complaint about our room,' the female half of the couple, a vision in jeans and fanny-pack, announced in an American accent.

'It overlooks the railway station,' added her husband, in tones of disgust.

Nicolas looked perturbed and Laura listened to him explain, as best he could in his halting English, that the view of the magnificent Victorian concourse was the pride of the establishment and usually preferred by guests to the glamorous aspect of the Euston Road. The couple looked unconvinced. 'I'm not paying good money to look over a railway track.'

Laura melted away up the stairs, shooting Nicolas a sympathetic smile as she went.

On the top floor, all was silent. Blocking her view down the long carpeted corridor was one of the cleaning trolleys pushed by housekeeping staff around hotels the world over. It was piled with sheets, towels and small bottles of bath foam and body lotion. The bottom level was a forest of cleaning products.

Laura sat down in an alcove to wait. Perhaps the cleaner it belonged to might lend her their phone. But as the minutes went by and no cleaner appeared, a new idea now occurred to her.

If she could get into a hotel room, she would be able to use the telephone. And the trolley was the perfect means of entry. Laura balled up her trenchcoat and shoved it between the bottles on the lower level. Taking a pillowcase from the top, she tucked it round her hips to look like an apron. Then she headed to the lift, which mercifully opened immediately.

It was large, mirrored and contained two chattering women in hijabs accompanied by a large boy who rummaged through Laura's trolley. He seemed to be looking for something. 'Chocolates!' he pronounced eventually, wielding a catering pack of foil-wrapped sweets in triumph. Watched fondly by the chattering women, he shoved the box in his rucksack. Laura didn't argue. She got off on the next floor down.

The corridor here was long and thickly carpeted, its cream walls picked out with gold. The air hummed slightly. Laura pushed her gently rattling conveyance slowly along.

She was starting to doubt her plan. Would she be able to get into any of the rooms? The doors were all shut, presenting glossy mahogany faces to the world, and there was no skeleton key on the trolley, no card that slotted into every lock.

A movement in the distance made her heart jump. A woman was coming down the passage: dark-haired, smartly dressed and with an air of belonging. Laura's hands clenched on the trolley's handles; was this the head of housekeeping?

Laura kept her head down, her mien submissive and her eyes on the approaching feet in shiny high-heeled black shoes. Her worst fears were realised when the woman paused beside her cart and stared her in the face. Then she opened a shining trophy handbag, crammed in all but a handful of the trolley's complimentary toiletries, and stalked off.

Laura pushed on past more closed doors. Perhaps if someone would rob her of her towels next, then her sheets, and she would be reduced to nothing at all. She saw that she was drawing up to a door that was ajar.

She stopped and listened. No sound was coming from inside. She knocked. 'Housekeeping!' But answer came there none. It was the work of a second to slip inside with her trolley and close it after her.

The room inside was enormous and seemed to lead off into several other rooms. A vast and ornate window dominated the far wall. Shining buttoned-leather sofas and matching chairs were arranged companionably round a coffee table. A screenprint of the Queen hung over a carved fireplace; adjacent to that was a black lacquered baby grand piano.

There was no time to admire all this, however, nor to pause at the glimpse of a luxurious blue-draped bedroom and a bathroom with a free-standing gold tub. Laura's eyes were on the telephone on the desk beyond the sofas.

Hastily she dragged out Harry Scott's card. Please answer, Laura prayed as she punched in the numbers, hoping that he wouldn't be another Caspar.

A couple of rings, then an answerphone kicked in. The voice was not Harry's but the generic female tones of the service provider. Laura's shoulders slumped in defeat.

She left a message anyway, her eyes scanning the room as she spoke. Might she hide under the bed and sleep there? Even the risk of discovery and arrest seemed preferable to a night taking her chances on the concourse.

'Hello?'

The woman on the other end had changed into a man. The other end had picked up. 'Harry?' she gasped.

'Who is this?'

His voice, though impersonal, made her want to cry with relief. She struggled for control. 'It's Laura. Laura Lake. We met on the train?'

The tone changed, subtly but instantly. 'Laura. Good to hear you.'

'It might not be when you find out why I'm calling.'

'Is this about Caspar?'

Laura took a deep breath. 'In a way, yes.'

'You've found a cache of jewels in his flat?' He sounded ironic, but hopeful.

'No. But he's disappeared,' Laura firmly pushed away any feelings of guilt. Caspar had let her down.

'Interesting,' said Harry. 'You don't know where to?'

'No idea. He's not answering his phone.'

'Can you give me his address?'

'I don't have it.'

'But you were staying with him.'

Laura agreed that she was.

'And you're a journalist.'

'Yes,' Laura said with a flash of pride. This fact was the only bright side to her current predicament.

'Your father was a famous reporter and you hope to follow in his footsteps.'

'Absolutely.'

'But you have no idea what address your friend lives at?' There was dry amusement in Harry's tone.

Laura's face flamed. 'It was all a bit of a rush,' she started defensively, before realising there was no point. Harry was right. It did all sound pretty silly. And she needed his help, and fast. Someone might come into the room at any moment. She took a deep breath. 'Look, I'll be honest.'

'Always the best policy. Except when it isn't.'

'I need a bit of help. Well, a lot of help really. Just for tonight. I start my new job tomorrow, so I'll be fine after that—'

'Stop gabbling. Slow down,' the other end instructed.

The other end was so silent after she finished her garbled account of her adventures that it seemed Harry had hung up. Laura couldn't blame him. Her story had sounded ridiculous even to her own ears. The lack of address, the careless loss of her bag with everything in it. He was right. What sort of hopeless reporter did that? She was a disgrace to the family name.

'Harry?' she asked, in a small voice.

'Go to the front desk,' the other end instructed.

'What?'

'The reception. There's a room booked in your name.'

Laura squeezed her eyes tight shut and opened them again, but things were as confusing as ever. 'What room? I can't afford a room here. Or anywhere. I just told you.'

'It's paid for,' the other end said, with a slightly testy air. 'I've just done it online.'

'But you can't...' Laura began. But then she stopped. She was in no position to argue. 'Thank you,' she added, sincerely.

'Look, I've got to go.' She could tell he was reading a text message. His voice had the same distant, distracted quality she remembered from the train. Then the line went dead.

Laura, calling it back immediately and repeatedly, could only get the answerphone girl again. 'Thank you,' she told her. 'I'll pay you back, I promise.'

She replaced the receiver, feeling at once vastly relieved but also hugely embarrassed. Laura was accustomed to thinking of herself as the capable sort, a strong woman, so it was humiliating to reflect on how she must seem to Harry. A scatty girl with pretensions to be a reporter. Who had come to London on the say-so of a virtual stranger, now missing and a presumed jewel thief. And who had compounded this folly by losing her every possession and means of identification. And who was now hiding in a hotel room pretending to be a cleaner

Well, she would show him! She might be down now, but she would get up again! As well as paying him back, she would make him respect her. Show that she was her father's daughter, somehow.

Voices passing outside the door reminded her of the precariousness of her situation. She held her breath, dreading that whoever it was would come in. Being discovered as an interloper now would be a disaster; the hotel might refuse to put her up, paid-for room or not...

But the voices passed on and Laura slipped outside, left the trolley where it was and took the lift to the ground floor. Hurrying across the large, lamplit lobby to the front desk, she hoped Nicolas would not see her. There was someone else who might find her behaviour suspicious.

'Here you are, Miss Lake.' The smooth-haired girl behind the reception smiled at Laura as she handed over a card key. The contrast with Kayleigh the Visitor Welcome Officer could not have been starker.

The room Harry had booked was on the top floor,

but she had no fear of going up there now. While much smaller than the splendid suite she had called him from, it seemed like paradise nonetheless. It was warm, clean and above all, safe. Nor did it lack comfort, with its wide bed covered with a folded silk drape, its padded armchair and its marbled bathroom. The view of the station through the Victorian stone tracery of the window was best of all. How the American couple could not have liked it was beyond Laura. Shining platforms, gleaming trains, glowing shops and moving people spreading into the distance. But while it looked romantic and exciting from up here, not to be down there, at the mercy of whatever or whoever might happen to her, seems the greatest luxury of all.

Her first act was to run a bath. She washed her hair and luxuriated in the scented bubbles for a while. Beneath the warm water, her stomach growled insistently. She had eaten the shortbread that came with the room, but she was still hungry. There was nothing she could do about it, however.

She was examining the TV channels, her hair wrapped in a white towel, when there was a resounding knock on the room's mahogany door. Laura clutched her bathrobe around herself; had her role in the theft of the trolley been discovered?

A familiar face stood outside.

'Nicolas!'

He looked just as surprised to see her. 'I thought you were here for a job.'

Laura cleared her throat and looked down at her bathrobe. 'Er…' She could imagine what sort of job it looked like.

Nicolas said nothing, but his disapproval was obvious as he proffered something at her: a tray with a silver dish cover on it, plus glasses, cutlery and a small bottle of red wine.

'I didn't order this,' Laura muttered through her blushes.

'A Monsieur Harry Scott did,' Nicolas said tartly before turning on his heel and disappearing down the corridor. Laura watched his retreating back and bit her lip regretfully. Oh well. It could not be helped. As Mimi sometimes said, you could not make an omelette without breaking eggs.

The delicious scent of whatever was beneath the cover, definitely not an omelette, swirled around her nostrils. She went back inside, full of hungry anticipation. On an elegant gold-rimmed plate lay a rib-eye steak the size of a foot, cooked *à point*, just as she liked it. Her favourite; how did he know? And the red wine was a Burgundy, her favourite, again.

She ate ravenously, overlooking the shining station and feeling utterly relieved. Tonight, unlike so many people in this city, she had been rescued from wandering the streets.

Tomorrow was another day, and her first at *Society*. There she could sort out her bank card and her passport and find somewhere else to stay. Pay back Harry Scott, as well. Impressing him would just have to wait.

Lying back, soon afterwards, on the smooth, cool, cotton pillows, listening to the hum of the air conditioner and, beyond that, the faint boom of the station, Laura smiled as she drifted off into a deep, relaxing sleep.

Chapter Eight

Five minutes later, or so it seemed, Laura was opening her eyes and wondering where she was. As she focused on the room's grand window and felt the crisp white linen beneath her, the events of yesterday rushed back, along with a feeling of swooping excitement. Today was her first day in her new job!

It was followed by a rather more complicated sensation, in which gratitude to Harry Scott was mixed with pure embarrassment. Laura threw back the covers and leapt out of bed. Oh well. When she was a great reporter, he would be able to reflect that he had helped her on her journey.

She stood before the window and stretched. The station's shiny floors, empty last night, were black with hurrying people. A sense of energy and anticipation filled her. Today was the first day of the rest of her life. Everything would be sorted out. Her start in London had been rocky, but it would be plain sailing from now on. She hurried into the bathroom. Caspar, even if he had been around, would never have had such an amazing power shower. Still less such an array of luxurious body lotions and possibly not an iron, although he probably had a hairdryer, judging by how full and shiny his mane always was. Laura felt triumphant. She had survived without him, after all.

She made full and glorious use of every facility and by the time she had finished looked and felt better even than when she'd set off from Paris. Her hair fell to her shoulders in a shining sheet, her dark shirt and jeans looked sharp and well pressed. Thanks to the hotel shoe-cleaning kit, her Chelsea boots gleamed. And Mimi's trench, while it was old, always looked good however badly it was treated.

Although Laura had been ready to brazen it out if Nicolas was on duty in the breakfast room, his absence was a relief. It meant that she could properly admire the grand Victorian room, with its chandeliers, Gothic touches and tables swathed in snowy linen set with gleaming silver- and glassware. More importantly, she could properly admire the breakfast. Ravenous again, despite last night's steak, she ordered the fullest and most English one on the menu. A plate of sausages, black pudding, bacon and eggs duly arrived and Laura wolfed everything down along with gallons of excellent coffee.

She flicked through her favourite mid-market tabloid as she did so, pausing on the gossip page. It was edited by a tough-looking blonde called Sarah Salmon, whose byline picture grimaced out at the reader.

The hand raising a forkful of bacon now stopped in mid-air. A familiar face smiled up at Laura from the gossip page:

Amy Bender, complete with cutlery-stuffed dreadlocks and wearing Irina Pushamoff's fishnet-tights top.

'TRIPP GOES ON A BENDER' was the headline to the main story. The bacon cooling on her fork, Laura read on.

Regular readers might recall my exclusive, 'Romancing the Stone', in which I revealed how multimillionaire contemporary sculptor Spartacus Tripp had married a large boulder in his Italian garden. But at last night's party launching new London hotspot Grope, Mr Tripp confirmed they had divorced. 'It was heavy going,' he revealed. 'But we want to stay on good terms. In many ways she's my rock.'

Mr Tripp's new love is fellow artist Amy Bender, who he met recently at the Kazakhstan home of billionaire art collector Igor Ripemov.

'Somehow, we just clicked,' says twenty-two-year-old Miss Bender, a recent graduate of Cleethorpes College of Art. 'Spartacus and I just chatted over supper and it was as if we had known each other for ages. I was absolutely amazed when a friend told me afterwards that he had an estate in Italy, several Picassos and a massive fortune.'

Miss Bender was in the former Soviet republic with her touring installation *Call This Art?*, whose Parisian launch earlier this month culminated in the dramatic theft of her mother's diamonds. The perpetrators of the robbery are still at large.

Miss Bender, however, is putting this unhappy affair behind her in the most practical of ways. New jewellery is being commissioned for the wedding. Mary-Bliss Skinner, a favourite of this column and *haute joaillier* daughter of rock star Brian Skinner, is creating zero-impact bespoke wedding rings for the happy couple from her Hell line of ethical jewels mounted on found objects.

'Sid and Nancy, Spartacus's pit bulls, are going to be the ringbearers,' Miss Bender adds. 'They'll look so cute!'

The happy couple divide their time between Tripp's Italian estates and his London home, a former typhoid hospital in Hoxton, recently given a multimillion-pound refurbishment by interiors guru Buzzie Omelet.

A glittering gathering of the great and the good, from fashion to finance, and art to the aristocracy, seems certain to attend the coming happy event. But will they get the right day? 'I have told people lots of different dates so that no one knows exactly when it is, not even me,' reveals Spartacus.

There was a picture of Spartacus Tripp beneath the article. He wore a frogman suit complete with flippers and spear gun and was holding a glass of champagne.

How utterly ridiculous, Laura thought. Thank God she wouldn't be seeing Amy Bender ever again. Placing her knife and fork together on her empty plate, she took a final gulp of coffee. She felt ready to take the world, and *Society* in particular, by storm.

As she would be walking to *Society*, lacking money for the bus, Laura consulted an *A to Z* in a station WHSmith's. Using one of the store's pens, she sketched a quick map on the back of a receipt found on the floor. Then she pushed back her shoulders, raised her chin and set off.

The bright morning reflected Laura's own bounding optimism. A blue sky stretched over the city. The buildings shone white in the sun; windows winked, gilding flashed. London, which for a time last night had looked threatening, now looked glamorous and full of promise.

The sun beat down on her back as she walked through Bloomsbury's elegant Georgian streets and shady garden squares. By the British Museum, a herd of spotty teenagers was being rounded up by a beleaguered-looking teacher. They were all staring into their screens and it seemed unlikely that any of them would be swooning over the Rosetta Stone.

In Soho, the streets were small and felt intimate. Fashionable people hurried past.

'Millie, call my mobey!' a redhead in a striped dress was shouting into a smartphone. Her hair reminded Laura of Clemency Makepeace, and a feeling of triumph filled her. What would the school bully think if she could see her now? Skinny Laura Lake with the wingnut ears, about to launch herself into the world of the glossies. About to go to the parties, ferret out the stories, win the awards. She had prevailed in spite of everything.

Grinning to herself, Laura continued on past the film-production companies, the voiceover studios, the marketing firms, the agencies.

'We've had requests from ITV's *Good Morning Britain* and *This Morning*, 5 Live and Sky News,' a dark-haired girl was saying outside a cafe.

A waiter came out. 'Chai-seed tea with a wheatgrass shot? Skinny nettle coffee?'

And here was the square with the statue in the middle, the one with *Society*'s elegant twenties building at one end of it.

A different guard at the desk glanced up at her. 'Cleaning staff go in the back.'

Laura was nonplussed. After all the effort she had made with her appearance too. 'I'm not cleaning staff. I'm editorial.'

The guard stared. 'But it's just past nine. Editorial never get in before ten.'

'It's my first day. I'm keen.'

'Makes a change. Fifth floor.'

It was the smell that hit Laura first. A powerful punch of the perfume of hundreds of bunches of flowers. The office seemed filled with them.

There were masses of them, heaps of them, blooms of all shapes, sizes and sorts. Bouquets in baskets, and bunches in fancy boxes with silk handles and bright tissue paper. Or wrapped in cellophane and bound with ribbons, plastic bags of water bulging around their stems.

Laura stared into bright yellow sunflowers and was stared back at by dark-eyed anemones. There were burgundy lilies and coral gladioli and purple delphiniums. There were peonies in every shade of pink, leaves in every shade of green and roses in every colour, every size, everywhere.

At which desk – at which flowers – would she sit?

It was obvious where Carinthia sat. A great bunch of giant white lilies was propped against the doorway of a small glass room, a sort of office within the office. Inside it was a big desk, with a long primrose-yellow sofa opposite. Thick white shelving covered the wall to the right of it, while a hugely blown-up *Society* cover was fixed to the wall behind the desk. The picture was black and white, sixties-style, with the magazine title in popping pink. The high-cheekboned model had blonde windswept hair and was smiling a huge, happy, pearl-toothed smile.

Laura grinned back, imagining herself on the primrose sofa talking Carinthia through her features suggestions. The hooded, snake-like eyes she remembered so well would glint with approval from behind the big desk. 'Laura Lake!' Carinthia would say. 'I really think that is the best idea I have ever heard in my life!'

The desk just outside the editor's door was dominated by a huge pile of post strapped with rubber bands. The red light of the answerphone was flashing agitatedly.

'This is the office of Bob Dylan,' a female American voice was announcing. 'Mr Dylan thanks you for the invitation to guest-edit your magazine but regrets he is unable to oblige.'

Pity, thought Laura. That could have been interesting. She started to immediately think up alternative guest-editor suggestions to present to Carinthia when they met. Adele? The Dalai Lama? Michele Obama? Prince Harry? Yes, he would be good...

In and among the flowers there were glimpses of computer screens; beneath the paper and ribbons there were keyboards. Perhaps the labels on the flowers would tell her who sat where.

The ones on the nearest desk were all to someone called Saffron. The beauty editor, presumably. Beneath the foliage were shiny boxes of make-up and skin products. This was the land of triple-oxygen facials, epidermal growth factors and volcanic Icelandic mud. One moisturiser contained 'hypodermically extracted blister juice, the new wonder ingredient that sets back your skin's ageing clock by ten years'.

Blister juice? As in that yellow stuff inside blisters? Yuk!

The bouquets at the next desk were all addressed to 'Darling Lucia'. That she was the interiors editor was obvious from the life-size black resin horse with a lampshade for a head that dominated the area. Scattered around it were cushions printed with Kim Kardashian in a crown and a large birdhouse shaped like Moscow's St Basil's Cathedral, right down to the twisted gold domes. Laura picked up a scented candle: 'Lime, Sage and Pizza Margarita'.

The heaps of flowers next door to all this were more numerous than anywhere else in the office. No prizes for guessing whose desk this was.

To Harriet, with love from Karl
To Harriet, with love from Miuccia
To Harriet, with love from Stella

The fashion editor did not seem to run an especially tight sartorial ship. The department was a mess. All over the desk and on the floor, designer carrier bags were tangled up with tissue paper, bubble wrap and shoes. More mess spilled from the open door of a small room nearby. Laura peered in. It was piled with great heaps of clothes and looked like a fashion avalanche, or perhaps a landfill site bristling with famous logos. She moved on, glad that clearing it up wouldn't be her responsibility.

The bank of desks in the middle of the office were the only ones that seemed to be used for actual work. No one sent the people here any flowers. The desks were covered with printouts of magazine pages. This must be where the sub-editors sat, the writers of headlines and checkers of facts. Here was a cover mock-up. A blonde in a big red coat beamed out above a coverline that read: 'HOW TO WEAR THE NEW STATEMENT GOAT'.

Someone had crossed out the G, put a C above it and scribbled, 'Whoever did this is fucking fired. Carinthia'.

Grinning, Laura slid the cover aside. Some girls with large teeth, tiaras and black leather jackets looked out haughtily from a photograph. The accompanying piece was about three heiresses who all dressed in identical clothes. How lame, Laura thought. She had much better ideas than that.

Beneath it was an article about how fencing was fashionable. Four superior-looking youths in tight white breeches stood holding their masks and foils. This didn't seem terribly original to Laura either. It also brought back a horrid memory.

That first term at St Margaret's. She had fallen foul of Clemency Makepeace immediately, although completely by accident. One night, walking into the dormitory they shared, Laura had found Clemency savagely pillow-beating one of the room's other occupants, a new girl like herself called Ella. The weeping Ella, her thick glasses shattered on the carpet before her, was being held by Kate, the fourth girl in the dormitory, and, like Clemency, an older girl.

Laura had not paused to think. Her instinct, to grab Clemency by the hair and smash her face into the wall, was one she followed to the letter. It marked the end of Clemency's campaign against Ella and began the one against Laura herself. Word soon got around the school of how the all-dominant school bully had been shown up by a new girl, and that funny, skinny French one at that.

As the vicious attacks began, no one, not even Ella, came to Laura's rescue. Fear of Clemency and her henchwomen was too great. Laura fought back as best she could but made no complaint to the teachers. There was no point; authority was always on Clemency's side. When not snarling and beating Laura, she sat in the front of the class paying wide-eyed attention and answering questions in a high-pitched little-girl voice. The teachers loved her.

As the campaign against her stepped up, Laura got used to finding her bed soaked with cold water and her clothes serving as bedding for the school's rabbits and hamsters. Efforts to track down missing shoes led to lateness, for which she was punished. As, at roll call, the housemistress rebuked her, Laura would see, out of the corner of her eye, Clemency smirking.

Trying to keep out of her way, Laura had taken up obscure pastimes. Fencing was one of them. The sport had been started at St Margaret's under the auspices of a housemistress who had been in the national team. Once it was known that Laura had an especial aptitude for it, Clemency struck. Literally.

It had all happened so quickly. One moment she stood in her fencing whites, reaching for her mask. The next, she felt a sharp bite of pain in her face. Raising her hand in its protective glove, Laura was shocked to see red blood running between the fingers, soaking the white fabric.

She pulled off the glove and touched her cheek. It felt swollen, wet. She could feel the blood pulsing out and taste its brassy flavour on her lips.

Laura had thought herself alone in the sports hall, but she saw now that she was not. Retreating, sabre in hand, was a masked figure, also in fencing whites. The black mesh meant that identification was impossible, but as the figure turned, Laura caught a glimpse of auburn hair tucked into a collar. Then darkness swirled over her eyes and she fell.

She woke to find herself in bed. Not in her usual dormitory, but in a small white room by herself. Her face throbbed and felt heavy. She raised a hand; her cheek was thickly padded. She was no longer in fencing whites but the pyjamas Mimi had sent her. They had Eiffel Towers and poodles on them. Laura stared at the poodles.

'And how are you feeling?'

She looked up into the friendly gaze of Matron. 'Someone slashed me in the face.'

Matron gasped. 'Of course they didn't! You blacked out just as you were putting your mask on. You fell on the sabre blades in the rack.'

'I didn't!' Laura protested, raising herself up. 'And I couldn't have done anyway. The blades point down, not up.'

'Well, *one* of them was upright.'

'Who found me?' Laura asked. There was more than one way of approaching this mystery.

'Clemency Makepeace,' Matron said fondly. 'She raised the alarm, the dear girl. She was awfully shocked herself, poor thing. But very helpful. She found the sabre that you fell on. Apparently it was absolutely covered in blood.'

Laura jumped, jerked rudely back into the present as someone now entered the office. She hoped it was Carinthia. To be alone in the office with the editor would be a wonderful opportunity. She could present some of her ideas.

It was not Carinthia, however, but a slight, tanned girl in a leather waistcoat and denim miniskirt. With her side-parted dark hair in a single plait which ended in a neon-pink feather, there was something of the squaw about her. Dreamcatcher earrings and brown gladiator sandals completed the look, along with a great heap of dry-cleaning.

Laura took a deep breath and gave the girl a broad smile. 'Hi. I'm Laura Lake. I'm the intern.'

The girl nodded. 'I'm Demelza. Carinthia's assistant.'

'I thought she was called Xanthe.'

'Xanthe was the one before me. None of us last long. Working for Carinthia's like being married to Henry VIII.'

'Surely it's not that bad,' Laura said brightly.

Demelza chuckled. 'You'll find out.' She snapped off the elastic band around the post and began to open it. 'Just watch out for The Gaze.'

'The Gaze?'

'Kind of a freezing thousand-yard stare. If you get that, you're in trouble.'

Laura immediately resolved never to get it. 'Where should I sit?' she asked.

'What department are you?'

Laura did not hesitate. 'Features,' she said firmly.

'Oh well, here's your answer!' Demelza said cheerfully. 'The features editor's just come in!'

Laura turned, and looked. And blinked, disbelieving. It could not be true. Please let it not be true!

'God, how bad was the Tube this morning?' exclaimed the familiar, breathy, little-girl voice. Clemency was busy shrugging off a tiny gold leather jacket. She hadn't yet glanced at Laura.

Laura was still struggling to gather her wits. It felt as if her brain had blown up and the pieces were floating back down only slowly. Clemency Makepeace, her long red hair flowing glossily over her shoulders, was the *Society* features editor? The disappointment was shattering. It was as if a plug had been pulled and all Laura's happiness and excitement had drained out. Her heart banged painfully in her chest and the scar on her cheek burned and throbbed.

The smell of the flowers rose overpoweringly up her nose. The room started to whirl. She gripped the edge of the desk. She would not faint! She stared at the spinning carpet, willing it to stop. She wouldn't let this stop her. She had overcome so much already. What could a school bully from years ago do to hurt her now?

Clemency was looking at her, she could feel it. 'Who's this?' asked the breathy little voice.

Laura looked up, pushing back her hair to reveal her

face, plastering on the calmest smile she could. This was the moment.

It was an anti-climax, however. The green stare that met hers looked merely bored. Clemency had not recognised her!

'Your new intern,' Demelza said cheerfully.

'*My* new intern?' Clemency sounded put out. 'Carinthia never said anything.'

'Carinthia never does.'

'Name?' Clemency glared at Laura, whose mind was whirling. As Clemency had no idea who she was, might she somehow remain anonymous? Invent a nickname?

'Laura Lake,' Demelza helpfully put in.

The green eyes flexed in shock. 'Laura *Lake*? It can't be!'

'Hey,' said Demelza, delighted. 'You two know each other?'

'We were at school together,' Laura managed, as Clemency remained silent.

'How great is that? Aw, look at Clemency! She literally can't speak, she's so thrilled.' Demelza's fond expression now changed to one of panic. She gave a sharp gasp. 'Someone's put *poppies* in Carinthia's office! She thinks red flowers are common. She'll freak.'

The executive assistant hurried off.

Laura turned to Clemency. 'So,' she said, brightly.

'So what?' Clemency snarled, conclusively abandoning the fetching lisp.

It wasn't an especially promising start, but Laura was determined to try. 'So perhaps we can put school behind us? It's a long time ago, after all. Let bygones be bygones and all that.' It seemed to her a magnanimous offer; she had been the injured party after all. Quite literally, and on many occasions.

Clemency did not reply. Hopefully she was considering the suggestion.

'Do you know where I'm supposed to sit?' Laura asked genially.

Clemency's green glance was full of derision. '*Sit?*'

'Sit, yes.'

'As in sit, as in have a *desk*?'

'That's right.'

'What the actual fuck do you think you're going to do here?'

The olive branch had clearly been declined. Laura raised her chin. 'Carinthia liked my writing.'

'Well I don't and I'm the features editor.'

'You haven't seen it yet.'

'I don't have to,' Clemency hissed. 'You're not writing anything for me. You might as well leave now.'

Anger was rising in Laura. 'Says who? You're not the editor. It was Carinthia who gave me the internship.'

Clemency's lip curled. 'Carinthia's always giving people internships. It's all part of her power trip. She loves that excited look in their bright little eyes when they think their great magazine career has begun.'

Laura stared at the floor. Obviously sensing she had landed a blow, Clemency stepped forward. 'But then when they turn up she doesn't have the foggiest who they are.' She shook her head, mock-pityingly. 'It's awful really. Poor little things get terribly disappointed.'

A knot of dread was tightening in Laura's stomach. Was this what lay ahead? She would not believe it. She could not.

Clemency was warming to her theme. 'Only the other week this poor girl rocked up who Carinthia had met in some hotel. Didn't work out though.'

Laura had heard enough. She met Clemency's glittering stare with a determined one of her own. 'You're not in charge.'

Clemency tittered. 'Well, I'm in charge of *you*. Given that you think you're on features.' She paused. 'But I think I'll send you to, ooh, let's see.' She folded her arms and glanced appraisingly round the office. 'Beauty? No. You're too ugly.'

The sheer childishness of it was hard to believe. 'We're not at school now,' Laura reminded her.

Clemency's lips, which seemed fuller than they used to be, curved in a nasty smile. 'You're right. And by the time I've finished with you, you'll wish we were.'

Her expression changed suddenly to a syrupy smile. 'Lucia?' she called in her lisping, little-girl voice. 'Need a slave on the interiors desk, do you, darling?'

Laura saw that the woman Clemency was calling to was Penis, Pigeon and Pout from the foyer.

'No, thanks,' Lucia called back as she draped her handbag round the neck of the horse with the lampshade head. 'The last one was a disaster. That business with the upside-down rose trees.'

Clemency gave a tinkling titter. 'Oh, yes! With their roots in the air and the roses in the ground.'

'Well that was how they were supposed to look, for the shoot.' Lucia groaned. 'But this idiot girl took them all out and planted them flower end up.'

Other members of staff were now drifting in. They stared curiously at Laura as she stood beside Clemency. She hated feeling such a spare part, and so powerless. But for now, of course, she had no choice. She would await her opportunity. If Clemency thought she had beaten her, she had another think coming.

'Travel?' Clemency was musing. 'We could send you on a luxury weekend in... ooh, let's think. Kabul? Aleppo.'

'Ha ha,' Laura muttered under her breath.

'Except that the travel editor's away trying a didgeridoo course in Venice. So that leaves fashion,' Clemency concluded.

While she knew that resistance was pointless, Laura had to try. 'It's not something I know much about.'

'Who said you need to?' Clemency demanded. 'You'll only be tidying the fashion cupboard.'

Laura pictured the bombsite in the little room behind the door. If that was the fashion cupboard, tidying it would take weeks. A person could go in there and never come out. Her heart was sinking, but she raised her chin. Clemency would never break her.

The fashion department was deserted apart from the heaps of flowers. Some bunches were still in their cellophane. They looked wilting and airless, obviously needing water. Other flowers were actually dead.

Sorting them out, Laura decided, would make her look proactive. It would also delay the evil moment of tackling the fashion cupboard. By the time she had finished putting the living flowers in water and throwing the dead ones away, someone might have arrived and given her something more interesting to do.

There was no tap in the office, but she had earlier spotted a loo sign on a door down the corridor. She now discovered it was as sumptuous as her hotel bathroom that morning, and about four times the size.

Power-shower heads the size of dustbin lids glinted through a row of shining glass-doored cubicles. White-painted woven baskets held piles of snowy towels. There was downlighting, muted whale music and underfloor heating, which was why the soles of her feet felt hot. There were shelves on which bottles of luxury shower gel and body lotion gleamed.

One wall was entirely mirrored and mounted with

expensive-looking hairdryers. Below them marched a line of basins, each full of yet more abandoned bouquets. Laura removed a couple of rusty-looking mixed posies so she could rinse out her vases.

The girl in the mirror rinsed too. She looked, Laura thought, more poised than might have been expected in her fitted navy shirt and narrow black jeans. Her freshly washed dark hair shimmered in the downlighters and, while her make-up-free face looked pale, there was a determined set to her jaw and her dark eyes held a hint of fire. Clemency messed with her at her peril, Laura thought.

Returning with her vases to the office she began to unwrap the flowers, some of which had been practically steamed in their bags. The smell of rotten stems filled the air, although one bunch, made up of twigs, chives and carrots, reminded her of the *bouquet garni* Mimi put in soups and casseroles. Laura pictured her grandmother at her stove and imagined what she would make of Clemency. *Plouc*, she knew Mimi's term for anyone charmless or vulgar. *Comme elle est plouc, cette Clémence!*

'Raisy and Daisy should turn up at some stage,' Demelza said, drifting past. Her former breeziness seemed to have restored itself; the poppy crisis was obviously over.

Laura had no idea who Raisy and Daisy were, or whether their advent would be good or bad. She carried on with her flower arranging, registering from time to time Clemency's tinkling laugh from across the room.

Her work finished. Laura surveyed with satisfaction the rationalised display of blooms, half its former size now she had thrown out the dead ones.

Two figures loomed at the cupboard entrance. 'Tweed, denim and diamonds,' one was saying.

'With thigh-high boots, a personality tee and a flouro-pink beanie,' answered the other.

Laura recognised the blondes she had passed yesterday at the entrance. Today, one wore a blouse with leg-of-mutton sleeves combined with hotpants and clumpy men's shoes. The other wore a high-necked pale pink coat composed entirely of ruffles and frills. At the end of her thin legs were high-heeled rubber clogs. This, presumably, was Raisy and Daisy. They stared doubtfully at Laura.

'What do you look like?' asked either Daisy or Raisy. It seemed like a genuine question.

'I've been living in Paris,' Laura said hastily.

'Paris, wow,' said either Raisy or Daisy, big eyes wide beneath her centre-parting. They looked like a pair of Scandinavian pixies by way of a manga cartoon.

'That's so cool,' said either Daisy or Raisy. 'But it's kind of obvious now you say it. You've got that whole tomboy androgynous Patti Smith thing going on.'

'Jane Birkin.'

'Gallic swagger.'

'Restrained allure.'

'Sartorial realpolitik.'

'Thanks,' said Laura. She felt almost cheerful now. 'It's good to meet you, Daisy. And Raisy. Which is which?'

'I'm Daisy.'

'Hello, Daisy.'

'I'm Raisy. Daisy's sister.'

'Hello, Raisy.'

'It's Raisy, actually.'

'Isn't that what I said?'

'No, you said Raisy. As if it rhymes with Daisy. But it doesn't.'

Laura was confused. 'How do you spell it?'

'R.O.S.I.E.'

There was an exclamation from Daisy. She pointed behind Laura with a shaking finger whose tip was painted with orange neon varnish. Raisy's green neon fingernails now flew to her face as well.

Both sisters were staring with wide and horrified eyes at Laura's flower arrangements. 'So we were actually going to use the dead ones on a shoot?' Daisy said, when she had collected herself sufficiently for speech. 'So they were, like, the theme?'

'Noble rot?' joined in Raisy. 'Kind of lots of wilting flowers in a kind of crumbling stately home?'

They looked at each other. 'Harriet's going to go mad,' Daisy said gloomily.

'She'll fire us.' Raisy sighed.

The fashion editor sounded like the Red Queen in *Alice*, prone to summary executions. Laura felt terrible. She had only been trying to help, but she had already blown it.

Daisy brightened slightly. 'But Hazza's in Pyong Yang shooting the new exacting silhouette.'

'And her deputy should tell her really,' reasoned Raisy.

'But Jazzy's in Kathmandu shooting the new playful pinks.'

'And her assistant, Fuzzy, is in Mumbai shooting the new fur skirt.'

Daisy twiddled one of several medals attached to her blouse. 'So that leaves the intern.'

They both stared at Laura. 'Which is only fair, as you threw the flowers away,' said Raisy, twisting a toy nurse's fob watch pinned to her coat sleeve. 'You ring Hazza and she can sack you.'

Laura did not want to ring Hazza and get sacked. There

had to be a way out of this, but what? She couldn't get the flowers back; she had shoved them all in the bathroom bin and it had been emptied almost straight away.

She remembered how the basins were crammed with rotting bouquets. Perhaps they would do for the noble-rot shoot?

'Genius!' pronounced Raisy.

Laura breathed a sigh of relief. Saved, for now. 'Shall I start tidying the fashion cupboard?' She had hated the thought before, but it seemed now a welcome chance to retire from the front line.

Daisy glanced at her in surprise. 'Why? Does it need tidying?'

The cupboard was far worse than Laura thought. As labours went, even Hercules might have balked at tidying it.

It was more interesting work than she had expected, even so. The clothes smelt and felt beautiful. They all had famous labels in the collar and were exquisitely made with colourful silk linings and wonderful details: buttons, pockets, sequins, embroidery. Laura held up shimmering dresses against herself and studied the effect in the mirror. Did they look funny with her Chelsea boots or just very fashion-forward and fabulous?

She slipped on a gossamer-thin silk jacket which felt like cool water against her skin. As she took it off she noticed a little message stitched inside the collar: 'Love Like You've Never Been Hurt and Be the Best that You Can Be.' Was it a cliché or just very, very deep?

She could hear, from the main room, the banter among the other members of staff.

'... couldn't find my slippers, had to open the door in heels and a bathrobe. And it was seriously the most ginormous cactus...'

'... lives in this amazing castle. It's got a slavery garden, with manacles and everything...'

The conversation that Daisy was currently having with the North Korea-based fashion director had been going on for some time. Laura had employed all her snooping skills to find out what the issue was but had so far drawn a blank. Something about a shoot in London that afternoon.

'Dongle', 'budget' and 'PDF' were bouncing off the fashion-cupboard walls. Laura was unsure what any of them meant, but it was clear Harriet was getting frustrated and Daisy was getting upset.

'But Harriet... Oh God, the line's gone *again*.'

Raisy stuck her head inside the fashion cupboard and swore volubly. Things were evidently getting tense.

'What's up?' Laura asked.

A pair of distracted eyes met hers. 'Hazza's trying to run this Lulu shoot from Pong Thing when she should really just leave it to us.'

'You're doing a shoot with Lulu?' Laura smiled. As well as cheering her up, the laundry-Fed-Exing socialite had been the inspiration behind her night in the hotel.

'"Is This the Most Spoilt Girl in Britain?"' Raisy nodded. 'That's the angle. Well, our angle anyway.'

'You mean she doesn't know that's the angle?'

Daisy swished her pale yellow hair from side to side. 'Not exactly.'

'She's doing it to...' Raisy made quote marks with her fingers. '"... address the misconceptions people have about her".'

Laura stared. 'But how's that going to work? If it's saying

she's the most spoilt girl in Britain, surely it'll make the misconceptions worse.'

'Exactly!' said Daisy triumphantly.

'But that's horrible.'

Raisy looked defensive. 'Well it's nothing to do with us. We're not in charge.'

'We just had to hire the photographer,' Daisy added. 'We've got Grimston.'

It was not a name Laura recognised.

'Seriously? You haven't heard of him?' Raisy passed her a book of photographs.

Grimston's Girls was the title. Laura turned over black-and-white images of shaved vaginas, close-ups of nipples and photos of women with their hands down their pants. She hastily passed it back. 'It's quite pornographic.'

'People have said that,' Raisy allowed. 'But Grimston says he doesn't objectify women, he subjectifies them.'

'What's the difference?'

'About twenty thousand quid.'

Chapter Nine

Things worsened shortly afterwards when Jazzy called from Kathmandu with her thoughts on the Lulu shoot as well. She seemed to have entirely different ideas to Harriet. The stress of brokering a compromise via intermittent and unpredictable connections between two shrieking women in two different countries eventually sent both fashion assistants to the loos in tears and Laura was left alone in the fashion department.

It was now that Demelza put her head inside. 'Features meeting!'

'Raisy and Daisy are in the loo.'

'Crying?'

'I'm not sure.' Laura was reluctant to drop them in it.

'Well you'll have to come then.'

'To the features meeting? *Me?*' Laura could not believe her luck.

'Someone from fashion has to be there. And you're the only one around.'

Laura's stomach was tight with excitement as she followed Demelza into Carinthia's office.

There was space on the yellow sofa and she headed there. Demelza grabbed her shirt.

'Not there! That's editors only.'

Laura gasped at a sudden sharp pain in her side. Someone pushing past had jabbed her hard by accident.

'What are you doing here?' Clemency snarled. The jab had been no accident.

'Raisy and Daisy are in the loo,' she growled back.

'Well don't even think about saying anything,' the features editor hissed.

She would say what she liked, Laura vowed, as Clemency reached the editors' sofa and sat down, her heart-shaped face with its disingenuous eyes the very picture of sweet innocence. She nudged the person next to her and nodded at Laura, who, feeling her face start to redden, stared at the shelves against which she rested.

They held a lot of arty ornaments: strange abstract shapes in glass. No, they were trophies, they had Carinthia's name inscribed upon them. The ones nearest to Laura said: 'Lifetime Achievement Award for Services to Dry-Cleaning' and 'Luxury Spa Guest of the Year, 2016'.

Carinthia was not yet here. Nor was her chair, oddly. Laura had expected some imposing piece of furniture, tall-backed, black and padded. Perhaps on a swivel, so the editor could swoop terrifyingly from one side to the other, as editors were supposed to. But all she could see behind Carinthia's desk was a large ball of pearly-blue rubber.

'Bad back,' Demelza explained. 'She's always trying new things for it.'

An elfin woman with perfectly streaked and mussed brown hair hurried in and draped herself gracefully over the editor's sofa. She wore multicoloured high heels and jeans covered in glittery appliqué poppies. Laura remembered Mimi's hatred of embroidered trousers.

'Who's that?' she whispered to Demelza.

'Saffron.'

'Beauty editor?' Laura remembered the cards on the flowers.

Demelza nodded. 'Oh dear. Here we go.'

Saffron was making a horrible gulping noise and had clamped her hand to her mouth. Her eyes bulged as she pointed at something on the floor, got up and rushed out.

There was a widespread groan. 'Honestly, Dora.'

A red-faced girl on the floor, presumably Dora, was clutching a take-out cup of coffee.

'What's wrong?' Laura hissed.

Demelza rolled her dark blue eyes. 'Saffron can't bear to look at anything ugly. She literally freaks if she sees polystyrene.'

Laura snorted. How did one not look at ugly things in London? Perhaps Saffron got chauffeured everywhere and just sat in the back with her eyes shut.

Demelza nudged her. 'Carinthia's here.'

Laura straightened immediately. She could feel Clemency's laser stare on her, but she ignored it and tried to catch Carinthia's eye. Or, rather, catch the lens of the big black sunglasses she wore with her biscuit-coloured shift dress. It was probably the nearest to biscuits Carinthia ever got.

Carinthia did not look at Laura, disappointingly. She

hurried past carrying a leather bag full of papers. Absolute silence fell as she slid behind her desk and balanced herself gingerly on the exercise ball. Then she yanked out a newspaper, waved it in the air and demanded, 'Everyone seen this?'

Laura recognised the picture of Spartacus Tripp in his wetsuit. 'Yes!' she said loudly.

'I feel an in-depth investigation coming on,' Carinthia announced in thrilling tones. 'This one will be seriously huge. Huger even than "Get Me a Unicorn! Inside Top Concierge Companies".' Her voice was rising. 'For which I got Editor of the Year!'

'You want to investigate sub-aqua gear at parties?' Dora, on the floor, looked puzzled. 'But suits of armour are the new thing. I was at a festival last weekend where everyone wore pig-faced basinets.'

'Wasn't that some Agincourt re-enactment society?' the girl next to her put in. 'I remember you said you were going.'

Dora looked even more puzzled. 'Was it? Did I?'

Carinthia cut in furiously. '"The New Society Wedding!"' The fat black fountain pen shoved between her teeth rattled like gunfire. 'That's the story!'

Laura was beginning to get the picture. And, as obviously no one else had, here was her chance to shine. She waved to get Carinthia's attention. 'You mean that top people these days don't get married the way they used to?'

'Exactly! The old-style grand wedding is over!' The editor's tone now had a ringing, Churchillian resonance. She pounded her desk with her fist. 'It's no longer about chinless wonders at churches in Chelsea! It's about well-connected hipsters getting hitched in Hoxton. Or at boho festival bashes in mystic forests in Wiltshire!'

Laura could see immediately how Amy's wedding fitted the

pattern. 'I think that's brilliant,' she said, still determinedly blanking Clemency.

Carinthia was wobbling wildly on her ball. 'You bet it's brilliant! Even more brilliant than "Pigs' Heads and Penises: Initiation Rites Investigated".'

'You got Editor's Editor's Editor for that!' Clemency sycophantically pointed out.

'Yes! Yes!' Carinthia was now almost screaming. 'Has anyone any contacts for Spartacus Tripp? Or Amy Bender?'

Laura shoved her hand unhesitatingly in the air. 'I know Amy Bender.'

'Great, you can write about the wedding!'

Laura gasped. Just like that, the world had changed. She had been given a commission in front of everyone. Not even Clemency could take her off the story now.

Carinthia was bouncing up and down crazily. Her nostrils were flaring and her bared teeth glinted in the striplights. 'This will scoop *Vogue*! This will beat *Tatler* into a cocked tiara! Carinthia Gold still has it! I will fight them on the newsstands! I will never surrender!'

'This has "award-winner" written all over it!' Clemency shouted. 'This is even going to beat "From 'Articulate' to A & E: When After-Dinner Games Go Wrong".'

'Which got me Magazine of the Year!' Carinthia ripped off her sunglasses in excitement. The hooded, snake-like eyes that Laura remembered were blazing feverishly. They closed, and the editor took some deep breaths. Then they opened again and swung to Laura. 'I recognise you.'

So Clemency was wrong. Carinthia knew her after all. 'Yes. We met in—'

'Aren't you Binky Bottomley's daughter?'

'No, I'm—'

'Wait, I've got you now.' The pen between the editorial teeth rattled. 'Your father bid for the placement in that raffle. £20,000. At the Small-Growth Champagnes charity ball?'

'I'm Laura Lake,' Laura said boldly. 'We met in Paris. You gave me a job as an intern.'

More pen-rattling. 'I don't remember.'

'Well you did,' Laura said firmly.

There was a collective gasp in the room. The snake eyes were freezing. Laura held them without flinching. Her heart was drumming, however. Was she about to be fired for insolence?

Carinthia blinked first. The thin lips spasmed. 'Hmm. Well, make a good job of this and I might put you on the staff.'

Laura gasped and stared at her benefactress with shining eyes. 'Oh I will,' she assured her fervently.

'Good,' Carinthia said shortly. 'See Clemency afterwards.'

It was difficult to concentrate on the rest of the meeting. All Laura could think was that if she made a success of the Amy's wedding piece, a permanent magazine job was within her reach! She wanted to hug herself. So great was her joy that she even smiled at Clemency. Clemency didn't smile back.

After the meeting, the features editor was nowhere to be seen. 'Probably in the loos,' said Demelza. 'Everyone else is.'

It seemed that this was the usual consequence of a features meeting. It was less to do with bladders than tears of frustration, humiliation and rage. Carinthia certainly didn't mind who she upset. During the last hour she had shot down most of her staff.

'I want to do "New Ways to Wear Old Jewels",' explained Amicia Le Carotte, the jewellery editor. She was resplendent in a T-shirt that said 'Make Poverty History', to which was attached with safety pins an enormous diamond necklace.

'Looks ridiculous,' said Carinthia decisively. 'Do a piece on Mary-Bliss Skinner instead.'

Amicia's face fell. 'But her jewellery's awful. She takes perfectly lovely diamonds, sandblasts them, drills a hole in them and sticks them on bits of old rubber.'

A pair of freezing snake eyes focused on her. 'So what? Her father's a rock star.'

'And she's a rock-wrecker,' Amicia muttered.

Mary-Bliss Skinner, Laura mused. It rang a bell. Wasn't she designing Amy's zero-impact wedding ring?

Lucia the interiors editor had had her idea for inverted libraries refused.

'Inverted in what way?' Carinthia had demanded.

'The spines are all turned to the wall? So only the edges of the pages show? It produces a lovely effect of mixed milk tones.'

'No.'

'O-kay.' As The Gaze was turned on her too, the interiors editor swallowed. 'Well, this is definitely the year of the scented clock.'

A wide-eyed beauty assistant had suggested a sought-after bag. 'There's only one factory making them and only one man in that factory and he only works one day in every seven and even then only until lunchtime. You have to be an A-lister to get on the waiting list's waiting list...'

The editorial fist had slammed the desk. 'Boring!'

Someone else had suggested vagina-steaming. 'It's the hottest thing...'

'Disgusting!'

'We should do something about posh builders. Scything is

massive right now and there's this duke's son who does dry stone walling...'

'Oh God!'

'This amazing restaurant, it looks just like a shed and you can only get to it by ski-lift, but when you go inside it's full of hedge-funders eating truffles...'

'Next!'

Even Clemency had come under fire, for the Lulu feature. It seemed that the 'spoilt' angle was her idea, which was possibly no surprise.

'"Is This the Most Spoilt Girl in Britain?"' Carinthia glared at her features editor. 'Bit obvious. We're *Society*. We're counterintuitive. We need an unexpected angle. One that will get people's attention.'

Clemency smiled sweetly. 'Don't worry. Grimston's doing the pictures. He's thinking of shooting her in a dustbin.'

The corridor with the loo on it was hung with framed *Society* covers featuring supermodels. Yasmin Le Bon beamed encouragingly as Laura hurried past.

Demelza had told her that the luxurious bathroom featured special Vitamin D lighting to combat depression. It didn't seem to be working today. There was someone sobbing loudly behind every closed stall door. 'Clemency?' Laura called softly, even though she doubted Clemency was one of the weepers. No answer.

Laura returned to the office. She would take matters into her own hands. Now she was officially writing a feature, she would remove to the appropriate desk. There was no Raisy and Daisy to say goodbye to as she closed the door on the half-tidied fashion cupboard and walked across the black office carpet to her new department. She knew which it was because she had seen Clemency sitting at it earlier. There were a couple of other girls there, a pair of glossy blondes. They introduced themselves as Pim and Hum.

As there was an empty desk, Laura sat down at it discreetly and fired up the computer. It felt reassuring to finally have a keyboard. Now she could really get going. After some thought, Hum remembered the office password and Laura launched herself on to the superhighway. She intended to track Amy down through her gallery and dealer; presumably she had both by now. Getting an invitation to the wedding would be easy. It would be free publicity, something Amy had always been keen on.

Pim and Hum's conversation floated over to her. 'Seriously,' Pim was saying, 'it's this shop in Chelsea no one can go to. It's so exclusive that it's never actually open.'

'Awesome,' said Hum. 'But come on, Pim. We'd better get on with rounding up those Lulu interviews. Clemency wants all the worst ones. For inspiration, she says.'

Laura felt sad for Lulu. Despite Carinthia's doubts, the *Society* interview was obviously going to be worse than any she had read so far. But there was nothing she could do about it, and besides, she had the Bender wedding to think about.

Finding Amy online did not take long. She was clearly now in the artistic ascendant and being represented by a mega-gallery called Gagillion Globalart. The homepage featured explosions, rubble and smoking holes in the ground, which was a new work called *#GodOfWar* by an artist called Zeb Spaw.

Amy had her own tab, on which *Call This Art?* appeared in all its glory. There it was: the bed, the rubbish, and the overhead spotlight shining down on a Chinese couple, presumably from the recent tour.

There was a shriek from Hum. 'Lulu alert!' she exclaimed to Pim. Then, adopting a grating foreign accent, '"My diet is the three Cs. Champagne, caviar and cabbage!"'

'What the fuck do you think you're doing here?' The vicious whisper came from above. Laura looked up into Clemency's furious face.

'Researching my feature.' Laura's smile was genuine, even hopeful. It would be easier to be civil. There was a lot at stake now.

'Well you can research it somewhere else. Get off my desk!'

'But why? There's plenty of room.'

Clemency reached for some magazines and laid them over Laura's space. 'No there isn't. Get out!'

Laura made one last effort. 'Don't you want to talk to me about this wedding thing? Give me some editorial direction?'

Clemency's scowling expression was all the answer she needed.

Laura returned to the fashion department. There was still no sign of Raisy and Daisy, so she sat down at Raisy's desk and started up her computer. She would not be stopped.

The paragraphs on Raisy's screen made no sense to her. Presumably they were notes for some fashion piece, but they read like sixties free verse:

futuristic synthetics artisanal threads optimistic texture pairings. Brave new world morphing with trompe l'oeil embroidery, flamenco ruffle jeans soothsayer old-fashioned anti-fit. Pheromone of authenticity think Debbie Harry in 505s the original androgyny utility staple dude-ranch denim hold a perfect bottom take your thrift-store boy jeans to a tailor and get them fitted denim woven in Japan using machines from the 50s. Futuristic aesthetic, radical new potency, sartorial realpolitik reworked in tablecloth plastics zing zigzags and zip worn with rigour, baggy trousers in boiled liver and an oversized sweater can look incredibly sexy and respond to changes in the role of woman. Transitional style ease hardwired into the fashion zeitgeist chunky flatforms, prairie dresses plastic pool slides androgynous boiler suit endorphin-releasing tote by Anya Hindmarch

'Hello?'

Laura looked up, blinking at Demelza.

'Bad news, I'm afraid.'

A host of horrid possibilities skittered through Laura's mind.

'Raisy and Daisy have resigned.'

'Resigned?'

Demelza rolled her eyes. 'People are always resigning. They'll be back tomorrow, don't worry.'

Laura stared. 'But what about the Lulu shoot today? They're styling it.'

'No they're not. You are.'

Chapter Ten

The taxi drew up outside the address Demelza had given her. It was halfway up a street whose entrance had a barrier with a guard beside it and whose individual houses looked the size of Mimi's entire block in Paris.

Not much of the houses could be seen, however. All were set back behind huge gates and some were further disguised by builders' screens and equipment. A huge crane reared up like an inquisitive yellow metal bird from the very next garden to Lulu's and the roar of drills came from all directions. Being wealthy in London, it seemed, meant being part of a constant construction project.

'Thanks,' Laura said, walking away from the taxi. Having less than zero interest in football, she was glad the lecture on Arsenal was over.

The driver banged on the window. 'Oy. Where you going?'

'I've got a meeting here.'

'And I've got an unpaid fare here. That'll be £10.60.'

Laura gasped. It had never occurred to her that she would need to pay for the taxi. Demelza had just told her to hail one. £10.60! That left her with precisely £9.40 to last the rest of the week. And she hadn't had lunch yet. Thank God she had gone for the full English breakfast; it might have to last all day.

The driver handed her the change, which she hastily pocketed. 'No bleeding tip?' he could be heard snarling as he wrenched the vehicle round.

Laura turned to the gates, which, being close-set cast-iron bars, had something of the prison about them. Looking up, she saw that the movements of her head were echoed by security cameras fixed above. She pressed the intercom.

'Good afternoon.' A polite female voice seemed to be coming from a distant galaxy. Lulu?

Laura explained who she was, and was let in.

Behind the gates, a short gravel drive led between manicured borders to a large house of vaguely Queen Anne style. It was three storeys high and redbrick with white-painted windows. The front door, flanked by bay trees in pots, had a white pillared portico and was painted a bright glossy pink. It rather clashed with the brickwork, Laura thought.

Something had been trembling beneath her feet for some seconds, but what she had assumed was a subterranean Tube line was clearly not. The ground was actually moving. Looking down, she saw that the stretch of gravel she stood on was sliding to the side to expose a large hole. An earthquake? She gave a small scream and jumped off.

The hole widened. Laura, standing astonished on the edge of it, now saw that something was coming up it on a platform powered by some softly clicking, whirring machine.

A gleaming candy-pink sports car now appeared. It had blacked-out windows and the numberplate was LULU1. An underground garage, Laura realised. Of course the girl who had everything was going to have one of those.

Her smile faded as, with the soft rev of its powerful engine, the car moved off towards the gates. If this was Lulu, and she was going out, where did that leave the interview? Had she forgotten? 'Miss, er, Lulu?' Laura yelled, rushing to the driver's window and tapping on it frantically.

The window slid down to reveal someone with big blonde hair, massive black sunglasses and a cleavage like a tanned, even Grand, canyon, rising from a tight coral dress. Hands covered with sparkling rings clutched a steering wheel padded with coffee-coloured leather. The pattern on the leather was one that Laura recognised. The slanting intertwined initials and the repeating quatrefoil of the Louis Vuitton logo were repeated endlessly all over the seats, the fascia, the handle of the gearstick, even the seatbelts and the back of the rear-view mirror.

While Lulu was not quite international A-list, Laura had read and heard enough about her to feel excited at seeing her in the heavily tinted flesh. She smelt wonderful too: a strong, fresh scent that suggested fabulous bathrooms and hours of pampering.

'What you want?' asked the growling accent familiar from all the newspaper articles. As one of them had said, or sort of said, it was a distillation of international first-class lounges. Lulu was a citizen of the world.

'I'm here from *Society* magazine,' Laura gasped. 'We have an appointment.'

The window shot back up. Lulu was hidden behind black glass. Double black glass, if you counted the shades.

The powerful engine revved again. The car's thick tyres were right by Laura's toes. If Lulu's Louboutin slipped, she would be jam. But if Lulu drove away, she would be jam as well, so far as *Society* was concerned. When Clemency deigned to turn up, she would be furious to find her interviewee gone. The consequences of that were easy to imagine.

Lulu pounded on the window again.

Again it slid down. 'I don' wan' do interview,' growled Lulu. Up close, and despite the huge sunglasses, Laura could see that the illusion of cheekbones and chin was a product of clever make-up. Lulu's actual face was as round as a ball.

'Why not? What's the matter?'

'Is no point, hmm? These magazines, always they make me look stupid. Call me rich idiot. Stupid socialist!' The enormous diamonds in her ears flashed agitatedly.

'You mean socialite,' Laura suggested gently.

'Socialite, socialist, what does it matter?' Lulu shook back the pile of blonde hair, which wobbled strangely. It evidently contained a lot of hairspray. 'What is difference?'

Quite a lot, but this was probably not the time to point out why.

'This interview won't be like that,' Laura soothed, knowing perfectly well that it would be. Doing Clemency's dirty work felt ghastly, but what choice did she have? It was Lulu or her. 'Can we go inside and talk about it?'

She needed to get this woman out of the car. The engine was revving in time with Lulu's agitated foot.

'Don' wanna talk.' Lulu pouted. 'Talking is what gets me into trouble. Interviews, they always come out wrong, hmm? My father go crazy. I do another to make the first one okay, but is worse. My father go crazy again. I do another. Is bishop's circle.'

'You mean vicious circle.'

Lulu shrugged and gave a sort of hiccup. Laura saw now that fat tears had appeared from beneath the heavy black sunglasses and were coursing silently downwards through the thick foundation on Lulu's cheeks. Suddenly she felt terribly sorry for her. As well as terribly guilty. 'Here.' She rummaged in her trenchcoat pocket and handed over a packet of tissues.

'Thank you.'

'*Je vous en prie...* I mean, you're welcome.'

Lulu had raised her head. 'You speak French?'

'I'm half-French.'

'Like me, hmm? I too am many countries. A mongoose.'

'You mean a mongrel?'

'Perhaps. So you are from Paris?'

Laura nodded. Lulu beamed.

'Paris, it is my second house. Place Vendôme, avenue Montaigne...'

The ultra-luxurious streets where the couturiers had their flagships and ateliers. Laura knew where they were, if nothing else. Yet she had clearly made a breakthrough. 'About the interview,' she began, cautiously. 'It will be nice, I promise.'

What was she saying? The intention was to make Lulu 'The Most Spoilt Girl in Britain!'

Lulu was having none of it anyway. The blonde mane wobbled firmly. 'Is not just words, is pictures as well. Always I think that if I am nice with the photographer and do what he want, he'll make me look good. But always he make me look like a slaphead.'

'Slaphead? Slapper?'

'Yes. Like cake, hmm?'

This one Laura couldn't decipher. She looked at Lulu quizzically.

'Tart. Then my parents go crazy and I feel so ashamed...'
Lulu sobbed again into the tissue, and Laura handed over
another. She tried not to think of *Grimston's Girls*.

There had to be a way out of this, but she would have
to think of it fast. Once Clemency and Grimston got here,
events would have their own momentum.

'It'll be fine,' she soothed. 'I can help you. Just let's go
inside and talk about it. I promise you the interview will be
your best ever. The best pictures, too.'

'Huh.' Lulu snivelled disbelievingly. 'Have heard that
before, hmm? But always they lie to me. Drag cotton over my
eyes and take me for jog.' The car revved again, threateningly.

'Trust me,' Laura insisted. 'And turn off the engine, can
you?'

After a few tense seconds, Lulu did as requested. The
sports car's long, gleaming, pink door opened.

Lulu was much taller than expected. Or maybe her shoes
were. They were the bizarrest Laura had ever seen. Black,
peep-toed and with thick platform soles which angled
upwards to accommodate a heel of about six inches. The
heel itself was not there, however, and so the shoe looked
like the side view of an escalator. Had Lulu left her heels in
the car?

'By Lambrusco,' Lulu said, seeing Laura staring. She lifted
one leg to show a neon-pink sole beneath the clumpy black.
'Is original, hmm?'

She bent over to rummage in the car, revealing an expanse
of solid brown upper thigh. She was quite well built, Laura
thought, certainly compared to the rickety waifs in the
Society office.

Lulu had produced a green snakeskin handbag and
was feeling around inside it. The diamond-ringed hand

re-emerged clutching a large bar of Galaxy, into which she ripped eagerly.

'Chocolate make everything better, hmm?' she mumbled through a full mouth. 'Wan' some?' She proffered the bar.

Laura shook her head. She preferred hers intense and dark. Her mind was darting about but coming up with nothing.

Lulu had almost finished the bar now and was looking much more cheerful. 'So you help me, hmm?'

'Absolutely!' Although how, Laura still had no idea. Her gaze slid to the Lambrusco shoes. How did one help the unhelpable? By thinking the unthinkable?

Suddenly, she remembered Carinthia's words about the magazine being counterintuitive. That was it! Saved!

'You just have to show your more serious side!' Laura's whole body was rushing with relief, not to mention self-congratulation. This really was a brilliant idea. She was a natural at this job!

'I would like to be taken seriously,' Lulu allowed, wiggling up to the pink front door in her tight dress and footwear.

'Absolutely!' Laura enthused. 'Show the Lulu no one's read about yet. The one to whom designer labels don't matter and—'

Her words were drowned out by a violent crashing. For some reason, Lulu was banging on the door of her own house. There was something familiar about the door-knocker's design.

'You like?' Lulu pointed to the shining interlocking Cs. 'Is solid gold. Chanel make it for me as special favour. Am good customer, hmm? They do letterbox too, and bootscraper.'

Laura was still looking at Lulu's fingernails. They were covered in tiny Gucci Gs.

The door was opened by someone broadly built, dark-suited and with a grave, respectful mien. A butler, Laura guessed excitedly. She had only ever encountered them in books.

Lulu's butler had a serious, even mournful face that could have been any age from thirty to sixty. His hair was plastered down and had a liquid shine and a side-parting so straight it seemed a ruler had been used.

He inclined his head gravely. 'Madam has forgotten something?'

'Have come back. Am doing interview, hmm?'

There was a hesitation, so slight as to be almost undetectable, before the butler said, in his sonorous tones, 'Very good, madam,' then bowed and glided away.

Laura entered the hall of Lulu's house and thought instantly of her grandmother. 'Letters are for the optician's chart. You are not a billboard.' But Mimi would never have imagined that a house could be a billboard too. Lulu had taken her logomania as far as it would go.

The hall walls were white and covered all over with the black Cs of Chanel. The Louis Vuitton logo from the car interior was echoed in the coffee-coloured carpet. Above it all, a vast chandelier dangled with gold letters of different sizes. They turned in the air, variations on D, I, O and R.

'This way, hmm?' Lulu picked her way up a flight of glass stairs that, like her Lambruscos, had no visible means of support. Given her powerfully black sunglasses, this seemed a risky undertaking.

In the huge first-floor sitting room, the shagpile carpet was Tiffany blue, stamped with the store name in white. The walls were Hermès orange and had the brand's coach-and-horses logo driving all over them. As none of these design houses usually did carpets or wallpaper, Lulu had to be a spectacularly good customer.

In the corner of the room was a large gold upside-down penis. It was hanging from the ceiling and almost reached the floor. Laura stared. What label was this?

'Is famous artist.' Her hostess yawned. 'Have forgotten name. Is long, though.'

'Very long,' agreed Laura, admiring the work, which made her think of Caspar and then, by extension, her enduring homeless state. But she would have to cross that bridge later. Sleep under it, if it came to that.

Lulu giggled. She had a warm, low, infectious laugh. 'No, is long *name*. One I have forgotten, hmm?'

Now she was tottering off again. Wading through the Tiffany shagpile in the Lambruscos looked like hard work. And, frankly, ludicrous. Laura's faith in her great idea was fading. How could Lulu show her serious side in a setting like this?

Or in her bathroom, which Laura was shown next and which seemed the size of an aircraft hangar. A round bath with integral Jacuzzi was reflected in walls comprised entirely of illuminated mirrors. Lulu demonstrated a special delay-photography function that enabled her to examine herself from behind.

'See if your bum looks big in this?' Laura joked. Her smile faded as she saw that, beneath the sunglasses, Lulu's face was stony.

'Is for hair, not bum. Bum's mirror in bedroom, hmm?'

The loo featured a bidet, which made Laura feel strangely at home. The English rarely had them. 'Is joke! By Miuccia, for me!' Lulu pointed at the loo paper, which was soft pink and had 'Liu Liu' stamped in black.

'Is even better joke!' she added, pointing to the 'Stella McCarpet' floor covering. Laura gave an obedient giggle. What cards these designers were!

The taps were jewelled and said 'Van Cleef' on hot and 'Arpels' on cold.

'Now I show you my bedroom.' Lulu announced, beaming. She clearly adored her house. It was like being taken round by a very enthusiastic, very oddly dressed estate agent.

The colossal bedroom was a logo mash-up. The carpets were Prada, the fringed, swagged, floor-length curtains, Armani. The only thing not designer branded was a cushion on the bed which said, 'Why Choose? Just Order One in Every Colour'. However, Lulu hadn't. Everything in the room was in shades of rose.

'You like pink,' Laura remarked.

'Is chop suey.'

Laura could translate fairly easily by now. 'Feng shui?'

The blonde pile of hair nodded in assent. 'This guy, he is friend of my interior designer. He told me pink, it will attract positive powers of cosmos. Also I must put healing crystal under bed.'

She pushed a button on the pink Burberry-check headboard and a large drawer of gleaming wood slid out silently from beneath. Row upon row of Cristal champagne bottles shone in the soft light.

'So I put under three cases! Better safe than sorry!' Lulu looked thrilled with herself.

Laura closed her eyes briefly. What Clemency was going to make of this was easy to imagine. The best thing would be not to let her in at all, but that would mean doing the interview in the garden, where presumably all the roses were Ralph Lauren and every tree was Tiffany.

One entire wall of the bedroom was reflective glass – the bum mirror, presumably. As Laura watched, the wall split in two and slid back to reveal what looked like a small shop.

'My clothes!'

A few seconds later, Laura was revising 'shop'. Lulu's wardrobe, with its many rooms, was more like a department store. A very grand one, all gleaming mahogany, brass rails, mirrors and soft downlighting. Only the oleaginous sales staff were missing.

The first room was devoted entirely to footwear. From a deep, cream, Gucci-stamped carpet, five shelves stretched all the way round from floor to ceiling. Arranged neatly on each, according to type, were designer shoes of every imaginable colour and style. One row was entirely trainers, including a green-laced pair with gold wings attached. Another held variations on the Lambrusco shoes: high-heel-less ankle boots and, rather amazingly, flip-flops. Other shelves held serried, gleaming, glittering, multicoloured ranks of shoes, sandals, ballerina flats, kitten heels and a bewildering array of boots. There were flat ones in gold rubber and mid-heels in pink snakeskin.

'Is great, hmm?' Lulu pointed to a pair of teetering denim top-of-the-thigh constructions with attachments to connect to a belt. 'By Coco Poudre.'

The next room was dedicated to hats, belts and bags. Lulu evidently had a weakness for baseball caps smothered in diamante. There were a number of crystal-encrusted Stetsons as well. It suggested a past as a failed country-and-western singer.

Lulu selected a cap which spelt out, in glitter capitals, 'God Bless VIP Rooms'. 'Is 'orrible, hmm? My last stylist. She had to go.'

'Because she wanted you in diamante?'

'Because she wanted my diamonds. Is in jail now.'

Lulu's tone was wearily matter-of-fact, but Laura blinked

at this glimpse into a world where everyone was on the take. Being rich clearly had its downsides.

'Need new stylist.' Lulu was looking at her speculatively. 'Maybe you do it, hmm? You have good style. Paris style. Birkin look might suit me, hmm?'

'Well you've certainly got the bags.' Laura gestured at an entire wall of gleaming gilt and leather.

Lulu glanced at them and groaned. 'Bring back bad memories. Father go to mad over article me lying on them, hmm?'

Laura remembered the magazine cover with the headline about private jets.

'Come!' Lulu urged, heading into another room, where Laura found her running her hands over the delicate ruffles and pearly sequins of row after row of dresses. Short, long, with sleeves, without them. One shift dress seemed to be made entirely of banknotes, overlapping like feathers.

'You like Ditzy Furtwangler?' Lulu waved a maxidress in violent swirling colours.

'I've never heard of her.'

Surprisingly, this seemed to be the right answer. 'Is new designer. She throw paint in blades of fan. Perfect for cruises, hmm?'

One whole row was dark denim jeans, another white and another leather trousers. One rail was devoted to leather jackets. Lulu opened a glass door. Against a lining of pale wood, rows of furs hung plumply from their hangers.

'Wow,' said Laura. There seemed little else to say. Lulu's designer wardrobe – glittering, gleaming, radiating money at every turn – made the *Society* fashion cupboard look positively drab. As well as horribly messy. Did the butler keep this place so tidy, Laura wondered. It was almost military in its order.

'Now I show you cinema.' Lulu waddled off. 'Is in basement. Very big, with reclining sofas by—'

'No time. We need to talk about the interview,' Laura called after her. Clemency must surely be due soon. She might even be here already. Wandering around downstairs, laughing at the logos.

'Okay. We go have tea.'

This sounded a much better idea. Laura felt ready to kill for a cup of Earl Grey. A biscuit would not go amiss either.

There was a small, mirrored lift whose buttons had labels like 'Gym', 'Pool', 'Treatment Room' and 'Salon'. Laura looked for one marked 'Library'; books would make the perfect counterintuitive Lulu setting. Perhaps unsurprisingly, there wasn't one. But there was something else.

'Can we have a look at this?' She pointed to a button that said 'Music Room' and imagined harpsichords, a wooden floor, a gleaming black baby grand.

'Sure.' The sunglasses flashed proudly in the light. 'Is studio, hmm?'

'Studio?' She used the music room to paint? Sculpt? Well, that could work. Lulu, interviewed amid her creations. Optimistically, Laura pictured the scene. Perhaps in an artist's smock, holding a brush.

'Yeah, mix album there. Wannabe singer-songwriter.' Lulu started to pump the air and swish her hair from side to side. 'Oooh, baby, baby, baby, wan' you so bad,' she crooned, wildly off-key. 'Oooh yeah, yeah, la, la.'

'On second thoughts,' Laura said firmly, 'let's just stick with the tea idea.'

The lift opened into a large kitchen. A vast breakfast island surrounded by high stools was flanked on each side by marble-topped units. Laura's hopes rose that this might make a neutral backdrop, but discarded this idea on spotting the Chanel saucepans, the Victoria Beckham cake tins and the logo on the solid-fuel stove. 'Is great, no?' Lulu beamed, waving a hand at the gleaming installation. 'My Balenci-Aga!'

Beyond the kitchen was a big, light conservatory where another Dior chandelier dangled over enormous padded armchairs upholstered in Burberry check. Lulu clacked across tiles whose logo matched her fingernails and collapsed in one with an air of happy exhaustion. 'You sit there,' she commanded Laura, pointing at the one opposite. 'Now we do interview.'

'Er, I'm not doing the actual interview. Someone else is.'

Beneath the sunglasses, Lulu pouted. 'Don't wan' someone else. Want you, hmm?'

Laura smiled encouragingly. 'I'm here to help you with what you're going to say.' Although God knows what that was going to be. The entire house was a PR disaster. The only good thing was that Clemency and the ghastly Grimston had evidently not arrived yet. There was still time, but the clock was ticking. The Céline cuckoo clock behind Lulu, to be precise.

Her hostess picked up a gold dish and proffered it. 'Champagne-cocktail truffle?'

Laura took one. It was delicious but hugely rich.

Lulu was stuffing them down like Smarties. Her capacity for chocolate seemed infinite. She had swung her non-heels up on a crystal coffee table and the combination of her bright dress with the Burberry background was doing strange things to Laura's eyes.

'So,' Lulu said, chomping noisily on truffles. 'About my serious side.'

'The main thing is for you not to say anything they can use

against you,' Laura explained. 'Anything that can be twisted to make you look stupid.'

But it wasn't going to take much twisting to make Lulu look stupid.

'Yeah,' said Lulu. But her attention was wandering. Her ring-heavy fingers were tapping restlessly on a cushion which read, 'Wealth Isn't a Sin, It's a Miracle'.

'Glass of champagne?' she suggested.

'No, thanks.' It wasn't that Laura didn't want one, but on her empty stomach it would make her fall over. The cocktail truffle was making her woozy as it was.

Lulu smiled knowingly. 'But this is England! You will like a cup of Josie Dee?'

Laura wasn't going to bother correcting this. All her energy and ingenuity had to be directed into saving Lulu from herself. But how?

'The Geordie rhyming slang, yes? Plates of pork, daisy leaves, ha ha.' Beaming, Lulu reached for a remote control on the sparkling table. 'Vlad? Some Posy Gee please. The usual for me. Thank you. My butler is amazing,' she added to Laura.

'Maybe don't mention your butler in the interview.'

Lulu nodded seriously. 'Good point. Is tough getting good staff, yes? I don' want anyone roasting Vlad.'

'Poaching him, you mean?'

The black sunglasses were cocked at a surprised angle. 'Him? Vlad is she, yes? Is lady.'

The butler was a woman? But there was no opportunity to express her surprise. The butler was even now coming in from the kitchen.

Really a woman? Laura watched the dignified figure unloading the contents of the groaning tea tray. Vlad was built like a rugby player and her hands and feet were huge.

'Please,' Lulu urged Laura, 'stick yourself in.'

The biscuits were beautifully made, each one shaped like a handbag, a skirt, a dress, hat or shoe, all carefully iced in pretty colours and detailed right down to the last bow and button.

'Vlad makes them. We look at new collections each season.' Lulu reached for an icing stiletto. 'Here is new season Diane von Furstenberg. And Christopher Kane. Vlad loves playful asymmetrics, right, Vlad?'

Vlad was adding a tall glass of champagne to the table. 'Indeed, madam. Will that be all, madam?'

It was, and the butler glided away.

Laura closed her mouth, which had fallen open. 'What an amazing character.'

Lulu leant forward confidingly. 'Vlad is short for Vladmira. Was Vladimir, but she's transmogrifying.'

'Transitioning?'

'Is what I say, no? She was nervous about telling me, but I am happy for her. Am equal opportunities employer, hmm!' Lulu beamed and reached for a bikini in blue icing.

Laura felt a warm surge of liking. So what if Lulu wasn't exactly a mastermind? She was warm-hearted, guileless and generous. But how to get this across in the interview?

She watched Lulu raise a glass of champagne to her lips. 'Probably not a good idea.'

Lulu looked astonished. 'But gives me fudge courage.'

'You've got to stay sober if you want them to take you seriously.'

Lulu's great pear-shaped diamond ring glittered despairingly as she put the glass down. 'But they never will do that,' she said sadly. 'They will say I am just a clothes donkey.' She popped a Prada handbag in her mouth, tugged her microscopic dress over her long, tanned legs and contemplated the Lambrusco heel-less platforms. 'Is so unfair!'

Anger was a start. Perhaps Lulu had other strong views, on the international situation, for example? 'What else makes you pissed – I mean angry?' Laura prompted.

Lulu thought. 'When moths attack my cashmere?'

'Try again. What really upsets you?'

Above the sunglasses, the brow furrowed.

'When break nail?'

'More serious than that.'

'When they've walked out of my size on Net-a-Porter?'

Laura groaned. In the corner, the Céline clock bonged the quarter hour.

She leant forward. 'Do you have any ambitions, Lulu? Something you'd really like to do?' She paused before venturing the words, 'A career?'

Lulu, who had been examining her Gucci-patterned fingernails, looked up and smiled. 'Would like to be ambassador,' she said brightly.

Relief flooded through Laura. That Lulu harboured diplomatic ambitions was a surprise. But perhaps it made sense given her international childhood. 'What country would you most want to be posted to? As the ambassador?'

Lulu seemed puzzled. 'I mean, you know, brand ambassador. Like for perfume or make-up, hmm?'

Oh God. Laura took a deep breath. 'Do you read?' It was the last hope, really. Just one book would be enough to hold in a photograph. Give a serious impression.

Lulu waved her hand proudly at the pile of magazines on the coffee table.

'I mean books. Do you have a favourite book?'

The blonde hair wobbled in a negative. 'Have never time.'

The heiress stretched and yawned on the Burberry armchair. 'I'm thinking of taking a pill for it, actually.'

'A pill? To help you read?'

'Mmm hmm. Vlad has one. Says is very good. Times Literary Supplement.'

Vlad now reappeared. 'Excuse me, madam. The people from *Society* magazine have arrived.'

Alarm shot through Laura. Clemency was here, and Grimston, and they hadn't got anything like a strategy. 'Don't show them in!' she exclaimed. 'Please!'

'Why not?' Lulu demanded, offended. 'Is what wrong with my house, hmm?'

Laura, face throbbing with embarrassment, was staring desperately at Vlad. There was something in the butler's face which hinted that she understood.

'Perhaps, madam, I could conduct them to the garden? As we have good weather, the interview could perhaps take place there.'

Laura leapt up and hurried to the conservatory windows. She needed to check it first. There might be a Louis Vuitton padded swing for all she knew. Some branded Yves Saint laurel bushes. To her relief, the park-sized garden was surprisingly tasteful.

There were herbaceous borders packed with stocks and delphiniums. Blooming rose bushes surrounded a large green lawn in whose centre a cedar of Lebanon stretched wide, elegant limbs. There was a little pond with lily pads, and in one corner a little white summer house peeped invitingly from a background of bushes and trees.

'Great,' Laura said, feeling that she rather wanted to hug Vlad. As she glided away, the faintest of smiles crossed the butler's broad, impassive face.

Laura turned to Lulu. She was really going to have to come up with something now. As ever, necessity had forced the issue and a plan was finally forming. But would it work?

Once Laura was satisfied that Lulu was ready and fully briefed, out they marched to the garden.

There sat Clemency like an unexploded bomb, at a table under a parasol, calmly tapping into her phone. Next to her was a padded recliner upholstered in gleaming white and, sprawled on it, heavily booted feet planted on the cushions, was the prone, plump, lounging, black-clad figure of what had to be Grimston. A sprawl of photographic equipment lay on the sunlit flags beside him. His stubble was visible even from a distance and his arms, crossed behind his head to expose fat white flesh, were dark with tattoos.

A fat girl wearing a lot of make-up was talking to a skinny boy in black under the cedar. Hair and make-up, Laura guessed, and Grimston's assistant.

As they approached and Clemency looked up, Laura had the joy of seeing the features editor's jaw drop.

Lulu stood barefoot on the lawn. She was dressed in a simple white T-shirt and jeans, both of which had seen better days. They were in fact Vlad's – the sole remainder of her Latvian, male wardrobe and about to be thrown out with the recycling.

Lulu was smiling now, but Laura's idea had taken some accepting. Lulu had never in her life before worn clothes that were not designer. She had seemed to actively fear them. If jeans she must wear, she had begged, could she not wear her £1,000 vintage AssManns?

But that would defeat the object, Laura had pointed

out. And the object had been achieved. Without her usual cartoonish carapace, one could imagine there was more to Lulu than just clothes.

Not wearing make-up had been even more of a struggle, and not wearing sunglasses the worst struggle of all. But the end result, Laura felt, was pretty good. Far better than she had hoped. Lulu's skin glowed dewy pink from all the scrubbing. Her hair, simply clipped up, revealed a face of surprising and endearing innocence. Free of the Lambruscos, Lulu looked 50 per cent the height and 100 per cent less silly.

Clemency's acid-green stare rolled slowly up and down the faded jeans with a tear at the knee. The crumpled T-shirt with the faint name of a Riga garage run by Vlad's brother-in-law.

'Well, how fabulous do you look, Lulu?' the features editor cooed. 'But you need to get ready for the shoot. We need to go and choose you some clothes.'

Lulu smiled at her sweetly. 'Is what I'm wearing, hmm?'

'Lulu, darling, I'm afraid that won't do.' An edge was creeping into Clemency's voice. 'We want you all dressed up, don't we?'

The green eyes flicked for the first time towards Laura. Presumably she was expecting to see her because they registered no surprise, only narrowed and returned to Lulu, who had crossed her arms and pushed out a stubborn lip.

'Am bored with being dressed to elevens all the time. Is real me.' Lulu swept a hand down her front.

Lulu was an unexpectedly good actress. Laura watched Clemency realise she actually had a problem on her hands. 'The real you?' she repeated, scathingly.

A pair of enormous, dirty boots now planted themselves on the patio. Grimston's face looked baggy and grey and his hair was not so much rumpled as matted. A less prepossessing figure was hard to imagine, even without his predilection for shaved pubes and sequinned nipples.

He yawned hugely, exposing uneven and yellowing teeth, and finished rubbing his eyes. He stuck a finger up his nose and then wiped it on the recliner's snowy padding. 'That's a great look,' he said.

Clemency's mouth fell open. 'Great look? Your brief was to do something like *Grimston's Girls*. Nude, shaved. You know.'

'Nah.' Grimston took something from behind his ear, put it in his mouth and chewed noisily on it. 'Been there, done that.'

'*What?*'

'*Grimston's Girls*,' the photographer went on, snapping his gum. 'Flesh, tits, lady bits. That were me old girlfriend anyway. Me new one's a feminist.'

'But that's the *brief*.' Tears of rage and frustration brimmed in Clemency's green eyes.

'Look, love, I'm Grimston, yeah? I brief me bloody self. Fuck off out of here if you don't like it.'

The hysterical urge to laugh was building within Laura. She did not dare look at Clemency. Trembling with anger, the features editor stood her ground. 'I'm going nowhere.'

'You said it, love.'

'I mean,' Clemency said, struggling for control, 'that I'm doing the interview.'

'Well I'm not bloody well interfering with that, am I?' Grimston was letting off bulbs at reflector screens and squinting at the results in his monitor. 'So don't you bloody interfere with me...'

Clemency had no choice but to obey. She returned to the table, where she swiped agitatedly at her phone.

'Okay,' Grimston added, in a milder tone, to Lulu. 'Just

stand still, yeah? Arms by your sides. And for God's sake, don't bloody *smile*. Like you said, this is Lulu as no one's ever seen her.'

Laura leant against a tree and breathed a great sigh of relief. Half the battle was now over. But there was still the interview to go. She had a plan for this too, but one even more high-risk than the photographs.

Her first plan had been to make Lulu learn intelligent answers to likely questions. But Lulu had become confused.

'Okay, got it. My favourite place is Wuthering Heights, my favourite book is *Mary Beard* and celebrity I most like to meet is Tintagel Castle.'

'Er...'

Sheer desperation had brought the idea skidding into her mind. It was mad, but it might just work. She could easily imitate Lulu's slow, heavily accented drawl and she had forgotten none of Caspar's tips about throwing her voice. It was worth a try, certainly.

'Do you know,' she had asked Lulu, 'what ventriloquism is?'

Chapter Eleven

The ventriloquism trick had saved the day. Caspar would have been wildly impressed if he had seen it. At least she had got something useful from the liaison, Laura thought.

Clemency's face when 'Lulu' had claimed that her favourite website was NASA had been a picture. As it had when she had described her favourite neurotransmitter molecules. Then they had moved on to crafting. 'Is very satisfying,' Lulu had drawled. 'Take my bunting everywhere with me and knit as well. Made Karl lovely bobble-hat last time went to Chanel. And matching one for Choupette. His cat, hmm?'

As Clemency had struggled to reply to this, 'Lulu' had swept blithely on. 'Do nice, spread happy and be the change. Do what feels right for the soul.'

Clemency's eyes had widened in disbelief. 'You're into mindfulness?'

'Yes! Am loving simple life!'

Laura had been glad to find a use for the many interviews she had read with ex-celebrities coping with not being famous any more by valuing the everyday and living intensely in the moment.

Clemency had not given in without a fight. She had attempted to reclaim lost ground by asking Lulu what she most desired in the world. Laura had not missed a beat.

'To walk along ringing beach, breathing in with each step the buffeting wind.'

But the master stroke had been the Wonder Supermarket. 'The *what*?'

'You have not heard of it?' Laura threw herself into a description of Native American talking sticks and Sense of Awe magnifying-glass pendants for looking at ants and houseflies. She had no idea if such a place really existed. But if it didn't, it definitely should.

By the time they had moved on to Lulu's love of Dostoevsky, Clemency was gathering her things together. She could not get out of the security gates fast enough.

As they had clanged shut behind her, Laura and Lulu had held each other in shuddering laughter. Vlad, in the background, had allowed herself a satisfied smile.

Grimston stayed longer. He and Vlad turned out to have a lot in common. One of his former girlfriends was Latvian and he had travelled widely through the country.

'Look at them,' Lulu said fondly. 'Getting on like house in smoke.'

'I'd better go,' Laura said, rather regretfully. After the afternoon's excitement and adventure, reality was starting to bite.

Clemency had not offered Laura a lift back to the office, nor had Laura asked for one. She would walk instead, and take the time to revel in her success. The afternoon had been a triumph. Thanks to her ingenuity and quick thinking, Lulu had been saved from more humiliation, and Laura's first ever celebrity interview would be exactly the kind of counterintuitive article Carinthia wanted.

She felt exhausted, even so. It had been a difficult experience. Glossy-magazine journalism was more demanding than she had ever imagined. Carinthia was right; it deserved respect, and Harry Scott's lofty disdain for it could not have been more misplaced. It might not quite be serious reporting or foreign corresponding, but it certainly had its challenging aspects.

Clemency being one of them. The interview, to put it mildly, had not gone to her plan. The consequences for Laura would not be good. But she had other, more immediate problems. Such as where she was going to sleep. It was late afternoon now and the £9.20 left over from the taxi fare was hardly going to buy her a room.

Lulu, now back behind her sunglasses and wearing jewelled stilettos with the jeans, waved her off from the glossy pink front door. 'Was good to meeting you.'

'You too,' Laura said sincerely. Lulu was by far the nicest person she had met since arriving in London. It crossed her mind that they might be friends, but she pushed it away. They were from different worlds. Lulu had a mansion – one of many – with a cinema room and Chanel saucepans. Laura was, well, homeless.

Lulu lingered in the doorway. 'Am very grating, hmm?'

'You don't need to be grateful.'

'No, am owing you one, seriously. If I can help you, let me know.'

It was very tempting to say exactly how Lulu could help her. But it would make for a very awkward moment and Laura had her pride. She would fend for herself somehow.

Besides, Lulu had helped her in other ways. After the interview, she had rushed to her wardrobe and pulled clothes off the coat hangers. 'I couldn't possibly,' Laura had protested, as Lulu pressed on her a thick red satin Valentino dress.

'Okay, these more your style.' Lulu had piled Céline skinny jeans and white Charvet shirts into her arms and then, opening some glass-fronted drawers, added sets of underwear with labels like La Perla and Dolce & Gabbana swinging on narrow bits of ribbon.

Then she had opened a door to reveal another room in the back of the wardrobe. Lights instantly sprang on inside. Laura followed.

'Is luggage room.'

It was the same size as the wardrobe and smelt powerfully and deliciously of expensive leather. Floor-to-ceiling shelves held rows of gleaming designer holdalls.

'I come with lot of baggage, hmm?'

'Er…'

'Is good joke!'

Seeing Lulu grab a vast Louis Vuitton and start shoving the clothes in, Laura stepped forwards. 'It's too much,' she said, meaning that it was too generous.

'You prefer Hermès? Okay, no problem.' Lulu reached for a big, bright orange holdall.

Laura set off back to the office. It was a warm evening and if she took enough time to get there, Clemency would, with any luck, have gone home.

Kensington Gardens were lush with summer: the grass glossy, the trees big and shaggy, the flower-beds full to bursting. Evening scents snatched at Laura's nose as she dodged the in-line skaters and crowds of Prommers awaiting the opening of the Albert Hall. But her attention was less on the ambience than on the practicalities of her situation. She was looking at the benches which lined the long paths. Would they be comfortable to sleep on?

But no. Outside was dangerous. Laura walked on.

Crowds of people passed her; many were workers heading for the Tube, the bus. All with places to sleep. It felt unreal, still being homeless in a city so full of homes.

She could of course always ring Harry Scott again. But if pride forbade her from asking Lulu for help, it doubly forbade asking him. She had yet to repay him for the room, and to go back to him in yet more trouble would just look pathetic. She wished she could, even so. Not just so he could rescue her, but so she could talk to him about her father. It would be wonderful to sit in some bar with him and have him tell her what he knew, what he admired, about Peter Lake. And perhaps there were other reasons too, reasons to do with those broad shoulders, that steady gaze, that glint of red in his hair. But for the moment, it was not to be. Not until she had got back on her feet.

Laura's feet now finally turned the corner into the square with Society House in it. For all her problems, it still sparked a flash of excitement. To go through the revolving doors and have the reception guards greet her remained thrilling. Even if they did call her Lorna.

She went upstairs in the lift, examining in the mirror the great dark shadows under her wide and worried eyes.

Now she was alone, the mask had slipped. She looked every bit as vulnerable as she felt.

The *Society* office, as expected, was empty. It was just as it had been that morning, silent and peopled only with flowers. A fresh tide had evidently come in that afternoon.

If only Caspar had answered his phone! She would be in his flat now, without a care in the world! Where was he? He had, she was by now certain, run off with Mrs Bender's jewels.

An idea struck her. She had not yet looked for him online. He might have posted something on Facebook. Or on that site that Raisy and Daisy were always consulting. Initially mishearing it as Pinteresque, she had imagined a website of loaded silences, tramps and people picking up their papers from Sidcup. It later turned out to be a photo-sharing site full of images of cupcakes and shabby chic.

Choosing the nearest empty terminal, Laura logged on. She used social media mainly for research purposes and had no photographs of herself on her accounts, only the blank egg. Online self-revelation had never been her thing. Mimi regarded it with horror and as absolutely the opposite of what a woman, or any person, should be. 'Always a little mysterious. You should never give too much away.'

To Laura's amazement, 'Caspar Honeyman' brought up page after page of links. She was even more surprised to see that, on opening them, Caspar looked different. Very different.

He had changed his hair colour. It was now platinum, and he had additionally acquired a deep tan. He had also plucked his eyebrows, veneered his teeth and waxed and oiled his chest. Was this, Laura wondered, what the blonde who'd sat next to him in the train wanted her men to look like?

Or was there another reason? Was there something Caspar had not told her about his career? Reams of film titles were listed. In many of the images, Caspar was surrounded by naked women, some with unfeasibly large breasts.

More stunning still were the movie titles: *Routemaster Ravers*, *Fare Stage Fanny*, *Replacement Bus Service Babes*. No wonder Caspar didn't want to face her. He was not a jewel thief, or anything like. He was working in what must be the specialist-interest area of public-transport-themed porn.

Laura suppressed a series of snorts. Her inner feminist should obviously be outraged, but it was hard to remain furious with someone starring in *Members of the On-Train Team* and *Coach-Trip Threesome*. And what an undignified end – as it were – for what had been a promising career.

No wonder he hadn't been in contact. This was seriously embarrassing. But even though, obviously, she wouldn't be seeing him again now, solving the mystery was a relief. It also meant that she could call Harry Scott with some proper information. It wasn't exactly Watergate, but it showed journalistic chops to some extent, and that she was her father's daughter. He might be impressed, even.

Five minutes later, Laura was less sure. She had now looked Harry up on the internet and found the enormous number of links to newspaper stories he had written. His byline was on investigations into everything from miscarriages of justice to phone-hacking and frauds in the climate-change lobby. He had exposed criminals in the Middle East and big-pharma profiteers in the USA. From the *Guardian* to the *Sunday Times* Insight Team, he had worked for most of the big British newspapers.

But on the *Press Gazette* list of 'Top Investigative Journalists' he was described as freelance. He was also described, by the peers who had nominated him, as 'the very top of the investigative journalism tree' and 'absolutely unstoppable'. On the same website, Harry's own comment on his profession was suitably short and sober. 'It's pretty simple. Your job is to be society's eyes and ears. You are there to verify what did and didn't happen. You are the watchdog.'

Laura felt awed. Harry didn't look much older than her, but he had to be. The only other possibility was that he never slept, or had a portrait in the attic like a reporting Dorian Gray. How else could he have packed this much in? He was a one-man wrong-righting, exposé-writing machine. Compared to him, she was nothing and never would be. How could she possibly call him about *Members of the On-Train Team*?

And yet, he admired her father. What was more, he had said that her father was his great inspiration. Laura took a deep breath and picked up the phone.

'Films called *what*?' Harry asked, when finally she got through to him. It had taken a few attempts as the line kept disconnecting itself. The one she eventually got was crackly and emitted strange bleeps. She had to shout to be heard.

'*Coach-Trip Threesome*. It's porn, I think,' Laura yelled. She was glad no one was in the office to hear.

'I see. Well, thanks.' Despite being distant and muffled in static roar, Harry's voice still had its trademark tone of dry amusement. 'How are you, anyway? Got somewhere to stay now?'

'Yes, thank you,' Laura lied. 'I'm absolutely fine.'

The line dropped out again and she did not try to reconnect. It now struck her that he might be abroad. He had sounded sleepy when he answered. No doubt he was somewhere being society's eyes and ears. Its watchdog. Would she ever be able to call herself the same? She sighed. The gulf between them seemed more than mere miles.

Oh well. While she was on the computer, she could at least try and sort out her bank and passport problems. Except – damn – it was out of office hours. She had better leave. She couldn't stay here all night after all.

Or could she?

It was such an amazing thought, it made her gasp.

But – seriously – why not? Where else did she have to go?

The door to the fashion cupboard was closed and she opened it. Hopefully no one would have messed up her hard work. No one had, and even better, no one had continued it. The tidied racks were as neat as she had left them, but there was still a nice big heap of unsorted clothes to hide behind.

She really could stay here. Actually, it was perfect for her purposes. It was big enough, warm and carpeted. It had an iron and ironing board and several mirrors. She could make up a bed from the cushions and rugs piled on Lucia's interiors desk, and just down the corridor was a five-star luxury bathroom stuffed with top-of-the-range toiletries and professional-level hairdryers.

All she needed apart from this was a small supply of food. A toothbrush, toothpaste, a cheap hairbrush. She'd just have to get by without make-up. She never wore much anyway – only red lipstick and a flick of eyeliner.

But hang on, there was a whole beauty department just a few feet away!

Laura exulted. Clever old her, she had found a way through yet again. She was not homeless. She was going to live in the fashion cupboard! She had a roof over her head, and not just any old roof either. She imagined what an estate agent would say. *Compact city-centre pad with all mod cons and minimal commute to the office...*

Who needed Caspar? Or even Harry Scott? Laura could look after herself.

Things were working out, after all.

Chapter Twelve

'We just have to have Tinky de Tiffany,' Demelza was exclaiming. 'She can limbo in Chanel, talk gorilla language and she's introduced broth bars to the Congo.'

It was the next morning. The features meeting was tackling the burning question of who should and should not be on the list of '*Society*'s Top Single Totty'. People were yelling out names from all over the room.

'Poldy von Biedermeier! His father's a count.'

'Bit harsh.'

'A c.o.u.n.t. And Poldy's a psychic-trance DJ. He never knows where he's left his keys. On the hall table, in the Lotus or in Lichtenstein!'

'Erik Beserker! He can roll his tongue into a figure of eight and his twenty-first birthday party had dwarfs, strippers and guns.'

At the editor's desk, Carinthia, resplendent in white and gold, was making notes with her fat black fountain pen. Behind her rose the back of an enormous chair, newly delivered that morning to replace the ball. According to Demelza, it exercised the back muscles as you sat there, by means of frequent electric shocks. Carinthia twitched constantly and her pen shot across the pad.

Suggestions were flying thick and fast.

'... can fart in Chinese. Invites a hundred friends on his yacht every summer.'

'... hedge-funder and serial mooner. Famous for his disco knee-slides.'

Laura smiled to herself. She was in tearing spirits having passed a surprisingly reasonable first night in the fashion cupboard. She had slept deeply on Lucia's Kim Kardashian cushions and woken only to the sound of the cleaner's hoover. The cleaner, fortunately, had made just the most cursory of rounds and had not ventured into the cupboard.

Her pen was moving even faster across her pad than Carinthia's. She was making notes on everyone mentioned. They could be useful for the New Society Weddings feature, and who knew what else. Some of them sounded positively unsavoury. Laura's inner reporter was on high alert.

'... likes to hunt the villagers on his father's estate. Once wore a pair of size 18 lace knickers as a cravat. Throws wild parties, not all of which end terribly well...'

Carinthia held a hand up. 'There I must draw the line. Sebastian Hunter may be a lord, but he is not the type of single we want in *Society*'s list of Top Totty. He's absolutely disgusting.'

'Repellent,' agreed Pim. 'Didn't someone die in his flat once?'

'And he's notorious for running after women with money so they can support his various habits,' added Hum.

Clemency put her head on one side. 'Is he really so bad?' She swung her hair winsomely. 'Isn't it just youthful high spirits?'

She got The Gaze for her pains and a chill now descended on the meeting. *Sebastian Hunter*. Laura underlined the name in her book. One to watch, clearly.

She looked up from her notes to find the piercing editorial stare now turned on her; it widened slightly as it took in what she was wearing. Lulu had shoved some Chanel pumps into the bag alongside the jeans and shirt and Laura felt like a different person in these expensive new clothes. From across Carinthia's office she saw Clemency looking her up and down suspiciously.

'So how are the weddings? You've fixed up the Bender one, I take it?' The editorial throne gave another violent jolt, which pitched Carinthia sideways.

'I'm working on it,' Laura said, evasively.

She had spent much of the preceding evening working on it, in fact. In the deserted office, the screen had glowed spookily into her face; a small pool of light in the surrounding darkness. The only other illumination was from the street outside, blades of sulphurous orange slanting across the flower-heaped desks.

Laura had tried her best not to remember what she'd heard someone say earlier, that the magazine building was on the site of a plague pit and the dead haunted the offices. She tried not to think that the flowers lying on the desks looked like funeral wreaths on the tops of tombs. Her stomach rumbled; her supper of sandwiches from Boots seemed hours ago, which indeed it was. She would have loved some soup, but that would have smelt and maybe alerted someone.

Laura had spent hours contacting the many Bender social media sites, some of which she had had to join especially for the purpose. She was confident of success, however; from past form she knew that Amy monitored herself exhaustively and any new message was sure to be seen.

Strangely, though, none of Laura's postings was answered. Undaunted and diligent, she left greetings and congratulations throughout cyberspace, including even via the 'Contact Us' tab on Amy's dealer's website.

Amy, hi, it's Laura Lake. Remember me from Paris? Where it all took off?

That was meant to remind Amy that Laura had contributed to her success.

Congratulations on everything, and especially on your wedding. I'm in London, as it happens, and I'd love to come along and wish you well!

Laura had consulted her various sites throughout the night, but nothing had come by way of reply. Perhaps Amy was asleep and would get back to her later that morning. She had to. She owed her. Her career just might depend on it.

The Gaze, with all its chilly, intimidating power, was trained on her. 'You *are* going? You have been invited?'

Conscious as she was of Clemency's smug smile from the sofa, Laura still couldn't lie outright. 'Honestly,' she reassured the editor, 'I'm on it.'

Carinthia now shuddered violently. Her chair had reached a stage in its programme not unlike the spin cycle of a washing machine.

'You had better not let me down,' she said ominously,

just as the chair shot upwards. 'You've allowed me to get my hopes up.' The seat plunged back down.

'I let you persuade me that you could do it!' The editor's dire warning was counterpointed by another lurch from beneath. 'You told me it would get me another award!'

'And I will. And it will.' Laura spoke with a calm certainty she was far from feeling. Actually, and as she well knew, Carinthia had persuaded herself about the article and award. But she had hinted at a staff job if she got the result she wanted. That was the thing to concentrate on. 'It's going to be brilliant,' Laura added.

Carinthia, now clinging to the bucking seat, was looking at Clemency. 'Okay. Make sure this story gets as much space as we can give it.'

Clemency replied with a wordless nod.

'I've had enough of it.' Carinthia hit the chair arms.

'I have to say, I think that's absolutely the right editorial decision.' Clemency's voice was syrupy with mock-regret. 'I'm really not sure this piece is going to work.'

Carinthia, clenching her teeth as her head juddered violently, glared at her. 'Not the feature,' she gasped. 'This chair. It's like effing Alton Towers. Turn it off, Demelza!'

The secretary dived under Carinthia's desk. 'I can't work out which plug it is.'

'Pull them all out!' Carinthia screamed as the chair threw her from side to side. It suddenly stopped and sank down, bringing her head to a level just above the desk's surface.

'Are you alright, Carinthia?' Demelza's tone was concerned. The editor's face was green. 'Can I get you something?'

'A small vodka perhaps,' Carinthia said weakly.

Demelza opened the fridge. It was crammed with clear glass bottles covered in twin-headed eagles and Cyrillic script. A clink, a slosh and Carinthia, despite being seated almost at floor level, was suddenly looking much brighter.

'Okay,' she said, looking at Laura. 'But if you balls it up, you're out.' She shook her brass-coloured bob. 'Okay. Let's talk about the Lulu interview.'

Laura crossed her fingers. On the sofa, Clemency straightened. The verdict on yesterday's adventures was about to be delivered.

'Grimston sent me the pictures last night,' Carinthia began.

'Laura styled them,' Clemency put in quickly, evidently feeling attack was the best form of defence.

The editor turned to Laura, who raised her chin, expecting the worst.

'Well you did a good job. They're fantastic. Fresh, simple, completely counterintuitive.'

Laura beamed. There was a gasp from the sofa, which Clemency did her best to turn into coughing. It went on so long, Carinthia eventually stood up to pass her the vodka tumbler. Clemency gulped it down, eyes bulging.

'Your interview,' Carinthia said, when she had finished.

'I'll be sending it over later,' Clemency managed between spurts of coughing. 'It's nearly done.'

'No need.' Carinthia waved a thin hand grandly. 'I've decided to run just the pictures. Worth a thousand words and all that. They speak for themselves and they'll have more impact on their own.'

Clemency's heart-shaped face went blank with shock. 'But…'

Carinthia relented. 'Okay. You can write a few captions. The best bits. Did she say anything especially unexpected?'

Laura held her breath. This was a dangerous moment. Clemency might yet twist Lulu's words. She might, even now, be able to persuade Carinthia to run a mocking piece.

As, possibly through sheer anger, Clemency had started coughing again, Laura seized her chance. 'She talked about her interest in crafting,' she said eagerly. 'Making bunting, doing scrapbooks. Oh, and shopping at the Wonder Supermarket and running along the ringing beach.'

'The what?'

'Relishing the buffeting wind.'

The editor clapped her beringed hands. 'Perfect.' And with that, the meeting was over. Laura grabbed her notebook and hurried out, Clemency's furious explosions still sounding in her ears.

After the meeting, Laura returned to the fashion cupboard, where Raisy and Daisy had unresigned, as Demelza had predicted. Neither seemed to suspect that their intern had spent the night in their workplace. They had not noticed the drying pair of La Perla pants, laundered in the washroom's shower along with Laura herself that morning. They seemed to wave at her like a flag now. She snatched them off, just in time.

Laura's mind was full. While the Lulu feature was an absolute success, the Amy Bender one, on which her future depended, was anything but. Clemency Makepeace, meanwhile, hated her more than she ever had before. She would now stop at nothing to get her into trouble.

'Got some new clothes, have we?' Talk of the devil. The devil was pausing by the door. From sneering at Laura, Clemency smiled sweetly at Raisy, who was just putting the phone down. 'Nothing missing from the fashion cupboard, I take it?'

Tears were rolling down Raisy's face. 'Yes, Hazza and Jazzy. Jazzy's stuck in a military cup...'

'You mean coup?' Laura pushed away the image this suggested of a fashionista wedged inside a silver trophy engraved with a squadron coat of arms. 'Oh no! How awful!'

'… and Hazza's in prison in Ping Pong,' added Raisy, hiccupping with grief.

'Pyong Yang,' snapped Clemency. 'God, don't you know anything?'

'She put a pink feather boa on a statue of Him Wrong-un,' Raisy said tearfully.

'Kim Jong-un,' the features editor snorted.

'Hazza said it really suited him,' Raisy wailed.

'More fool her,' was Clemency's unfeeling response. She walked off.

Laura comforted her colleague as best she could. Raisy's distress was exacerbated by having absolutely no idea about politics, or geography or why any of this might have happened. Presumably Hazza and Jazzy were equally ignorant. What a disaster.

Demelza now appeared. 'Call for you,' she said to Laura, whose heart instantly leapt. Amy! At last!

'Go to Raisy's phone and I'll put it through.'

Laura gently detached herself from the wailing, clinging fashionista.

There was a yell from the editor's office. 'Demelza! You forgot to plug the fridge back in, you bloody idiot.'

The secretary's eyes widened with alarm. 'Oh dear. Her vodka won't be chilled. Heads down, everyone.'

'Hello?' Laura gasped into the receiver a few minutes later. 'Is that you, Amy?'

'Amy?' answered a sleepy voice with a thick accent. 'Is not Amy. Is Lulu.'

'Lulu!' It wasn't the call she was hoping for, but it was still a delight. 'I've got great news for you!'

'Is surpriseballs!' shrieked Lulu, when Laura had finished. 'Amazeballs?'

'Is fantabissimo! My parents happy fatly.'

'Thrilled skinny?'

'Yes! Yes! Hardly can I believe it. Thank you, thank you, thank you—'

'What did you call about anyway?' Laura cut in. Lulu's thanks were as overwhelming as the rest of her.

'I remember who make my sculpture. The penis, you know?'

'Oh... yes.'

'He sent me wedding invitation. Today. Made me remember.'

'That's nice for you.'

'You think so? He marry Amy Bender.'

A gear now meshed in Laura's mind. A connection fused. A giant penny dropped. 'You mean Spartacus Tripp?'

'She do portrait of me once,' Lulu complained. 'Was expecting nice oil painting and she produce turd.'

'Turd?'

'Made of plastic, ran on battery. She say is bold artistic statement, but she get from joke shop, I think.'

'Hang on,' Laura said. 'This wedding. When is it?'

'I think this week. Is too small notice.'

Short notice. Laura's white knuckles clutched the receiver. 'When this week?' Not today, surely? If it had already happened...

'Um, Vlad? Vlad?' Lulu's voice went faint, then returned. 'Is Saturday.'

That was tomorrow. Laura's insides sagged in relief. 'Are you going, Lulu?' If so, was there the faintest hope that she could go with her?

'No, am going to ear spa in Switzerland. Have lobes lifted.'

'I'll call you back,' Laura said hastily, making a note of the number on the phone display. It was impossible to have a conversation under the suspicious stare of Clemency, especially as she had now passed the desk accidentally on purpose with the obvious intention of eavesdropping.

A few minutes later, in the lift lobby of the floor below, Laura called Lulu on Demelza's mobile. She had another plan by now.

'Look, Lulu, your lobes are just perfect. They don't need lifting. And if you go to this wedding, it will help people take you more seriously. Make you look like an art collector.'

'Maybe,' Lulu agreed.

Laura pressed her advantage. 'Spartacus is a pretty important artist. There'll be all sorts of intellectuals there. Your parents will be pleased if you get photographed talking to, ooh, David Hockney or someone.' She was inventing wildly now, but the stakes were desperately high.

'Papa like Hocker Knee,' Lulu conceded.

'And the *Society* cover *is* going to be amazing.' Time to remind Lulu of what she owed her.

'Yes, yes, and am so grating.'

'So you'll go to the wedding and take me with you?'

'Is not possible,' Lulu countered flatly. 'Diamonds girl's best friend but real bad news for lobes. Really big stones, they drag them down, hmm?' She sighed. 'If only I had clone!'

The words sent pure radiant inspiration flashing through Laura's brain. 'Oh my God, Lulu! You're a genius!'

'You think?'

'Yes! You do have a clone! Me!'

'Huh?'

Laura took a deep, steadying breath. This had to be

explained absolutely the right way. But it was hard not to gabble with excitement.

'What would you say, Lulu, if I went to the wedding disguised as you? I can fit into your clothes and I did all the talking for the interview.'

'You did,' Lulu agreed. 'Was amazeboards.'

'And this is an artists' wedding! And I know a bit about art. I've been to all the Paris galleries! Lots of times! I could make you look really knowledgeable...'

Laura stopped, aware she was sounding conceited. The other end was silent. Was Lulu offended? Had she put the phone down?

At last the reply came, in slow, heavy tones. 'But you have wrong hair, too skinny and big gap between front teeth.'

'Yes, but—'

'But maybe you not smile,' the other end interrupted brightly. 'Also, I have wigs. You know, for bad head days.'

'You have?' Laura's heart soared. This sounded like a yes.

'Mmm hmm. Have special wig bathroom in house. On top floor, next to present-wrapping room.'

'So it's a plan? You're happy for me to go to Spartacus Tripp's wedding and pretend to be you?'

'Is fine. You very good at being Lulu. Better than me, ha ha.'

Laura decided to take this as a compliment. She felt optimistic again. Things were back on track. She would go to the ball, or at least the wedding.

'Come to my house tomorrow morning,' Lulu instructed. 'Vlad help you with hair and make-up.'

Laura doubted it. Vlad, built like a prop forward, was hardly the lady's maid sort. She must have misunderstood.

It was difficult to sleep that second night in the fashion cupboard. This was partly because of excitement about the morning and partly because a new consignment of dresses kept slithering from their hangers and on to her makeshift bed. They were the work of a designer called Olympia Jagerbomb, who seemed to specialise in bum-skimming, glittery, multicoloured creations with cleavages down to the navel.

Raisy and Daisy had been very excited about them.

'Fabulously unexpected,' said Raisy.

'Energising primary brights,' said Daisy.

'Next-level traffic stopper.'

'Showy virtuosity.'

Both seemed to have quite got over the fact that their superiors were currently being detained by the Nepalese army or languishing in a North Korean jail. They had possibly taken their lead from Carinthia, whose response to the news had been that a fashion story on dictator chic was long overdue and Harriet was finally in a position to do some proper research.

'Hardwired into the fashion zeitgeist,' was Raisy's final word.

Laura thought Olympia Jagerbomb's clothes were hideous. Every stitch contravened Mimi's opinion that sensuality beat sexuality. 'Why wear corsets and truss yourself up? You are not a chicken!'

Something else was keeping Laura awake too. The possibility that she might be discovered. She really couldn't stay here over the weekend. Tomorrow being Saturday, the office might close altogether. Would she have to escape to Amy Bender's wedding through a window somewhere? And once out, how would she get back in?

Chapter Thirteen

On Amy Bender's wedding day, after a series of dreams about tight and tarty dresses, Laura got up early. Her lack of money meant that she was going to have to walk to Lulu's, so the sooner she started the better.

Her fears that the magazine building would shut at the weekends were not borne out. The foyer was open as usual and the guards were sitting behind the desk. Laura hung around at the back by the lifts and waited until they were engaged with a parcel delivery before scuttling past. Being noticed was not something she wanted.

Outside, the London sun had decided to shine on the Bender wedding. Laura hurried along the now familiar route towards Kensington, trying to not to think about how hungry she was or how much she would have welcomed a stop at one of the many cafes along the way.

Hyde Park was full of straining, grim-faced people thundering by in Lycra, their ears stuffed with plastic buds. By the time she emerged into Lulu's road, Laura felt exhausted. Under the swivelling gaze of the security cameras, she pressed the entryphone button in the broad stone gatepost.

Five minutes later, she was under the chandelier in the basement kitchen, holding an espresso with a kick like a mule. Vlad certainly knew her way round a coffee maker. She was handing Laura a second even as she finished the first.

Laura sipped, and felt life returning. 'Thanks, Vlad.'

The butler bowed slightly. 'If I could just ask madam to follow me upstairs?'

Amid the pink Armani drapes of the billionheiress's bedroom, spread out on the rose damask four-poster bed, was a multicoloured minidress barnacled with lace and sequins, cleavage slashed to the navel.

'It is by a Miss Olympia Jagerbomb,' Vlad intoned. 'A new designer much favoured by madam. I gather that she has won particular plaudits for her brazen glam and her dialling up of the kinetic fringing.'

The urge to giggle seized Laura, but then she remembered Vlad's fashionable biscuits. People in this house took clothes very seriously. 'Hardwired into the fashion zeitgeist,' she agreed.

'Indeed, madam. A refreshing palette with cyberpunk influences and a divinely decorative intarsia. Here is the wig, madam.'

A head-shaped mould stood on the multi-mirrored dressing table. Perched atop it was a cascade of long blonde hair, the tresses twisting with curls. It looked like a small dog.

'But first, madam, we must complete the spray tan.'

'Spray tan?' Laura repeated in horror. Mimi would have a fit. Nothing was more vulgar, in her view.

The butler stopped. The broad, dark-suited back turned. A pair of level dark eyes met her own. 'If I may be permitted to be so personal, madam's skin colour is a slightly different shade to madam's. Should this remain the case, the illusion of verisimilitude will be difficult to achieve.'

'But Lulu's had a life reset,' Laura pointed out desperately. 'That's what the *Society* article, sorry, pictures, are about. She's given up fake tans. Now she wants to craft and run along the ringing beach.'

Vlad's eyes met hers. The expression was part exasperation, part scepticism and entirely doubtful that Lulu would do any such thing. 'May I respectfully suggest that wearing Olympia Jagerbomb without a tan is inadvisable.'

'*I* have to wear that?' Only now did Laura make the connection between the dress on the bed and the wedding.

A few minutes later Laura found herself standing, stark naked and legs apart, in a small room covered in the Versace logo. Challenge was part and parcel of being a journalist, she reminded herself as Vlad, crouching before her with a nozzle, expertly sprayed her brown from head to foot. She had clearly done it many times before.

'Ow!' cried Laura. 'It's freezing.'

'I apologise for any discomfort, madam. Could I respectfully ask you to turn to the side? Present your back? Splay your fingers? Thank you very much, madam.'

It was hard to imagine Jeeves doing this for Wooster.

The spraying done, Laura was offered a white waffle robe and ushered back into the bedroom. Her skin felt unpleasantly sticky and smelt of pork pies.

The zeitgeisty Jagerbomb dress still lay on the bed. Up close, it seemed mostly slits and gaps; the cleavage in particular was a couple of feet wide. Desperately, Laura thought of another objection. Her bra and pants would show.

'If I may be so indelicate, the items you refer to are quite unnecessary, madam.'

Laura groaned, again thinking of Mimi's reaction. Showing a little, not a lot, was the essence of attractiveness.

She had heard about tit tape, but not until now had she personally experienced it.

Vlad, clearly a mistress of the art, pushed her breasts to the sides and lashed them securely down so the flat exposed panel of her ribs was front and central. It was like looking at her back, at the front.

'The sternum is the directional look of the moment, madam. Now the shoes.'

The mirrored entrance to the wardrobe slid back and Laura followed the impeccably British Estonian. Vlad was standing before the rows of evening pumps, pulling out a model with Perspex heels, straps bristling with crystals.

'I won't be able to walk in those,' she protested. The heels were a good eight inches and there was a three-inch platform to boot, as it were. How was she going to manage the Tube in these, supposing she found the fare to start with.

But perhaps she should think herself lucky. At least Vlad hadn't chosen the Lambruscos.

'Madam will not be required to,' said Vlad. 'Madam will take the lift to the basement garage, where the chauffeur will be on hand to meet her.'

Laura was so relieved, she tried the shoes on without complaint. While they were less agonising than they looked once silicone pads had been slipped into the soles, the feeling of her toes at ninety degrees to the rest of her foot took some getting used to. Standing before Lulu's mirror, she watched the butler lower on the wig. She felt like a dystopian Cinderella. She stared at the reflected creature, all blonde hair and dark brown legs, with a tiny sparkly dress in between. Was this really her? Who knew that journalism involved all this?

Vlad loomed behind her. 'If madam is now ready to proceed to make-up?'

Madam was. In yet another room, before a mirror framed with lightbulbs and surrounded by hair appliances mounted all over the leopardskin walls, Laura felt like a diva being prepared to go on stage. She half-expected a gang of waiting beauticians to lay her out and take one limb each, working like a team of mechanics at a Grand Prix pit stop. Certainly this was what Lulu in all her splendour suggested. So when Vlad calmly slid out a series of inbuilt drawers containing brushes and make-up, she was surprised.

'You're pretty good at this,' she said as the butler expertly sculpted her cheekbones with three different shades of blusher. 'Were you a make-up artist before you came to Lulu?'

'Since madam is kind enough to enquire, I was in the army.' This seemed only to deepen the mystery.

The butler selected a lipstick from a tray containing what looked like several hundred. Before Laura even knew it, Vlad had attached false eyelashes and was separating them out with a pin.

Gradually, beneath this assured, practised and enormous hand, what remained of Laura Lake disappeared completely and became Lulu.

Eventually, the butler stepped back and surveyed her critically. 'The preparations are complete, madam.'

Laura stood up, wobbling wildly in the shoes. It seemed unlikely she would take one step without breaking her neck.

'Forgive me, madam. One more thing.'

Laura's world suddenly went black. Only after a second or two did she realise Vlad had added a pair of Lulu's trademark huge sunglasses. How did Lulu manage, crippling herself with such shoes while hampering her sight in this way? There was, Laura felt, a sort of crazy heroism in it all. Or was it just crazy?

The lift to the garage was different from the one with the Music Room button in it. It was smaller and lined with snakeskin and mirrors. Stepping in was like entering a designer handbag.

She studied her reflection, beamed in from all four sides of the lift and from another mirror on the ceiling. Lulu pouted back at her, inscrutable behind her shades and beneath her pile of hair, and holding a jewelled clutch in which Laura's tools of the trade, a notebook and pen, snuggled into the satin lining. No one was going to stop her now!

The lift was so smooth, Laura only realised it had stopped when the doors slid open and she found herself looking over several gleaming car roofs. The cars were ranged on top of each other, parked on hydraulically operated shelves. She had heard of stacking garages, but this was the first time she had seen one. How very James Bond.

Lulu's pink sports car was there, plus a Maserati and a Lotus, one red, the other black. All had LULU numberplates. There was a large pink motorbike and, even more improbably, a couple of bicycles, Hermès orange and covered in that fashion house's logo.

Laura looked about for the advertised chauffeur. A figure in a buttoned grey uniform and a cap with a shining patent brim approached.

'Your car, madam.' The voice, with its faint East European accent, was familiar.

'Vlad?' The butler was standing beside a gleaming black limousine. LULU4.

'This way, madam.'

The interior was impeccable and smelt of expensive leather. Laura could just about see, through her sunglasses, polished wood and chrome gleaming dimly. The windows appeared to be entirely black; she could see nothing out of them at all.

The car rose up on its platform and emerged outside. The platform revolved to face the gates. As the gates slid back, Vlad started the engine and the car moved forward into the tree-lined street.

Laura peered hard from behind her sunglasses through the dark windows. No wonder people like Lulu got accused of not knowing how normal people lived. It wasn't that they didn't care, more that they couldn't see.

London glided by. The car passed through areas she recognised and into a neighbourhood she did not. There were steel tower blocks and glass-fronted buildings and signs to the City.

Eventually the streets narrowed and the buildings got lower. Vlad drove past Victorian terraces bookended with retro-smart restaurants called Sourdoughista and The Labourers' Canteen.

There were rows of restored period shopfronts containing ethical taxidermists, steampunk upcyclers, vintage boutiques and hand-letterpress printers. A gastropub on the corner, The Shoreditch Samurai, featured a guy with a man-bun on the sign.

'It is indeed Shoreditch, madam,' Vlad replied in answer to Laura's question. They were slowing down now.

Laura was interested to see this famously fashionable quarter of London. Not much was visible through the double screen of tinted glass, but she could make out The Old Street Salumeria, its window dangling with a cancan line of ham legs with little white drip trays fitted underneath. Her stomach rumbled. It was a welcome surprise that Amy was having her party here. Was anything better than the melting saltiness of thinly sliced ham, washed down by chilled dry fino?

A door or two away was Death Becomes Her. Its window was dominated by a huge Warhol-style screenprint; four colourful upended coffins replaced Elizabeth Taylor.

'A hipster undertaker?' Laura exclaimed.

'Indeed, madam. It is my understanding that as the denizens of the locale shuffle off this mortal coil, a gap has emerged in the market for burials with style and irony.'

'I see.'

'The venue for Miss Bender's celebration is between the two buildings, madam.'

'So not ham and fino, then?' Laura said disappointedly.

'I fear not, madam.'

Laura had hardly noticed the low brick structure between the salumeria and Death Becomes Her. She squinted at it now: a tiled roof, black-painted Victorian railings and gates, and framed signs saying 'Men' on one side and 'Women' on the other.

Amy Bender's wedding was taking place in an East End lavatory.

Chapter Fourteen

F ortunately, the convenience's capable Victorian builders seemed to have anticipated, a century and a half in the future, fashionable weddings where guests wore impenetrable sunglasses and cripplingly high heels. The narrow iron staircase leading down to the toilets was equipped with a sturdy railing.

Laura was about halfway down when she heard, above her in the street, a taxi door slam and some people get out.

'Oh my God, it's an actual bog,' a man exclaimed.

'So Marcel Duchamp!' answered a woman excitedly. 'But even better, as it's plumbed in and everything.'

Laura squinted up from beneath the staircase's curving cast-iron treads. The man had green hair and a T-shirt saying '#FirstWorldProblems', while the woman had what looked like a chandelier on her head.

The door at the bottom, towards which she was edging, said 'Men' on it. She had inadvertently edged down the wrong staircase, but there was no possibility she was edging back up it to go down the 'Ladies' steps. She pushed the door open.

A great gale of noise greeted her; laughing and shouting and the sound of champagne corks popping. It was hard to see the decor over the mass of people, but the walls were white-tiled and in between the pressing bodies the odd glimpse was afforded of urinals stuffed with white flowers. Laura was reminded of the washroom at Society House.

Waiters dressed as East European secret police were doing the rounds with trays of glowing green champagne. Laura took a glass and a cautious sip; it tasted normal enough, which was all that mattered.

On the other hand, perhaps it was making her delusional. Everyone looked strangely familiar. Laura wasn't as well versed in famousness as she had been as a full-time UK resident. Her once-sharp awareness had been blunted by France's celebrity culture, which was proudly nationalist and centred round ancient icons like Johnny Hallyday.

But these people... Laura looked around her. It was difficult to be sure, under her thick, dark shades, but wasn't that Elton John over there, in his regulation Nehru collar and huge yellow sunglasses? And Robbie Williams, complete with signature naughty smirk and biceps bulging from a studded leather waistcoat? Kylie Minogue? Beyoncé?

She had not realised that Amy Bender's crowd, while presumably wider and more influential these days thanks to the success of *Call This Art?*, included such superstars. She was struck by how absolutely celebrity-ish the celebrities looked, dressed exactly as one would expect.

My God, she thought, doing a double-take. Was that actually Prince Harry? There, by an open lavatory door, in a red military uniform with a blue sash across it; the very same one he'd worn for his brother's wedding to Kate Middleton. Laura had still been at school then and the entire boarding house had crowded round the day-room telly, oohing and aahing at every detail. As Clemency had blocked her view throughout, she had seen fewer details than most.

Her heart was racing with excitement. She had struck celebrity gold! What an opportunity; Carinthia would be thrilled. It might make the cover, perhaps even be picked up by a national paper. But only if she got quotes from the stars. Exhilarated yet determined, Laura plunged into the crowd.

Moving forward was tough, however. Hundreds of people were packed into the narrow space between the urinals and the lavatories. People who Laura guessed were either fashionable artists or had a connection to that world, judging by their ill-fitting clothes in terrible colours, their silly hats, and their spectacles of such profound thickness, bigness and ugliness that they could only have cost a fortune and come from the most recherché of sources.

Despite all this, they seemed to feel free to look her up and down and make derogatory remarks. 'I mean, just what do you do all day?' a man in a black fedora and a suit rioting with Marvel characters asked her.

Laura was about to explain that she was a journalist when she remembered she was disguised as Lulu. Her first thought was to respond defensively, but then a more amusing possibility struck her. 'I am working in lab all day,' she drawled in Lulu's trademark thick accent. 'Coding human atom.'

'Coding the human atom?' repeated the man in astonishment. He wore a black shirt and a tie printed with Captain America.

'Is my passion, yes. Science. Have four degrees in physics from University of Murmansk. What do you do?'

'I'm a steampunk poet.'

'Is what?' Laura asked. 'What do you do all day?'

She had similar exchanges with a muse in silver headphones and a jeans historian in a leopardskin playsuit. Having learnt that Lulu was a qualified heart surgeon, both stumbled off looking befuddled by more than the green champagne.

Some canapés now passed, borne aloft on a tray by a Stasi officer. Realising she was starving, Laura grabbed a handful of retro Ritz crackers, orange cheese on sticks and ironic vol-au-vents.

Strange music could be heard at intervals above the din; disjointed and jangly. She asked a man with guybrows what it was.

'It's the Eight-Legged Orchestra of Great Britain. The composer takes spiders from their webs, puts them in other spiders' webs and sticks them in boxes. Then he mikes up the boxes and records the sounds their feet make on the webs. It's kind of twangly, like free jazz.'

Laura wrote this down. 'I didn't realise you could read and write,' the young man remarked. Besides the guybrows, he wore a vintage Soviet tracksuit with CCCP motifs, teamed with a tweed flat-cap.

'What?'

'Aren't you Lulu? That socialite?'

Laura was about to reply when an elderly man in tight leather trousers placed a warm hand on her bottom. 'You, my dear, are a work of art,' he announced to where her cleavage would have been had sternums not been so directional.

She wrenched the hand away. It didn't discourage him in the least. 'Want to see my erection?' he asked, retrieving his smartphone from a pocket. 'It's in Tate Modern.'

Laura looked at a photograph of a huge bobbing inflatable cat. 'It's called *The Universal Unaddressability of Things*.' He swiped to the side. 'And here's the companion piece.' It looked like a pile of blow-up sex dolls. 'They symbolise moral decline.'

Laura continued squeezing towards the celebrities. Getting quotes from Elton, Robbie and especially Prince Harry was absolutely essential.

The spider music had now changed to a loud, insistent pounding. 'It's the Hackney Collective of Non-Binary Samba Drummers,' someone behind Laura said.

'Well, can someone turn them down?' shrieked an American accent. A glossy woman in a fitted dress with gleaming spike-heeled shoes held a smartphone to each ear.

A Stasi officer tapped her on the shoulder. 'No photos. You can draw the party, but that's all.'

The woman spun round so fast and furiously it almost dislodged her chignon. 'Draw? Why the hell would I draw? I'm from Gagillion Globalart! Spartacus Tripp's dealers?'

The group Laura was now edging past was discussing wedding presents.

'I've bought them a painting by Hitler,' a man in oversized glasses and a Morphsuit was saying proudly. 'Rather nice, a view of distant hills. No figures, but I guess he wasn't a people person.'

'I'm giving them a toaster,' said a woman with a flashing neon 'Open' sign on her head. 'Covered in dead houseflies.'

Laura made a mental note to write down these gems later and approached the first of her targets. Elton John was only feet away, taller than he appeared in photographs.

Up close, his Paisley silk Nehru jacket looked worn and stained, unexpectedly so for someone so famously wealthy. Perhaps it was his lucky jacket, Laura thought. She tapped him on the shoulder, excited and nervous. She had never spoken to a megastar before.

'Sir Elton!'

Sir Elton whirled round. Up close, his face was less round than anticipated, his nose less snub. Perhaps it was her sunglasses. Or perhaps, in the age of Photoshop, celebrities rarely looked like their pictures.

'Can I ask you few questions?' Just in time, Laura remembered to add her Lulu drawl.

'Course you can, love.' His own accent was northern, which seemed strange. Wasn't Elton a Londoner?

But perhaps all that was put on. Perhaps he had a sordid northern past ready to be uncovered by a journalist-in-disguise who would ferret out his deepest secrets and write an exposé about the 'real Elton'... Laura snapped out of her daydream and began her interrogation.

'How you know Amy Bender? Spartacus Tripp?'

Behind his yellow glasses, Elton's eyes widened with amazement. 'Who the 'eck is that?' he asked bluntly.

'Bride and groom?'

'Oh, right. Got no idea, love. My agent booked me, see.'

Laura supposed this made sense. Elton famously did a lot of wedding gigs, for vast fees. He probably didn't always know the people involved.

She noticed that he was staring fixedly at where her breasts would normally be, which seemed out of character. 'Let's talk about your career, hmm?' she said hurriedly.

'Going great guns,' Elton declared. 'Hell of a lot better than being a plumber, let me tell you.'

Laura racked her brains. She wasn't an expert on Elton but hadn't realised he'd been a plumber. Hadn't he been to the Royal College of Music?

She gasped in shock as Elton's clammy hand grasped her shoulder. 'What you doing later?'

Laura ducked out of his reach. Desperate she may be, but not that desperate. She looked down. Kylie Minogue was beaming up at her, trademark quizzical eyebrow aloft. Up close, it looked drawn on.

'Can we talk about your career?' Laura asked her. 'Hmm?'

'It's better than it was. Last year I was in a Girls Aloud tribute band.'

Laura laughed. Kylie was of course famous for her refreshingly Australian sense of humour.

She felt a hand on her shoulder and turned to find herself looking at a familiar grin, above a ginger beard and beneath a braided military cap.

'I say, wench,' said Prince Harry. 'One finds you seriously hot, what?'

Laura's mouth fell open.

Prince Harry gave a self-satisfied smile. 'Don't be too over-whelmed. I'm just a guy, you know.'

'Wench,' Laura said.

The Prince looked puzzled. 'Eh?'

'You call me wench.' Laura made full use of Lulu's heavy accent. 'Is sexist, no?'

HRH looked apologetic. 'Soz. Sorry. Joke.'

'I do not think it is funny.'

'I know. But people expect it, you see. They think the royal family are dinosaurs. Even me, and I'm the trendy one.'

'And are they dinosaurs?' Laura was feeling triumphant. She had him on the back foot now, and this was a promising line of discussion. It would make a brilliant few paragraphs, maybe even the coverline. 'MY FAMILY ARE DINOS, BY PRINCE HARRY'. Her heart was beating fast. This was her biggest ever opportunity. It wouldn't just help her career, it would shoot it into orbit.

The Prince looked amazed. 'How the hell would I know?'

'You are Prince Harry, yes?'

Harry looked at her in astonishment. 'You having a laugh?'

His accent was possibly more mockney than expected. But as he'd said, he was the trendy one.

'Bunch of twats,' Harry added. 'Must be one of the worst gigs ever.'

Laura could hardly breathe; was this further criticism of his family?

'A party in a downstairs bog! God knows why I do this. '

'But you have to do it, yes?' Laura sympathised, still in Lulu's voice. 'Boost British business and culture, yes?'

He stared at her again. 'Is that your actual accent? I thought you…'

'Thought what?'

'Oh, never mind. So you're really Lulu? I've always wanted to meet you.'

'Really?' Laura was delighted. This would make things a lot easier.

'You bet. Ever since that sex tape that went viral.'

'Oh.' Laura jumped as a royal hand began hovering around her hemline. It seemed quite a practised move.

'That's an awfully nice dress you've got off.'

'Off?' Laura struggled to shove away the exploring digits.

'Well, it is more off than on.' Prince Harry guffawed. 'Are those real?' he added, staring at her breasts, which had now started to edge back into position. 'My grandfather taught me to always ask that of a lady. The perfect icebreaker, he reckons.'

Laura smiled through gritted teeth at Prince Philip's celebrated wit. The enquiring hand was back again.

'What are you doing later?' Beneath the shining peak of his cap, the princely eyes gleamed. 'I could show you some of my medals, if you like?' He flashed her a suggestive grin and lifted his free hand to ripple the discs on his chest.

Laura considered. Unlike many, she had never found Harry all that sexy. Ginger men did not appeal to her. But she was a journalist with a job to do and keeping him talking might help her avoid what else he obviously had in mind.

'Okay.' Whatever happened, it would be a story. 'I'd love to.'

'Sick.' He looked at his watch,

'Six?' Laura queried.

'Sick,' repeated the Prince. 'As in well rad. As in bad. As in good. I'm the trendy royal, remember.'

'Oh yes.' Laura's mouth was twitching.

'I clock off at five. Laters, bro.' He disappeared into the crowd.

Lulu now felt a firm hand gripping her exposed shoulder. Expecting it to be Elton again, she whirled crossly round. The face looking into hers was not that of the 'Rocket Man' singer, however. It was bright orange and surrounded by long, snaky, dark hair set off by a plastic tiara.

'Lulu! Darling! It's Irina! Irina Pushamoff!'

The designer who had come to *Call This Art?*, Laura remembered. Who had provided Mrs Bender's zip-festooned gold trousers.

'It's so wonderful to see you,' Irina cooed, her sharp eyes raking Laura's dress, or what there was of it. 'Is that an Olympia Jagerbomb?'

Laura nodded.

'She steals all my ideas!' Irina exclaimed with a flare of Slavic nostril. 'Muah!' As she received two loud kisses on her cheeks, Laura got a blast of powerful perfume. 'Darling, I must go. The bridal party are arriving and I, as the designer, must be on hand. But I will see you in my atelier? My new collection launches soon and you are, as ever, my inspiration!'

It was only now, as Irina pushed off through the crowds, that Laura saw what she was wearing. The tight sheath of pearlised blue rubber reminded her of Carinthia's exercise ball, as did the prominently shaped buttocks beneath. If this was from the new collection, being the inspiration was a backhanded compliment, if not a backsided one.

Laura watched Irina pause beside someone. A someone she recognised, with punky white hair, high cheekbones and dark eyebrows. The designer seemed to be talking to him very intently, with none of her usual gesticulating exuberance. Where, Laura wondered, had she seen him before?

She was distracted by a kerfuffle at the door. As if at a prearranged signal, all the lavatories flushed simultaneously. You could, Laura thought, call it a saloot.

The non-binary samba drummers struck up what might have been a version of 'Here Comes the Bride'.

Amy and Spartacus had arrived.

'Woo-hoo!' shouted a female artists' collective in orange ISIS-prisoner boilersuits, waving their arms in the air. 'Let's pump it up to turbo!'

The Stasi waiters were moving through the crowd handing out fistfuls of torn-up paper from large bowls for use as confetti. It looked like a ripped-up book. Laura, examining hers, saw that it was *The Iliad*. Classics had been one of her best subjects.

The blushing bride looked very blushing indeed; Amy was in fact bright red from head to foot. She was dressed as a lobster in tight pearlised coral rubber with sparklers stuck into her dreadlocks. Irina Pushamoff had clearly surpassed herself.

Spartacus, for his part, wore a suit of armour and carried a surfboard. Two snarling Staffordshire bull terriers brought up the rear. Sid and Nancy the ringbearers, Laura remembered from the newspaper report.

She peered at the happy couple's fingers, eager to see the rings by the famous Mary-Bliss Skinner. Both Amy and Spartacus were wearing what looked like the ring-pulls of Coke cans, set with small, dusty rocks.

'Amazing, aren't they?' someone breathed reverently behind Laura. 'Mary-Bliss drilled them off the same sustainable diamond. They're worth about half a mil each.'

Bits of Homer fluttered through the air as the guests hurled confetti at the happy couple.

'Amy!' shouted Laura, as she neared. But the lobster swept on with the devil dogs in her wake. A familiar figure brought up the rear of the bridal party.

'Mrs Bender!' Laura yelled. Not as valuable an interviewee as her daughter, but could be good for background information.

Mrs Bender too was sporting the Pushamoff pearlised rubber range. As she was less pneumatic than Irina and less artistic and experimental than Amy, it was correspondingly less of a success. But, as mother-of-the-bride outfits went, definitely unusual. The clinging violet dress exposed wrinkly knees and crêpey arms and pitilessly outlined the rigging of underwear. It made a strange farting noise as Mrs Bender clomped along in Perspex shoes whose heels were formed of metal spirals. She was hanging on unsteadily to Mr Bender, who was looking, as ever, as if he wished it was all over.

Amy's mother proved a mine of useful information. Laura now found out that the Bender-Tripps had plighted their troths in a window-cleaner's cradle at the top of the Shard. After the lavatory celebrations, they were heading off on honeymoon. An ironic one, naturally.

'A senior-citizens' coach trip to the Italian Lakes,' explained Mrs Bender.

Mr Bender had covered his eyes and was shaking his head.

The lavatory celebrations themselves were to be followed by an afterparty in a hospital A & E department. A fleet of ambulances was due to convey the guests.

Laura could hardly suppress her glee. It was all so crazy; Carinthia was going to love it. And Prince Harry would be the icing on the cake.

Not that there was a cake. According to Mrs Bender, each departing guest was to be given a Tunnock's Caramel Wafer. 'Whatever that is.'

'I'm so sorry about your jewellery,' Laura said, moving the conversation on. Mrs Bender's remarks on the robbery would be a useful addition to the piece. 'Hmm?' she added, remembering that she was still meant to be Lulu.

As Mr Bender let out a hollow groan, Mrs Bender sighed. 'They still haven't caught whoever did it. What really hurts is those people who say it was all faked to publicise Amy. As if she would do such a thing!'

Laura caught another glimpse of the bride in her rubber lobster dress, her dreadlocks spitting fire. She was posing for a selfie with Tracey Emin.

'She's such a shy creature at heart,' her mother went on sorrowfully. 'Self-promotion doesn't come easily to her.

Other people use her all the time. Take this wedding. Who else but my Amy would agree to be given a free Irina dress and let that jewellery designer give her a discount on the rings?'

Mr Bender now spoke for the first time. 'Can I smell something burning?'

He could. As could other people. There were screams. The crowd started to panic and head towards the exits. 'Fire! Fire!'

The Benders were suddenly gone. Laura felt a sharp heel jam down on her foot. 'Let me through!'

It was the dealer from Gagillion Globalart. 'Hold that price, I'll get back to ya,' she shouted into one of the two smartphones she still had clamped to her ears. Laura watched as she shoved Spartacus aside on her way to the exit. He tottered, then collapsed in a deafening crash of metal.

The stairs were now jammed solid with people desperate to escape. Fights had broken out. The chandelier hat was hurled into the stairwell. Fashionable spectacles crumpled under flying fists. The silver headphones sailed through the air. Above it all, Amy could be heard screaming that her zero-impact Coke-can ring had fallen off in the crush.

Laura, stuck in the crowd, was unable to move. Across the smoke-filled room, she saw the cubicle door open and a distinctly rumpled-looking Kylie emerge with the elderly artist in leather trousers. Her expression of sated wonder gave way to horror. 'What's going on?' she screamed. 'Oh my God! We're all going to die!'

Were they, Laura wondered. Had her last hour really come? After all that had happened, was this how it would end, in a Victorian loo in Shoreditch?

A ripple of relief now seemed to pass through the assembly.

The panic and screaming died down as the news got through. The blaze was a purely local one. Local to the bride. The sparklers had set Amy Bender's dreadlocks aflame.

Further reports came in. A real ambulance had been called and Spartacus, now upright, above ground and still in his armour, was clanking between the afterparty conveyances, trying to discover where it was.

Everything was back on track. So much so that, by the time Laura dragged herself up the iron stairs, everyone had gone. Only a few shreds of *The Iliad*, stuck to the pavement, hinted at the fashionable revelling that had been.

She looked up and down, annoyed. Where was Prince Harry? They had a date, after all. No doubt it was the fire scare; his security detail must have whisked him away at the first sign of trouble. He had deserted her, like a rat deserting a sinking hipster.

So much for her groundbreaking, cover-worthy, front-page-dominating interview. Another chance gone, she thought glumly.

Still, she had the rest of the information, and it was a glorious, golden evening. Rich sunshine flooded the windows of the hipster funeral parlour and lively chatter came from the salumeria; there were a few skinny tables outside, with even skinnier people sitting at them.

Laura was aware of curious gazes being directed at her over the fino and *pata negra*. She stood, anchored in her shoes, wishing that Vlad would appear to save her, but no such arrangement had been made. She would have to make her own way back to return the clothes at some point, and her own way back to the fashion cupboard right now. How on earth did one get to central London from here? Was there even a Tube station?

She summoned her strength and was about to totter off, when a familiar figure in a red jacket appeared from around the corner.

'Your Royal Highness!' exclaimed Laura, as he clasped her in his arms.

Chapter Fifteen

'Look,' Prince Harry said, 'the party's over. Can't we drop this?'

'Drop what?' They were in a taxi. The Prince had, curiously, directed it to an address in Brixton. Must be a royal safe house, Laura thought, having read somewhere that such places existed. Somewhere he could go where no one would disturb him.

'This whole Prince Harry thing.'

'What do you mean?' Laura looked at him from under her sunglasses. She was still in the character of Lulu as unmasking herself had no obvious advantage. Who was Laura Lake to the fifth in line to the throne?

The Prince now tugged off his ginger beard and removed his hat to reveal a full head of contrasting dark curls. Laura now realised what else about the royal appearance had been strange: his dark eyes. Prince Harry had light blue ones;

he was also, unlike this man, unusually tall. She had been suspending her disbelief so hard that she had utterly failed to see what was staring her in the face.

'Caspar!'

'You know me?' Caspar stared at her in amazement.

'Of course I do!' Just how short was his memory?

'But I've never met Lulu.'

'I'm not Lulu.' Laura ripped off her sunglasses and pulled off the blonde wig.

Caspar's large mouth dropped open. 'Laura!' he yelled. 'Laura effing fucking bloody Lake!'

'Oy!' remonstrated the taxi driver. 'Language, if you don't mind.'

Laura and Caspar stared at each other, half-laughing, half-shocked. 'This is like one of those Shakespeare comedies,' Laura said eventually. It was a relief to speak in her normal voice. 'Where all the women are really men and they're all in disguise on top of that and they don't recognise each other and—'

'Don't!' Caspar groaned. 'That's just what I've been doing for the past two weeks.'

Laura looked at him sternly. 'Come off it, Caspar. I know exactly what you've been doing. And I have to say, it's pretty awful.'

He groaned again. 'You mean the porn?'

'Look, I realise you have to eat and everything, but must you stoop so low?'

'Laura, you don't understand.'

But Laura was warming to her theme. 'I know porn's supposed to be practically mainstream now, but it shouldn't be. It's sexist and degrading and it twists people's minds, especially young people's.'

'Well, you can talk, I must say,' huffed Caspar.

'Meaning what?'

'I tried to call you loads of times. But you always put on a foreign accent and asked if I wanted spanking, full sex or a threesome.'

Laura gasped. 'My mobile was stolen. In King's Cross. That wasn't me.'

'And that porn thing isn't me!' Caspar shouted.

'Keep it down, willya!' admonished the driver.

'It's not me,' Caspar repeated, in a rasping whisper. 'He's just got the same name as me, that's all. That guy in the films.'

Laura stared. 'There are two Caspar Honeymans? Honeymen?'

The tousled dark head nodded. 'And it's just my luck that the other's a particularly crap porn star. Why can't he be a brain surgeon?'

The urge to smile was pulling at the corners of Laura's mouth. She believed him, but it didn't explain everything. Where had he been since Paris?

'Hey nonny no,' Caspar said.

'Is that meant to be funny?'

He rolled his large brown eyes despairingly. 'No. That really is what I've been doing.'

He described touring Scotland with the Hey Nonny No Men, a five-strong troupe of male actors who did Shakespeare in the original fashion, with men dressed as women. 'Our mission was to boldly go and perform *A Midsummer Night's Dream* where no Shakespeare had been performed before, boldly or otherwise.' Caspar sighed. 'But there was a good reason why it hadn't. No one wanted it.'

At least, not in numbers sufficient to comprise a profitable audience. Bad weather, on the other hand, had been a keen supporter of their efforts.

'It was neither midsummer, nor a dream. More like a nightmare in an exceptionally bitter December.'

When not playing in freezing, wind-blasted, midge-infested gardens before a handful of people invisible under umbrellas, the Hey Nonny No Men had drunk away their misery and profit in silent Highland pubs. Or played the ever popular game of Hunt the Mobile Signal.

'Poor you.' Laura was trying to sound indignant as Caspar clearly considered himself the worst off, despite having condemned her to penury and homelessness. But her anger at him was melting in the heat of his charm and the circumstances, which were funny enough to forgive almost anything. 'And there was me thinking that you'd run off with that blonde you sat next to on the train.'

Caspar looked rueful. 'I did. She was the Hey Nonny No Men's manager. She told me that they were an actor short. It was only after I'd signed up that I found out she was staying in London and not coming on the tour.'

'Can't you hook up with her now you're back?'

'Hardly. The Nonnies have broken up. One guy criticised another guy's Bottom.'

'Spare me,' groaned Laura.

'So it's all Oberon between us.'

'Stop it!'

Caspar grinned. 'So I've had to do whatever work my agent comes up with. My last gig was handing out leaflets by the Shrek Experience dressed as a Grenadier Guard on stilts.' His voice had worked its way up various registers of anguish and now it reached its crescendo. 'Oh God!' he wailed. 'My career's vaporised! Now I've descended to the final circle of thespian hell! I'm with a lookalike agency.'

Laura was laughing now, but suddenly her smile vanished. Lookalike agency!

A rush of heat went through her. Of course. Now he said it, it was obvious. How could she not have realised?

'You mean all those people there were lookalikes? Not just you? Tom Jones, Elton John, Beyoncé?'

Caspar stared. 'Wait, you can't seriously have thought...'

Laura had her face in her hands and was groaning and rocking back and forth.

'Laura, you must be joking. They were all terrible. It was deliberate, they were meant to be ironic...'

'I know. I know. I've been away too long. And I had the sunglasses on. You can't see a thing through them. And anyway,' Laura added, looking up, 'you weren't at all bad. You were quite a good Prince Harry. Strangely convincing, considering you're so much smaller and—'

'Thanks,' cut in Caspar. 'I'll take that as a compliment. I thought you were winding me up, but I went along with it because...' He stopped. His glance flickered over her exposed sternum.

'Because what?'

'Well, I thought you were Lulu, basically. That celebutante or whatever she is. I've always quite fancied her.' He paused and frowned as the thought clearly occurred to him for the first time. 'Why are you dressed up as her anyway?'

'It's a long story. I'll tell you when we get back to yours.'

He looked startled. 'To mine?'

'Well, you owe me a place to stay,' she pointed out. 'You promised me. It's the whole reason I'm in London.'

Caspar looked panicked. 'Things have changed a bit. My flatmate's thrown me out...'

'Again?'

'Another flatmate, but, yeah. So now I'm sleeping on another mate's floor. You wouldn't like it, he shares with four other guys. They don't wash much and they eat a lot of curry.'

Laura said nothing. It looked like it was back to the fashion cupboard after all.

'Look, if it helps, you can have these.' Caspar was fishing things out of his pocket. 'They were giving them away as I left.'

Laura looked at a piece of card with silver blobs on it. It bore an image of the happy couple and the words 'WIN! WIN! WIN!' It was, she realised, a themed scratchcard.

'You can win a work of art by Amy Bender,' Caspar said encouragingly.

'But I am a work of art by Amy Bender,' Laura pointed out. 'Or I was.'

'Me too, but you wouldn't have thought so. She looked right through me when I tried to say hello.'

'What are these?' Laura studied the shiny black packets he had also tossed into her lap.

'Misfortune cookies. Kind of a dystopian version of fortune cookies. Let's have a look, shall we?' Caspar ripped them open to reveal small white slips inside. 'You will meet stranger who steal all your money!' he read in a cod-Chinese accent.

Laura's face remained unmoved.

'Here's another. You will get new job and find rurst enemy rurk there!' Caspar laughed again. 'Hey, come on, Laura. Where's your sense of humour?'

Where indeed? Laura looked out of the taxi window.

She suddenly realised how tired she was, and how hungry. She had no money and the ironic party food had been terrible.

She looked at Caspar, lounging in the cab, his legs in their side-striped military trousers nonchalantly crossed. The gold braid on his red jacket shone in the pink evening sun. He had unbuttoned it to reveal the muscled chest she remembered. He was smiling suggestively, a lock of glossy hair flopping into brown eyes full of erotic promise. 'God, you look hot in that dress,' he said.

'Thanks,' she said stiffly.

'You haven't got any knickers on, have you?'

This occasioned a warning clearing of the throat from the taxi's front seat.

Caspar grinned and shifted across the seat towards her. 'I know I said I couldn't put you up, but the other guys are away this weekend. Dune-bashing in the Arabian desert with Ben Fogle.'

'What?'

'Or maybe Ben Fogle-bashing in the dunes. Stag do, anyway.'

'Oh.'

'Point I'm making,' Caspar said, his hand warm and heavy on her thigh, 'is that you could stay for a couple of nights.'

He was up close to her now. He bent his head and brushed her lips with his. A hot rush of longing swept through her. Caspar was a shit, but a handsome one who knew exactly how to push her buttons. 'You know I love you really, Laura Lake,' he murmured, his expert fingers already at work.

'Sure,' she snorted, but softly.

His kiss was long and slow and she responded with increasing enthusiasm.

The taxi driver knocked on the glass again. 'Get a bleedin' room.'

Caspar lived in sexy squalor. So Laura thought at first. But after five minutes she decided it was actually just squalor.

It was the top floor of a battered terrace and had grimy

windows with peeling CND stickers. Thin, dirty curtains hung drunken and half-hooked. The loo lacked paper, a hand-towel or even a seat. The sole utensil in the kitchen was a spatula. They used it, Caspar explained, for eating cold beans out of tins.

The floor of the sitting room was so cluttered, none of the carpet was visible. 'Take it from me, you don't want to see it,' Caspar said when Laura pointed this out.

Unconvinced, she looked critically at the scatter of trainers, dirty plates and clothes. 'It looks like they use the floor as their wardrobe.'

'They do,' Caspar confirmed. 'First up, best dressed.'

Caspar had a blow-up mattress in one corner. It was heaped with rumpled blankets and twisted sheets and made a farting noise whenever you moved. It reminded Laura of Mrs Bender's dress and added an unwelcome comic element to their lovemaking.

Caspar had lost none of his sure touch, however. And after so much recent worry and uncertainty, losing herself in pure physical pleasure came as a profound relief to Laura.

Over the weekend, Caspar showed her the glories of Brixton. Laura loved its air of crumbling grandeur, although it was, her host huffily retorted, coming back up in the world and very middle-class these days. Laura especially loved the lively market, full of music, exotic vegetables, and stalls selling Caribbean food.

'This is amazing!' Laura dug into a takeaway carton of soused pork made with limes and scotch-bonnet peppers. 'How can you just eat beans with a spatula?'

Their trip to the famous Ritzy cinema struck the only sour note. It was showing Orlando Chease's latest blockbuster, a gunfest action movie called *The Kalashnikov Protocol*.

'Oh come on,' said Laura, trying to cheer Caspar up. 'It's macho rubbish. Blokes with choppy runs blowing people up. You don't want to be in anything like this.'

'Try me,' said Caspar bitterly, adding that *The Kalashnikov Protocol* was effectively Orlando Chease's audition for the Bond role. He was also trying every publicity stunt known to man, including dating a famous American singer called Hudson Grater.

'Is that a man?' Laura asked. She had never heard of Hudson Grater, but it was quite usual for celebrities who were massive elsewhere not to make an impression in her adopted country.

Caspar stared. 'Are you seriously joking? Hudson Grater's huge. She sings about break-ups. You must know "You Fat-Shamed Me on Facebook"?' He began to hum.

''Fraid not.'

'She's a serial celebrity dater,' Caspar went on. 'That she's bothering with Chease shows how big he's become. People are calling them CheaseGrater.'

On the Sunday night, after a prolonged session on the mattress, Caspar rolled a huge joint and offered it to her. 'Camberwell carrot?'

Laura shook her head. She had never much taken to drugs. Marijuana made her feel sick.

As Caspar smoked it for the two of them, she told him about Lulu and the magazine. They had been too preoccupied to discuss it until now.

'So you took my advice,' Caspar said smugly.

'What advice?'

'That if you started on a glossy you could work your way up to newspaper reporter. Maybe even the foreign pages, like your papa.'

Laura smiled. 'Funny thing is, I like the glossy stuff. Actually, I love it. You have to think on your feet; it's a lot more derring-do than I expected. And absolutely hilarious.' She told him about the features meetings, and the Lulu interview.

'Caspar strikes again,' gloated Caspar. 'You'd be nowhere without me, you know. I'm the guardian angel of your career.'

'Huh?'

'The ventriloquism?' He threw his voice to the other side of the room.

Laura folded her arms, annoyed. How dare he take credit for everything? A thought now struck her. 'Okay then. I bet you can't help me with this.'

'Try me.'

She told him about the New Society Weddings article. 'The editor's wild about it. Convinced it's going to get her a Pulitzer Prize or whatever. And she's given it to me!'

'Great.' Caspar shrugged. 'So?'

'So I've got to get it right. If I do, she'll give me a job. My life depends on it, basically. On you.' Laura gazed at Caspar, her eyes bright with longing.

Caspar's own eyes were puzzled. 'But what's it got to do with me? I'm not getting married.'

'No, but you can help me. Seeing as you're the guardian angel of my career and so on.'

Caspar's expression was cagy. 'Still not quite making the connection here, I'm afraid.'

Laura groaned. She would just have to spell it out. 'Okay. So, I've done an arty wedding. You follow?'

Caspar drew hard on his joint and nodded.

'Next I need a boho-aristo one. And one in a castle, with tiaras and ancestral coaches. Just to show that that sort of thing still goes on.'

Caspar narrowed his eyes as he blew out the smoke. 'And does it?'

'I don't have a clue. But if I don't find one of each, the whole deal will be off. She'll sack me. You've got to help me.'

Caspar inhaled again. He was looking vaguer by the second. She wanted to throttle him. 'Any ideas? You're not being Prince Harry anywhere?'

The words had an electric effect. Caspar sat bolt upright. Then he put a hand to his head. 'Woah. That was a bit sudden.' Looking green, he started to slide down the wall.

But Laura pulled him back up. He had obviously remembered something. Something that might help her. 'Prince Harry?' she prompted, shaking him. 'You're dressing up as Prince Harry again?'

'Midsummer faun,' Caspar muttered, his eyes closed. 'At some wedding in the West Country. Under a mystical oak. Sometime this week.'

Laura gave a high-pitched squeal of triumph. Bullseye! Perfect!

'But I'm not going,' the limp body in her arms went on.

'Yes you are.'

'I may be desperate, but not so desperate that I'll wear wings and a tunic and have my legs sprayed silver.'

'Well you just did it for a fortnight in Scotland,' Laura pointed out.

'Exactly. I rest my case.' Caspar closed his eyes.

Laura let him drop back on to the mattress. 'Don't you want to help me?' she demanded, crossly.

'No.'

There was, Laura realised, only one thing for it now. She had tried threats, tried appealing to Caspar's non-existent conscience. One tactic alone remained.

She prised his arms apart, rolled on top of him and pressed her lips to his. 'Remember,' she whispered. 'I'm a journalist. Laura Lake, Ace Reporter. I'll do anything to get my story.'

Caspar did not respond. She raised herself slightly and traced a nail down his stubbly cheek. 'And when I say anything, I mean… *anything*.'

She could tell already, through certain failsafe signs, that this was having an effect.

Caspar spoke, but his eyes remained shut. 'Including all the things you just did anyway?'

'Yes.' Laura giggled into his chest.

'And the things you didn't?'

Laura knew what was being referred to. There had been a couple of positions even she had drawn the line at. 'Yep.'

His eyes opened. They were full of lustful speculation. 'The Greek Vase?'

This was particularly extreme. But he had, Caspar swore, seen it on some pottery in the British Museum.

'Fine.' If it meant she could write her piece and get her job, it would be worth it. 'But you drive a hard bargain.'

'A hard something. Definitely.'

Chapter Sixteen

On Monday morning, Laura returned happily to central London. The weekend had gone well. She and Caspar had had a ball – quite literally – and, on the professional front, she had lots of material from the Bender wedding. Plus the mystical boho marriage was also in the bag. Carinthia was going to be thrilled.

It was just past eight when she emerged from Oxford Circus Tube. Lots of time to write up her notes, as well as investigate the possibilities in the fashion cupboard. Besides serving as her temporary home, it was about to play another role in her life. An actual clothes-related one.

She needed something to wear. At the moment, her look was jeans and a T-shirt borrowed from Caspar's floor. In other circumstances they might have passed as the 'boy-friend' look, but it wouldn't be the sort of boyfriend anyone at *Society* was interested in.

With any luck there would be something low-key – some smarter jeans, a plain T-shirt – that she could borrow until she could get up to Lulu's and get her own clothes back. And return the Olympia Jagerbomb wedding ensemble currently folded inside a Lidl carrier from Caspar's kitchen.

As expected, no one was in the *Society* office. Laura headed straight for the fashion cupboard. Leaving the light off so as not to draw attention to her presence, she examined the clothes on the racks as best she could in the gloom. Good; here was a plain white shirt and dark jeans, both of which closely resembled the ones Lulu had given her. In the unlikely event that Raisy and Daisy noticed anything, they would think them the same ones.

Laura peeled off Caspar's musty clothes. As he had been unable to provide underwear, and she would have anyway thought twice about accepting any he might offer, she stood naked on the carpet. She inspected her long, pale body in the mirror; there were scratches and bitemarks all over, especially around her breasts, she noted ruefully. No one could describe Caspar's lovemaking as gentle. On the other hand, she had given as good as she'd got...

She smiled, then froze. She could hear footsteps outside. Her mind went blank and panic thundered round her body. Was she about to be discovered naked in the fashion cupboard? It would look weird at the very least; at worst it might mean serious trouble.

She crouched down on the carpet, behind a wall of boxes. Just in time. The light in the cupboard was suddenly switched on and a piercing brightness flooded the room. She suppressed a sudden, crazy urge to scream. Whoever it was seemed to be looking for something. The hangers were rattling on the racks. They jangled in Laura's ears, mirroring her jittering nerves.

Who was it? From where she crouched, she could see the occasional flash of the top of a head as it came close and went away again. A red head. Clemency!

The knowledge that her worst enemy was so close made her situation all the more dangerous. Had it been Demelza, she might have been able to talk her way out of it, but in Clemency's hands, her predicament would certainly end in a sacking.

Though not if she could get Clemency sacked first. The features editor seemed to be helping herself to the clothes.

Through a chink between the boxes Laura watched her slip a couple of blouses off the racks and stuff them in her bag. Now she picked up the Lidl carrier with Lulu's wig and dress in it. Laura swallowed. If Clemency took that, how would she explain it to Vlad?

But Clemency, clearly having spotted the supermarket logo, dropped the bag with an expression of disgust. She moved on, out of Laura's sight.

Was she getting nearer? Impossible to tell. Laura pressed herself close to the carpet, wishing she could disappear into it. There was a dress by her foot; a white cotton scrap with a £6,000 price tag. This had previously struck Laura as excessive. But now, if she could pull it over herself, it would be worth every penny and more.

She raised herself up an inch or two. Her fingers touched the soft fabric. It slithered easily, silently, towards her, covering her feet and ankles. She pulled it further, and then disaster struck. The dress caught on something, and one of the boxes beside her moved.

Laura crammed her fingers into her mouth to stop her gasp of horror. If the boxes tumbled down it would sound, in the silence, like a bomb going off. And she would be revealed, in all her highly suspect, naked glory.

The box wobbled. She closed her eyes. Her heart hammered in her throat. But Clemency was rustling somewhere over by the door now. The box fell still, the light went off, the door squeaked and the latch clicked shut.

Laura breathed out but didn't move. She waited, then dressed hastily in the dark. Once she had clothes on, it was a simple matter to switch on the light and gradually edge the fashion cupboard door open so it seemed as if it had been ajar all along.

The morning went on, much in its usual way. And yet things weren't at all usual. Laura detected distinct disapproval in the air. People weren't meeting her eye.

Immediately she was on the alert. Had Clemency spotted her after all, but said nothing?

'Is everything alright?' Laura asked, going up to Demelza's desk after even Raisy and Daisy had cold-shouldered her.

Demelza gave her a look of wary sympathy. 'Actually, I was just coming to find you. Carinthia wants to see you.'

Laura's heart sank. There was no doubt that this meant trouble. She turned away miserably.

'Be warned,' Demelza added.

'Yes?' Laura whipped round, anxious for any intelligence. Forewarned was forearmed.

'Carinthia's got a new seat.'

This seemed a bit of a side issue. 'Right. Well, thanks for that.'

Her worst fears were realised when she entered the editor's office to meet the icy gaze not only of Carinthia, but Clemency too. The features editor sat on the yellow sofa, radiating malevolence in a short red dress that matched her lipstick. Combined with her flowing red hair, this gave her the appearance of a vengeful flame.

Laura reminded herself that she had one weapon in her arsenal at least. She had seen Clemency stealing from the fashion cupboard. Should she fire first, Laura wondered. Fire now?

What would Mimi do? She racked her brains, and some of her grandmother's words floated back to her. 'Always look as if you are admiring a ravishing sunset. Especially in a tricky situation.'

Laura arranged her features into an expression of suitable ecstasy.

Carinthia, as befitted someone all-powerful, was dressed in goddess white, accessorised with gold bangles and earrings. Her brassy bob gleamed as her head moved back and forth. She appeared to be wobbling, but on what, Laura could not see. No part of the new chair was visible.

'Sit down,' the editor snapped, waving at the sofa. Lowering herself down beside Clemency, who shifted away as if she were something nasty, Laura now saw that her boss was sitting on an exercise bicycle. Her legs were pumping up and down under the table.

'You wanted to see me?' Laura maintained her thrilled expression and did her best to sound confident.

'Yes.'

'May I know what about?

'This!' With an almighty shove, Carinthia propelled a pile of newspapers in Laura's direction. She lost her balance and bicycled wildly before righting herself and glaring. 'Well?'

Only now did Laura look down at the papers. Shock rolled through her. Every front page was dominated by the same large photograph. Two people, kissing. The girl wore a tiny dress and huge hair and heels. The man wore a ceremonial military uniform and an unmistakable ginger beard.

WHEN HARRY MET LULU
It Girl Lands Prince at Wedding of Art-World Royalty

Laura bit back an incredulous laugh. That she, through sunglasses darkly, had believed Caspar to be Prince Harry was just about understandable. But that Britain's famously sharp-witted national newspapers had made the same error was extraordinary.

She guessed immediately who had taken the photos. The hipsters with smartphones sitting outside the salumeria. Presumably they had sold them to the papers.

Something now hurled through the air towards her from Carinthia's direction.

A magazine whose glossy cover flashed in the light. It landed on the floor by her feet. Smiling up was Lulu, simply dressed in Vlad's old jeans, her windblown hair shining in the sun, her make-up-free face fresh and beaming. The coverline, in green neon capitals, read, 'LULU: WHY I'VE TURNED MY BACK ON HIGH SOCIETY'.

'Great,' Laura said. It was bang on-message. Lulu would be thrilled.

She looked up, only to encounter the full icy force of The Gaze. 'Great?' Carinthia repeated.

It was clearly the wrong thing to say, but why? She had been mad keen on it before.

'It's a good picture,' she hedged, hoping to bring Carinthia round to her former position. 'Very counterintuitive.'

From the sofa, Clemency gave what ended as a cough but had almost definitely begun as a chortle.

'Counterintuitive!' cried Carinthia. 'You bet it's bloody counterintuitive! Lulu in jeans and no make-up. Saying that she has turned her back on high society.'

'Yes!'

'Just as every newspaper front page reports she's started an affair with the fifth in line to the throne.'

'Oh.'

'Exactly!' Carinthia slammed the desk so hard with her fist that she slid right off the bicycle seat and landed with a crash on the floor. There she lay like a beetle with her legs in the air as the other two looked on, perplexed. 'Will someone bloody well help me up?' she howled from under the desk. 'My bloody back's gone again.'

Clemency got there marginally before Laura and stamped hard on Laura's foot with her stiletto to prevent her from assisting. Laura reeled away, tears of pain in her eyes, as Carinthia was helped up, cursing. 'It's so *bloody* embarrassing,' she raged, heaving herself back into the saddle.

'Don't worry,' Clemency soothed. 'It's hard to keep your balance on these things.'

Carinthia stared at her in disbelief, before exploding with rage. 'Not the effing bike!' she screamed. 'The story! My reputation as Editor's Editor is built on exclusives! I don't get scooped. Ever! This undermines everything I've achieved! It's the most appalling humiliation! I'll be stripped of my titles! How's this going to affect my DBE for Services to Journalism? I'll never be on *Desert Island Discs* now!'

It was hard not to smile at this. Laura knew from Demelza that Carinthia kept a list, constantly updated, of the eight records she would play when the radio-show invitation came.

'I can give you a scoop,' she said. The time required to get the editor upright again had given her a valuable few seconds. She had put them to good use and now had a plan. 'I can call Lulu. Get you the exclusive. The real story about her and the Prince. She trusts me.'

Dead silence followed this. Had it worked? It seemed so. The furious snake eyes were now blazing with crazed hope. 'You're serious?'

Laura nodded. 'She'll tell me all about it, I promise you. I got to know her really well. Actually, I felt like I'd known her all my life.'

She'd just have to square it with Lulu somehow. Hopefully the celebutante would see it as a trade-off for the wonderful magazine coverage. What the real Prince Harry would make of it was another matter, but so much rubbish was written about him, one more thing wouldn't make much difference. Or so Laura told herself. She was glad, even so, that people weren't slammed in the Tower for treason any more.

It was worth it, anyway, to see Carinthia's face. Her expression was now as ecstatic as if she too was gazing into Mimi's sunset. Clemency, meanwhile, was as pale and stony as the White Cliffs of Dover. The effort of trying, for appearance's sake, to maintain a smile was obviously killing her.

'Fantastic!' Carinthia shouted. 'This is going to blast everyone else off the newsstands! It'll be the scoop of the century! Pull this off, and...' She paused, seemingly searching for the words.

'You'll give me a staff job?' Laura slipped in.

'More than that!' Carinthia screamed. 'I'll make you features editor!'

'But I'm features editor!' Clemency pointed out, alarmed.

Carinthia turned on her the full force of The Gaze. 'Not for much longer! You're useless!'

Laura actually felt sorry for her old enemy now. Her back-up plan, to expose Clemency as a thief, was unnecessary. She had the upper hand in every sense.

And Clemency knew it. 'I'll get you,' she hissed through gritted teeth as they left Carinthia's office.

Laura pretended not to hear.

Back in the fashion department, a pleasant surprise awaited her. A large orange Hermès bag sat on her desk; her bag. Vlad – it must have been Vlad – had sent it back by messenger. Along with her few possessions, there was a card inside with Lulu's address engraved on it, and 'With Compliments'.

Laura felt a rush of gratitude at such thoughtfulness. Tonight, after work, she would return the Olympia Jager-bomb and thank the butler with all her heart. And explain, hopefully convincingly, about the Prince Harry feature.

The question of how exactly she would write this occupied Laura all that afternoon. She could not concentrate on anything else, not even the fashion shoot she was required to assist Raisy and Daisy with, which was to take place at an abandoned warehouse by the side of a canal.

The shoot had originally been Harriet's, but events in that respect had moved on. It was now known that the fashion director was in solitary confinement in a Pyong Yang jail. Her deputy, meanwhile, was at the mercy of the Nepalese justices.

'It's just so terrible!' Raisy wailed in the taxi, shortly after the news came through. She clutched her hair, which was plaited, sprayed blue and worn with tinfoil trousers.

Daisy, in frayed denim ruffles and a neon fascinator, grasped her sister's tiny wrist. 'But we've got to carry on. Do what they would have done. In their memory. They would expect us to.'

'They're not dead,' Laura pointed out, feeling that all this was a little extreme.

'Well, no,' Raisy admitted, possibly regretfully.

The shoot was chaos. A gang of decorative youths, who looked like models themselves, ran everywhere, waving light reflectors and call-sheets. The photographer was Grimston. Laura greeted him enthusiastically, having got quite fond of him in the course of the Lulu shoot. Anyone who was so rude to Clemency was a friend of hers.

Grimston was not pleased to see her, however. He too had read the newspapers and seen that the counterintuitive Lulu had been overtaken by events. He hated being scooped as much as Carinthia did and expressed his annoyance by roaring at everyone, even the famous model.

The model's famously thick dark eyebrows were scrunched together in fury. She hurled the steamed ice-cube prepared for her lunch by her assistant across the warehouse. 'It's the wrong water!' she screamed. 'You should have used fizzy.'

The shoot was meant to showcase the new season's couture. Laura had sat in the taxi under a plastic-swathed pile of sparkling sequins, delicate feathers, shimmering silks and floating gauzes, all exquisitely hand-stitched by the *petites mains* from some of the most famous ateliers in the world. The hand-painted hem on one dress had taken a week to complete.

Every piece was now liberally splashed with black paint. It was Raisy's idea. 'This look's so much more directional!' she exulted, hurling another can at the model.

'And editorial!' agreed Daisy, prising the lid off another.

They returned to the office to find Carinthia in a mood even darker than the stains on the clothes that it would be Laura's responsibility to return.

This was a surprise, given the blithe spirit the editor had been when they'd left. 'What happened?' Laura asked the fount of all knowledge, Demelza.

Politics, was the surprising answer. Demelza had been delivering the editor's onion-dust salad at lunchtime and had heard part of Carinthia's conference call with the Foreign Office about the missing fashion team. It had not gone well. It seemed that the Foreign Secretary was not prepared to risk nuclear war over people who made their living from combining knuckleduster gloves with knee-skimming kilts.

'Looks like Hazza might be fashion's first martyr,' Demelza added.

'St Harriet of Selfridges,' agreed Raisy cheerfully. 'But it's an ill wind that blows nobody any good. Think of all that weight she'll be losing in prison.'

Behind her, in the fashion cupboard, Daisy was scrabbling about. 'Have you seen those Anna Reksic blouses?' she asked her sister. 'The ones that came in on Friday? For the Belgravia Punks shoot?'

Ask Clemency, Laura wanted to say, but didn't. Not yet, anyway.

Raisy looked alarmed. 'We need to find them. I'm ripping them up and reversing a car over them for a transitional urban look.'

Laura hoped that, in her rummagings, Daisy wouldn't come across the Olympia Jagerbomb dress in the Lidl bag. If that was ripped up and reversed over too, she would be in trouble. Even more trouble than she might be in on account of the Prince Harry article. As evening approached, she was becoming more concerned about how to put the idea to Lulu and Vlad. Especially as it wasn't an idea, it was a *fait accompli.*

She packed up the paint-stained couture as neatly as she could. But the tissue paper stuck to it horribly. She sent it down to Despatch with a sinking heart.

Just before the end of the day it was clear that some new drama was going on in Carinthia's office. The door was closed and the Venetian blinds were down and closed, as they always were when something important was going on, like Carinthia sleeping off one of her hangovers.

Raisy and Daisy had been called in. Perhaps something even worse was happening to Hazza and Jazzy. Laura wanted to ask Demelza, but the secretary did not seem to be meeting her eye, quite.

It was like the morning all over again. Something, once again, was very wrong, and Laura did not have long to wait to find out what. Soon, and with a great rattle of Venetian blinds, the editor's door swung open. Demelza came over. 'Carinthia wants to see you.' She had walked away before Laura could ask why.

As she trudged towards the editor's sanctum for the second time that day, Laura noticed that her bag, the orange Hermès holdall given to her by Lulu and returned by Vlad, was not by her desk.

Worry tugged at her. It had everything she owned in it – precious little, it was true, given that most of her stuff had gone with Mimi's bag. Had she lost this one too? She realised that she hadn't seen it since leaving earlier for the shoot. Had she left it at the warehouse? No, she hadn't taken it. She had left it in the office.

Laura entered Carinthia's lair. Opposite the desk, on the yellow sofa, was Clemency. It was like a rerun of that morning, except that the editor was now sitting on a normal office chair. And the features editor, no longer angry and defensive, now looked like the proverbial cream-possessing feline.

Against the wall, commensurate with their non-sofa-qualified status, were Raisy and Daisy. They looked as serious as one could in ensembles Raisy had earlier described as 'the runway edit'.

It was now that Laura noticed her bag. Sitting on Carinthia's desk, it seemed to glow and throb an almost neon orange. What on earth was it doing here?

'You wanted me?' she asked Carinthia, trying to conceal her confusion.

The editor came straight to the point. Unzipping the bag dramatically, her fingers dived in and out, pulling with them a succession of shirts. It was like a magic trick; all that was missing was the rabbit.

The shirts, of course, were the ones Laura had seen Clemency stealing that morning.

'The Anna Reksic blouses!' exclaimed Daisy.

'Scrunched up and completely ruined!' added Raisy, as if her intentions had been other than to rip them up and run them over.

Carinthia fixed Laura with glittering eyes. 'Care to explain this?'

Laura could, of course. Easily. There was no doubt who had planted the shirts in her bag. Clemency had sworn to get her and, during the afternoon, when Laura was off at the shoot, she had done just that. She wanted to kick herself. How could she not have seen this coming? To have thought for a nanosecond that Clemency would stand idle while Laura took her job?

She would keep calm, however.

'Clemency put them there,' she said flatly.

The features editor snorted. 'I most certainly did not.'

Laura surveyed her. Her old enemy's eyes were positively sparking with spite. It was as if the intervening five years had not happened. Here she was, back in the headmistress's office, set up once again by the girl whose loathing for her seemed infinite.

'Yes you did,' she said. 'I saw you steal from the fashion cupboard.'

Clemency seemed surprised by this and perhaps Laura might have prevailed, but then Raisy interrupted. She was staring, narrow-eyed, at Laura's shirt. 'That's from the fashion cupboard as well!'

'And those jeans!' chimed in Daisy, accusingly.

'I can explain,' Laura assured them. 'I was only borrowing them.'

'Borrowing!' snorted the features editor. It was clear from Clemency's tone that she knew she had been saved. She moved quickly to secure her victory.

'She was like this at school,' Clemency went on in sorrowful tones. 'Always trying to shift the blame. So terribly sad. But not really her fault. The school doctor was of the view that she was mentally ill. Delusional.' Clemency shook her head pityingly.

'That's completely untrue,' Laura exclaimed, outraged at such a barefaced lie. But glaring at Clemency was no good. She had been outmanoeuvred.

Carinthia delivered the expected verdict. 'Obviously I'm going to have to let you go after this.'

A hard ball was blocking Laura's throat. But she would not cry in front of Clemency. Never. A desperate idea occurred to her.

'What about the New Society Weddings feature?' she blustered. 'I've got all the info on the Amy Bender one. And this weekend I'm going to a boho-chic one under a mystical oak in Wiltshire!' It sounded almost comical, but Laura had never been more serious. She stared desperately into Carinthia's snake eyes. 'It's going to be brilliant!' she pleaded. 'You'll almost certainly get an award for it.'

Carinthia glanced towards her shelf full of glittering trophies. Her expression became wistful. 'It really could be an amazing story,' she mused. 'Amy's ring was stolen, of course. And Spartacus's.'

'Is that right?' Clemency looked at her boss, surprised. 'It wasn't in the papers.'

Carinthia smugly tapped her suspiciously straight nose. 'We top journalists have our sources!'

As Clemency subsided, reddening, Laura spotted an opportunity. 'Absolutely,' she declared. 'I heard Amy scream out that she'd lost hers – that it had been stolen, I mean. And Spartacus was so shocked, he fell over in his full suit of armour.'

Carinthia gasped. 'An inside-track account!' She looked at Clemency. 'If she's got this far with it, perhaps we can overlook the stealing thing?'

Hope soared within Laura just as long as it took for her oldest enemy to shake her red tresses in syrupy mock-regret. 'Trust is so vitally important, don't you think?' she sighed to the editor. 'And after the events of this afternoon, I fear that most precious of commodities is damaged beyond repair.'

Laura boiled inside. She longed to pick up Carinthia's strangely shaped glass awards and hurl them at Clemency's lying head.

Carinthia looked back at Laura. 'She's right, of course,' she said reluctantly. 'I'm still sacking you.'

Laura held her gaze. 'Okay. I'll just do the piece for someone else then.'

'It's mine! You can't!' Carinthia exploded.

'Just watch me,' said Laura, as she headed for the door.

Chapter Seventeen

What now, thought Laura, emerging from the lift into the Society House lobby.

Her reflections got no further. Something white and gold now loomed before her. Carinthia had moved like lightning. Her bad back was clearly no impediment when the editorial chips were down. She dragged Laura away from the lifts and into the stairwell behind.

'Shit, sorry,' Laura said, assuming this was about the clothes and starting to unbutton her blouse.

Carinthia stared. 'What are you doing?'

'Getting changed. You want these back.'

Carinthia held nothing for her to change into, however. No T-shirt or jeans belonging to Caspar. Was she to walk into the street in just her underwear? It would be the final humiliation.

'Oh God, it's not that,' Carinthia cried, her skinny chest heaving, her snake eyes wide with the effort of racing down the stairs. 'It's the bloody weddings article. If you're still interested in doing the piece freelance,' she gasped, 'I'm still interested in publishing it.'

Laura considered. Yet again, she had pulled victory from the jaws of defeat. But how much of a victory? 'Might I still get a staff job if it all works out?'

Carinthia looked cagy. 'I can't promise anything.'

Laura folded her arms. 'Perhaps one of your rivals can.'

The snake eyes rolled. 'Okay, okay. Yes. If it's good enough.' And with that, Carinthia turned on her heel.

Laura reeled joyfully out of the revolving doors of Society House. Her feeling of triumph was short-lived, however. What exactly was she so pleased about? She had still been sacked.

Standing in the early-evening sunshine, Laura wondered if now, finally, was the moment to throw in the towel and go home. Mimi, once she had heard her adventures, could not dispute that she had tried her hardest. She would not be judgemental about the point of it all. 'Just because you have only one life,' Mimi often said, 'doesn't meant you should be scared of wasting it.'

Someone was walking towards her. It was Saffron in heavy black sunglasses, possibly with special filters to bar anything unsightly. 'Think Turkish baths and Russian banyas,' she was urging into her smartphone.

Laura felt a powerful pang of longing for the world from which she had just been ejected. She shaded her eyes and glanced up to where the fifth-floor windows of the *Society* office glinted in the rich evening light. Even though it had devils like Clemency in it, it seemed more than ever a magazine paradise in all its silly, glittery, scented glory.

It was so unfair. She had tried so hard and been so brave and ingenious. But she mustn't forget that there was still a chance. Tempting as it was to give up altogether, she might yet prevail. If she went to the boho wedding with Caspar, wrote up the Amy one, and somehow found a castle-and-tiara one into the bargain, she might still manage to land the magazine job she needed in order to get the newspaper one she longed for. She might emulate her father yet.

Laura took a deep breath. No, she wouldn't return to Paris just yet. Clemency may have beaten her for the moment, but the war was far from over. To return to Paris would be to leave the field.

She looked down at her hand, from which a Lidl bag dangled. She had snatched up the Olympia Jagerbomb dress on her way out. It was all she had; the Hermès holdall remained in Carinthia's office and would no doubt become part of the tribute which flowed in daily from those trying to court the editor's favour. That must be nice, Laura thought wistfully, as her own dream of journalistic eminence seemed to recede yet further.

Well, she had better return the Jagerbomb dress. Vlad might even give her a cup of coffee. And the one good thing about being sacked by Carinthia was that she no longer needed to write the Lulu and Prince Harry exclusive. So she wouldn't have to have that conversation, at least.

Would this, Laura wondered as she crossed Hyde Park, be the last time she followed this familiar route? Every time she came here, the sense of *rus in urbe* surprised her. It was so big and so green, with only a few tall buildings at the perimeter to show you were in the middle of the city.

To her surprise, Lulu's normally quiet road was seething with life; loud, shouting, jostling life. At first Laura thought it must be a demonstration coming down the road, then she realised the action was centred round Lulu's gates. Was it some sort of protest? Animal rights activists, taking issue with Lulu's extensive collection of snakeskin?

But the people looked unlikely protestors. They were too well dressed, for a start. There were smart suits, big hair and lots of tan make-up – and that was just the men. Whatever was going on?

As she got closer, Laura saw microphone booms and recording equipment. Tall men in headphones shouldered TV cameras. The smartly dressed people, she realised, were television reporters. And not just mere reporters either. Royal correspondents.

A chill went up her spine as she remembered the newspaper headlines. In the drama of her sacking, she had completely forgotten. Poor Lulu. Through no fault of her own, she was now in the eye of a media storm. The whole world thought she was going out with Prince Harry.

'... Buckingham Palace has yet to release a statement,' the BBC's Nicholas Witchell, resplendent in suit and tie, was saying loudly.

'... Lulu, while a familiar fixture on the London social scene, might not be familiar to the man in the street,' Jennie Bond, in a little blue suit, was adding.

'... I'm talking to you today from outside the palatial London home of the girl everyone's saying is Britain's newest princess,' a much-maquillaged American with coiffed blonde hair was excitedly informing her viewers.

Something along the same lines was being said in what seemed like hundreds of different languages. Logos of international news agencies were clipped to the handles of the microphones. CNN; Al Jazeera. Agence France-Presse in a Chanel suit and a perfect gamine bob. Crews from Spain, Greece and Germany. Lulu was under siege by royal correspondents from all over the globe. Even Vatican TV was there.

Knowing that she, Laura, was the reason for all the fuss, the origin of the story, and even had the clothes and wig in her bag, felt bizarre. But what was more worrying was the possibility that Lulu was within, no doubt terrified at the press pushing around her perimeter.

Paparazzi were leaning on the security buttons; hacks were stabbing at the bells. The noise of bleeps and buzzers inside must be considerable, and the background roar of royal reporters even more intimidating. The view on the security cameras would be like that of an invading army. Bared teeth. Shouting. Gesturing. Wild eyes.

It was mayhem. And it was all her fault! But what could she do to help them? Laura told herself that Lulu might not even be there, might still be away having her lobes done. But that still left Vlad, imprisoned in the house by what was basically a baying mob, even if dressed in suits and covered in make-up. The calmest of butlers might find that a challenge.

She looked up at the big house beyond the gates. Its red brickwork shone cheerfully and its windows gleamed in the sunshine. But the rooms behind them looked dark; if anyone was there, she could not see them. She raised both arms and waved reassuringly, even though it was very unlikely that Vlad would spot her in such a huge crowd. More people seemed to be arriving all the time. Onlookers were now gathering to watch the journalists watching the house. People were photographing on their mobile phones the photographers taking pictures of Lulu's security gates.

Small wars were breaking out among the national TV

crews. A loud stream of violently abusive French now filled the air; the impeccable French presenter had just had her impeccable toe crushed by NBC.

'What's she saying?' the American blonde snapped at Laura.

Laura coughed and looked down. 'You don't really want to know.'

More and more people were coming. Laura felt herself pushed and crushed this way and that. She was not a claustrophobic person usually, but this was panic-inducing. What must Vlad be feeling? And Lulu, if she was there?

She could remember the gate code, she realised. If she was subtle about it, she might be able to slip inside. Perhaps she and Vlad could make a daring exit in one of Lulu's sports cars. The sheer surprise of it might make people spring back, buy them some time.

The entrance area was seething with bodies though. Someone might follow her in, or push the gate open to allow the whole pack through. But not if the whole pack was directed somewhere else. Where though? And how?

Inspiration struck, suddenly and dazzlingly. Laura struggled out from the crowd and crossed the road into the park. She chose a suitable tree a few feet from the entrance, and opened the Lidl bag. Seconds later she had on the wig and the sunglasses. She was ready.

Her heart was thumping violently. The disguise had worked before, but would it work again? And if it did, would she be able to escape and get back to the house before the rest of them? Or would she be torn to pieces by the mob?

She took a deep breath and summoned up her Lulu voice. She stuck her head out from behind the tree. 'Hey! You people!' she yelled. 'What you do outside my house? Hmm?'

It worked like a charm. *'Elle est là! Elle est là!'* screamed the Frenchwoman, felling her American rival with one jab of her Chanelled elbows as she darted across the road, leading the mob. Vatican TV was hot on her heels, followed by Al Jazeera and the BBC, neck and neck. They poured into the park like a pack of hounds, pushing and shoving at the narrow gate, climbing over the fence, shouting, slipping, kicking, cursing and fighting. That royal reporting was this physically dangerous was amazing. Was this what went on behind the genteel coverage of all those babies and weddings?

By now Laura had darted into the bushes and was out the other side, back through the gate and on to the pavement. Across the road, alone outside Lulu's, she punched in the code with trembling fingers. A roar now met her ears and, glancing towards the park, she realised she had been spotted.

'She's getting in!'

'*Elle rentre! Vite, vite!*'

'Quick! Before she shuts the gate!'

'Lulu! Lulu!'

'Señorita Lulu!'

'LULU!'

Laura had meant to tear off the wig and glasses. But now it was too late.

Fists were raised and bloodcurdling screams reached her ears. The army of reporters began to thunder back towards her.

The gate had not moved; had the code been changed? The journalists were getting closer; she could see the whites of Nicholas Witchell's eyes. Laura flattened herself against the gate, half-resigning herself to a hideous death at the hands of the international royal reporting mob. Then, to her vast relief, she felt the gate give under her hand. She pushed it back just enough to slide through and felt almost sick with gratitude to hear it click shut. She was in! She was safe!

She closed her eyes and leant briefly against the gate, which was now being pounded and shaken in fury by those left outside. There were roars and curses. Laura hurried across the blessedly empty paved patio and rushed up the steps to the front door. Standing before the double-C knocker, she ripped off the wig and sunglasses. That particular charade was over.

The varnish on the door flashed brightly in the late sun as it opened. Vlad appeared even more unruffled than usual. Her black suit and tie were perfectly pressed, her shirt was a blazing white and the side-parting in her cropped black hair looked more than ever as if it had been made with a ruler.

Laura, dispensing with ceremony, flung her arms round the butler. Vlad's figure was as solid as a stone pillar. It felt as if she was wearing a steel corset. 'Oh, Vlad! I'm so sorry. This is all my fault.'

'I must beg you not to concern yourself, madam.' Vlad detached herself with dignity. 'Madam is not at home. All is well.'

'Well?' gasped Laura, flinging an arm in the direction of the booming gate and the baying mob beyond it.

In the kitchen, Vlad began unscrewing the Dolce & Gabbana coffee maker on the BalenciAga.

'An espresso, madam?'

'That would be great, Vlad. And,' Laura added as her stomach rumbled violently, 'might you have one of your lovely biscuits?' She had eaten nothing since the turnip sashimi at the fashion shoot.

The butler shook her head apologetically. 'I regret to say that madam embarked on an air diet just before leaving.'

'An air diet?' Laura felt strangely reassured. The familiar insanity of Lulu's life was somehow saner than what was going on outside.

'There is, as a result, no food in the house.'

'No food in the house?'

'None, madam.'

Laura met the butler's calm gaze with her own distracted one. 'So what's going to happen? What are you going to live on? These people might stake you out for days.'

It was now that Laura saw something move. Something outside. She crossed to one of the windows, then recoiled in shock. A photographer stood mere feet away. He was not looking at her, fortunately, but squinting up at the front of the house. He was holding an enormous camera, with a long, magnifying lens.

He was joined by someone else, similarly dressed and also with a camera. Then a woman with a smartphone appeared. They all looked up at the house. More people came, now with TV equipment. Laura recognised the French royal reporter. Then Vatican TV appeared, hot on her Chanel heels.

'They've got in!' she exclaimed.

Chapter Eighteen

Vlad, behind her, was watching the TV monitors. Laura scuttled to her side and looked up at the bank of screens at the kitchen's rear. Tight suits and little dresses notwithstanding, royal reporters and their teams from all over the known world were climbing over the top of the security gates, negotiating the spikes with ease and dropping down into the patio. Their hair remained immaculate throughout.

'Is the house locked?' Laura demanded.

Vlad assured her that it was, although if the journalists had got through security, a mere house door and flimsy glass windows were hardly going to stand in their way.

'But what about all this security?' Laura waved agitatedly at the cameras. 'Doesn't it work? Isn't it connected to, I don't know, the local police station or something?' She had read about such arrangements, whereby celebrities were accorded special treatment. This had always seemed to her less than democratic; now, however, she was prepared to exchange scruples for survival.

'Indeed it is, madam, but it may be that the local police station is unavoidably detained elsewhere.'

Laura swallowed. Her thoughts were flying, apparently by themselves, to Harry Scott. His card was in her jeans pocket, in the bag in Carinthia's office. But strangely enough, she found she could remember the number.

Vlad coughed gently. 'May I suggest that we hide upstairs, madam?'

As the butler led the way up the glass staircase, the death-defying nature of glossy-magazine work impressed itself again upon Laura. She had imagined it to be all face creams and drinks parties, but she could not have been more wrong. From downstairs came the sound of glass shattering. 'It's like war!' she exclaimed as Vlad opened the door to an upstairs room and politely waited for her to go through it.

'That there are similarities is undeniable, madam.'

Vlad closed the door. The room was small and lined with shelves on which coloured rolls of paper and bright bolts of tissue lay alongside boxes of ribbon rosettes and labels.

Laura had half-thought Lulu was joking about the present-wrapping room.

As there came, from downstairs, the sound of another breaking window, accompanied by ominous thumping on the door, she and Vlad moved to the middle of the room, to avoid being spotted from below.

'Where are the police, Vlad?' she said, panicked.

'They will be on their way, madam,' replied the butler, imperturbably.

Laura wished she had such faith. But the possibility seemed to her an increasingly unlikely one. Perhaps a great number of the rich and famous were currently experiencing security issues in Kensington.

She swallowed. Those people on the TV monitors had definitely looked unhinged. The reporters were holding their microphones like machetes, and the boom mikes were swinging like pickaxes. She had to do something.

'Vlad,' Laura said urgently, 'have you got your phone on you?'

Vlad had. As she pressed in the numbers, the background noise of baying crowds and banging grew exponentially louder.

'Harry, I'm really sorry to bother you again, it's Laura by the way, but I'm sort of under siege by some international TV crews and I seriously think they might kill us...'

She handed the butler her phone back, now wishing she hadn't bothered. Harry would think she was insane at best. At second best he would think she was drunk. At worst he would laugh.

More loud thuds came from downstairs, ending in a conclusive smash that was unmistakably the front door caving in. Footsteps followed, and shouting. Someone – lots of someones – were coming up the stairs. The door of the wrapping room flew open.

Laura gasped and shrank against the shelves of tissue paper. Vlad, meanwhile, remained steadfast at the ribbons table, a Gucci-printed length twisted round one finger.

A tall young man in jeans and a black leather jacket stood in the doorway. It took Laura a few seconds to realise who it was.

'Harry!' she screamed, leaping to her feet in an ecstasy of gratitude. He had answered her call! He had come!

Harry did not return her salutation. He closed the door quickly behind him and pushed a chair under the handle. It was a small padded pink one covered in Prada logos. Then he turned to face them, arms crossed, face serious.

'You've saved us,' Laura gasped.

'I haven't actually done anything,' Harry wryly pointed out. 'And you're not out of danger yet.'

'How dangerous is it?'

'Lethal. Royal correspondents are notorious, the worst of the lot. Normal hacks are bad enough, but this lot are really vicious. Red in tooth and claw, and with absolutely no mercy. We have to get you out fast.'

Laura felt the colour drain out of her face. 'But how? There's no route out apart from the window.'

'If I might be so bold as to suggest it,' Vlad offered, 'we could shin down the drainpipe.'

Laura went to the window. The lawn surrounding the drainpipe seethed with royal reporters ready to tear them limb from limb.

There was a giant crash from the door. Their assailants were practically upon them now. The little padded chair shook and shuddered under the force of the blows from the other side. For the moment, however, it held firm.

'Help!' whimpered Laura.

Harry looked up from his phone screen. 'Come on. Think of your father. He endured worse than this.'

It was on the tip of Laura's tongue to ask Harry what Peter Lake had endured, exactly. Her father's death in action had never been described to her, no more than his life in journalism had. From the distance of France, at least, reading his articles had been difficult. And Mimi had always discouraged questions. On the subject of this quintessential newsman, there had been, in effect, a news blackout. But now was hardly the time to seek revelations. Not when it looked likely she might follow in the family tradition.

Harry was tapping into his smartphone. 'I've got an idea. It might just work.'

'Teleporting?' Laura demanded. It seemed about the only hope left.

'Bit simpler than that.' Harry spent a few more minutes tapping, then put his phone away and looked up. 'I know people at the international news agencies. I've asked them to put out a message that this is a false alarm.'

Minutes later, the thunder of feet running upstairs was replaced by the thunder of feet running the other way. What doors remained downstairs slammed, and all was silent.

Laura went to the window once again. The lawn stretched emptily in all directions. A few solitary cigarette packets, scattered about, were all that remained of the crowds and chaos. A scrap of pale fabric, possibly from a Chanel suit, waved like a pennant from the top of one of the gate's spikes.

She turned to Harry. 'I can't thank you enough,' she began, before realising that the pink padded chair had been moved from beneath the doorknob and the door now stood open. Harry had gone. It wasn't that she couldn't thank him enough; she couldn't thank him at all.

'A most remarkable young man, if I may say so,' was Vlad's verdict.

Laura could only agree.

'Brave and decisive and possessed of quite extraordinary initiative. Most regrettable that he was unable to stay. Perhaps, madam, you would be kind enough to pass on my thanks when you see him again.'

'I won't see him again,' Laura said gloomily. All that now

remained was to dispatch the matter that had brought her to Lulu's in the first place. Once the Lidl bag containing the Jagerbomb dress was handed over, she need only say goodbye. She had grown genuinely fond of Lulu the crazy socialite and her East European Jeeves. But there would be no reason to see them again after this. She would be back to square one. On her lonesome in London. Homeless, jobless and penniless.

Laura made her farewells in the kitchen turned over by the just-departed mob. Some of the Chanel pans had departed too, and there was no sign of the Victoria Beckham biscuit tins.

'May I be so bold as to make an enquiry, madam?' Vlad spoke as Laura headed glumly for the door.

Laura turned. 'You may.' Anything to delay the dreaded moment of departure.

'Might you consider the possibility of staying with us here? If it was convenient, naturally.'

Convenient? It was some distance beyond that, it was heaven-sent. Had Vlad guessed?

Time, Laura thought, to put her cards on the table. 'I may as well be honest with you. I've lost my job on the magazine and I've nowhere to live.'

'My condolences, madam.' The butler inclined her neat dark head.

Laura waited. Now she was unemployed and of no fixed abode, that was sure to change things.

'But the offer remains,' Vlad finished.

'Wow. That's fantastic. But what will Lulu say?'

'Madame would approve wholeheartedly. Her parents are extremely gratified about the magazine article.'

Laura was unable to believe her luck. Saved again. 'It's so generous of you to suggest it.'

Vlad now cleared her throat. 'Not entirely, madam. I have my reasons.'

Laura's mouth went dry. Was the butler about to confess to having the hots for her?

Vlad held her eye steadily. 'Madam, as you may be aware, is subject to strong and sudden impulses. Some of which result in less than positive outcomes.'

Laura was confused. Was Vlad talking about her or Lulu? 'Can you be a bit more specific?'

The butler coughed delicately. 'I apologise for not making myself clear, madam. You will appreciate this is a sensitive matter. What I am attempting to convey is that madam is occasionally vulnerable to the advances of those whose motives are less than honourable.'

Light dawned, sort of. 'You mean people try to take advantage of Lulu?'

Vlad nodded. 'While madam is very sociable and enjoys the company of others, her wealth can make relationships problematic. Romantic relationships in particular.'

'The guy in the tape on the internet?'

'That gentleman, yes. And others. I do what I can to monitor the situation, but my area of surveillance is necessarily limited.'

Laura got it now, entirely. 'You want me to keep an eye on Lulu? Look out for her?'

'Exactly that, madam.'

Laura was struck by this new image of the exuberantly wealthy and colourful Lulu as a lonely and vulnerable figure. She remembered the glittery hats, the pilfering personal stylist, Lulu's weary acceptance of it all. 'I'd be happy to. Glad to help.' It all seemed a bit vague, even so. 'What would it involve?'

'Madam has a busy social calendar. Parties. Dinners. Engagements. Appointments.'

'Oh, right. You want me to, what, organise it all?' Planning wasn't her greatest strength, but she would try her best.

'That won't be necessary. I handle madam's diary. Your role would be that of a companion.'

Laura stared. 'You'd want me to go as well? With her? To all these swanky bashes?'

'Precisely, madam.'

'Wouldn't Lulu mind?' Laura looked down at her creased jeans.

'There is, as you know, a large wardrobe here. And madam would be very pleased to have your company. She doesn't have many genuine friends, for the reasons I have already alluded to.'

Laura hesitated. Vlad was basically asking her to live Lulu's life. Was that what she wanted? It wasn't exactly the glittering career in journalism she had planned and had got so close to realising. On the other hand, it was a job of sorts. More importantly, a place to live. She could stick it until Saturday and the Wiltshire wedding, at least. After that, if all went well, anything could happen.

'If you would like to follow me, madam, I will show you to your room.'

Laura hoped she was not about to be shown to a room rioting with more logos than a duty-free. But she should be grateful, even if she ended up with leather-quilted walls and a loo pulled by a Chanel-bag gilt chain.

In the lift, Laura watched apprehensively as Vlad pressed a button marked 'Buzzie Omelet'. The name rang a bell. Hadn't she done up Spartacus Tripp's ex-typhoid hospital? The décor she could be facing might be worse than logos,

Laura realised. It could be narwhal tusks and directional rubber batwings.

'Buzzie Omelet' turned out to be a suite that took up the entire top floor. Laura's batwing fears were unfounded. It was furnished in restrained fashions with beige walls, a sage bed and armchairs in muted greige linen. The chairs held the only really Lulu touches: two linen cushions embroidered respectively with 'The Need to Own Prada Was the Reason We Evolved from Apes' and 'Save the Earth, it's the Only Planet with Chocolate'.

Laura listened as Vlad explained that while Buzzie Omelet had logo'd up the rest of the house, her signature style was neutral and as the work had taken some months and required her constant presence on site, she had adapted the top floor for her own use. 'I thought you might prefer it, madam,' the butler offered dryly.

Laura nodded. She couldn't help wondering why a designer specialising in beige, sage and greige had been chosen to cover a house in garish labels. Lulu would have been better off with a Selfridges window-dresser.

The view across the park was to die for. She could see Kensington Palace, the Round Pond, even the distant flash of the Serpentine.

Behind her, the butler cleared her throat.

'Madam returns from New York later tonight. In the morning she has a couture appointment in Chelsea. With a new designer who is very keen to work for madam. Perhaps madam would care to accompany madam?'

'New York?' Laura queried, once she had disentangled all the madams. 'I thought she was in Geneva, having her ears done.'

'Madam's plans often change at the last minute. As madam will discover.'

Something was being pressed into Laura's hand. She stared down at a wad of notes. 'I don't need paying. I'm staying here.' But only until the weekend, Laura reminded herself.

Vlad was now passing her a top-of-the-range new smartphone. 'You also might find this useful, madam. It's quite the latest model. I understand you can even use it in the bath.'

Laura stared at it. She certainly would find it useful. This was the type that had an internet connection on all fronts. The perfect reporter's tool. Her fingers itched to explore it; it was far more tempting than the cash. She might have lost her job, but she felt like a proper journalist now.

Chapter Nineteen

Laura had been looking forward to seeing the famous lobe lift, but it turned out that this had never actually happened. Lulu had left Geneva before her appointment. She had gone to New York to escape from her father.

'He cross me.'

'Annoyed you?' Laura translated.

'Right. So I leave Geneva and go to New York. Shopping, hmm?'

'Why did he annoy you?' Laura was uninterested in the shopping but riveted by Lulu's family life. So little was known about it. Her parents and background were utterly mysterious, although they seemed to live in Geneva. Laura imagined a vast house and gardens by the lake.

'He say that now I am taken seriously, with magazine cover, should take advantage. Make grass while moon shine.'

'Right.'

'Make me watch *Shark Tank*,' Lulu complained. This was the American version of *Dragon's Den*, apparently. 'Then make me talk business plan.'

'He wants you to start a business?'

'Mmm hmm. But he not like my ideas.'

Lulu's ideas ranged from launching a brand of pink caviar to opening a high-end sweet shop selling Bollinger lollipops. Laura could see where her father was coming from.

They were proceeding up a Chelsea street lined with small, obviously expensive shops. With their tasteful cream fronts, gleaming windows and restrained signage, they all looked pretty similar to Laura. The one that Vlad now glided to a halt in front of struck a different note, however. The name 'IRINA' was scrolled in sparkling silver across a gleaming black plastic fascia. A vast disco ball hung in the window, beneath which writhed a group of mannequins wearing very tight, brightly coloured rubber minidresses.

Recognising the house style, Laura groaned. She might have guessed that the couture appointment was with Irina Pushamoff.

Within the shop, beneath an enormous and glittering chandelier, against a background of swagged black rubber curtains held in place with thick diamante ropes, stood a familiar figure. Irina's big black hair looked bigger and blacker than ever, and her lipstick and mascara thicker. She was resplendent in a sequinned body-stocking and thick-soled diamante-encrusted high heels. Her bangles glinted and rattled as she held out her arms to Lulu.

'Lulu, my darling!'

'Irina!'

The air was full of air-kisses and exclamations.

'It was so wonderful to see you at dear Amy's wedding!' the designer crooned.

Laura felt a clutch of alarm. Would Lulu remember she had gone instead? Lulu looked bland, briefly, then beamed. 'Yes! Was so beautiful, so emotional. It move my bowels.'

Laura suppressed a guffaw, but Irina hardly noticed. 'Darling! I have the perfect dress for you! From the new collection, which you have inspired!'

Steered firmly by Irina, Lulu disappeared behind one of the rubber curtains and emerged a few minutes later in a purple ruffled miniskirt attached to a sequinned, plunge-fronted bodice. It was far and away the most hideous dress Laura had ever seen.

'Is great, hmmm?' Lulu was looking anxiously at her, seeking validation.

'Er...'

'She looks stunning, no?' Irina instructed. 'This is the "Lulu" dress. It is very her, don't you think?'

Laura said nothing.

'She want me wear this tonight,' Lulu put in. 'She give it me, for free. And in return I make fat her customers.'

'Expand my client list,' Irina put in smoothly.

'What's tonight?' Laura asked.

Lulu beamed. 'Tonight is dinner of elephants.'

Laura was appalled. 'Dinner of elephants? You're eating elephant?'

'Is good for them. Help them,' Lulu insisted. 'Is party for them.'

Laura was speechless.

'Make money.'

'Oh. A fundraiser.'

'Is what I say, hmm?'

Preparing for the dinner of elephants took up several hours of the early evening. A pink van labelled 'Glam Squad' arrived and disgorged a gang of beauticians in pink overalls. Led into Lulu's presence by the black-clad Vlad, they looked, Laura thought, like something from a musical.

Certainly, they were highly choreographed. Within seconds they had laid Lulu out on a towel-padded treatment chair and simultaneously set to work on different bits of her. There was someone at her head and a pair at her feet. Two separate Squadders worked on two separate hands. Good job Lulu wasn't an octopus, Laura thought, watching from a corner of the specially designed Treatment Room, its glass walls engraved with famous beauty brands, scented candles of all sizes crowding the pale stone floor, and murmurous whale music floating amid the fumes.

Lulu looked up from her fruit facial peel and winked. 'It take village, hmm?'

'What?'

'It take village. To make me look good. Like Hillary Clinton say.'

'Oh. Yes. Ha.'

Lulu's rare moments of self-awareness were always disconcerting.

Stepping deftly between the candle flames at their feet, the Glam Squad applied spritzes and balms, creams and oils, and massages with warm muslin from a heated cabinet. Then came a rice-powder mask, Japanese eye-whitening drops and a sublative-radio-frequency treatment. This did not involve broadcasting the World Service at Lulu's face but was about controlling wrinkles with sound waves.

Laura, meanwhile, amused herself with the new smartphone. It was amazingly useful. She could call up any website at will, look up anyone she wanted.

The first name she entered was that of Harry Scott. She scrolled through some more of his articles and felt, as before, a swell of admiration. Harry was a proper grown-up reporter. She noticed that there was nothing about the Bender jewel robbery in Paris. Did this mean he was still working on it? Perhaps she should have asked, but circumstances so far had not permitted that. Their phone calls had been all about her, Laura reflected guiltily.

She wondered if Harry knew about the second robbery; Amy losing her million-pound wedding ring. If Carinthia had her sources, surely he did too. Perhaps she should have mentioned it, nonetheless.

Hastily, Laura scanned for media mentions of a robbery at Amy's wedding. But what coverage had reached the gossip columns mentioned only the fire scare, the ironic honeymoon and the artistic luminaries in attendance. Which, Laura deduced, meant one of two things. Amy had either found her zero-impact ring-pull by now, or, if she hadn't, reports of its value had been wildly exaggerated. Carinthia had got the wrong end of the stick. It surely wasn't possible that so scrappy-looking a piece could be worth so much. Was it?

Laura frowned, trying to remember the jeweller's name. Mary-Bliss something. She could look her up, find out for sure. She swiped at her phone and typed in the keywords.

Her first thought was that she had been misdirected. Her phone screen went red and flames licked the edge of it. Black letters appeared, looking like they had been scratched with the fingernail of a dying hand. 'Welcome to Hell' they spelt.

It took a while to work out that Hell was Mary-Bliss's zero-impact jewellery company. How very offputting.

Mary-Bliss was offputting too. A black-and-white portrait of her had been shot in front of a barbed-wire fence which stretched away into the distance against a grey sky. Her dark eyes were heavily ringed with kohl and she glowered into the camera. She had long, lank, dark hair and a black leather waistcoat across which her pale arms, heavily tattooed, were folded tightly. Her knuckles were covered with ragged rubber rings of her own design; the effect was as if she had punched a melting tyre.

'At Hell, we use only settings *trouvés*,' ran the paragraph beneath. 'Things from the London street or shore; pieces of wire, rubber, wood, glass. Unique objects that tell a story.'

The story of the moment, Laura gathered, was 'male tiaras'. Mary-Bliss was launching a line of them 'imminently'. The photo on the website was of something wiry, nasty and spiky that looked like the Crown of Thorns.

The wedding-ring section featured settings *trouvés* ranging from the burned silver paper left by crack addicts to the Coke-can ring-pulls as favoured by Amy Bender. But how much these pieces cost was withheld; all prices were 'on application'. Which, Laura knew, meant expensive.

For those who couldn't afford to buy new, or *trouvé*, Hell offered a 'redesign' service. A photograph of an exquisite, glittering, perfectly cut stone mounted in an elegant ring was captioned 'Boring and conventional'. The photo of what resulted after Mary-Bliss had drilled through it, pebble-dashed it and mounted it on barbed wire was captioned 'Funky and Ibiza-ready'.

'Ow!' Lulu's squeal made her look up. Two smiling Squadders were injecting something into her armpits simultaneously.

'You OK?' Laura asked her wincing charge.

'Is Botox. Stop you sweating. You too?'

'No, thanks.' Laura wondered what her grandmother would have made of the suction-lift machine now rolling over Lulu's face. Or the scrubbing with a goat-hair brush and the needling of medical-grade oxygen into her forehead, which Lulu underwent next. Mimi always said that an hour spent sleeping or making love was better than anything at the dermatologist's. And even if it wasn't, it was impossible to tell: Lulu replaced her sunglasses immediately after each treatment.

But Mimi would have loved Jay. He was Lulu's hairstylist and arrived at the house on a bright red Vespa just as the Glam Squad were leaving in their van. Laura watched him greeting them – they all seemed to be old friends – from the window of the bathroom where Vlad was finishing Lulu's make-up.

Jay was a cheerful and wildly camp cockney with TV ambitions. 'Go on,' he urged Lulu. 'We could do a great programme together, you and me.'

Laura, foreseeing disaster, was about to interject. But Lulu got there first. 'My father go mad. He want me big business success, hmm? He lecture me in Geneva. He fed me up.'

'Made you eat?' Jay exclaimed in horror. 'Oh my days!' He was backcombing Lulu's locks over a series of plastic crescents he had placed on her scalp. The effect was quite literally hair-raising.

'Maybe I start salon!' Lulu resolved suddenly. 'Is good idea. You will help me do that, Jay, yes?'

Jay had paused to discipline his two dogs. They had arrived alongside the volumising spray in the top box. They were tiny, yappy, aggressive and wore Scandinavian sweaters.

From Lulu's house, Jay was going to the airport and flying with the dogs to Oslo, home of his ex-husband, who had joint custody.

'Start you a hair salon? Easy peasy lemon squeezy,' Jay said indulgently. His own hair was appalling, arranged in a windblown mullet, kept off his face by yellow metallic aviator sunglasses which he wore on his forehead. How they stayed in position was difficult to say.

Lulu, of course, kept her own sunglasses on even as Jay blow-dried her long locks with a big round brush. It reminded Laura of a microphone and she said so.

'Ooh, funny you should say that,' replied Jay. He was, he added, in talks about a TV show called *Hairbrush Karaoke*, in which celebrities would sing pop hits into hairbrushes.

Jay now stepped back and assessed his handiwork in one of the many mirrors. 'All done, sistah.' He beamed at Lulu. 'You can go to the ball now.'

'Is not ball, is dinner for elephants.'

Jay rolled his eyes. 'Don't you just hate fat people?'

Laura left them to it. The question of Harry and Amy's ring was nagging at her. Perhaps it had been stolen and for some mysterious reason Amy wanted to keep it quiet. In which case he might not know and she should tell him.

It took some time for him to pick up, and when he did, the line beeped in a distant-land sort of way. 'Uh?' said Harry tiredly, and Laura worried that she had woken him up again. 'No, I'm awake, it's fine,' he said, obviously untruthfully. 'What is it? You need some more money? Another room?'

Blushing at this proof of the encumbrance he saw her as, Laura started to explain about the wedding.

'Hold on,' Harry was evidently doing his best not to sound irritated. 'You dressed up as Lulu who?'

Perhaps she shouldn't have begun at the beginning. 'The point is, there was another robbery. Amy's ring got stolen. At least I think it did.'

'Slow down,' Harry instructed. 'Talk me through it. Tell me everything you remember.'

Laura recounted what she could recall about green champagne, Stasi waiters, non-binary samba drummers and the Eight-Legged Orchestra of Great Britain.

Harry sighed. 'What I'm getting at is: was there anyone there who was at the *Call This Art?* party too?'

Laura closed her mouth hurriedly. She had not thought what the consequences of this call might be for Caspar. He had been at both events.

'Was Caspar there, for instance?' Harry pressed.

Laura was reluctantly forced to admit that he was.

'So where was he when Amy yelled out about her ring?'

Laura explained that Caspar had disappeared some time before it happened. 'Which means it couldn't have been him,' she concluded triumphantly.

'Possibly.'

'What do you mean, possibly?'

'Well, there are two ways of looking at it, and neither of them are good. Either Caspar's the thief or you were talking to him and there was a fire scare and he basically left you to perish. Either way, sounds like a great guy.'

The elephant dinner was in the ballroom of a glittery Park Lane hotel. Huge, hideous posters showing dead and dying elephants hung on the gold and marble walls of the central staircase. As the two women ascended, Laura stuck close by her charge, less from the urge to protect her than because she couldn't see where she was going. The paparazzi at the entrance had completely blinded her.

Lulu, protected by her sunglasses, had taken the explosions of light in her stride. Quite literally, in six-inch heels attached to the soles of a pair of thigh-high see-through plastic boots. Laura had tried in vain to persuade her against these, but Lulu had insisted. 'Match Irina dress, hmm?' And there was no denying that the boots and the plunge-fronted ruffles struck a similar note. What note that might be was best not thought about.

Selecting a sober, black, long-sleeved number for herself – it had taken some finding – Laura had hoped to tone down the overall effect. But judging by the stares as they made their way to the ballroom, she had not succeeded. Everyone was whispering about Lulu, who showed no sign of caring, or even noticing.

Footmen in tailcoats proffered champagne at the entrance to the function room. Laura took one but had no intention of drinking it. She was here on duty.

Lulu, on the other hand, drained her first glass within seconds and was surrounded almost as quickly by an admiring crowd. It was like wasps to a honeypot. Wasps with smart-phones, converging from all sides to snap selfies. Lulu gave the same glassily indifferent smile to each. Was she enjoying the attention? Given her shades, it was difficult to tell.

Laura watched from a distance. Men, especially, were all over the celebutante like the apocryphal cheap suit. Not that any of Lulu's admirers wore one of those; it was Savile Row dinner jackets and animal-print bow-ties to a man. More nods to the theme of the evening came from the decor; tables spread with tribal bric-a-brac including shields, masks and things trimmed with beads and feathers. The effect, given all the chandeliers and Aubusson-style carpets, didn't quite come off.

But it was sort of apt, Laura found herself thinking. The gathering was in aid of an exotic, harmless creature, the prey of cynical hunters bent on profit. Was there really such a difference between the African elephant and Lulu?

A middle-aged man in a cravat went past, one red-lipsticked brunette on each arm.

'That's Titus Sloane,' someone behind Laura said. 'He founded the charity. They call him Elephant Titus.'

There came the sound of someone tapping a microphone. The speech part of the evening was about to begin. A throaty deb lectured the Clicquot-slurping crowd about endangered pachyderms. 'Like, uh, seriously, you might seriously not see one next time you go on safari?'

Laura sipped her champagne. She was trying not to dwell on her last conversation with Harry. The aspersions he had cast on Caspar's character were bad enough, but it was the implication that she herself was an idiot that really stung. She had only been trying to help, but it seemed that the more she tried to impress him, the more stupid she looked. Perhaps she had better just give up. Let him think what he liked about Caspar. Let him think what he liked about her.

She emerged from her musings to see that a tall, lean young man had homed in on Lulu. She recognised him, but it took a while for the penny to drop. Of course! This was the blond artist in the dark suit. She had glimpsed him at the wedding talking to Irina. And in the shadows at *Call This Art?* So, someone else who had been at both places! Why had she not remembered before?

Under the brilliant lights of the chandelier, she could study him properly. With his high cheekbones and full lips, he was strikingly good-looking. But was there something grubby about the contrast of spiked white hair and thick black brows? His eyes had a febrile glitter, as did his nails.

She moved closer to hear his conversation with Lulu, who was looking thrilled.

'Lord Hunter!' she was exclaiming.

So he had a title.

'My friends call me Seb.' His voice was low and amused. 'You're my friend, aren't you?'

Lord Hunter. Seb Hunter. Lord Sebastian Hunter. Now Laura remembered: the 'Society's Top Single Totty' meeting. Sebastian Hunter was mad, bad and dangerous to know. He rode down his father's tenants on horseback and wore knickers as cravats. He had 'habits' and someone died in his flat. Allegedly. He preyed on wealthy women...

Laura hurried, alarmed, to Lulu's side.

'Do you have the number for the National Trust?' Lord Sebastian was asking, earnestly.

Laura was surprised. This did not sound like the hard-partying lord of legend. Had his detractors got it all wrong?

'No!' Lulu giggled. 'Why?'

'Because I want to ring them and report a new Area of Outstanding Natural Beauty.'

Laura winced. But Lulu was clearly smitten. 'Oh, Lord Sebastian!'

Smirking, Hunter bowed to kiss Lulu's hand. It took him some time; was he, Laura wondered, assessing the worth of the diamonds on her fingers? They were chewed and covered in chipped blue metallic varnish. A large gold signet ring gleamed on his grubby pinky.

'Do you like parties?' he was asking Lulu.

'I lurve parties!'

'I give very good parties.' His eyes glowed.

Laura's heart was hammering. This was exactly the sort of man Vlad had warned against. The sort of man Lulu had fallen foul of before. The sort of man who went to parties where robberies took place. Was Lulu going to be next?

She had to stop him. But how? She hesitated. The noise of chatter and laughter in the room swelled in her ears. She felt very hot in the long-sleeved dress. Perhaps she should have had the sweat injections after all.

Lord Sebastian's face was now very close to Lulu's, or as close as anyone could get, given the sunglasses.

'Do you ever take those off?' he was saying.

'Sometime, yes.'

'What else do you take off sometime?'

People were taking pictures, no doubt pinging them round the world. The relationship would be official within minutes. The thought of Lulu, in all her innocent, good-naturedness, falling into such decadent clutches was horrible. As was the thought of Vlad seeing it in all the papers. Panic rose in Laura. She would have failed in her mission!

Inspiration suddenly struck. She rushed up, grabbed Lulu and kissed her hard on the mouth.

Lord Sebastian backed away immediately. 'Oh I say,' he drawled sardonically. 'Didn't realise.'

Feeling Lulu struggling beneath her, Laura put her mouth to the celebutante's ear. 'This is for your own good, Lulu. Seb Hunter would have killed you in three months. Did you know...' She briefly outlined some of what she had read.

Lulu stopped struggling. Laura let her go. Now she became aware of the clicking phone cameras, the lens being focused by the wasted-looking official photographer. But who cared? She had rescued Lulu, and that was enough.

Chapter Twenty

They had got home late after the elephant party. Too late, Laura figured, to call Harry, wherever he was in the world. Instead, she had texted him her suspicions from the back of the car, while Lulu dozed next to her amid the padded and polished leather. As she pressed send, Laura had glanced up to see that Vlad was driving through the square with Society House in it. Passing the building, she had felt a twisting worry. Would her career as a journalist ever get back on track?

She rose the next morning gloomily anticipating another day of shopping and pampering. She settled down at the shining marble table under the kitchen chandelier and reached for one of the neatly arranged newspapers. The topmost front page had a large picture of herself and Lulu.

'Oh God,' she said.

She grabbed the paper. The photograph made what had been an emergency move on a surprised, not particularly pleased Lulu look like a passionately sexual embrace. Lord Sebastian had been cropped, if not Photoshopped out.

The headline – 'LULU'S LIPSTICK LOVER: Billionheiress in Clinch with Mystery Brunette' – said it all. Well, most of it. Readers requiring the full story were invited to turn to the Sarah Salmon gossip column on page 65.

With shaking hands, Laura did just that. The story was the page lead and she read it in silent horror.

Celebutante Lulu (no surname necessary!) last night used a Hathi Foundation fundraising dinner to launch herself as a lesbian. The middle of a five-star hotel ballroom was the chosen venue for a private moment with a mystery brunette whom she kissed passionately in front of a glittering crowd including Lord Sebastian Hunter, Simon Cowell and Lady Clara Strumpett. The elephant charity's annual event provided an appropriate backdrop for the publicity-seeking blonde's latest effort to trumpet (geddit?) her private life to the world. Readers will remember the headline-courting billionheiress's recent appearance in *Society* in which she claimed to be turning her back on society (maybe she just meant the magazine?!), and her attempt to seduce what turned out to be a Prince Harry lookalike. Those with longer memories will recall that the fame-crazed celebutante's last heterosexual entanglement ended in an explicit tape going viral...

'Is disaster!'

Laura looked up to meet the furious glare of Lulu's sunglasses. 'Again I am laughing stocking, and this time is because of you.'

'I was trying to help,' Laura objected, hurt as well as shocked. Lulu had never blamed her for anything before.

In reply, Lulu picked up one of the red-tops and waved it. 'My father call,' she shouted. 'Say you are my Lebanese lover! So now again must I go to Geneva and tear my strip off.' She stamped out so hard, it seemed the Versace-logoed marble would crack.

Laura lowered herself from the high stool with all the dignity she could muster. If she wasn't wanted, she would leave.

'Breakfast, madam?' Vlad hovered at her elbow with a plate of bacon and eggs.

'At a time like this?' Laura looked askance at the butler. 'I'm supposed to be helping Lulu, but I'm just making everything worse for her!'

Worse for herself, too, as Carinthia was hardly likely to be thrilled either. The joke about *Society* would not go down well. And Clemency would be sure to make as much trouble out of it as she could.

'I should just go!' Laura cried, trying not to look at the bacon and all she would be leaving if she did.

'I think not, madam. If I may be permitted to observe, your actions were both prompt and imaginative.' The breakfast was placed swiftly on the bar.

'Do you really think so, Vlad?' Laura had now remembered that she had nowhere to go and was depending on staying here until the Wiltshire wedding at least. Hopefully Lulu – and her rage – would remain in Geneva until then.

'Indeed I do, madam.'

'Well, we certainly stopped Sebastian Hunter in his tracks,' Laura admitted, her urge to leave compromised by the delicious aroma of sausage. 'Which has to be a good thing.'

'Indeed, madam. Ketchup, madam?'

Laura started to calm down. The breakfast was even better than the lavish fry-up she'd enjoyed at the hotel, which sent her thoughts flying to Harry Scott. She hoped he would not see the Sarah Salmon piece. For some reason this was an even more alarming prospect than Carinthia reading it.

But Harry was obviously not the gossip-column type. And even if he did see it, he would not recognise her. She had now gathered her scattered wits sufficiently to study the pictures in the newspapers again and realise that, thanks mostly to Lulu's enormous hair, her identity was pretty much obscured.

'This marmalade is delicious,' she said, spreading it thickly on her toast.

'Thank you, madam. I make it myself, when Seville oranges are in season.'

Was there no end to Vlad's talents? Butler, chauffeur, make-up artist, fixer extraordinaire and now maker of top-notch preserves.

Afterwards, rather stunned by all she had eaten, Laura went back to her room. She was, she realised, free. Until Lulu came back from her strip-tearing visit to her parents' in Switzerland, she had no duties whatsoever. Which was just as well, as there was a lot to do. She had pressing personal admin, for instance, such as sorting out her passport and credit card. She had made progress on both fronts at *Society*, but there was still a fair way to go.

Most of all, though, she wanted to play on her new smartphone. She called Mimi, who didn't seem at all concerned not to have heard from her granddaughter for a week.

'Everything is fine,' her grandmother said. Laura pictured her in the little flat, the white Sacré-Coeur domes at the front and the sweeping view from the kitchen at the back. A pot would be trembling on the hob, letting out delicious smells.

'Are you eating well, *chérie?*' Mimi worked on the very French basis that if you were eating well, everything else would be going well too.

'Fine.' Laura decided not to go into the onion-dust salad, the steamed ice-cubes (fizzy) and the air diet. 'Good breakfasts.'

'Ah yes. The Full Monty. How I used to love them!' Her grandmother's voice was dreamy.

Laura was surprised. Mimi had never previously made mention of a passion for bacon and eggs. Before she could ask, her grandmother pumped her for news of London. Had she met up with Caspar? It was a relief to be able to answer yes, without going in to the details. Thank goodness Mimi never looked at the internet or the British press. She would have no idea that her granddaughter had appeared in two sensational front-page stories in the last week alone.

'You are staying with Caspar?' Mimi pressed.

'Er, no. With a friend in Knightsbridge.' Laura crossed her fingers, hoping Mimi would not ask any more.

'Dear old Knightsbridge!' exclaimed her grandmother longingly, her rich Parisian accent giving it four syllables. 'How I used to love it!'

'*Really?*'

But Mimi changed the subject again, and Laura learnt that Ernest, Ginette and Evelyne had been as good as their word and were looking after her. 'The Fat Four', as they now apparently called themselves, ate together every night, taking it in turns to cook. Evelyne's clafoutis had not gone down well with the group. 'She used cherries, not apricots,' Mimi grumbled. 'And cream, not crème fraîche.'

Laura felt she would settle for Evelyne's version. The fruit tart with its sweet batter base was one of her favourite puddings at home.

'Have you met any nice Englishmen?'

Mimi's question came from nowhere and Laura was unprepared. 'Er...'

The other end waited.

'No,' she said, firmly pushing away the image of Harry Scott.

'*Chérie*, I am not sure I believe you.' Her grandmother's voice was teasing. 'There is something in your tone. Who is it? Caspar?'

'God, no.'

'Then who?'

Laura hesitated. She knew of old that one could never hide anything from Mimi, even down a phone line from hundreds of miles away.

'He's just a friend.'

'Of course he is, *chérie*!' Mimi sang teasingly. 'So. Tell me about this... friend.'

'There's nothing to tell,' Laura maintained stubbornly.

'There is always something to tell,' Mimi corrected robustly. 'So, is he clean?' This was high on her grandmother's list of male priorities.

'Yes.'

'But not in too obvious a way?'

'Well, he's got a bit of stubble.'

'Good. And he is funny?'

Laura thought. 'He might be.'

'Has he got class?'

'Yes.' Those articles spoke for themselves.

'But is modest?'

'Yes.' Harry never spoke about them.

'Has he got something special?'

This of course was the million-dollar question. To which, in all honesty, there was only one answer. 'Yes.'

'And what does he do, *chérie*?'

'He's a journalist. An investigative reporter. And, as it happens, he's a great admirer of Dad.'

Something like a freezing blast now came from the other end of the phone. 'A journalist?' Mimi's voice was choked. 'No!'

'Mimi, what's the matter?'

'You must never fall in love with a journalist!'

'But he's only a friend! Mimi!'

'I must go,' her grandmother gasped, her voice muffled. 'I must check my soufflé.'

The exchange left Laura confused and unsettled. Clearly something had happened between her father and Mimi to provoke a reaction like that. What it might have been, she could not imagine. Her mother possibly knew, but to find out would mean a trip to Monte Carlo, which she could not afford, and lengthy exposure to Leon, which she did not want. All to discover something undoubtedly miserable. Better to think of her father as a hero, Laura decided.

She hurried out on her various errands. First up was the Foreign Office. There were papers to sign before a new passport could be granted.

Walking down Whitehall, she took out her new smartphone and called Caspar. As she keyed in the numbers, her eye caught a familiar outline. A dark-haired figure in a black leather jacket, disappearing into New Scotland Yard. A figure she had imagined being far away. She blinked, and Harry Scott – if it was him – was gone.

'Look, who *is* this?' Caspar, on the other end, had answered and was sounding agitated. Laura guessed he had asked a few times.

'It's Laura.'

'Ah! Lulu's mystery brunette!'

'How did you know?' Laura was shocked. She had convinced herself she had been unidentifiable.

'No one else snogs like you.'

It wasn't the reassurance she wanted, really. 'I just wanted to give you my new number,' Laura said stiffly. 'So we could liaise about this wedding on Saturday.'

'You mean tomorrow.'

'Tomorrow? Not Saturday?'

'Sweetie, no one gets married on Saturday any more.'

'Amy Bender did.'

'Yeah, but that was ironic. The loonies are proper posh. They don't need to try so hard.'

'The loonies? What loonies?'

'People getting married. They're called Loone. Eccentric Irish aristocrats, you know the sort of thing.'

'I'm not sure I do,' Laura said slowly. Loone wasn't a name that inspired one with confidence. Would Carinthia approve? Would she be wasting her time? 'What do you know about them?'

Caspar sighed irritably. 'Well, what do you want to know? Groom's called Gawain. Makes hand-carved spoons in Peckham. Stamps rude words on them with old printing blocks.'

Laura's heart sank. Abusive artisanal cutlery was never going to interest Carinthia.

'He's a friend of a friend, so I know him vaguely. Comes from a long line of rackety lords, artists' muses and some sixties aunt who ran a Chelsea clothes shop that supplied stovepipe hats to the Rolling Stones.'

Laura's spirits rose slightly. This sounded much more promising. 'And the bride?'

'Some edgy jeweller covered in tattoos. Dad's a rock star.'

'Not Mary-Bliss Skinner!' Laura excitedly broke in.

'Something like that.'

'Fantastic!'

'I wouldn't go that far, but it's a job, baby. Gotta go, anyway. *À demain*. Nine on the dot, outside the Natural History Museum.'

Laura lost no time in looking up the event online. Seconds later she was reading a Sarah Salmon column from some months ago, headlined 'I WANT TO BE A LOONE'.

Whispers have reached me that Mary-Bliss Skinner, celebrity gemsmith daughter of rock legend Sir Brian, has the intent (geddit?) to marry this summer. Mary-Bliss and her beau, Peckham spoon carver Gawain Loone, are planning a festival-themed wedding on a mystical site in Wiltshire. Gawain proposed by firework, Mary-Bliss confides at the launch of hot new London hotspot Mingers. 'It was supposed to spell out "Will You Marry Me", but the "You" and the first four letters of "Marry" didn't go off.'

There was a photograph of the future Mr and Mrs Loone. Yes, here was Mary-Bliss alright, her long white face staring unsmilingly out from the depths of an Afghan coat. Round her neck was something horrible in rubber. Beside her was an effete-looking young man in flowery bell-bottoms. He was doing his best to smile, despite having a male tiara from Hell on his head.

Laura wanted to turn cartwheels in the street. What a stroke of luck! It wasn't just any old mystic boho wedding she had hit on, but the mystic boho wedding of a rackety aristo spoon carver to an artisan jeweller rock princess. Carinthia was going to love it, especially as there were pop connections on both sides. *Society* was obsessed with rock and roll – the Stones had seemed to come up every five minutes, although never the Beatles, who were for some reason considered common.

Why hadn't Caspar told her? Very possibly because he hadn't known or cared. He was many things, or wasn't many things, including reliable. But he wasn't a snob. She had had to talk him into going – well something him into going, anyway.

Tomorrow! Hopefully Lulu's angry father would keep her in Geneva one more day at least.

Chapter Twenty-One

It was nine on the dot, and the queue at the Natural History Museum was already colossal. In front of Laura, a blonde mum in a denim jacket looked up from a phone in a bright pink cover. 'Atom!' she admonished a sullen-looking child engaged in kicking his companion. 'Do that again and you'll get a red dot.'

As Atom carried on kicking, Laura looked about her. She was meant to be meeting Caspar on the steps, but they were cordoned off. Even if he were there, it was doubtful she would see him. All of London's many Nappy Valleys had evidently emptied themselves out on to Museum Mile, and Caspar was too short to be spotted over so many heads. Just as she was thinking this, however, she suddenly glimpsed him in a gap in the crowd and plunged in his direction, praying he would not move before she got there.

There was no danger of that. Caspar had been pinned to the spot by a bearded young father in a T-shirt that said 'I Like to Party, and by Party I Mean Read Books'. Two small, bespectacled girls tugged at his hands. 'I know you!' the man was saying to Caspar. 'You're an actor.'

'For my sins!' In his faded RSC T-shirt, Caspar was positively radiating fake modesty. 'Seriously? You recognise me?'

'Course I do. I was at university with you. Tenebris Dark, you must remember.'

'Oh, er, yeah. Yeah! Tenebris, of course! Great to see you, mate!'

Laura hung back, grinning. This was too entertaining to break up.

'Can't quite recall your name, I'm afraid,' she heard Tenebris say next. 'But I'd know you anywhere!'

Caspar was looking less thrilled now. 'Yeah? Well, that's very kind...'

'You were in that double-act with Orlando Chease, weren't you? Blimey, how well has that guy done? Left you miles behind, right?'

Caspar's smile faded.

'Is it true he's going to be the new James Bond?'

'I wouldn't know, we've lost touch,' Caspar snapped. 'Look, I've got to go...'

'Going out with Hudson Grater, isn't he? They're calling them CheaseGrater.'

'So I've heard. Anyway, nice catching up, Tennyson.'

The bespectacled girls were singing something which might have been the lyrics to 'You Fat-Shamed Me on Facebook'.

Tenebris ruffled their unbrushed heads. 'This is Forest and Temple. They're wild-schooled.'

This was surprising enough to halt Caspar's attempts to escape. 'Wild-schooled?'

'Home-educated, but in the garden. My partner Willow and I believe in them taking ownership of their own direction of learning. Today it's dinos, but last week Temple wrote a novel and Forest directed her own film. Maybe she could give you a part, eh?' Tenebris nudged Caspar hard in the ribs.

'Ha ha. Yes. Maybe.' Speaking through gritted teeth, Caspar shoved his way towards Laura.

Laura had imagined that he would tease her about the Lulu kiss, but Tenebris seemed to have dampened his spirits. She followed him as he pushed moodily through the crowd and, finally, out into the wide thoroughfare of Exhibition Road.

'There it is,' Caspar said ironically. 'The Resting Actors' Express.'

A battered people carrier was parked outside Imperial College. A handful of people stood around it, being ticked off a list by a pretty girl in a pink dress and black ballet flats. Her blonde hair tumbled around a cherubic freckled face and big blue eyes.

'Hot, isn't she?' Caspar said.

'I didn't know Sloanes were your type,' Laura teased.

'Not Jess. She's the event organiser. I mean Georgia. Georgia de Mowbray. The dark-haired one.'

A pretty brunette was standing some distance from the others. She wore a clingy red crêpe dress and Converses. She looked twitchy, highly strung and disdainful.

'I know her from way back,' Caspar said. 'We were in Footlights together.'

'With Orlando Chease?' Laura said, before she could stop herself.

Caspar's face scrunched in annoyance. 'Actually, Georgia used to go out with him. They went to Hollywood together, in fact. Two Brits taking the town by storm.'

'Laurence Olivier and Vivien Leigh,' said Laura, who had a soft spot for old movies.

'Yes, until he made it big and traded her in for more famous and more useful models.'

'Hudson Grater, you mean?'

'And lots of others before her, Georgia says. She got left in LA trying to do that posh English girl in Hollywood thing. Problem is, there are more posh English girls in Hollywood than in Chelsea. You can't move for people banging on about Peter Jones and boarding school.'

'So now Georgia's come back?'

'And trying to get work, like the rest of us.'

The blonde in the pink dress spotted them and bounded up like a friendly Labrador. 'Thank God you're here! Jasper and Dora, yes?'

'It's Laura, actually. Laura Lake. And Caspar,' Laura added, as Caspar had slid away to stand beside Georgia.

'I'm Jess from Trance Events.' The girl stuck a pencil in her hair and attempted to twist it up. 'Thanks so much for stepping in, Dora. My other faun's now Second Harlot at the Globe.'

'Talk about typecasting,' interjected Georgia, sourly. But it wasn't surprising she was bitter, Laura thought. The more she heard about Orlando Chease, the worse he sounded.

Jess beamed round. 'Right, well, everyone's here. So let's get this show on the road, shall we?' She went to the driver's window. 'That okay with you, Reg?'

Reg, large and lugubrious-looking, wordlessly folded up his copy of the *Sun* and started the engine. Everyone climbed aboard. A dapper older man sporting a cravat beamed at Laura and patted the neighbouring seat. 'Hello, I'm Michael and I'm Sagittarius. Sit next to me?'

'I wouldn't, he's got wandering hooves,' warned Georgia.

As Caspar was next to Georgia, Laura sat down on the only free seat. This was next to Jess, whose brown knees were heaped with files, a tablet and several mobile phones. The vehicle had barely moved off before she'd started on her first call.

'Hello, is that Trance Events?' she said brightly. 'Hi, Tess, Jess here. Fine, thanks. All good. Just setting off with all these actor guys. Actor guys, yes. You know, for the ceremony under the mystic oak.'

Laura's fingers tapped restlessly on the smartphone in her palm. Would it look obvious if she started making notes?

Behind her, Caspar and Georgia were indulging in their mutual loathing of Orlando Chease. 'One minute he was begging me to marry him,' Georgia hissed, 'and the next he'd blocked me on Instagram.'

'Smug arse. I'd deck him if I saw him.'

'Not if I saw him first,' said Georgia. 'I wouldn't piss on him if he was on fire. Although I might if he wasn't.'

'Everything going well on site, Tess?' Jess was chirping. 'The Gothic morris dancers have come early? No, God, don't send them away. Get them to do something. We need all the help we can get. Ask them to put the teepees up.'

'What is Trance Events?' Laura asked, when Jess clicked off her call and started scrabbling frantically through a pile of notes.

Two distracted blue eyes met hers. 'We do high-end niche occasions. Well, hopefully. We've just started. Actually, I'm doing this wedding for free. As my present to Gawain and

Mary-Bliss. But I came on board quite late and it's all a bit chaotic. Oh, 'scuse me, that's my phone. Hi? Tess? A great pile of weeds? No, Tess, don't throw it away, it's the lunch. It's all been foraged. Someone's supposed to turn up and make it into salads... Oh damn, lost the signal.'

'Strip him naked and chain him to a lamppost in Oxford Street.' Caspar's voice came from behind. The Orlando Chease conversation was still going on.

'Having first stuffed him with laxatives,' Georgia agreed with relish.

They both laughed, wildly.

Jess, in the next seat, had reconnected with Tess. 'The main course is stew cooked over the open fire. Beef stew. Yes, round a giant campfire. What, Tess? There isn't a fire? Or a stew?'

This was all too good not to make notes on. As subtly as she could, Laura tapped on her phone screen. She loved the notebook facility, and also the recording one. You could make oral notes if you wanted; she could even record Jess and cut out the middleman, although that seemed a bit sneaky.

It was doubtful that Jess would have noticed, anyway. She clearly had other things on her mind. 'It's not the bunting? It's too big for bunting? Might be hammocks. Have you thought of that? That's the seating. Hammocks and hay bales. Are the hay bales there? They're supposed to be coloured. Sprayed pink and blue. No?'

Coloured hay bales? Hammocks? Laura tapped away. This was all excellent material for her article.

'Okay, so next on the list is the softly fluttering ribbons. Softly fluttering ribbons, that's right, Tess. The bride appears at the hand-fasting ceremony in the ancient mystical forest through a screen of softly fluttering ribbons... Damn. Lost her again.'

'What's a hand-fasting ceremony?' Laura asked, seizing the opportunity.

'It's kind of pagan. You make promises and the priest binds your joined hands. Mary-Bliss and Gawain are both a bit...'

'Crusty?'

'I'd prefer to say alternative.' Jess sighed. 'But I can't tell you how much I wish it was a bog-standard parish church. Organised religion has a lot going for it. It's organised, for one thing.' Jess's phone was ringing again. 'So, Tess, this ribbon curtain, okay? Gawain's supposed to have made it, as a gesture of love sort of thing. What, there's no sign of it? Can you hear me?' Jess stabbed frantically at the screen.

'It all sounds a bit stressful,' Laura said sympathetically.

Jess turned to her, wild-eyed. 'I'm really starting to wish I hadn't got involved, let alone done it for free.'

'Can't they pay you? It sounds like they should.'

Jess shook her hair, which had fallen down from its pencil twist again. 'It's all so hand to mouth,' she sighed, putting her hair up again. 'Nobody realises, but Mary-Bliss and Gawain are completely skint. The original distressed gentlefolk.'

'But isn't Gawain rich? From a long line of Irish lords?'

'Myth-making but not money-making.' Jess shook her head. 'They used to have some castle in Ireland, but Gawain's grandfather gambled it away on a bet about two beetles crossing a saucer.'

'That's crazy.'

'The Loone family are crazy. Gawain's dad is a pagan priest called the Fluid Druid. He's performing the ceremony. His mother lives in the Arctic Circle with a reindeer herder. We've had to get some whale blubber in especially for him, and it's not easy to get in Earl's Court, let me tell you.'

Laura itched to write all this down but knew she couldn't.

Instead, she subtly activated the recording button. Needs must. She was a reporter, after all. 'But what about Hell?'

Jess looked blank, and rather alarmed.

'Mary-Bliss's jewellery business?' prompted Laura.

Jess looked relieved. 'Oh. That Hell.'

'Doesn't that make any money?'

Jess bit her lip. 'Don't tell anyone, but not really. Her pieces are a bit, well—'

'Directional?' suggested Laura, invoking Raisy and Daisy's favourite word.

'Exactly. And those Coke-can diamond rings getting stolen really hit the business. Amy Bender never paid for them, and after the robbery she refused to.'

Typical, Laura thought. And that explained, of course, why Amy had failed to make a fuss about the theft. 'So what about Mary-Bliss's father? Surely Brian Skinner's hugely rich?'

'Yes, but she doesn't talk to him. They're not in contact. Well, he wants to be, but she won't have it.'

'Why not?'

'He's just had a midlife crisis – or extreme-old-age crisis in Brian's case – and left his wife for a teenage waitress. Mary-Bliss has taken her mother's side, not surprisingly. Brian's desperate to make things up, but M-B refuses. Won't have him at the wedding or let him pay for anything. Says she doesn't want his money and she'll manage everything on her own.' She sighed. 'But, frankly, it's all very well for her to say that when I'm the one managing everything on my own!'

Laura sympathised with the hard-pressed, good-natured events organiser. Mary-Bliss sounded rather selfish to her.

Jess's phone rang again. 'Oh, sorry. My assistant again. Tess, is that you? Right, where were we? Oh, the ribbons.

Just forget them for now. Let's talk about the tractor. Tractor? This guy was supposed to show up with one? To take the guests into the forest? Oh. Well, just ring him and check, would you? And could you ask him about the hay bales?'

As discreetly as she could, Laura called up the Mary-Bliss story on her phone. It was roughly as Jess had described. An ancient Brian, his bandy legs in tight leather trousers, stood with a soppy expression on his wrinkled face beside a wolfish teen in a miniskirt. There was a picture of Babs, too, a handsome blonde with a face possibly not the one she had started out with. Her name was, though; she had reverted to her maiden one, which was Bloggs. Her hobby, according to the article, was collecting vintage Cartier jewellery.

'The puppet show is there, Tess?' Jess exclaimed beside her. 'And the clowns? Great. Get them to do the campfire and the hammocks. Or the ribbons and the bunting. It's all hands on deck, tell them. What? No sign of the tractor? Well you'll have to get one yourself then, Tess. From where? From anywhere. From off the road. Just go out and flag down the first one that comes past.'

Chapter Twenty-Two

Some time later the people carrier turned off the main road and went down a narrow lane through thick, shady woodland. They had arrived in the ancient mystical forest where the wedding was to take place.

It was certainly mystical, Laura thought, looking out through the people carrier's grubby window. Or maybe just mistical. So dense was the swirling vapour that you could hardly see the massively thick and ancient tree trunks twisting up and out of it as if making some agonised appeal. Shafts of light stabbed at the cloud but made little impact. Was that normal? The season of mists was autumn, was it not?

'It's incredibly foggy for July,' she observed to Jess, who was looking out of the window, exhibiting every symptom of dismay.

The party organiser turned dismally towards her. 'It's not

fog. It's dry ice and it cost a fortune. We got the *Game of Thrones* people to do it. Mary-Bliss wanted atmosphere, but…' Jess sighed. 'Possibly not quite this much.' She took up her trusty smartphone and began to text frantically.

Laura tried to comfort her. 'It's very… dramatic. It'll make great photographs.'

Some of the shadows between the trees almost looked like people. Laura pressed her own phone against the window and took a couple of shots.

'This place gives me the willies.' Georgia shuddered.

'I was rather hoping that would be my job,' remarked Michael, who had a way of making the filthiest remarks in tones so impeccably polite, you wondered if he'd really said them.

It was a relief when the *Game of Thrones* gloom gradually gave way to a bright shimmering among the leaves and branches. This resolved itself into a stretch of water and they drove up to a lakeside whose bank bustled with flags, bunting and activity. A group, dressed identically in long black leather coats, mirror shades and top hats, pale blue make-up giving their faces a ghastly hue, were struggling to erect a vast tent. The Gothic morris troupe, she guessed.

A man with a red nose, green Afro wig, yellow baggy trousers and comically long shoes was up a tree tying a hammock while another, similarly dressed, attached its other end to the trunk next door. As the actors disgorged from the bus, the first clown fell out of the tree. Everyone laughed.

'It's not fucking funny!' snapped the clown, rubbing his head.

Not far away, a middle-aged man in a T-shirt saying 'Mr Sweeting's Splendidly Traditional Puppet Show' was tending a large fire, over which a vast pot had been hung.

'Burning much better now we've got some nice dry wood,' he said cheerfully to his neighbour, who wore a bowler hat, a black waistcoat and red-and-white-striped trousers which seemed strangely over-long. His expression changed as he looked at the fire. 'You've put my fucking stilts on, you moron.'

'Oh good,' said Jess. 'There's Tess.'

A dark-haired girl was pleading with a sharp-eyed man in braces who stood beside a tractor and trailer. 'Honestly, I could buy one of my own for that,' she was wailing.

'Hold on,' Jess shouted. 'I'm coming.'

Michael sighed and stirred. Georgia eyed him. 'Don't say it, you filthy old man.'

Tess now came over to Laura and the actors. Plump and pale to Jess's plump and tanned, she had a big red-lipsticked smile and short, shiny dark hair. Her impressive cleavage was shown to its advantage in a fifties-style fitted black dress with a big flared skirt. She started to hand out costumes from a large trunk. 'I love your enormous chest,' said Michael, appreciatively.

'What's this?' Caspar asked, looking in horror at the items he had been allocated: a silver bowler hat covered with netting and a pair of silver-sprayed leather trousers.

'Your costume. You're Water.'

'Water?'

'The handfasting ceremony,' Tess explained. 'There's a bit where the priest invokes the energies of the four elements. You come out from behind the trees when your element is invoked.'

Laura thought bleakly of Demelza, back at Society House. Was this really the way to regain her job there? It seemed hard to believe, as Tess handed her some multicoloured wings, a red sequinned Venetian mask and a skirt of mismatched frills. 'You're Fire,' she explained. Then she passed Georgia a fringed silver playsuit and a pair of antlers. 'And you're Air.'

Michael was examining his Earth costume: a green Morphsuit teamed with tall brown boots and a wide-brimmed feathered hat. 'Hope it's clean,' he said mildly, shaking the suit. 'I once got the most frightful crabs from one of these.'

A cider bus turned up; a red London Routemaster complete with pumps and barstools. Caspar made a beeline for it. 'Oo arr scrumpy,' he growled, emerging with a pint in each hand.

'You'd make quite a good Poldark,' said Georgia, giggling, as she swigged back a pint herself.

The toilets had now arrived and they all went to change. Caspar, fuelled by cider, could be heard loudly singing 'Porta-loo Sunset'. Everyone was laughing when they re-emerged.

'Now off you go into the wood,' Tess instructed, 'and wait by the mystic oak for the bridal party.'

'Misty coke?' repeated Caspar, hopefully.

'Mystic oak,' repeated Tess, with crisp RSC diction. 'The oldest tree in the forest. Where the wedding's happening.'

The *Game of Thrones* mist was persistent stuff, Laura thought. Expensive though it was, you certainly got your money's worth. The sun was quite high now, but the fog remained, a low level of dense cloud billowing about the forest floor. It was cold too, and damp. The trunks of the trees shone wetly. Great dripping boulders stood about a forest floor of sodden leaves. It seemed strangely quiet. Even though she knew the mist wasn't real, Laura had started to feel nervous and sensed the others had too.

She could still see shadows between the trees, slipping in and out of the shafts of light. It was easy to imagine evil spirits in a place like this. Laura raised her phone and took more pictures. It would help set the scene for her article. The flash of her phone camera also felt protective; a sort of stubby light sabre. The conviction that she could see people in the mist had not entirely gone away. Like the Wild Wood trees in *The Wind in the Willows*, the vapour had the unnerving ability to form itself into faces; faces she knew, even. A few moments ago, for instance, she had imagined she had spotted Lord Sebastian Hunter, crazy though that was.

Laura's heart was racing. Before she could stop herself, she had texted Harry with her thoughts. He could take it or leave it; leave it, most probably. Hang on, though. Wasn't that...? Having pressed the send button, Laura looked up into the swirling fog. That face she had just seen, or thought she had. Harry's face. But it couldn't have been. That really was crazy.

'Bloody midges,' exclaimed Georgia, swatting at a shapely thigh.

'Let me do that,' suggested Caspar. 'There. Got it.'

'No you haven't,' said Michael, clamping a hand on the top of Georgia's leg. 'That's it.'

The two men glared at each other. Things were definitely getting tense.

They walked on, into what seemed an ever-thickening mist. They would come across the mystic oak within five minutes, Tess had said. You couldn't miss it. It was huge and stood in a clearing. But they had been going for more than ten and no tree looked bigger or more obviously set in a clearing than any other.

'Let's ring Tess,' Georgia suggested.

Everyone got out their phones, then looked at each other. 'No signal.'

'Literally, nightmare on Elm Street,' said Georgia, patting a trunk. 'These are elms, aren't they?'

'God knows,' said Michael. 'I'm hopeless on trees.'

'I'm surprised,' said Caspar. 'Thought you'd be an expert on wood. Given your acting.'

'Let's not fall out,' said Laura, hurriedly.

They walked on. Time passed. The mystic oak remained elusive.

'We're going to miss the wedding at this rate,' Caspar said, putting into words what they were all feeling.

'One could go mad here, lose all reason, die!' Georgia burst out dramatically.

'It's not the dying that bothers me.' Caspar looked down at his silver trousers. 'It's the thought of being found dressed like this.'

'Look!' Laura pointed. 'Over there!'

The gathering, mostly obscured by the trunk of a vast tree, looked like a meeting of the Round Table. Through the mist, pointy wizard hats could be made out. Knights' helmets and crowns. And a tall stovepipe hat, as sold in Whirligig to the Rolling Stones in the sixties by Aunt Oenone.

The four of them hurried over the slimy forest floor and took up positions behind different trees. Peering out from behind hers, Laura could see that Tess and Jess had performed miracles. The tractor and trailer had evidently been acquired. The coloured hay bales were there. Even the curtain of ribbons was present and correct and softly fluttering, with the young couple now emerging through it.

The groom, somewhat inevitably, wore another of Mary-Bliss's male tiaras over his unkempt long dark hair. Noting with concern that it had a lot of dusty, drilled, Ibiza-ready diamonds on it, Laura glanced about her for signs of a predatory Sebastian Hunter. Gawain had rounded off his look with daisies in his beard, a flowery shirt and half-mast white trousers suspended above long, thin, bare, white feet.

Mary-Bliss was also shoeless, although she sported on one skinny ankle what looked like a rubber manacle on which the treads of car tyres were clearly visible. Ugly as it was, Laura felt it was an appropriate piece. Marrying Gawain would be like shackling yourself to something – something utterly useless – she imagined.

Mary-Bliss, despite her name, was still having trouble cracking a smile even on her wedding day. From either side of her narrow, sulky face, her hair streamed darkly to her skinny shoulders, as lank and lifeless as ever and not really requiring to be held in place by what was presumably a female version of the male tiara: a plastic bag, twisted to thinness, in violent aquamarine and wound round with a necklace of more Ibiza-ready diamonds threaded on to dirty string. Her something blue, Laura imagined, eyeing the bag.

Her gangling frame was shoved awkwardly into a short white dress whose hem barely skimmed the tops of her thighs and whose sleeves barely got below her elbows. Laura heard someone behind commenting on Mary-Bliss's amazing courage, and could only agree, before working out that the dress was actually Courrèges and a vintage piece belonging to her much shorter mother.

Babs Bloggs was sitting on a baby-blue hay bale beside the ribbon curtain. She presented a magnificent spectacle in silver lamé elbow-length gloves, a pink fur bolero and a crown with grey feathers exploding out of it. Perhaps she had emerged the winner of the marital spat after all, Laura thought. She was here and Brian wasn't. The vintage Cartier was here too. A spectacular emerald collar held her wattled neck securely in position. Again, Laura glanced around for possible jewel thieves, but none seemed in evidence.

The person beside Babs was the stovepipe hat, beneath which was a striking older woman in a rainbow velvet kaftan. She had the same high pointy cheekbones, long pointy nose and huge pointy feet as the groom. You didn't need to be Sherlock Holmes to identify this as the legendary sixties aunt who had hung out with the Rolling Stones.

Rock rebel or not, the aunt was reverting to type now. A collar of enormous pearls hung round her long, scraggy neck. Some Loone family jewels? They looked strange against the rainbow kaftan, but Mimi would approve, Laura thought. Her grandmother was a big fan of *haute joaillerie* worn with casual clothes. Diamonds with jeans, not evening dresses. 'The Parisienne mixes it up!'

Click, went Laura's concealed smartphone camera. *Click*. *Click*.

Other members of the Loone clan were much in evidence. A bearded man in a paisley dressing gown held a fuchsia fan next to a man in a kilt with a green Mohican. Next to him was a woman in thick Cleopatra eye make-up, ghetto-fabulous earrings and a jumper with sewn-on knickers from which dangled granny tights. They all looked like Gawain too; his brothers and sister, possibly.

Click. *Click*. The pictures were going to be *amazing*.

A tall figure now appeared suddenly out of the mist. Laura started; was this the expected thief? If so, he was unusually dressed in a sweeping purple robe with leaves on his head. 'We thank you, tree, for being here,' he intoned, facing the mystic oak.

The Fluid Druid, Laura realised. Gawain's father.

'Thank you, tree,' echoed the congregation.

There was a snort from Caspar and Georgia.

The Fluid Druid raised his hands. 'Finula Finn Flaherty will now sing "The Fiddler's Dream" by Conn Connbain McConn O'Connor.'

A woman in a latex bra and a skirt made of leaves stepped forward and began to wail in unearthly fashion. As she finished, the Druid's long arms rose once again in the air.

'Mary Storm will now respond to the occasion with a spontaneous verse work.'

A woman with burning eyes, tangled hair and flared velvet trousers leapt up and ran to the front. She took a deep breath and began to shout wildly. 'I have seen the finest minds of my generation struggling with the Sainsbury's self-service checkouts...'

Caspar and Georgia were clinging together helplessly. 'I'm going to pee myself,' Georgia gasped.

Laura, meanwhile, was clicking away and making notes. Her position, concealed behind the tree, was perfect for this. She could see everyone, but no one could see her. She noticed that she was not alone in her note-taking and picture-snapping. A black-basqued woman in a neon tutu and silver DMs was doing the same.

A red-headed woman.

Oh God.

It couldn't be.

Laura snapped her hurriedly and examined the image on her phone. She pawed the screen to enlarge it. There was no doubt now. No mistaking those sharp green eyes. That piquant, deceptively innocent little face. And that tutu and those shoes had definitely come from the fashion cupboard.

Clemency Makepeace was here. At the wedding. There

could be only one reason. The note-taking said it all. She was covering it as well.

The Fluid Druid had raised his arms. 'We move now to the most sacred part of the ceremony. The fasting of the hands.'

Mary-Bliss and Gawain stepped forward and joined their four hands together.

The Fluid Druid intoned over them. 'Blessed be this union with the gifts of the East and the element of AIR.'

'That's your cue. You're on, darling,' whispered Michael, pushing Georgia out into the open. She stumbled slightly, shot a furious look backwards and righted herself.

The crowd on the coloured hay bales applauded. Laura, her eyes on Clemency, saw her raise her phone to take a picture and make a note on her screen. Bugger. She had to stop her somehow. Or beat her. Do a better piece. She had the unique perspective of being Water, after all.

'And so the first binding is made.' The Fluid Druid tied Mary-Bliss and Gawain's hands together with a ribbon that had lately been part of the softly fluttering curtain.

'Blessed be this union with the gifts of the West and the element of WATER.'

'You now, ducky. Break a leg!' Michael shoved Caspar so hard, it looked as if he actually might.

He reeled out into the clearing and collided with Jess as she ran forward with a ribbon. The crowd laughed. Clemency took another picture.

'Blessed be this union with the gifts of the North and the element of EARTH.'

'Wish me luck!' trilled Michael as he tripped out in his Morphsuit.

It would be her in a minute, Laura thought. There she would be, front and centre, before the audience on the pink and blue hay bales. Before Clemency. Would she recognise her? Thank God for the Venetian mask.

'Blessed be this union with the gifts of the South and the element of FIRE.'

Laura took a deep breath, and stepped forward.

Chapter Twenty-Three

The handfasting was well under way. Mary-Bliss and Gawain had now vowed to share the truth, to meet all new experiences with a smile and to partake jointly in each other's pain. The Fluid Druid had placed five ribbons on the happy couple's hands. He seemed to be tying them up pretty firmly.

Laura's heart was still racing. But the Venetian mask seemed to have done the trick. Clemency had cast her a cursory glance as she had entered; no more.

The final ribbon was put in place. Mary-Bliss and Gawain smiled dreamily at each other, then back at their hands. Mary-Bliss, still beaming, gave a gentle tug, and Gawain, beatifically, did the same. The cat's cradle of white satin did not immediately untangle and some nasty moments followed until the sixties aunt produced a Swiss army knife from under the stovepipe hat.

The ceremony over, the party returned to the trailer parked some distance off in the trees. It was attached to a tractor in whose cab sat lugubrious Reg from the people carrier, still perusing his copy of the *Sun*.

Everyone had to sit on the trailer floor for the journey back to the lake. People lurched and sprawled across each other as Reg hurtled over the uneven ground. Caspar and Michael were taking full advantage of this. Laura averted her eyes resignedly as Caspar fell back with Georgia in his arms. If she had hoped that they might rekindle their own occasional romance, she had evidently hoped in vain.

She cheered herself up by watching Michael try his luck with a clearly disgusted Clemency. 'Do you like twerking?' he asked her brightly. 'You look the type.'

It was a relief to emerge from the misty green gloom of the woods into a beautiful ripe summer's afternoon. The lake, reflecting a hot blue sky, looked like an expanse of azure silk. On its banks, the teepee was finally erect. A bar called Good Libations had been set up on an enormous table made from upturned doors. Gin was being served from a roll-top bathtub. Bunting and flags fluttered colourfully in the breeze. The row of Portaloos was now beautified with a whimsical sign reading 'The Great House of Easement'.

Laura climbed off the trailer and looked around. People were milling around the bar or capering along with the Gothic morris dancers as they laid into each other with large sticks to the strains of an accordionist dressed as the devil.

Clemency seemed to have disappeared. Hopefully Michael had scared her off. Caspar and Georgia, meanwhile, were making off into the woods behind the teepee. He was so disgustingly unsubtle, Laura thought, wounded in spite of herself.

Jess and Tess were heading for the lakeside, drinks in hand. Which looked to Laura like a good idea. 'Well, that's part one over with,' Jess said in relief, plonking herself down on a pink hay bale and raising her tumbler of hipster gin. 'Here's to part two.'

'What happens in that?' Laura asked.

'Well, basically, everyone jumps in the water.'

'Naked,' Tess added.

Laura looked at the glistening lake, mere feet from where she sat. Up close, it looked rather brackish.

'It's a kind of pagan baptism,' Jess explained. 'Gawain's father's doing it.'

Laura had been wondering what was so fluid about the Druid. No longer. 'Is it compulsory?' she asked nervously.

'It's optional. But Mary-Bliss and Gawain hope everyone will join in.'

Their optimism was misplaced, Laura thought. Certainly so far as she was concerned. She had work to do; there was a lot to write up on her phone, and good photo opportunities were plentiful. The pagan baptism would make the best one yet.

'Get well soon!' someone was writing on the big white piece of cardboard, propped up on an easel, intended for messages to the happy couple.

A sudden, earsplitting noise now drowned out the hubbub of the crowd, the thump of the Gothic sticks and the wheeze of the infernal accordionist.

Thubathubathubathuba. It dinned in everyone's ears. The trees shook and the leaves roared. Three helicopters could now be seen, hanging in the blue sky, blades whirring, like in *Apocalypse Now.*

'Might be some oligarch who's got lost,' Jess suggested.

The morris dancers had stopped. The crowd rushed to the lakeside, the better to view the descent of the huge, gleaming machines. They sank from view, the blades wheezed to a halt and there were rumbles and slams, as of doors being pulled back. From between the trees a group of huge men in black now appeared. As they walked menacingly forwards there were screams from the crowd.

'Oh my God, terrorists.'

'It's a vigilante army!'

The huge men had shaven heads, arms as thick as the branches of the ancient trees that surrounded them, and chests so broad they looked inflated. They wore black uniforms and straps across their bodies that undoubtedly held guns.

Someone was emerging from the trees behind them, a skinny man in leather trousers.

'Isn't that Brian Skinner?' someone shouted.

'It is! It is!'

'Brian Skinner!'

'Sir Brian, to you!'

The ancient rocker, who'd looked raddled enough in the photograph, looked positively Methuselan under the pitiless glare of a summer's afternoon. The chains on his tight leather trousers gleamed and rattled as he walked, as did the bracelets on the leathery arms beneath the 'Anarchy' vest straining over his little pot belly. Under hair dyed a determined black, eyes buried in wrinkles and ringed with kohl looked around cagily. 'Where's my princess?' he rasped. 'My little girl?'

The crowd near Laura parted and Mary-Bliss now appeared, stepping deliberately over the grass with her long pale feet. The sandblasted diamonds on her plastic-bag tiara glinted dully in the light. She said nothing.

The crowd, too, was silent. Laura raised her phone's

camera expectantly. Was it about to capture a touching celebrity reunion?

Brian Skinner took another tentative step forward. 'Wotcha, princess,' he growled. 'Good to see ya. Know things ain't been too good between us lately.'

'No,' Mary-Bliss agreed, calmly. There was a movement in the crowd behind her and someone else stepped forward. Babs, Laura saw. In her silver crown and grey feathers.

Brian raised his hand and gave his estranged wife a nervous wave. 'Wotcha, babe. How's it going?'

'Just great,' said Babs tightly.

Brian nodded. 'Good to see ya, yeah?' He looked at Mary-Bliss. 'Now listen, princess, I know yer didn't want me involved with the wedding or nothing, but I wanted to bring a little something to get the party started. Or a little someone.' He turned to the side and gestured at a small blonde female, now surrounded on all sides by the huge men in black. 'Ta-dah! My new best friend. We're doing an album of blues songs together.'

There were shouts from beside Laura. 'That's Hudson Grater! OMG!'

The blonde now stepped forward, beaming round at the crowd. She wore a pair of denim shorts and a Union Jack T-shirt. She tucked one side of her shiny bob behind one shell-like ear. She looked about twelve, Laura thought. Was this really the world's biggest-selling recording artist?

The hands holding her phone were trembling. What a scoop! This was a truly massive story. Never mind Carinthia; there wasn't a paper or magazine in the world that wouldn't want it.

And it was *her* exclusive! Again, Laura glanced around for Clemency, but again she was nowhere to be seen. She was beginning to wonder if she had imagined her.

'Hello, everybody! It's really great to be in West England!' Still beaming, Hudson shot out a small hand, on which, despite the shorts, a huge jewel flashed, and snapped her fingers. One of the huge men hurriedly handed her a guitar. It was almost as big as she was.

'Brian and I were just flying over on our way to London's world-famous Abbey Road Studios,' Hudson began in a broad Texan drawl, threading the guitar strap over her tiny shoulders. 'We thought it would be kinda fun if I dropped by and sang you a few songs, get the party started.'

Huge cheers greeted this. 'Theee-ank yee-oo.' Hudson beamed, twanging a guitar string. 'So let's kick things off with my last hit, "You Fat-Shamed Me on Facebook", still riding at Number One in the international charts, I'm glad to say.'

The crowd whooped. Without further ado, Hudson struck up. 'You said you loved me,' she sang in a yearning falsetto. 'And then I logged on / And saw you'd done me wrong...'

People were singing along and holding up their phones. Laura dodged here and there to get the clearest possible pictures. The song was finished to wild cheering.

'Thee-ankyee-oo. Thee-ankyee-oo so much!' Hudson held up a tiny but commanding white hand. 'Now, before my next song, "You Trolled Me on Twitter", I'd like to dedicate my appearance to the guy who's come to mean so much to me and who I'm happy to say is here with me today. My very own English gentleman and the world's next James Bond, my boyfriend of the moment, Orlando Chease!'

The crowd gasped. 'They're both here! CheaseGrater!'

Laura was shaking all over now, so much so that she could barely hold her smartphone. All her journalistic Christmases had come at once. This was a scoop on a scoop on a scoop. The reporting equivalent of a Baskin-Robbins parlour. Amazing. Unbelievable. She snapped away, making notes in between.

Hudson turned and beamed towards the teepee and the trees in the rear, between whose trunks Caspar and Georgia had disappeared. They were missing everything, and serve them right, Laura reflected. That would teach Caspar to seduce one woman right under the nose of another.

Orlando had not yet appeared, but everyone was eagerly awaiting him. Even Reg had got out of his van, the *Sun* clamped under his arm.

Hudson tried again. 'The man currently licensed to thrill me, Orlando Chease!' Her voice had a steelier note in it now.

Still no one. The only things moving to the rear were the flags and the bunting. The pretty, imperious little face darkened with annoyance. 'Orly?' she shouted. 'Get your ass out from back there!'

There were titters from the crowd. 'ORLY!' yelled a clearly incensed Hudson. The burly security men were looking at each other worriedly and peering confusedly between the tree trunks. It was clear that, her size notwithstanding, Hudson's fury was a force to be reckoned with.

An answering cry came from somewhere at the lakeside. Beyond the crowd of wedding guests, just behind where Laura stood, there was a commotion. A tall man in a leather jacket was struggling with someone in silver trousers. His accomplice, in a fringed playsuit and antlers, was helping to drag him to the water's edge.

The crowd's attention immediately transferred from the angry little pop star. 'It's Orlando Chease!' people were shouting. 'They're throwing him in the water!'

'Help! Help!' the putative James Bond was squealing at the lakeside as he struggled desperately against his assailants.

Laura was near enough to see the determination on Caspar's face and the glee on Georgia's. 'You've had this coming for a long time, mate,' Caspar was growling.

The Fluid Druid stepped out from the crowd and raised his hands. 'May the union with the elements commence!'

There was a mighty cheer and the click of a hundred phone cameras as the male half of CheaseGrater sailed through the air and into the lake.

The Fluid Druid raised his arms again. 'And where he leads, let others follow.'

His words had hardly died away before another commotion became evident. Round the side of the crowd came Babs Skinner, grim-faced and resolute, with an equally determined Mary-Bliss. Behind them tripped Gawain, looking alarmed in his flowered trousers, while gripped firmly between them was an elderly man in an 'Anarchy' vest. 'Aw, come on,' Brian Skinner was pleading with his estranged wife and daughter. 'You can't mean it. You can't chuck me in there. Me hair's a weave. It'll knacker me barnet.'

The noise of rock legend hitting water coincided exactly with that of rotor blades starting up. Hudson Grater had clearly seen the answer that was blowing in the wind. The tremendous noise of her helicopters lifting off was accompanied by cheers and more splashes as wedding guests stripped off and dived into the water to join the sodden celebrities.

Laura was not among them. She was at the edge of the lake, taking photographs and making notes. This was going to make one amazing story. And her story alone, she permitted herself to gloat. She had definitely imagined Clemency Makepeace. Perhaps it had been the stress of it all.

There were scores of people in the lake now, some of them

naked, all of them filthy. They were roaring 'Mud, mud, glorious mud,' like a rugby crowd. *Click, click*, went Laura.

Someone now burst on her from behind, snatching the phone out of her hand. 'Thought I didn't recognise you with that mask on, Laura Lake?' Clemency hissed. 'Thought you'd write the story anyway and get your job back? Or *my* job? Fat chance!'

Laura whirled round. Her old enemy stood before her, eyes glittering with venom. 'Only one of us is doing it,' Clemency snarled. 'And it isn't you!' Her arm gave a sudden jerk upwards. Something silver flashed in the sun.

'Give it back...' But Laura had not finished the sentence before her phone was whirling through the air. She twisted towards the lake just in time to see it land in the middle of the mud-covered, squealing scrum. She felt a sickening dismay. Her phone! All of her notes and, much worse, her pictures!

A great shove in the middle of her back now knocked all the breath out of her. She tipped helplessly forward, arms flailing emptily in the air.

'Laura Lake!' cackled Clemency. 'Meet... the lake!'

Cold water hitting her warm skin was a shocking and horrible sensation. It flooded her mouth, dirty and sour. It closed over her head, filling her ears and nose. For a moment everything was thickly silent, cloudy and green. Then her head was out in the air again and she was gasping for breath, thrashing with her arms, kicking her feet free of the slimy weeds which had fastened around them.

Her phone! Could she see it? Laura pushed the filthy wet strands of hair back over her ears and stared desperately down into the water. It was waterproof; it would survive, it was just a question of spotting it. But so brown was the water, so thick with churned-up dirt, that it was impossible to see anything. It was deep, too; she could not feel the bottom, only horribly greasy weeds beneath her paddling bare feet. Her shoes had slid off on impact and were presumably nestling far below, never to be seen again.

Damn Clemency. Damn her to hell.

The mask had disappeared on impact, as had the wings; she could no longer feel the gentle restraint of the elastic. She wasn't Fire any more, but she was definitely Water. Every inch of her was stewed in filthy brown liquid.

She would get Clemency for this. Get her phone, more to the point. If her own phone had gone in the lake, Clemency's would follow. And then Clemency herself. The years of fury and unsettled scores boiled up in Laura with such violent heat, she expected the whole lake to seethe and bubble.

Fired up by these murderous thoughts, she started to plough her way back to shore. It was hard going; the frills of her skirt were heavy with water and the lake was choppy with waves caused by mud-wrestlers screaming and splashing and evidently having the time of their lives. The one nearest to Laura was making more noise than any of them. He was yelling madly, occasionally disappearing beneath the surface of the water, then coming back up again, gasping and flailing his arms.

The cold, prickly feeling that now gripped Laura's scalp had nothing to do with the water. He could not swim, she realised. Or he was stuck. He was not waving, anyway, but drowning.

Wet, muddy people larking about in lakes looked remarkably similar to one another. It was almost impossible to distinguish if the flailing and filthy figures were men or women, let alone who they were. It was only now she got close to him that Laura realised the person struggling just beyond her reach was Orlando Chease. Thanks to Caspar's obsession with him, she knew his face – the curved nose, the full lips, the assured gaze, although his eyes looked anything but assured now. His gaze was desperate.

'Help me,' he gasped. 'I'm caught on something.'

Then he went under again.

Laura, hurling herself towards him, felt her clothes pulling her back and dragging her down. She would have to take them off. Orlando Chease was clearly running out of steam now; he sank more often and came to the surface much less; the gaps between the two were getting longer.

As Laura reached him, he sank and did not come back up at all. She took a deep breath and went under. In the thick brown-green gloom she could at first see nothing, but then she spotted Orlando beneath her feet, sinking slowly and softly to the distant bottom of the lake. His pale lolling limbs and closed eyes suggested complete surrender. Perhaps he was already dead.

Charged with a desperate energy, Laura shot back up to the surface, dragged in a lung-bursting breath of air, then propelled herself down again. Her hands grabbed Orlando's shirt and started to pull him up; he was unmoving, as heavy as a ship's anchor. Her own lungs were beginning to strain and a terrible pressure was pushing in her chest. She, too, was running out of breath. Was Orlando Chease going to pull her down with him?

His legs were the problem; they were trapped in weeds, she now saw. It was as if the weeds were winding round him, dragging him down. Laura tore at them until they surrendered, loosened and billowed away. Orlando's body was finally free.

Gasping, she broke the surface of the lake once more. The actor bobbed beside her, head tipped back, eyes still closed. She started to drag him to the shore. 'Help!' she screamed, when she had the breath to. For a while it was just the heavy water they were moving through, but then Laura's knee made contact with the muddy side of the bank. She looked up and saw feet. Wearing shoes. Rather battered shoes, she couldn't help noticing. A pair of capable hands were stretching down to her.

Dazed and nauseous from terror and exertion, she looked up. Harry Scott looked back down. 'You called?' he said, poker-faced. 'Or should I say texted?'

Laura dimly recalled that she had; it seemed years ago now. And there had been no need, anyway. Sebastian Hunter had not appeared after all. Other disasters had taken his place.

Including this one. Yet again she had wasted Harry's time. Yet again she looked stupid; more stupid than ever before in these ridiculous clothes! For a second she considered swimming away again.

But Harry now had firm hold of her. 'Come on,' he said shortly. 'Let's get you out.'

Standing up, hair streaming, Laura remembered that, actually, she wasn't even wearing the ridiculous clothes. She had taken them off in the water. She was in her underwear, dripping and covered in lake slime like some dystopian Ursula Andress.

'Shit!' She clamped her arms around herself, and crouched down. But then, in the midst of her embarrassment, she heard her grandmother's voice. '*Mais, chérie*, things could be worse. Your lingerie matches, is even a little racy. *C'est bon!*'

But Harry, rather to her disappointment, was not looking. His face was turned resolutely away. 'Here.' He passed her his leather jacket and as she threw it on, the warmth of the quilted lining, so recently against his body, sent a bolt of pleasure through her.

'Is he okay?' But even as she asked, she could see Orlando sitting up and coughing violently, as the woman who had been pumping away at his chest sat back on her heels. An apologetic, shocked-looking woman in antlers and a silver playsuit. Georgia.

'Come on.' Harry shot her the briefest of glances. 'I've got a car. I'll take you home.'

'But I've lost my phone,' Laura bleated, remembering. 'How am I going to write my article now?'

The look Harry gave her, which conveyed 'Why bother?' more eloquently and succinctly than words ever could, only increased her despair.

Harry drove a battered and elderly Golf whose foot well was full of rubbish. Poking her naked toes gingerly into the mess of crisp packets, sweet packets, empty water bottles and other journey-related jetsam, Laura realised she had grown rather used to the polished and scented interiors of Lulu's limos.

'I'm sorry,' she said, after they had driven in silence for a while. 'I got you there on a wild goose chase.'

Her reward for this admission was the briefest of glances from the steering wheel.

'Not necessarily,' said Harry, blowing a dark lock of hair out of his eye.

'Caspar was there,' Laura admitted, thinking that was what he meant. 'Although I'm not sure anything was taken. Apart from my phone,' she added gloomily.

'I wouldn't worry about that.'

'Of course I'm worried!' Laura exclaimed. 'It had my article on it. My whole future as a journalist!'

Harry said nothing, which irritated her further, although most annoying of all was the knowledge that he could not be blamed for it.

'Anyway, I was happy to come,' Harry now said unexpectedly, changing gear to overtake a filth-belching tractor.

Within her chest, under the jacket, Laura's heart speeded up, and not only because she could not see what was coming round the bend. She only hoped that Harry could. She also hoped he'd been happy to come because of her. 'Really?'

'Yes. I love the countryside round here,' Harry demoralisingly explained, passing the belching farm vehicle with aplomb.

Laura looked out of the window. She could see why; it was very pretty. Smooth, rounded green fields flanked a road which wound in an ancient sort of way. The occasional villages had square-towered churches, and houses with thatched roofs and tiny windows in the eaves. Tall flowers – stocks and hollyhocks – stood sentinel either side of low doors and roses burst out everywhere.

'I grew up round here,' Harry added, unexpectedly. 'Cut my teeth on the local paper.'

Laura smiled. 'The rubbish on the playing field.'

Another look from the steering wheel. 'You remember that.'

Laura blushed. 'Yes, and that my father inspired you,' she said quickly, playing her ace card.

Harry did not reply. The car purred along and Laura, convinced she had said something wrong, looked out at duck ponds and elm trees, hills and valleys, imposing gateposts and estate walls. Had he changed his mind about her father now that he had met his hero's daughter?

They had turned on to the motorway before Harry spoke. 'Your father was an amazing man. And it's even more amazing that I am in the car with his daughter. What was it like growing up with him? It must have been incredible.'

Laura stared at his profile in surprise. Every straight line of his face radiated sincerity, however. He meant it. And while part of her wanted to glory in this unexpected tribute, to milk it dry, to paint a picture of a childhood sitting under her father's desk as he banged out award-winning reports on his ancient lucky Remington, or ricocheting round the world in an if-it's-Wednesday-it-must-be-Saigon sort of way, she knew the time had come to admit the truth. Even if it made her look like a fraud.

'I never knew him,' she admitted flatly. 'He and my mother divorced when I was very little. He died soon afterwards, but I never found out how. I never found out anything.' She bit her lip, hard, as the hot tears stung her eyes. Laura rarely cried, and never about this. She had long since trained herself out of it. But as Harry passed her a somewhat crumpled tissue, she took it gratefully.

'No one will talk to me about him,' Laura went on, when she had collected herself. Harry himself had said nothing, yet she sensed his silence was sympathetic, not disapproving. 'My grandmother, for instance...' She recounted to Harry the story of Mimi's recent reaction, realising too late that it involved admitting that she had told her grandmother about Harry himself. 'She hated him, for some reason,' Laura finished, mortified. 'But I don't think he was awful to my mother. I imagine, if anything, it was the other way round. But I'll probably never find out,' she added, bleakly.

'She probably didn't hate him,' Harry said, sounding so sure of himself that Laura was almost more indignant than surprised. What did this stranger know of her family history? But then, what did she know herself?

'What makes you think that?'

He looked at her for some seconds before saying, gently, 'Has it ever occurred to you that your grandmother was trying to protect you?' The expression in his deep-set dark eyes was warm, almost tender. Her heart rose into her throat again, making it difficult to speak.

'Protect me?'

He nodded, and the lock of dark hair fell into his eyes again. He tossed it back. 'She doesn't want the same thing to happen to you. She didn't want you to follow in your father's footsteps and do such a dangerous job. Probably she thought that talking about him would encourage you. That you would want to avenge his death.'

'But she encouraged me to be a journalist,' Laura pointed out heatedly. 'She was mad keen for me to go to London.'

'Yes, to work on a magazine. There's no danger in that at all.'

'Oh, I don't know,' murmured Laura as some of her recent scrapes flashed through her mind. She could see his point, however. Perhaps Mimi's apparent madness had had method in it. And perhaps, too, her grandmother had seen an even bigger truth, that she was no good at journalism anyway. She pictured her phone arching through the air, glinting in the sunshine, taking her photos, notes and future to a watery and premature grave. Proper reporter? Well, she had definitely put the 'pond' in 'correspondent'.

Then she remembered something Harry had just said. 'Avenge his death?'

'What?' said Harry, vaguely, as if he had been thinking very deeply about another matter entirely.

'You said I might want to avenge my father's death. What happened to him?' An urgency had gripped Laura. She had to find out. The sound of the tyres on the motorway rose in her ears.

'I don't know,' said Harry, not particularly convincingly.

'You're a rotten liar,' Laura told him.

He raised his level brow. 'Probably my worst failing as a journalist. But I'm telling you the truth. Well, sort of.'

'You do know what happened!' Laura accused.

'Not entirely. Anyway, it's something you need to look into yourself. It's not my story, it's yours.'

Laura subsided into angry silence. Just where was she supposed to start? Mimi, her mother, and now even Harry. Brick walls, every one.

The motorway was now bathed in a fiery glow. A sun like a huge red penny was sinking into an invisible slot just below the horizon. Stripes of coral, gold and duck-egg blue spread across the sky. An enchanted evening, Laura thought, but beside her, Harry kept his eyes on the road. Now that she had nothing to tell him about growing up with a famous reporter, he was probably desperate to get the journey over as soon as possible.

The engine whined in her ears. The motorway stretched ahead. Exhaustion overcame Laura and she fell asleep.

She awoke to find that it was dark and they were back in the capital. And that she felt much warmer. Looking down, she saw that a car rug had been placed across her knees. Harry must have put it there. How had he done it? Matter-of-factly? Or with a tender glance at her sleeping face? Recognising the dark mass of Hyde Park, she realised that the journey was about to end and felt a mixture of relief and regret.

They were turning into Lulu's road now. The great houses loomed in the streetlights. Only now did he break the silence. 'We're here.'

'Thanks for bringing me back,' she said politely.

'You're welcome.'

She climbed stiffly out and stood barefoot on the pavement. What must she look like in a leather jacket, skimpy underwear and a car rug? No doubt Daisy would have a name for it. The thought made her smile in spite of herself. She shrugged off the jacket.

'No, keep it on,' Harry said. 'You'll freeze without it. And besides,' he added, 'it suits you.'

For all her frustration with him, Laura was suddenly filled with pure delight.

'You can give it back to me tomorrow.'

'Tomorrow?' It was the last thing she had expected.

'If you're free, that is.'

Laura remembered. Lulu. Geneva. Oh God. Please don't let her come back. Or be here already. 'I'm free,' she said firmly.

'Good. Come and meet me at the most exclusive club in London.' He was writing something on a scrap of paper and now held it towards her. 'I'll be there anyway, so don't worry if you can't make it.'

Laura took the paper. The most exclusive club in London, according to Harry's sloping ballpoint, wasn't Mingers, Shag or Grope, but somewhere called the NDY.

He had driven away before she could say another word.

Vlad had opened the door before she could even knock. She did not comment on Laura's appearance.

Laura didn't either. 'Never explain, never complain,' was

another of Mimi's mottos. Instead, she summoned up what dignity she could. 'Is Lulu back from Geneva?'

She had her fingers tightly crossed.

'Not as yet, madam.'

Joy shot through Laura. She wanted to punch the air. She could go to the club with Harry.

Chapter Twenty-Four

JAMES POND!

Mud Larks for Chease and 'Pond Girl'
as Hudson Helicopters off in Huff

Laura read the front pages with a sense of grim familiarity. And irony. Of course, her entire professional ambition was to make headlines. But not in this way.

To have been a mystery brunette on the front page of every morning newspaper once was embarrassing. Twice was unfortunate. But three times definitely bordered on carelessness, especially as this time she was practically naked. Her breasts and bottom, barely restrained by scraps of lace and underwiring, were on every breakfast table in Britain.

The only good thing was that, covered in weeds and mud as she was, even the most prying telephoto lens had not been able to make her recognisable. This did not, however, prevent wild speculation about her identity. An ex-girlfriend was the favourite. 'A source at the scene confirmed it was Lady Clara Strumpett, former flame of the actor once tipped to be the new James Bond. "I'd know those tits anywhere."'

The coverage, which was exclusive to all newspapers, was intensely unflattering to Orlando. There was no sympathy for the real danger he had been in; no sympathy, either, for the physical shortcomings the episode had exposed. 'BALDFINGER!' blared one headline, whose accompanying huge photograph zoomed in pitilessly on Orlando's severe and previously unsuspected case of hair loss. The water had pulled apart what had clearly been a skilled combover. 'He's a rubbish swimmer too,' another 'source' was quoted as saying. 'Can a man like this really be James Bond?'

Similar points were made in other reports. It looked as if Caspar had, after all, killed off his hated rival's ambitions. And might have killed off Orlando himself had it not been for her, Laura thought, and perhaps more importantly Georgia. She wouldn't piss on him if he were on fire, yet had given him the kiss of life. Perhaps that evened things out.

There was lots of wild speculation about Hudson Grater's hasty exit. Photographs of helicopters whirling into the air above the mystical wood featured widely. 'None of Miss Grater's spokespeople could be reached last night, although a press release is expected later this morning.' The conclusion was that CheaseGrater was over.

Still, it was an ill wind that blew no one any good, and the one who had benefited most was the most unlikely candidate of all. There were plenty of pictures of Brian Skinner flailing about in the lake. The papers, apparently unaware of the real reasons for this, were full of praise for 'the vintage hellraiser's undimmed sense of fun' and were pleased at this proof that there was 'life in the old rock dog yet'. 'His joy at being reunited with his daughter on her wedding day was touching to see,' gushed one report, alongside a shot in which Mary-Bliss and Babs Bloggs watched from the banks in grim satisfaction as Brian went under again.

Laura turned to Sarah Salmon's gossip column. The main item on the page was headlined 'TURKEY TOFFS TO TIE KNOT'. Reading on resignedly, Laura thought that, had her prospects with *Society* not just spectacularly hit the buffers, this was exactly the kind of wedding she would have tried to include.

A little bird (or is it a large one with stuffing?!) brings news of feverish preparations at Creake Castle, north Norfolk, where Lady Sophy Creake, daughter of the 78th Earl of Screming, will marry Rupert Sturmdrang this weekend.

The ancestral Creake carriage, in which Lady Sophy will travel to the estate church, has been freshly regilded. 'It's taken the family to more coronations than you can shake a sceptre at,' an insider tells me, 'although last time it suffered a bit of damage coming back up the A1.' No less than three Countesses of Screming have served the monarch as Mistress of the Furs. And, as hereditary Groom of the Stool, Lord Screming is entitled to an annual delivery of Waitrose's finest lavatory paper as a perquisite.

Rupert's ancestry, meanwhile, is lost in the mists of nineteenth-century Birmingham commerce. His father, racehorse trainer Ernest Sturmdrang, and mother, the formidably social Lolita, have an estate conveniently close to Creake Castle and have encouraged the relationship between their son and the Earl's daughter at every stage.

Former property developer Rupert, 28, recently returned from the City to launch a paper-aeroplane business from a barn on his parents' land. 'A classic FILTN,' an uncharitable source lets slip. 'Failed In London, Trying Norwich'.

Like all Creake brides, Lady Sophy, 29, will wear the famous Creake tiara. Her wedding gown, designed by herself and based on a portrait of her great-grandmother by the artist John Singer Sargent, is her latest foray into ethical fashion. Lady Sophy's other creations include a range of Fairtrade fur-trimmed shooting capes to raise funds for the WWF and sustainable #IAmATit bags to promote Garden Birds Awareness Week.

Friends say the wedding is a marriage of true minds, 'or maybe a case of two half brains making a whole'.

Lips are sealed as to whether there will be royal guests at the wedding. Rupert and Sophy are part of the so-called Turkey Toffs set: young Norfolk-based bluebloods connected to the Duke and Duchess of Cambridge's inner circle.

Laura reread the item, thinking that the wedding was exactly the sort Carinthia wanted. It had castles and tiaras, royal connections and an ancestral carriage. Together with the Tripp–Bender nuptials and what she could remember of the Wiltshire one, this would round off the 'New Society Weddings' piece to perfection. Had she still been writing it, that was. But now she wasn't, not any more, and even if she had been she could not go. She knew no Turkey Toffs at all; certainly not Rupert Sturmdrang or Lady Sophy Creake.

As Lulu's continued absence meant that Laura was still relieved of her duties, such as they were, she went slowly back up to her room after breakfast. She thought of her lost smartphone whirling through the air, heard the sickening splash as it sank out of sight for ever. Curse Clemency.

Damn her to hell. She could have used it to research the Turkey Toffs wedding; find a way of crashing it. But what was the point? That dream was over. She had to accept it.

And yet, as Laura paced up the Stella McCarpet steps, the idea wouldn't quite go away. There *would* be a way to get into the turkey wedding. There had to be. If she could infiltrate it, it would give her the advantage and push her ahead of Clemency, who, for all her scheming, only had one wedding in the bag so far. At least, Laura hoped so. Chill panic swirled through her as she realised she had no idea what Clemency knew, or was planning.

The events of the day before had left Laura aching and with a stuffy nose. She decided that a few hours back in bed would help, and prepare her for the forthcoming night out with Harry. But the prospect of that filled her with a strange restlessness and after only half an hour she decided she'd had enough of lying amid Buzzie Omelet's tasteful sages, beiges and greiges. It was like being immersed in a bowl of pea soup. She would do something else instead. Something that just wouldn't stop nagging at her, for all her efforts to suppress it.

The urge to research the Turkey Toffs was strong, and growing stronger. The more she could find out about them, the better her chances of finding a way in to the wedding. Vlad, of course, would be able to lend her another phone, or let her use one of the house computers. But Laura felt she needed a change of scene. There were computers elsewhere – the library, for instance.

An hour later, Laura sat before the terminals at Knightsbridge Library. She had thirty minutes; the slots were in demand. Ten minutes later, she had ascertained the following about the Turkey Toffs. They were wealthy young people with aristocratic connections based on grand

Norfolk estates. Their families all knew each other and they had been to the same southern public schools and the same northern universities, at which, while normal students lived in halls, ate Pot Noodles and drank lager in the college bar, Turkey Toffs rented smart houses in town with other toffs. These houses had guestbooks and champagne fridges and were the scenes of spag bol suppers occasionally attended by royalty. 'We always used to feel *so* sorry for HRH's minders sitting outside in their horrid little car,' one Turkey Toffette was quoted as saying. 'So we'd slip down with plates of toast and mugs of tea.'

After university, TTs moved to London, where they worked for Richard Branson, joined luxury concierge companies or launched boutique businesses called Awesome Wellies. They lived in flats bought by their parents in smart parts of town. For some, city life was an education; 'Soph thought electricity came free out of the walls,' one ex-flatmate was quoted as saying.

Fascinating though this information was, Laura needed more wedding detail. Her spirits rose when she found an article about Rupert Sturmdrang's stag night. A group of assorted Hughs, Williams (but not that one), Charlies and Guys had gone to Las Vegas, where they had hired a fur-lined cabana at a nightclub called Hooters and played pool with naked pole dancers.

Laura enlarged the picture of Rupert; with his Ray-Bans, red trousers and dark floppy hair, he didn't look the fur-lined, pole-dancing type. It didn't take long to discover who had masterminded the jaunt. A large picture of Sebastian Hunter accompanied the piece. He stared into the camera from beneath his spiked white hair, his blue eyes coldly amused beneath the jet-black brows, the lips curved in a secretive smile.

Laura gasped. Him again! Was there no posh marital pie his grubby painted fingers weren't all over? She reached for her smartphone to text Harry, before realising that of course she didn't have it. It was at the bottom of a lake hundreds of miles away. 'Shit!'

'Sssh!' said a passing librarian.

Laura gave her an apologetic smile. She didn't want to get thrown out of here, at least not before seeing what Lady Sophy's hen night had entailed. Hastily, she consulted the oracle of the search engine. Up came the headline: 'SOPHY'S SPARM SURPRISE'.

Sparm? Did they mean sperm? How... graphic! It sounded worse than the fur cabin at Hooters.

It was not, she discovered, a misspelling. Lady Sophy's hen celebrations had been held at 'fashionable Cotswolds sparm the Portobello Farmhouse'.

A sparm, it seemed, was a conflation of 'spa' with 'farm', a luxurious country hotel combining the fashionably folksy with five-star levels of comfort and service and the very latest and most expensive beauty treatments. Sparm guests, Laura discovered, stayed in candlelit cow byres designed by Buzzie Omelet – her again – rode about on Hermès bicycles – those again – and were fed from a mobile van specialising in 'gourmet fry-ups'. Each cow byre had its own butler who dressed like a farmhand in clothes designed by Victoria Beckham. It all sounded very Marie Antoinette.

Lady Sophy's sparm experience had been organised by the chief bridesmaid, Lady Clara Strumpett. Laura looked closely at the picture of a sly-looking blonde in a flowing dress split to reveal long legs. Had this girl not been at the Skinner–Loone wedding? Snogging the owner of Gawain's rude artisanal spoon company all the way back in the haycart? And here she was at another wedding, walking up the church path with Pippa Middleton. According to the caption, Lady Clara was a model, actress and, under the name Captain Disco Pants, a DJ with a Monday-night slot at exclusive London nightclub Grope. She looked the bride-upstaging type, Laura thought, and poor Lady Sophy, who was chinless with a piggy nose, probably wouldn't take much upstaging.

Of the other hens, Lucy made hats, Rosie designed party bags and Neroli was a caterer. All were pictured wearing aprons printed with a pink hen and watching from behind their hands in mock horror as the Chippendales performed in the Portobello Farmhouse barn against a shabby-chic background of rag rugs, standard lamps and whitewashed walls. The Duchess of Cambridge did not seem to be present.

Laura read the piece another couple of times. An idea was forming in her mind. If Neroli was a caterer, there was a good chance she would be gracing the wedding with her services.

Laughter distracted her. At the screen next to hers a couple of London-sophisticate schoolgirls, all leggings, eyeliner and untidy hair, were looking at clothes. Laura recognised the brightly coloured leather minidresses as Irina's.

'Whenever I'm feeling down,' one remarked to the other in the husky tones of the privately educated, 'I look at this website. Never fails to cheer me up.'

'Designer to the stars!' the other chortled, pointing at the slogan emblazoned on the home page against the background of a neon-pink heart.

'Porn stars, more like.'

'*Haute tarte*, hee hee.'

Laura recalled the last time she had seen Irina, at the Bender–Tripp wedding. And before that, at *Call This Art?* At that stage, it now struck Laura, the designer could have been a suspect in the robberies. But not now. There had been no sign of her at Mary-Bliss's wedding, and she was clearly not involved in Sophy's. The dress had been designed by the bride herself.

Laura now prepared to research the catering. Looking up Neroli's website, she anticipated a cheerful plump blonde holding plates of petits fours and a rack of lamb with paper ruffles on the legs. She was surprised to encounter a lithe girl sliding across the screen to a slow, heavy backbeat. She wore a yellow retro-printed frock and had a fringe and glossy long dark hair. 'Hi!' said a speech bubble issuing from a bright-red-lipsticked mouth.

This image faded into ones of Neroli holding a dripping mozzarella at a farmer's market or arranged fetchingly over a high stool in a light-flooded kitchen, eating green soup from a white bowl. She was a clean-eating queen, Laura realised, reading the rolling Twitter feed on which Neroli was giving 'a big shout-out to my besties on the radiant juicing and wellness scenes'. It seemed to have been posted a couple of seconds ago.

Useless, Laura thought, clicking through recipes for crisped carrot peelings on spiralised cardoon root and chilli and swamp moss shots 'packed with invigorating heat and toxin-blasting pond vitamins'. Quite apart from the fact that she personally had had as many pond vitamins as she could take for the time being, there was no way that a grand English wedding would have faddish cooking like this. Green clean eating might have taken over the world, but it was almost certainly yet to scale the walls of Creake Castle.

Now there was an idea. Were the castle walls actually scalable? She glanced at her watch. Five minutes left to find out.

Creake Castle's website showed a huge, medieval building the size of a small town. The walls were sheer, cliff-height and clearly the sort that only a trebuchet could get over. So much for her brilliant idea. Before clicking off, Laura took the virtual tour. There was a Great Staircase gleaming with suits of armour, a Great Salon blazing with gold, and parkland stretching into the middle of next week. 'History's wheel has rarely turned without a Creake on stage,' the home page said. 'The de Crekes came over with the Conqueror and fought at both Agincourt and Crécy.'

Creakes, Laura discovered, were even mentioned in Shakespeare's history plays:

> Anne Boleyn: Forsooth!
> Sir Roger Creake: Odds bodikins!
> (*Henry VIII*, Act 3, Scene ix, line 389)

But the place clearly had no possibilities for her. Trying not to feel despondent, she returned to Lulu's. The day was sunny, she would think of something else. She would have to, or run the risk of Clemency getting the better of her.

The editions of the London evening paper were being handed out outside Knightsbridge Tube. Laura took one, expecting to see more James Pond headlines and herself in muddy underwear. The headline had changed, however.

HIPPY HEIST
Thief Targets Top-Notch Wedding
while Bond Splashes in Pond

Laura's hands gripped both ends of the paper, hard. It appeared that, while the gathering of guests watched the

Brian, Orlando and Caspar show, someone had been working what the report referred to as the 'haute boho crowd', detaching necklaces, removing rings, unhooking bracelets and removing earrings. Babs had lost her Cartier collar and Aunt Loone her pearls. Gawain's male tiara had gone missing, as had Mary-Bliss's female counterpart. The thief – or thieves – had even managed to grab Hudson Grater's ring.

From a strolling pace, Laura started to walk faster. How had this happened without Sebastian Hunter even being there? Had it been, could it be, Caspar after all? He was the only person who had been at all three occasions. Impossible though it seemed, it was the only conclusion left to draw.

Now she was allowing herself to consider it, she could see it made sense. Harry had been right after all. Why else had Caspar and Georgia disappeared into the woods? Laura had assumed they were going to have sex, but was she a thief too? Part of his gang?

The timing didn't stack up though. The stealing had been done while Caspar was throwing Orlando in the water. Unless that had been a distraction – a rather brilliant one, actually – while other people worked on site, among the guests. Had Michael been concealing marquise-cut emeralds in his Morphsuit? He had been very proud of his bulge. Or had the Gothic morris dancers been an international gang in disguise, which might explain their trouble with the teepee.

It was all very confusing. Being an investigative reporter was much more difficult than it looked. When you thought about it hard, as Laura was doing, just about anyone seemed a likely jewel thief. Orlando himself might have been part of it, working in league with Caspar even. Who would suspect that the two apparently bitter enemies were a team? Orlando could have agreed beforehand to be thrown in.

Even to pretend to drown. It had seemed realistic to Laura, but Orlando was an actor, after all.

Well, it would certainly be something to talk to Harry about later. It would be fascinating to get his seasoned reporter's view on it all. She spent the afternoon trying out looks for the evening. High heels or low? Hair up or down? What did one wear to London's most exclusive club?

Towards teatime there was a knock on her door. She opened it, half-expecting Vlad with a cup of tea. Lulu's face, without her sunglasses, looked disconsolately back at her.

'Lulu! You're back.' Laura tried to sound pleased but was inwardly aghast. Her evening was in ruins. She could hardly go out on her own now.

'I can come in?'

'Of course.'

Lulu was wearing some floaty grey cashmere leisurewear and very little make-up. It made her look prettier and somehow younger, a heightened version of the *Society* cover. Laura guessed she was straight off the plane. She pushed her tanned bare feet into the thick beige carpet, frowning.

'What's the matter?' Laura asked.

Lulu was by the window, looking out. She heaved a heavy sigh. 'What is sharp end?'

'What?'

Lulu's blonde hair was swishing restlessly from side to side. 'Every day I go shop, go party, go fly about world. Why? For what meaning, hmmm?'

'Oh. You mean what's the point?' It was a good question, and not one Laura could answer. Her heart sank. It wasn't just that her date was off, her charge had returned from Switzerland with an existential crisis.

The dark eyes, free of their usual heavy make-up, had a

lost, vulnerable expression. 'Is same always, hmm? Everyone want my money. Everyone love my money. But no one love Lulu. Have no real friend.' The bare, unglossed lip trembled and the billionheiress turned her face to the window.

Alarmed, Laura hurried over and put her arm around Lulu. 'Vlad loves you,' she assured her, sincerely. 'And I'm sure your parents do,' she added, more hesitantly.

She felt Lulu go rigid beneath her. 'Always criticise. And too busy always,' she muttered. 'Like having no parents at all sometime.'

Laura could relate to that. She thought briefly of Odette and Leon in their Monaco apartment.

'Everything, he always go wrong,' Lulu lamented.

She could relate to that too. It had been one disaster after another since she'd got to London. They were strangely similar, she and Lulu, for all the differences between them. Laura suddenly felt very affectionate towards her.

'First problems hashtag, hmm?'

'What?'

'Hashtag problems first world.' Lulu was smiling wryly.

She was making a joke, Laura realised. She smiled. 'You have me. I'm your friend.'

'You are? Real friend?' Lulu looked so thrilled, Laura's vision became suddenly misty. Friendship was a rare thing for her too. She blinked hard. 'Yes. You're a good woman, Lulu.'

'But cannot find good man, hmm?'

'You don't need a man, Lulu. You're better off without them.'

Lulu looked wistful. 'But everyone want be loved, hmm? Get married, have children?'

Laura did not reply. She hadn't the slightest urge to have the latter. And her efforts at the former were doomed to failure. Her relationships were so casual, they hardly existed at all. Caspar, from whom she had not heard since leaving him in silver trousers in a field in Wiltshire. Harry, who probably thought she was mad, and whom she would not now be seeing anyway.

'You know,' Lulu was musing, 'sometime I think that simple life would be best, hmm? Like magazine interview? Run along ringing beach, hmm? Shop at Wonder Supermarket and not Harvey Nichols.' She slapped her cashmere knee and let out a bark of laughter. 'Feel better now. You want we go out tonight? Go club, hmm?'

Laura's heart sank. Lulu's idea of a club would be her idea of hell. It would have people like Lord Sebastian in it.

'Mingers? Grope?' Lulu was thinking aloud.

'What about the NDY?' Laura suggested suddenly.

'The what?'

'It's the most exclusive club in London.'

'Never have heard of it.' Lulu was looking doubtful. Then she smiled. 'Must be new place. Is good idea. We will go us both, yes?'

By the time they were in the car and on their way to the club, Lulu's spirits were quite restored. She was cackling at something on her phone.

'Look!' She held it out to Laura. It was a link to a newspaper website on which a short film of Orlando Chease, open of mouth and flailing of limb as he hit the water, had been uploaded, clearly from someone's mobile.

Laura watched the little scene unfold over the course of a few seconds. 'Is good-looking guy, hmm?' Lulu remarked.

'Orlando?' Laura asked doubtfully. The footage was not flattering. He looked more like someone from a *Carry On* film than a spy licensed to kill.

'No, guy in silver pants throwing him in.'

Laura hadn't paid much attention to the figure Caspar cut. But it was true that he looked strangely magnificent in his blazing metallic trousers. He had obviously come off best in the encounter, both physically and in terms of public approval. 'Who's the hotty with the tinfoil botty?' was typical of the comments below the clip.

The question was, was he a jewel thief?

Chapter Twenty-Five

'Is here, you are sure?' Lulu said as Vlad stopped outside the dilapidated old building which corresponded to the address Harry had given. It looked completely closed up and dark. A mixture of dread and anger pulled at Laura. Had he been teasing her? Did the club simply not exist?

'We go Mingers instead, hmm?' Lulu suggested. 'Tonight they have chocolate wrestling. Good for laughing.'

'Let's give it a minute,' said Laura, desperately. Perhaps someone would turn up, unlikely though that seemed. The walls before her rose blackly to meet a slice of moonless sky. A dying streetlight fizzed and flickered over cobbles gleaming with rain. It was quiet, but not in a good way; the distant roar of traffic only made the silence more menacing. They were parked in the shadows in a darkened, dead-end street, with big hair and even bigger make-up.

Lulu had insisted they dress to the nines. She had dragged Laura into her wardrobe and picked out any number of unsuitable outfits. Laura had managed to escape with a thick cream silk shirt and skinny jeans, but there had been no stopping Jay, who had been hastily summoned to zhuzh up her hair, nor Vlad, who'd given full vent to her make-up skills. She had ended up with more contouring than an Ordnance Survey map. Fortunately, Harry's battered leather jacket, worn over this ensemble, helped tone it down.

Lulu herself wore a tiny multicoloured skirt and a see-through black blouse over a black bra. Her signature huge black sunglasses were firmly back in place. 'Louboutin soles very slippery in wet,' she was saying, peering doubtfully at the cobbles. 'You can drive nearer door, Vlad?'

'Look!' said Laura. A thickset stranger now appeared at the end of the road, the light behind him casting a huge shadow towards her over the greasy cobbles. He had closely shaven hair and a black eyepatch.

'Look like pirate,' Lulu said. 'We go Vomit, hmm? Tonight is burlesque disco.'

'Just give it another minute,' Laura pleaded.

The burly figure went to the door opposite. He raised his arm, as if pressing something. There was a snap as a lock was released, then a creak as the door opened. Laura saw a naked bulb and a dingy interior, then it closed again. The building went back to being dark and silent.

'Looks like the club's open,' she said.

'Not look smart,' objected Lulu. 'No clipboard. No VIP area.'

Someone else was coming up the road now. Another man, tall and thin, limping and with his arm in a sling. He appeared to be wearing a flak jacket.

'Like back from war,' Lulu remarked.

It was hard not to agree. All these sinister, injured people – was this the HQ of some vigilante militia? The possibility that Harry had been teasing her lurked unpleasantly at the back of Laura's mind.

There now came the sound of light heels on the cobbles. Someone in a pale Audrey Hepburn mac belted tightly round a tiny waist appeared. The sulky streetlight shone on glossy long dark hair.

'Is Maribeth Collins!' gasped Lulu.

It was. She was with her tall and handsome husband and the two of them were laughing softly. They pressed the buzzer and as the door opened, the light fell fully on the faces of the famous actor and his almost as celebrated barrister wife.

'Okay, we go in.' Lulu was out of the car now and hurrying over the cobbles in her heels. Laura, scrambling after her, expected to see her fall over at any moment.

Lulu pressed the buzzer. 'Yeah?' someone snarled.

'Is Lulu,' Lulu announced grandly, as if this should be enough, which presumably it usually was.

'Who?'

Laura leant forward to the battered answerphone.

'I'm here to meet Harry Scott.' She spoke hesitantly, still half-sure it was all a joke. But the door buzzed, and she pushed it open.

'Harry Scott, is who?' Lulu demanded as she tottered in.

'Good question,' Laura muttered, following her.

This was the most exclusive club in London? Well, it definitely wasn't Annabel's.

The inside of the NDY Club looked, if anything, even

shabbier than the outside. Worn wooden stairs led upwards. The panelling on the walls was split and peeling, last painted in the late 1790s, it seemed. Surely she hadn't just spotted the cream of Hollywood here?

Clearly she had, though, as Lulu was clattering excitedly up the stairs in her Louboutins towards a battered black door with faint noise coming from behind it.

By the time Laura caught up, Lulu had already pushed it open. A burst of noise came out, followed by a thick cloud of cigarette smoke. Lulu plunged inside, Laura hurrying after her.

What seemed like a thousand people were crushed into two tiny rooms. Just inside the door was a diminutive bar with dimpled half-pint glasses hanging above it in dusty rows. Grimy football pennants were stuck to the ceiling. Laura was reminded suddenly and powerfully of Ginette's.

The presiding spirit had none of Ginette's sharp humour, however. Nor was he a suave, buttermilk-jacketed, bow-tied bartender with a shining silver cocktail shaker. He was shrunken and skinny with a few strands of greasy hair combed over an intensely miserable face. Laura had no doubt he was the answerer of the buzzer. He moved slowly and reluctantly at the behest of his shouting customers.

'Ron! Two pints of Stella and a packet of cheese and onion!'

'A double Grouse and some peanuts, please, Ron.'

There was no sign of Harry. The smeared bar mirrors reflected other faces, however. There was the wife of the famous film star, with her glossy black hair and lean limbs, deep in conversation with the man with the eyepatch.

'I drank goat's piss for breakfast,' someone was saying behind her. 'And slept in a car guarded by kids with AK47s.'

What sort of club was this? Who were these people?

'Laura!' Her heart jumped into her throat as a tall figure with a quizzical smile pushed into the crowd beside her. 'I wasn't sure you'd come.' A pair of deep-set dark eyes flicked over her. 'Wow, you look great.'

Harry looked great too, handsome in a white shirt and jeans. Without the dark leather shell of his jacket he looked brighter, fresher, younger.

'Really... polished,' Harry went on, a flicker of amusement twitching his long mouth.

Beneath the layers of foundation, Laura reddened. He meant she had overdone it, but how could she explain she'd been in the pitiless grip of an ex-army transgendering butler and her lipstick tray? Her heart was racing and a strange, sharp, excited feeling was piercing her lower belly. 'Here,' she said, struggling out of the jacket. The crowd was so pressing, it was difficult even to move her arms.

'Leave it on for now,' Harry said. 'There's nowhere to hang coats here anyway.'

In contrast to her awkwardness, he seemed completely at ease.

'Like it?' He nodded towards the riot surrounding him.

Laura wasn't sure she knew what 'it' was. Another famous face flashed at her from between two shoulders, then disappeared as the shoulders met. 'Was that really...?' she began, astonished.

'Yes,' he said, as if this was entirely to be expected. He swirled his tumbler of Famous Grouse.

Laura gasped. She had just caught sight of Hudson Grater. She seemed to have entirely recovered from the humiliations of yesterday and was laughing loudly at something a famous writer was saying. 'What are they all doing here?'

Harry grinned. 'You walk off stage in the West End, you come here. You duck out of your Leicester Square première, you come here. You're bored with Kensington Palace, you come here.'

'But why do you come here?' Laura asked. 'What does NDY actually stand for?'

'Not Dead Yet. It's the foreign correspondents' club. They come straight here from the battlefront and drink like fish.'

'What battlefront?'

'Take your pick.'

Now it all made sense. The people at the bar – mostly men, but the odd woman too – were knocking back whisky like there was no tomorrow. They were shouting and laughing and their faces were tanned and shiny, as if back from somewhere very hot. Camouflaged gilets were unzipped over grubby white T-shirts; a bulletproof vest hung loosely open. And was that a rifle she could see, slung over a shoulder? The strap of a shoulder holster? Laura's eyes widened.

Foreign correspondents? Like her father? Might her father actually have come here? Looked at the same things? It was an incredible thought, and it made the stuffy, riotous room seem not strange but welcoming. A place where she had every right to be. It was hot, but Laura felt shivery all over. She looked at Harry wonderingly. 'You brought me here because of my dad?'

He seemed not to have heard her, and as the noise around them was tremendous, it was possible that he really hadn't. But now he leant towards her, and his breath on her cheek made her shiver in a different way. She looked at the long, strong fingers clutching his whisky glass and suddenly imagined them touching her.

'See that guy over there? Under-Secretary of State at the Foreign Office. You get diplomats here from all over. Gathering intelligence from people straight back from the field.'

The door had opened to admit yet more revellers and the noise levels had suddenly soared. The atmosphere was one of near-hysterical excitement. Around her, people were shouting about ISIS, the UN, NGOs, MSF...

The film star's wife had finally succeeded in getting her round in. You had to hand it to Ron, he clearly didn't have favourites. He treated everyone equally rudely.

'Ron's a spy too, of course.' Harry leant in confidingly and Laura caught his aftershave: clean, classic cologne. 'Or was.'

'Ron?'

'Burnt out, though, years ago. So the FCO put him here. He's a far better landlord than he ever was an agent.'

He must, Laura thought, have been a truly terrible spy. She grabbed her chance now Harry's head was close. 'My father...?' But he just smiled and pulled away.

There were shouts about some press awards going on elsewhere. 'Come on, Jezza. Time to get your gong.'

Harry pointed up at the bar ceiling, with the football pennants. 'People bring those back from their tours. Aleppo United, Kabul All Stars, Sporting Homs, you name it. The people that don't come back, we commemorate over there.' He pointed, and Laura could see, on a wall behind the crowd, rows of small brass plates.

She felt the hairs on her neck suddenly lift. Was her father there? 'Is...?'

'Yes, he is,' Harry said. 'Why else do you think I brought you here?'

He smiled down at her and for a few seconds, their eyes locked. The emotion balling in her throat meant that she could not speak, but as she had no idea what to say, that was just as well.

Gently he put an arm about her and drew her through crowds that looked impenetrable and yet parted before them. Laura was vaguely aware of some sympathetic smiles.

PETER LAKE

1962–2002

She stared at it, the small, shining brass plaque in the midst of many more. 'I didn't realise he had any memorial at all. There's no grave; at least, so far as I know?' She looked at Harry appealingly, but he only smiled.

'That's for you to find out,' he said. 'And here's the start of your journey.' His voice was low, and yet, for once, she could hear him perfectly well. There was no shouting over here.

Laura traced the letters with her finger. They had become blurred with all the polishing; this was, it suddenly occurred to her, the only polished area in the whole club. The thought made her smile through the sudden mist of tears. Before she could stop herself, she had turned and, with a spontaneous sob, buried her face in Harry's shirt.

For a brief moment his arms closed around her; then, realising what she was doing, she shot her head up, so fast she caught his chin.

'Ow!'

'Sorry... I...' Laura was raking her hair, confused, but it wouldn't rake, having been pinned and sprayed up by Jay. It was absolutely solid. What had he used? Glue?

Harry was banging the soggy bar with his fist. 'Ron! Got any wine?'

'Red or white?' Ron roared back, without looking up.

'Rosé?' asked Laura, then watched apprehensively as Ron bent and scrabbled in the murky depths before straightening with two bottles in his hand. Her apprehension turned to horror as Ron poured some white into a glass, then added some red before twisting round and shoving it at her. 'Here you are,' he said. 'Hand-curated rosé. Cuvée Ronaldo.'

There was an appreciative guffaw from round the bar. Laura was uncomfortably aware of being the centre of attention again. Had everyone watched her find her father?

'People usually drink the hard stuff in here,' Harry explained. 'Or lager. No steampunk ale or boutique gins at the NDY.'

Laura decided to get over herself. When you'd come back from some ISIS-held hellhole, you probably didn't want hipsters and craft beer. Conscious of Ron's sardonic gaze, she took a large swig of the hand-curated rosé. It wasn't as bad as she'd imagined.

'Delicious,' she said. Ron nodded, there were smiles from round the bar and Laura sensed she had passed some kind of test.

She turned back to Harry, determined this time to get to the bottom of things. 'Which paper do you work for?'

But Harry was waving at someone on the far side of the bar. 'Back in a sec,' he said, and ducked into the crowd.

He touched her fingers as he went, and an electric judder of excitement passed through her. As her eyes followed him, she noted ruefully that the smartphone poking out of his pocket was the same model as her own. She was possessed by a feeling of loss and longing, which ended in a sudden jerk of panic.

Lulu! She had forgotten all about her. She hadn't seen her for ages. And she was supposed to be looking after her.

She looked around wildly. There was no piled-up blonde hair, no flash of sunglasses. The sulphurous lights from the bar glowed on the billowing fug of cigarette smoke. That the prevailing law didn't apply here made sense, if you had half the government turning up.

Suddenly Laura spotted her charge. On the other side of the room, thank God. Where she had made a new friend, it seemed. Clamped round her was the arm of someone in vast mirror shades and a denim jacket so blazing with diamante that none of the actual denim was visible. On the someone's arm was a huge status watch. It had about three dials and you could see the diamonds from where she stood.

Laura caught her breath. He looked like Vlad's worst nightmare, an absolute vision of rampant materialism. All her efforts to get Lulu out of the frying pan had resulted in her walking straight into the fire. She shoved her way through the crowd in panic. It took some doing, but eventually she reached the table. Lulu was in peals of laughter, clearly smitten. She looked up at Laura, eyes shining.

'Laura, is South'n Fried. Is rapper. Own Motherf****r Records, big label, hmmm?'

Laura looked into the mirror shades and could see nothing but her own suspicious face. She forced a smile. 'Hi.' The shades nodded and a row of teeth were revealed: one gold and another in which a blood-red ruby flashed. Laura swallowed.

'He say my shirt is jiggy,' Lulu added proudly. 'He say that we vibe.'

Laura tried to look as if she knew what any of this meant, and that she shared Lulu's view it was the best possible news. She tried not to stare at the row of glittering skull rings on South'n Fried's knuckles.

'Says he has always wanted meet me,' Lulu burbled happily. 'Says I woman after own heart.'

Laura's eye caught the diamond dollar signs in South'n Fried's ear cuff.

'Father he is in prison. Is sad, hmmm? Drugs.' Lulu shook her head sorrowfully.

She had to act. 'Look, I hate to break up the party, but we'd better go, Lulu.'

Lulu twisted her head from side to side. 'Want to stay. South'n Fried tell me about his new album, *Nasty Ho*.'

'Er...'

Someone now tapped on Laura's shoulder. 'Sorry about just then,' said Harry. 'I had to speak to someone about a pair of magazine journalists from some stupid glossy. They've got themselves into a lot of trouble.'

Hazza and Jazzy, she guessed. The 'stupid glossy' bit stung. 'What's going to happen to them?'

Harry raised his eyebrows. 'Could be a prison sentence. North Korea in particular takes that sort of thing pretty seriously.'

'But it's only fashion,' Laura exclaimed.

The long grey eyes narrowed. 'What do you know about it? Oh wait. *Society*. That's your magazine, isn't it?'

'Not any more,' Laura said, but didn't offer an explanation. Harry didn't have the monopoly on being mysterious.

He looked at her curiously and added that Carinthia was planning to launch a campaign using posters of Hazza and Jazzy's faces behind prison bars fashioned from lipsticks. 'She's going to organise all-night vigils at the Chiltern Firehouse.'

Laura tried not to laugh. 'Will that help?'

'I doubt it.'

'Harry Scott!' A blonde woman in a fitted white shirt and red lipstick, her hair drawn back in a loose chignon, appeared from nowhere and planted a kiss on his cheek. 'I've been looking for you.'

'Ellen!' Harry turned to Laura. 'This is Ellen O'Hara. Just back from Mosul. This is Laura Lake.'

Ellen didn't look just back from Mosul. She looked just back from a Ralph Lauren fashion shoot. But she was older than she first appeared, Laura realised. Much older. Her hair was grey and the blonde streaks at the front were caused by nicotine.

Ellen drew on her cigarette. 'Any relation to Peter Lake?'

'My father,' Laura said with a burst of pride.

'You a journalist too?'

'Yes,' Laura said stoutly.

The other woman smiled an unexpectedly warm smile. 'Good, he'd be proud. It's the only thing. Who do you work for?'

She should have expected the question of course. But Laura was stumped for an answer. She found herself looking helplessly at Harry, who, without missing a beat, said 'Freelancing.'

Ellen nodded approvingly. 'Just like your father, eh?'

'Did you know him?' Laura asked, grabbing the chance.

Ellen smiled a red-lipsticked smile. 'I did.'

Laura's heart soared. Harry was right. Her journey towards her father was beginning. 'Can you tell me about him?'

Harry stepped in. 'Not now, Laura. Ellen and I have to talk.'

'Give me a call sometime. Here.' Ellen handed over a card, then turned back to Harry. They began a conversation in low voices. Laura was relieved Ellen hadn't enquired further. Harry had saved her from the necessity of revealing that her father's derring-do legacy was being honoured with an article about three increasingly preposterous weddings. One of which she hadn't even managed to get to. Still, baby steps, as people liked to say.

She now remembered Lulu and turned back to where they were sitting. But Lulu was no longer there. Nor was the proud proprietor of Motherf****r Records.

Pure fear juddered through Laura. She peered desperately about. There was no sign of them anywhere. This time they really had gone.

Harry was still deep in discussion with Ellen. She did not dare interrupt them: Ellen was talking rapidly, her expression terrifyingly intense. Harry's head was bent intently towards her. He had, Laura thought gloomily, more important things to think about than her. And she, for her part, had responsibilities.

Oh, where was Lulu? Vlad was going to be furious. She'd really messed up this time.

Chapter Twenty-Six

In the end, there had been no need to panic. Vlad had been waiting just round the corner, with Lulu and South'n Fried in the back. Laura had spent the whole journey home berating herself for not having said goodbye to Harry. And not just that; what with the excitement about her father and the general surprise of the club, her discovery that Sebastian Hunter was involved with the Creake Castle wedding had gone unreported too. She really was a hopeless journalist. And without her phone she had no way of reaching him either.

Inspiration struck her: she could contact him via the club. He would still be there; she could ring up Ron. Get Harry to the phone. Lulu handed over her smartphone willingly enough, but none of the searches Laura entered brought up anything about an NDY Club. It seemed that, so far as the internet at least was concerned, the place she had just been in simply didn't exist.

But it did exist. What was more, it had her father's memorial plaque in it. She had met someone who had known him. Laura rummaged in her pocket and brought out Ellen's card. She dialled the number, but it only rang out. Ellen did not seem to have an answerphone. Her spirits slumped. She had seemed so near to something, but now it had disappeared. If Harry's only purpose had been to show her the club, and reclaim his jacket, she might not see him again after this.

And she wanted to. Very much, and not only because of jewel thieves or her father. Again and again, in the course of the sleepless nights that followed, she saw his deep-set dark eyes, heard his low, amused voice, relived the moment when he'd taken her in his arms. It had been a mere few seconds, and such chaste seconds too – he had not even kissed her. But it seemed to Laura that there had been more genuine feeling in those seconds, more of a real connection, than in any of the exhausting physical encounters with Caspar.

Harry's quizzical smile, keen grey eyes and calm, measured voice now figured in her dreams.

A dreary hopelessness afflicted Laura in the days after the visit to the NDY Club. At first she thought it was flu from her dip in the lake, but the heaviness she felt failed to develop into the usual symptoms. Nonetheless, her energy and determination had deserted her. The days were counting down to the Creake Castle wedding, but she felt completely powerless regarding it. What could she do if there was another robbery? She was probably wrong about Hunter anyway. Only Harry would have believed her, and she was unable to contact him.

And as for its potential as a feature subject, Clemency would long ago have scooped her. She'd probably already been to the nuptials of an alternate set of Turkey Toffs, and found an arty Amy Bender one into the bargain. All three modern society marriages would be done, dusted and on their way to being bound between glossy covers. Carinthia would have moved on to some burning new topic.

One small comfort was that no one was yet writing stories about Lulu and South'n Fried. If that ever hit the press, it would be a disaster. The rapper's influence on Lulu had been dramatic. She had changed overnight.

A week after the tumultuous evening at NDY, Laura sat alone at the breakfast island, turning over the paper. She wondered if it was the absence of Lulu that was getting her down.

Vlad entered the room. They looked at each other. 'They got away okay?' Laura asked.

The butler nodded.

'Let's just hope no one sees them.' Laura groaned and rubbed her eyes. 'Why don't you have a coffee?' she added. Vlad was looking drained. Recent events had taken their toll on them both. As the butler pulled out a chair, Laura reflected that, apart from in the driver's seat of the limo, she had never before seen Vlad sitting down. It was an indication of the extremity of the situation.

'I still can't get over it,' she said.

Vlad silently raised a cup to her lips.

'It was all such lies,' Laura went on. 'A complete fabrication. Utter deceit.'

Vlad's shoulders heaved in a sigh.

'He believed everything he read in *Society*. Those captions that went with the pictures. About how she was a simple soul at heart. Wanting to stuff cushions, play tiddlywinks and run along the ringing beach.'

The butler slowly shook her head.

'And the great irony of it all, of course, is that now she actually does. Because he does.'

Laura had thought that her experiences with Lulu and Amy Bender had given her an insight into what it meant to be famous. The knowledge that all was not what it seemed. But that was before she had met South'n Fried and discovered that below the diamanted, designer-clad carapace of the Motherf****r Records front man there beat the heart of a devoted homebody and keen crafter.

This aspect of his personality had been for years carefully hidden. As his rap empire had grown and flourished, his preference for flower-pressing over Ferraris had been determinedly disguised. His many social media sites showed his custom-built David Linley sneaker closet and collection of high-end timepieces. He spent as much time as he could bear to in penthouses and yachts and was regularly photographed with the world's most famous and beautiful women. And yet he had, South'n Fried told Laura, despaired of ever meeting a woman who shared his true passions.

And then, in a private jet taking him to the launch of a range of watches for dogs, he had read the *Society* interview with Lulu. A flame had been lit in his heart and that flame was now a fire.

Lulu, for her part, was just happy to be loved. And that South'n Fried adored her blazed from every crystal on his jacket, glowed from his gold teeth and shone from his every gleaming pair of mirror shades.

The two of them were out shopping at that very moment. But not among the glittering designer stores of Bond Street, Manhattan or Rodeo Drive. They were in the Brent Cross Hobby World megastore, where they were buying scrapbooks and unvarnished frames on to which they would stick the seashells they'd recently collected in Wales.

They were, of course, both heavily disguised. Lulu was doubly unrecognisable in flat shoes and no sunglasses, while South'n Fried wore chain-store jeans and that eternal trope of the fashionably clueless, a Ramones T-shirt. These precautions were about more than merely being recognised, however. South'n Fried's fans ran into the millions and all of them believed he was a bad-boy rapper with a heart full of anger and a mouth full of swearwords. If they discovered that he preferred to spend his nights playing Bananagrams, there would be uproar. There was, Laura knew, a plan for South'n Fried to come clean eventually, and for him and Lulu to launch their Motherf****r Children's Foundation. But not quite yet.

Not while he and Lulu were having so much undisturbed fun below the radar. No one expected to find them on the tops of hills in Derbyshire or paddleboarding in small Cornish coves. And so, even though they were there, no one did.

Laura finished her coffee. It was all very well, Lulu being so happy, but it left a vacuum. Her role in the household had been to protect its mistress and make sure no one with avaricious intentions got near her. This task had been completed, and Laura was now redundant.

Perhaps now was the time to return to Paris. She had had many adventures but still had no job and, in real terms, nowhere to live. Lulu had assured her that she could stay in the house as long as she liked, but Laura didn't want to hang around like some twittering retainer in a Jane Austen novel. She was a woman of action, but the action was now elsewhere.

As Vlad exited the kitchen with a bottle of Autoglym – she

spent a lot of time polishing the cars these days – Laura stood up. She would ring Mimi. After the madness of the past weeks, the sanity of her grandmother would be a welcome relief.

The phone in the Montmartre flat rang and rang. And rang and rang. Anxiety clutched at Laura. Had something happened? She was about to give up when finally Mimi answered, sounding rather out of breath.

'I've just run up the stairs,' she said.

'What? But Mimi, you should take the lift. You're over ninety.'

'As you were always reminding me.'

'What?'

'When you were here. Always fussing.'

Laura was hurt. She was only being a good granddaughter. 'I'm coming back,' she announced, her resolve now redoubled. If her grandmother was running up the stairs at her age, it was just as well she was going home.

She had expected Mimi to sound pleased. The last thing she'd anticipated was that she would say, flatly and in a tone that brooked no argument, 'You can't.'

'Can't?' Laura repeated. 'Why not?'

'Because I won't be there. I'm going on a year-long round-the-world cruise with the rest of the Fat Four.'

'What's brought this on?'

'I want to travel. See the world.'

'But won't it exhaust you?'

'Not at all,' Mimi averred stoutly. 'Since Ernest and I started jogging round Montmartre, I feel like a teenager again.'

'Jogging round Montmartre...?' Laura faltered, realising that life at the Paris end had changed beyond all recognition.

But knowing Mimi as she did, she also realised there was no point arguing. Besides, now she had her breath back, her grandmother did sound remarkably bright. 'But I can still come back, though? The flat will still be there.' And empty for a year, which had its advantages.

She sensed hesitation in Montmartre. 'Not exactly,' Mimi said cagily.

'What? You haven't sold it, Mimi?' Laura was horrified. The view over the front to Sacré-Coeur! The view over the back of the whole of the city! She had grown up in the flat, it was her life. She felt she was about to cry.

'Not sold. Rented. While I'm away.'

'You've rented it out for a year?' Laura gasped.

'Correct. Mademoiselle Burgwinkle has been very helpful.'

'You've rented it to Paradise in Paris?'

'Certainly. You always said that it charged the most exorbitant prices of any of them.'

Laura was angry now. 'You never told me! You never even thought to consult me!'

'*Mais, chérie*, remember what I've always told you. The Parisienne should always be surprising.'

For the first time in her life Laura was uninterested in her grandmother's stock of wisdom. 'It's a surprise, I'll give you that. What am I supposed to do while you're away? Where will I live?'

'You'll think of something,' was Mimi's airy answer. 'The Parisienne is always resourceful. I must go, *chérie*. Ernest is here.'

The line went dead. That, it seemed, was that.

As always when she was disturbed, Laura went to one of the windows and peered out across the trees of Hyde Park. It was a beautiful bright summer's day and she could see, between the leaves, people walking along the paths, lying on the grass, pausing in the gardens to sniff the flowers. In the distance, the Serpentine was busy with rowing boats and pedalos. It seemed to Laura that everyone was busy and having fun. Except for her. What on earth was she going to do?

There was a knock on her door.

'Come in,' called Laura.

Vlad appeared, phone in hand. 'A call for you, madam.'

Laura took it, puzzled. Who knew the number here?

Harry, it turned out. Her relief at hearing his voice was such that actual tears brimmed in her eyes. 'Thank God! I need to talk to you!'

'And I you,' replied the familiar, measured voice.

Laura felt suddenly energised, as if a switch had been flicked. All her lassitude evaporated and she felt newly engaged and focused. 'It's about a wedding this weekend. At Creake Castle.'

'What a coincidence,' Harry said lightly. 'I've been invited to it, as it happens. I can take a guest and I thought you might like to come.'

'I didn't know you knew the Scremings,' Laura said.

'You'd be surprised who I know,' was Harry's rejoinder, before he rang off. Laura danced around her bedroom, reviewing the instructions. He would pick her up on Friday afternoon. They would arrive at Creake Castle in time for a grand dinner in the Great Hall. She felt wild with excitement, even though Harry, rather crushingly, seemed to doubt her theory about Sebastian Hunter. 'A possibility,' was all he had said.

'You're not still thinking it was Caspar? He's not even going to this one,' Laura challenged, even though she had not heard from Caspar since the Skinner–Loone wedding.

But that was not surprising if he had been calling the phone at the bottom of the lake.

Another possibility, of course, was that she could now re-engage with the New Society Weddings feature. She had been given the perfect opportunity. But in her heart Laura knew that her excitement was about more than that. What was making her heart thunder and her stomach swoop with butterflies was the prospect of being alone with Harry all the way to Norfolk. She could barely wait for the days to pass.

'Just look at it!' Laura exclaimed to Vlad, calling up the picture of the castle on the butler's phone. The only fly in the ointment of her happiness was the fact she still had no phone of her own. All her observations about the wedding would have to be written down, and there would be no photographs.

'I recall it as most impressive, madam.'

'You've been there?'

'One of my former employers was a regular guest at Lord Screming's shoots. I became reasonably well acquainted with Creake Castle as a result.'

Laura was seized with curiosity as to whom Vlad had previously worked for. But Vlad was evasive on the subject and there were more pressing matters to sort out.

'What should I wear?' The few things Lulu had given her wouldn't see her through an event on this scale. There was the department-store-sized wardrobe, of course, but Laura didn't like to help herself. Lulu was away camping with South'n Fried, an experience which seemed certain to push their fledgling relationship to its limit.

'It would be my pleasure to look out some suitable attire for you, madam.'

'Oh, Vlad, would you?'

Vlad would, and had. Now perfectly wrapped in tissue paper and placed carefully inside a shining Vuitton weekend bag, the suitable attire sat by Laura's feet as she waited excitedly for Harry outside Lulu's gate. She went over it in her mind. For the dinner, Vlad had selected the glamorous red satin sheath Lulu had pressed on Laura the first time they met. For the wedding itself she had picked a perfect pink Jackie O suit. For the party after the wedding, a simple but astonishingly elegant little black dress had been chosen. Vlad had even thought about the journey; Laura's jeans and T-shirt were all very well, it seemed, but only with an Armani jacket over the top of them, a pair of huge Chanel shades and some patent Dior pumps. Shoes and jewellery for the other outfits had also been packed. She was ready; fabulously so. Her eyes fixed impatiently on the street corner, willing Harry's ancient Golf to round it.

Was this it? No, this was something sleek and grey. A convertible sports car with headlights like long eyes and a grille like a silver smile. It looked familiar, but so did the young man behind the wheel, his dark hair shining in the sun. Rumpled dark hair, dangling into his deep-set eyes. 'Harry?'

He leapt out, walked round and opened the passenger door for her. He looked, she thought, utterly delicious in jeans and a pink gingham shirt. A battered bag covered in aeroplane labels lay on the back seat next to a top hat and the inevitable black leather jacket.

'My God, it's an Aston Martin.' Busy admiring Harry, she had only just noticed.

'I borrowed it from a friend.'

'James Bond?' Laura quipped.

Harry did not answer directly, and Laura thought of the NDY Club. The idea was not as far-fetched as all that.

She strapped herself in and gaily surveyed the car's polished walnut fascia. 'If I touch any of these knobs, will a machine gun come out of the exhaust?'

She reached out a hand, which he seized with unexpected force. 'Don't!'

Laura glanced at him in panic, but then his face cracked in a smile. His hand, gripping hers, felt warm and strong.

'Let's go,' he said. 'It's a long way to Norfolk.'

They drove up through the sunny park and past the white blocks of Bayswater. Laura stared out at Edgware Road, Camden Town and Finchley Road. 'What's so interesting?' Harry asked. He seemed amused, for some reason.

'Everything,' Laura said fervently. 'You're probably used to it, but to me every street corner in London tells a story.' The moment the words left her mouth she regretted them. How naïve she must sound.

'Spoken like a true journalist,' said Harry, and gave her a sidelong smile. This unexpected praise brought a bright flush of pleasure to her cheeks, as well as the awareness that this was an opening, an opportunity.

'Speaking of journalists,' she said, 'I tried to call Ellen. But I didn't get through.'

At the wheel, Harry's broad shoulders went up and down in a shrug. 'Keep trying.'

It wasn't quite the reply she had been hoping for. But Laura pressed on. 'Sebastian Hunter.'

'What about him?'

Laura blinked. 'He's why we're going to this wedding, isn't he? Your investigation?'

'And your article. Looked like you needed a break with it.'
She stared at him, stung and gratified in equal measure.'
'But how…?'
'Rupert was at school with me.'
'Must have been a posh school,' Laura observed, once she had got over the double surprise.

He glanced at her, eyebrow raised. 'So what if it was? You went to a pretty posh one yourself.'

'Yes, but on a scholarship,' Laura retorted, before it occurred to her to wonder how he knew this. 'Which none of the other girls ever let me forget,' she added hotly.

'Me too,' Harry said. 'Got my head flushed down the loo, was locked naked out of my bedroom with my pubes sprayed blue, you name it. Rupe was the only one who was ever nice to me.'

He was grinning ruefully, but Laura felt her heart contract. It was hard, yet just about possible, to imagine the capable Harry as a small, scared, bullied boy. Just as she herself had been a small, scared, bullied girl. She felt a rush of fellow feeling, as well as being impressed by Rupert's kindness. There was clearly more to some Turkey Toffs than just red trousers and huge teeth.

'I'm looking forward to tomorrow,' she said. 'I love a good wedding.'

'You're a romantic.'

'I guess so.' Did that sound silly to the hard man of journalism?

'Me too,' Harry said unexpectedly.

'Really?' Laura looked at him teasingly. 'You want the house in the country, the wife and the dogs, the heir and the spare?'

He laughed. 'Not that sort of romantic. That's all completely unrealistic.'

'Is it?' She felt a faint pinch of disappointment.

'Well, maybe not for some. But I wouldn't want it.'

'No?'

'No. My sort of romantic is probably just believing that people aren't all that bad.'

She glanced at him in surprise. 'After all the bullying?'

'That was ages ago. And I've seen much worse since. Bullying on a major, international scale. But I've seen plenty of good things too. Courage. Generosity. Love,' Harry added, before putting his foot down and making the car zoom along a stretch of empty road. The wind buffeted Laura's head and rushed loudly in her ears. Further conversation was impossible.

Instead, she looked about her at the wide, flat landscape. The sky was huge and blue and billowed with white clouds. There were mighty oaks, rolling fields and distant churches. It was beautiful, like the background to a Gainsborough painting. Was this Norfolk? Land of the Turkey Toffs? Scene of the Creake Castle wedding, at which anything might happen?

Chapter Twenty-Seven

Creake Castle was even huger in real life than it had looked on its website. It reared up like a cliff above Great Screming, whose ancient buildings cringed at its feet like the generations of vassals who had doubtless lived in them. The castle towers were vast, grey, battlemented and punctured with arrow-slits.

'Well?' prompted Harry, as Laura had gone rather quiet.

'It's a bit...'

'Scary?' Harry flashed her a grin from the wheel.

Laura raised her chin. She wouldn't be intimidated by a mere building, however dark and grim. Besides, this was 2017; the place couldn't possibly be as frightening inside as it looked from outside. 'Feudal.'

'It's that alright. It's not long since any man who wanted to marry one of the Creake daughters had to sling her over the back of a horse and ride with her to the castle to ask the Earl's permission. In fact, Rupert had to do that only last week.'

'You're joking!' Laura was wide-eyed.

'Hang on, we're going over the drawbridge. Don't look down.'

Laura did, of course, and felt her insides lurch. From either side of a wooden bridge that seemed too narrow for the car, a fifty-foot drop plunged to a moat. It was full of dark green water which it seemed the sun never touched. Horribly easy to imagine the bottom of it littered with the skeletons of the family's enemies, Laura thought with a shudder.

A portcullis was raised at the bridge's other end, its sharp-pointed prongs facing downwards. She held her breath as they went under it. They drove on into a huge passage, the Aston Martin bumping on the cobbles.

'Feeling the atmosphere?' Harry asked, his tone faintly teasing.

Laura gave him her bravest grin. 'I can practically see the monster and I just know there are yards of mysterious tunnels underneath carved with the initials of forgotten prisoners.'

'You're spot on. The monster lives in one of the towers, apparently. The heir to the title gets to meet it on his twenty-first birthday and after that, they say, he never smiles again.'

Laura had burst out laughing before she realised Harry looked entirely serious. But he couldn't possibly mean it. Could he?

They drove on into a large inner courtyard where 'Wedding Guest Parking' signs, a reminder they were here for a happy occasion, cheered Laura up slightly. Other people had evidently arrived; a long row of cars was parked below the battlemented walls. Harry slid into a spot between a Porsche and a battered Land Rover.

He was out and retrieving his bag from the boot while Laura still sat in the passenger seat. She jumped as his smiling face appeared suddenly at the window. 'Come on! You're not scared, are you?'

Laura's hope that the inside would be better than the outside faded as they approached a vast and ancient oak door bristling with studs at the top of a flight of mossy steps. Harry yanked at a rusting chain, which set something jangling deep within the fortress. He then pushed open the door to reveal an entrance hall hung with huge paintings of dying stags and bleeding pheasants reminiscent of Caspar and his National Gallery-inspired sex positions. She snorted with sudden laughter.

Harry looked at her in surprise. 'What's so funny?'

'Nothing. My God, look at all these guns.' Between the bleeding and dying animals, weapons of every size were mounted in concentric circles on chicken wire. There was enough hardware to supply a small army.

'Lord Screming's one of the best shots in the country,' Harry told her. 'The Screming sandwich is to be avoided at all costs.'

'Why? What's it got in it?' A lot of venison, she imagined.

'It's when you've got Lord Screming shooting on one side of you and his brother blasting away on the other.'

'I'll watch out for that then.'

Laura, ever the optimist, was clinging to the possibility that a friendly, round-faced housekeeper might yet appear to dispel the place's forbidding spirit. She now conclusively abandoned this as a bent creature with fearsome sideburns and snaggle teeth appeared and introduced itself as Fogg, the castle steward. 'Follow me,' it coughed, and Laura and Harry obeyed, shadowing the retainer's unsteady path up a wide flight of stone stairs on whose every tread a huge and forbidding suit of armour stood sentinel. Laura studiously avoided looking either into the dark maws of the metal helmets or at the sharp edges of the enormous halberds held in the rusty gauntlets.

It was a relief – of a sort – to reach a passage lined with worn carpet. Until, that was, Laura noticed that the metal objects arranged in circular patterns on the walls were gruesome medieval artefacts which the Scremings of the time had obviously bought in bulk.

Dark oak-panelled doorways loomed between the maces, flails, thumbscrews and garrottes. Laura had wondered where the people from the row of cars were; hearing the sounds behind the doors, she knew the answer.

'There's only a bath!' exclaimed a gravelly, patrician, female voice. 'How are you supposed to wash your hair if there's no shower?'

More doors and more steps. Now they were following Fogg up a tight and uncarpeted stone spiral. Laura thought immediately of the winding staircase to Mimi's apartment, but there were no heartlifting views or reassuring smells of polish here. The way was shadowy and unlit, the air chill and damp.

Laura leaned into Harry. 'You were joking about that monster?'

He shot her an apologetic glance. 'I wish I could say I was.'

As Fogg stopped before a crumbling wooden door and fished out a rattling bunch of black iron keys, it took all Laura's courage not to turn tail and run out.

The door creaked open. That this was the first time in

a while was suggested by the blast of stale air that greeted them. A four-poster bed of carved oak hung with dark red curtains seemed to be the only thing in the room apart from a mullioned window set with three diamond-paned casements. Before disappearing, Fogg plonked Laura's bag down on the faded cushion of the windowseat, where it sent a large cloud of dust into the air.

'Cosy,' Laura remarked brightly, after they had both finished coughing.

The bed was big, but not wide. Two people sleeping in it would be very close indeed, particularly given the dip in the middle of the sagging mattress. The heat rose in Laura's face and anticipation twisted in her tummy. For the first time since entering the castle, she felt cheerful.

Harry did not seem to have noticed the sleeping arrangements. He was reading something on his phone.

'What are we going to do?' Laura asked, rather breathlessly.

Harry's eyes remained on his screen. In an absent tone he asked, 'About what?'

Laura gestured to the bed. Then, as he still did not look up, she said, ironically, 'The bed?'

'Oh, that. You can have it. I've got to go somewhere.'

'Go somewhere?' Laura repeated, astonished. 'But we've just got here. I'm your guest. Your fellow investigator, even,' she added wryly.

'Thing is, it's not the only investigation I'm working on.' Harry snapped his phone away. 'And something's come up on one of the others. Sorry.'

'So… you're leaving.' Laura swallowed. And leaving her in this creepy place, more to the point.

'But I'll be back. Don't worry.'

Laura was furious but could see from Harry's set face

that venting her irritation would not change his mind. She confined herself to an angry toss of her hair. Fine, then, if the great reporter was quitting the scene, she would just have to solve the mystery on her own. And if there was no mystery after all, she would at least have an article to show for it.

She unzipped her bag to unpack, before realising there was nowhere to put anything. Perhaps it was better to leave everything folded perfectly in tissue paper, as Vlad had left it, and get things out as and when she needed them.

Harry had disappeared with a creak of the door, but now it creaked again, and he was back.

'Sorry,' he said. 'Meant to give you this. You might find it useful.' He pressed something small and silver into her palm.

Laura looked down and took in a sharp breath. It was a smartphone. A top-of-the-range one, exactly like the one Vlad had given her and Clemency had thrown in the water. Was this, then, Harry's way of handing over responsibility for the investigation to her? Or was it a gesture with another meaning altogether? Laura tapped the screen and frowned at the image that appeared. Who were these ridiculous people? Then she recognised the selfie of herself and Caspar waiting to be summoned by the Fluid Druid. It was the last picture she had taken. It was her own phone!

'But it was at the bottom of the lake,' she stammered, looking up to see that Harry had gone. She felt less cross with him now, though. She had no idea how, but all her notes and photos had been restored. Her article would be complete, in all three of its glorious parts. Now she had her faithful reporting tool, there would be no stopping her. She would explore. Take notes. Set the scene.

She hurried down the spiral stairs and along the carpeted corridors, snapping the best of the flails as she went. Mere words would not do justice to that kind of detail, and here was a stag's head, its mount reading 'Loch Desolate, 1914', practically falling off a wall visibly shining with damp. And what was this? Laura paused by a tall glass-fronted case. Within was something long, half of it a piece of dirty white fabric stained with brown, half some sort of boot. 'Leg Formerly the Property of General Clovis Screming. Shot off at Waterloo' read a small brass plaque attached to the box's polished wooden top. *Click*, went Laura. Click, click.

At the bottom of the great main staircase, she paused. She could see into a huge room with a carved wooden ceiling. Faded tapestries and gloomy paintings filled the walls. What light could struggle in through the murky stained-glass windows illuminated a vast wooden table almost audibly groaning under the silverware, glasses and candelabras crowding its surface. At the distant end of the table were two people in green aprons wielding rulers. They appeared to be measuring the distance between each setting.

Click! Laura pushed the button on the smartphone screen. It was amazing, the confidence it gave her. And it had transformed her surroundings at a stroke. The castle was no longer creepy, it was wonderful material.

She shot the dead pheasants, the guns and the gloomiest of several gold-framed ancestors. A couple of selfies with the suits of armour and that was enough interior for the moment. Time to get some outside shots.

Maybe in the town. A few local images – and images of locals – to set the scene and build up the pre-wedding atmosphere.

Chapter Twenty-Eight

Laura wandered down the main street of Great Screming. In her newly positive mood it seemed even more comically Gothic than the castle. Amusing photo opportunities positively abounded. Posters for 'The Great Screming Ghost Walk' peeled off charity-shop windows. There was a grim-looking pub called The Poor Strugglers, its sign showing a line of condemned men dangling from the gallows like Christmas baubles. 'Family Hostile,' warned a blackboard outside. 'No Hipsters.'

Dark and sinister passages between the buildings had discouraging names like Gibbet Alley and Execution Lane. For all the bright blue sky and sunshine, there hung over Great Screming an air of ghastly retribution. Even the picturesque cobbled marketplace with its ancient cross had a whiff of witch-burning about it.

At the top of the town stood a dark church with a sharp steeple and spiked Gothic towers which jabbed the sky. Guessing that this must be the scene of tomorrow's wedding, Laura headed towards it. There might be photo opportunities there too; flowers being arranged by apple-cheeked old ladies and the like. Apple-cheeked and eagle-eyed, presumably, given that reaching the church meant risking the road ringing the marketplace, which seemed to be a racing circuit for the local disaffected youth. Cars were appearing at high speed from nowhere and Laura only narrowly escaped being run down. She reached the church gate in one piece, but it was a damned close-run thing, as the Duke of Wellington had observed after Waterloo. Perhaps he had observed it to General Clovis Screming.

Not entirely auspiciously, perhaps, the church was dedicated to St Jude, the patron saint of hopeless causes. It was built in the same black stone as the rest of Great Screming and exuded much of the same foreboding. The clock had stuck at five minutes to midnight and a squawking family of raptors had set up home in the tower. Laura walked up the path, which was paved with flattened gravestones; more gravestones lurched at crazy angles to either side. *Click*.

The iron-bound door was firmly shut. But not locked, Laura found, as it burst unexpectedly open following her shove, propelling her into the shadowy interior. The cold was bone-chilling, and the place dark and unlit. No apple-cheeked ladies seemed to be present, but as her eyes got used to the crepuscular conditions, Laura spotted something moving in the gloom. In the nave a pair of ancient crones were bent over the pews. Laura, finger poised over her phone camera, approached. The crones were muttering irritatedly to each other as they attempted, not entirely successfully, to attach bunches of daisies to the pew ends.

Laura watched them for a while as they tried to stick the weak little stems on with Sellotape. Then, as neither took the slightest notice of her, she cleared her throat. 'Is that for the wedding tomorrow?'

One of the crones looked up. She appeared to have just one working eye, which regarded Laura malevolently from within a mass of wrinkles. 'And what business be that of yourn?'

'I'm going to be there,' Laura replied brightly. 'And while I think what you're doing looks very nice, I don't think the daisies are really working. Why don't I go and pick you something a bit longer-stemmed? Scabious or valerian or something. You'd still have all that spirit-of-the-hedgerow thing going on, but it would be much easier to work with.'

The other crone looked up. 'Spirit of they 'edgerow?' she echoed in a gravelly hiss. 'And what might a flighty piece like you know about they ancient wisdom of they woods and fields?' Another single eye, more malevolent even than the first crone's, glittered from within its sagging folds.

The Fluid Druid and his antics skittered across Laura's mind, but she dismissed them. 'Nothing,' she said nervously. 'Nothing at all. Just trying to help.'

'Daisies be they Creake family flower,' said the first crone. 'It be they flower that Sir Fredegonde de Creke, what came over with they Conqueror, picked when first he came to they parts and fell to his knees and built they castle.'

'Great,' said Laura. 'Good for him.' She left them to it and hurried towards the chancel.

Within a stone chapel separated off by a stone screen, two rows of medieval tombs squared up to each other. Shafts of light fell like sword blades through the heavily leaded stained glass. Laura started to examine the carved stone figures, their heads lying on stone cushions decorated with stone tassels. They were all Creakes, or de Crekes, many of whom had been present at some of history's greatest rumbles. Small framed paragraphs propped up on the tomb-tops told how those lying within had reported for duty at Crécy and Agincourt and both Bosworth and Flodden fields. And here was Fredegonde de Creke, daisy fan and founder of the dynasty, chainmailed legs crossed as if desperate for the loo, the pair of hounds at his feet making it seem as if he was wearing novelty dog-shaped slippers. And here, on the floor, was a tablet informing the visitor that General Clovis Screming, or three quarters of him at least, was interred in a tomb 'near this place'.

Interested as she was, Laura could not quite shake off the feeling that she was being watched.

But by whom? There was no one in the church apart from herself and the crones, who were still bickering in the nave. A cold hand now grasped Laura's shoulder. She gave a strangled scream and whirled round.

'Calm down, dear,' said a familiar voice. The familiar person it belonged to was wearing a red summer dress, white tennis pumps and a blue cotton jacket; amid the long-dead Creakes she seemed vividly colourful and alive.

'Georgia!' Laura gasped, hugely relieved. 'But what are you doing here?' she added, more cautiously. At least one possible reason had shot through her mind.

'Well, don't sound so suspicious!' Georgia exclaimed. 'Anyone would think I was up to no good. Actually, I was at school with Shit.'

'Shit?' Laura was still not entirely convinced. That Georgia was here seemed a coincidence, to say the least. The proof, of course, would be Caspar's presence as well.

'Sophy's nickname. As in Shit Creake. Which is appropriate, given everything that's going wrong.'

'Wrong?' Laura was watching Georgia's face carefully. 'What sort of wrong?' Was she about to mention some missing jewellery? If so, was this some sort of double-bluff?

'Well, there's the hog roast for starters.'

'Hog roast?'

'The one for the cringing peasantry tomorrow night. It's tradition after a Creake gets wed, apparently. But some local vegans are threatening to sue. Say it's infringing their human rights. And now Shit's dress has gone wrong.'

Laura rummaged in her memory. 'The one based on a painting by John Singer Sargent?'

'That was the idea.' Georgia groaned. 'But the designer looked at the wrong painting and based it on the family Picasso. The sleeves are coming out of the skirt, the neckline's round the ankles and the whole thing's back to front. They've got some couturier coming from London to sort it out, but I don't get the impression they're Coco Chanel.'

Laura's distrust of Georgia was fading. This all sounded crazy, but authentic. 'Poor Sh… I mean Sophy, doesn't seem to be having much luck.'

'No, you'd almost think someone was trying to ruin it for her,' Georgia agreed cheerfully. 'It'll be a miracle if she gets to church in one piece. What are you doing here, anyway?'

Laura blushed as she scrabbled for an answer. 'An, um, friend brought me.'

'Oh yes?' Georgia's eyes were dancing and her tone was teasing.

'Not that sort of friend,' Laura insisted.

'No?' Georgia's head was on one side, her pixie face disbelieving.

'Anyway, he's had to, um, leave.'

'Leave? Leave you here on your own, you mean?' Georgia looked astonished, but then grinned. 'Oh, I get it.'

'You do?' It was more than she did, Laura thought.

'You've had a row!' Georgia pronounced triumphantly. 'Go on, admit it. You've had a lovers' tiff!'

Laura shook her head indignantly. 'How's Caspar anyway?' she asked, deep crimson with embarrassment.

'Don't try to change the subject,' Georgia admonished.

'I'm not, I want to know.'

'You mean you haven't heard?'

Laura's suspicions came instantly roaring back. 'So he's here as well?' She knew it! The Bonnie and Clyde of society weddings were about to strike again!

Georgia gave a bark of sardonic laughter. 'You must be joking.'

Laura stared. This was not the reply she had expected.

'Seriously? You really don't know?'

'Know what?' Laura's heart was thumping. Had Caspar been arrested? Was that why Harry had had to leave suddenly?

'Got time for a coffee? You'll need to be sitting down.'

In the Great Screming Costa, Georgia brought her up to speed. The film that Laura had seen on Lulu's phone, of Caspar pushing Orlando Chease in the lake, had been viewed by millions around the globe. More significantly, it had been viewed by the 007 powers that be. Whether Orlando Chease had ever seriously been in the running for the role remained unclear. But what was crystal clear was that Caspar Honeyman had now landed it.

'Seriously?' Laura gazed at Georgia with wide, amazed eyes. Could she have been more wrong? Caspar was not an international criminal mastermind, he was the new James Bond.

'They thought he looked hot shoving Orlando in, apparently. And that Orlando looked, well, less hot. Especially with his bald patch showing.'

Laura shook her head. She almost felt sorry for Orlando. He'd lost his famous girlfriend, the role of a life-time and his dignity all at the same time. She wondered which loss meant the most. Probably not Hudson Grater, who had since got through an astronaut and a senator and had released a top-selling single, 'I Thought You Had Hair', which was widely seen as a dig at Chease.

'That's amazing. Caspar must be thrilled. How exciting for you both.'

It was the wrong thing to say. Georgia's expression had darkened. The spoon in her glass of mint tea rattled against the sides as she stirred. 'We've consciously uncoupled. He dumped me when he got the Bond job. No doubt Hudson Grater will be after him now. Stand by for some globally syndicated spontaneous shots of him walking on some windswept beach with her, her agent, her PR people and her security detail.'

Laura laughed.

'As it happens,' Georgia added, 'I've been seeing Orlando again. My kiss of life at that wedding reminded him of what he'd been missing.' Her eyes shot to her watch. 'Omigod, we'd better be getting back. It'll be time for the dinner before we know it. Have you seen that hall? Reminds me of college. Hoorays throwing bread rolls and sitting sideways on the benches pretending to row.' She shuddered.

'I wouldn't know,' Laura said, entirely without rancour. The more she heard about university, the more convinced she was that she had missed out on very little.

They walked back to the castle together. 'See you later,' Georgia trilled, disappearing down the corridor in the opposite direction. 'Watch out for that monster! It lives in one of the towers, supposedly.'

Laura had temporarily forgotten about the monster. But now, as she hurried past the dismembered leg and the instruments of torture on the walls, her earlier sense of foreboding returned with added force. Oh, why had Harry left her alone? Every alcove and passage seemed suddenly full of dreadful possibility. A door she was passing swung suddenly and violently open and Laura, suppressing a scream, shot behind a handily placed suit of armour. Heart thudding, she bent forward just enough to allow, over the top of a savage-looking axe, a view of whoever or whatever it was.

A heart-stopping sight met her apprehensive gaze. The creature standing on the worn corridor carpet was wearing a clinging black PVC minidress, vertiginous high heels and red fishnet tights. There was only one person Laura knew who went in for this sort of look. But what was Irina Pushamoff doing here?

Laura had barely framed the question before she recalled what Georgia had said about a couturier coming from London to reconfigure the Cubist wedding dress. A chill went down her spine. But surely – *surely* – that couturier was not Irina? Laura's sympathy for poor Sophy deepened further. Things were bad enough for her already; they were about to get even worse.

Irina was looking up and down the corridor. She seemed to be expecting someone, someone late, judging by her thunderous expression. She tottered back into her room and Laura was just about to emerge and escape when another figure appeared; again, someone she recognised. Sebastian Hunter's spiked white hair seemed almost to glow in the corridor's gloom. Shrinking back into the shadow of the axe edge, Laura watched him pace along the corridor and pause outside the door recently closed by Irina. He twisted the knob and pushed it open and she caught his angry expression in the light.

'That bloody reporter's here,' he complained to Irina, before the door slammed shut and the passage was enveloped in shadows once more.

Chapter Twenty-Nine

Laura scooted out of her hiding place and bolted back up the tower's stone steps. Her mind and heart were thundering. Any thoughts of a legendary ghoul had been conclusively displaced by this evidence of real-life evil. Irina and Sebastian were obviously working together; as, Laura now speedily worked out, they had been doing all along. She had actually seen them at *Call This Art?* and the Bender wedding, and while Irina did not seem to have been present at the Skinner–Loone nuptials, Laura remembered being almost certain that she had glimpsed Sebastian there, in the *Game of Thrones* dry ice among the trees. She had taken photographs at the time. Was he in them?

Once back in her room, Laura sat on the bed, swiping wildly at her phone. Here were some images of the castle and a couple of Great Screming. 'Family Hostile', 'No Hipsters'.

It was impossible not to smile, even in these circumstances, and Laura was grinning as the sequence of Mary-Bliss wedding pictures began.

Here were the shots of drifting mist between the trees, of gnarled and twisted trunks lit by faint beams of light. No people though. Laura was beginning to assume, dejectedly, that she had been mistaken about Sebastian after all, when her eye caught something. Hold on, wasn't that a person? She scrolled back and enlarged the image. Yes. Definitely not a trick of the light. A figure, tall and lean, wearing dark clothes. You couldn't make out its face, or whether it was male or female. But it had a man's wide shoulders, and there was something familiar about the way it stood. It also seemed to have white spiky hair. Laura looked carefully through the other Skinner–Loone pictures, searching for Irina. There was no sign of her, however. Not so much as a flash of pearlised rubber. Had Sebastian been working alone in Wiltshire, or had La Pushemoff been directing operations from elsewhere?

Laura took a deep breath and stared up at the room's cracked ceiling, liberally festooned with dusty webs. Oh, why wasn't Harry here? She had made a breakthrough and had no one to share it with, or, for that matter, any real idea of what to do next. Especially as the couple had rumbled that Harry was on their tail. 'That bloody reporter' obviously referred to him. Hastily, Laura composed a briefing and sent it.

It was now, as she raised her head from her screen, that Laura realised Harry must have come back after all. Things in the room had been moved. The clothes in her holdall looked rumpled, as if someone had rummaged through them. Crumpled tissue paper poked out. But why would Harry have done that? Why leave the Jackie O suit scrunched on the floor? Laura picked it up hurriedly, shaking it out and slipping it on to the hanger Vlad had provided. Oh, if only she were there too! What she would not give, Laura thought, for the butler's imperturbable presence.

Unless, of course, it was not Harry at all. Had Irina or Sebastian Hunter been in here? The thought of those bitten blue nails pawing through her things was a hideous one, and Laura pushed it away. She had to calm down, get a grip. Especially as she was now investigating alone. She had to keep a clear head.

The golden afternoon was coming gradually to an end. Rich sunshine slanted through the ancient window, throwing amber diamond shapes on the white wall. Laura yawned.

She was overwrought and needed a rest. There was time for one before the dinner, and by the time she woke up, Harry might have returned. He hadn't said he would, but she could always hope. An intense longing for him rippled through her. It wasn't just that she fancied him, although she did, and something rotten, she now had to accept. She also missed his calm strength, his unflappable authority. In this unnerving situation, he would know exactly what to do. He was a grown-up reporter, whereas she was just starting out and had already managed to end up out of her depth and facing two possibly dangerous adversaries.

Laura took a couple of deep breaths to steady herself and calm the thoughts which were galloping out of control. She could be imagining it all yet. The presence of Irina and Sebastian might just be coincidence, and the reporter reference could be something and nothing, possibly concerning the restyled dress.

She climbed on to the bed, which was every bit as uncomfortable as it looked. She shifted about, but getting rid of the lump shoving up into her shoulder only brought a new one pressing into her thigh. Nonetheless, Laura had always been a good sleeper and it did not take long for exhaustion to overwhelm her. Within seconds, the lumps notwithstanding, she was unconscious.

She awoke in the dark. But not just any dark, she realised, sitting up on the bed and looking nervously about her. This dark was of a density and blackness she had never experienced before. It was like having a bag over her head. Alarmed, she stood up and took some cautious steps forward, hands outstretched in the direction she thought was the wall. As her fingers made contact with something damp and crumbling, she felt for a light switch and found one. It flicked on, but nothing happened.

Was there a power cut in the castle? She felt her way to the window. Through the thick, wavy glass, against a night sky of inky blue, the castle's massive dark walls glittered here and there with yellow squares and arches. There was electricity elsewhere. Just not in her room.

She swallowed hard to force away the fear crowding in on her.

She could hardly be a derring-do journalist if she was afraid of the dark!

She tried to think logically. What time was it? She remembered the dinner; had it started? How was she to get dressed? Where were her clothes?

She moved forward and something now enclosed her face; something thick and smothering, accompanied by a ghastly rattle. She cried out before realising it was just the dress hanging on the bed's curtain rail.

She undressed in the dark. The cold air washed over her

skin as she felt for the red silk. As she zipped it up, her warm body shrank from its slithery, freezing embrace. Hopefully she had it on the right way round. She padded over to where she thought the bag was and felt about for the matching shoes. She was not at all confident that she would find the right pair, or put them on the right feet if she did.

Her heart leapt as her fingers made contact with a small, cold, metal cylinder at the bottom of the bag. Vlad, who really did think of everything, had packed a torch!

As she switched it on, shadows jerked horribly about the room. She finished getting ready and left hurriedly, deciding to leave her hair to its own devices and not bother refreshing her make-up. Had Mimi not always urged her never to look her best, so that people would think how much better she would look if she really tried?

The dinner had started. Laura could hear it even before she had reached the end of the instruments-of-torture corridor. Once she got on to the main staircase the noise of shrieking and braying laughter echoed off the ancient stone walls. At the bottom of the stairs, grim-faced staff passed each other, carrying plates and bottles.

She paused on the bottom step and stared into the room.

It was an infernal sight. Candles blazed like a yellow fire, their light endlessly reflected not only in the glass front of what Laura recognised as the case containing Clovis Screming's leg – apparently serving as a table decoration – but also in the sweating, shining faces of the people at the table. There seemed to be hundreds of them, all red, roaring and shouting. The Turkey Toffs in full cry. Or full gobble, perhaps. Some were shoving in food so fast their cheeks bulged.

There was the bride. Lady Sophy's mouth was gaping open,

revealing crooked teeth. Her face was as red as her glass of claret – and possibly for that reason – and her glassy eyes were popping. She was evidently offloading some pre-wedding tension. And who could blame her, given how things were going, and how much worse they were possibly about to get.

Laura looked about for Irina and Sebastian, and felt for her phone. She had a job to do; two, now. Reporting the wedding and gathering evidence from what might very well become a crime scene.

Her fingers slipped into the chill silk insides of her clutch-bag for the slim metal bar of her phone. Subtly, she lifted it out and slowly raised the screen to face the gathering. *Click!*

'Haw haw!' Lady Sophy was roaring at some joke.

Click! Click!

Beside Sophy, Lady Clara Strumpett, the famous DJ, imperiously waved a bottle of champagne at a passing waiter. 'I say! This is impty!'

Click!

Elsewhere on the table, Laura spotted a disdainful-looking older woman with high cheekbones and a light tan. Was this the formidably social Lolita, Rupert's mother? Beside her, an old man with a deerstalker tipped over his weathered face had slumped forward, evidently asleep, and was dribbling on to an ancient green quilted gilet. The Earl of Screming, she guessed. He was snoring loudly, each intake of breath guttering the flames in the candelabra before him. No wonder Lolita Sturmdrang looked cross.

Click!

'Madam?'

Laura almost dropped her phone with shock. But the waiter who had glided up beside her seemed fresh-faced and perky compared to the other, rather sinister castle servants.

Perhaps he was a local schoolboy drafted in as extra help. She hoped so.

'Can I show you to your place?' the boy asked, in a contemporary version of the accent used by the crones in the church.

'Is it nearly over?' She nodded to the gathering, which was surely drunk and noisy enough to have been going on for hours.

'Wish it bloody was... Er, I mean, no madam.' The boy looked horrified at his lapse.

'Don't worry.' She grinned, sensing that here was another good source of background material. She rummaged in her clutch-bag and slipped him a fiver. 'What have I missed? Be honest.'

'The creamed blood soup. Old family recipe, apparently. Made me want to vom. You're in time for the mashed tripe though.'

'The *what*?' Laura's gorge was rising at the mere thought.

'Served with pickled scrotum. It's been buried in the garden since Lady Sophy was born. Waiting to get dug up for her wedding banquet. Family tradition.'

She didn't want to hear any more. She held her hand to her mouth as she was shown to her place. This was a practical precaution, given the thick smoke that hung like ectoplasm above a particularly riotous séance. Almost everyone had a cigarette, and some had one in each hand.

Someone looked up from the table as Laura was led past. Someone with red hair tumbling over exposed shoulders.

'Well, well, well,' sneered Clemency.

Laura's initial shock at the unwelcome presence of her oldest enemy gave way to a sense of resignation – didn't she always turn up, after all? And here, of course, was the answer to the 'bloody reporter' mystery. Sebastian must have meant Clemency.

Laura nodded pleasantly. 'Still working on the wedding story, are we?'

The green eyes glowed molten and malevolent in the candlelight. 'And making a better job of it than you, Laura Lake, Ace Reporter.'

Someone now spoke from across the table. 'She's a reporter as well?'

From below dark brows and white spiked hair, a pair of disconcertingly pale blue eyes drilled into Laura's. Her cover, such as it was, was blown.

Behind her, the waiter hovered. 'Red or white, madam?'

Laura remembered Ronaldo's hand-curated rosé at the NDY Club. She thought of her father. She would make this story work and expose the thieves. A feeling of strength suddenly filled her. She smiled up at the waiter. 'Both.'

Chapter Thirty

Laura awoke feeling as if she had been clubbed over the head. Pain pulsed from behind her eyes. When she moved, her brain hurt and nausea pressed in her throat.

At first, she had no idea where she was. The bed beneath her was hard. Which was odd, as she remembered it as lumpy. She put out a hand. No, it was hard, very hard, and covered in gritty dust. It was, in fact, the floor.

Had she fallen out of bed? She seemed to be lying between it and the window. On the other side, the far side, was the door.

Gingerly, she edged herself round to look. The mattress rose above her, red-draped, smooth – and empty. She hadn't even made it between the sheets. Perhaps she had stumbled round it, or overshot it. She lay where she must have fallen after returning from the dinner. God only knew how she had got up the spiral stairs.

She had stuck it out until the last bread roll had flown through the air and the last Turkey Toff had ripped his trousers doing a disco knee-slide down the table. Even when Clemency and Sebastian slid under the table, and orgasmic gasping had commenced, she had not moved. She would get every single scrap of colour for the piece she was going to write, and every piece of evidence for the theft she felt sure was in the offing. But Irina had not appeared at the dinner and Laura was now starting to wonder if she had imagined her in the castle after all. Or somehow mistaken her for Clemency. Perhaps, after all, nothing untoward was going to happen. Had Harry realised this, and was that why he had left? Hastily Laura felt for her bag – on the floor beside her, thank God – and checked her phone. He had not replied. Laura remembered the long, excitable message she had sent yesterday and felt the heat in her cheeks. No doubt she had sounded hysterical.

God, she felt bad. She groaned and rubbed her face, which felt as dry and gritty as sandpaper. She imagined that plenty of others must be waking up in much the same state. And today was the wedding; guests had to look bright-eyed and bushy-tailed, however appalling they felt. Of all wedding traditions, that was the most enduring.

Hopefully Sophy, who, as Laura left, had looked distinctly the worse for wear, standing on the ancestral table and belting out 'Jerusalem' while waving her napkin wildly, would be up to the job of riding in the ancestral carriage while sporting the ancestral tiara.

There had been much talk about the Creake tiara at the table. It was, Laura heard, absolutely priceless and made up of legendary stones including some from Richard the Lionheart's crown and Elizabeth I's ring. It also contained a huge rock called the Star of Bengal.

'Sounds like a not very good Indian restaurant,' Clemency cackled.

'Indeed,' acknowledged someone near them on the table, a 'family friend' in tartan trousers who seemed to know far more about the Creake family than could be good for anyone. 'But it was actually given by a besotted rajah to Sophy's great-great-grandmother.'

'How *wonderful* to have a rajah besotted with you,' exclaimed Clemency, who was drunk by this stage and making wild gestures, such as the one that now knocked the candelabra over and caused sheets of flame to shoot from several after-dinner brandies.

'Good shot!' exclaimed someone with smoking patches where his eyebrows had been.

Tartan trousers continued to an audience consisting of Laura, taking down every detail in her phone, and Sebastian Hunter, who sat smoking across the table, silent and still as a crouching jaguar.

'It was actually Sophy's great-great-grandfather he was besotted with. But he knew how to keep the old dear happy.'

Clemency slapped the table and hiccupped. 'Haw, haw, haw,' she barked, like a drunken seal.

Laura was looking forward to seeing the wonderful tiara sparkling with its huge diamonds. A bridal headpiece not made of rubber or plastic bags would be a welcome change. She rolled over on to her back, wincing at the hard wood against her shoulder blades and wondering what the time was. The room was thick with shadow and the bit of sky she could see through the window from where she lay was grey. Had dawn even broken yet?

The silence was so heavy, her heart thumped in her ears. Except that, Laura realised, it was not her heart. It was footsteps. Coming softly up the stairs. The wooden floor outside the door creaked. The door itself opened, with a strangled squeal.

Was it Harry? At last? Laura tried to raise herself, but felt too ill. She lowered herself down again. He would have to come and find her.

The incomer, whoever it was, had not entered the room. Laura sensed them standing in the doorway, looking round, and a hideous fear tightened her scalp. She suddenly knew, beyond all doubt, that this was not Harry. This was someone else altogether. Had the person who had come into her room yesterday come back? Or was it Clemency, now awake and aware that she had nothing on last night's events. Laura had not seen her make a single note, still less take a picture. She had obviously had her mind, and eventually her body, on something else altogether. Now, presumably, she wanted Laura's phone. The phone curled tightly in Laura's hand.

Should she confront her? No. For one thing, she couldn't have confronted a housefly in her present state, and for another, it wasn't beyond the bounds of possibility that Clemency was armed. She had form with dangerous weapons, Laura thought, as the fencing scar on her cheek throbbed warningly. And there were enough instruments of maiming and torture on the corridor walls to supply the Bloody Tower when, as it were, at full stretch.

Pressed into the floor, huddled against the bed, Laura held her breath, crossed her fingers and prayed that Clemency would not hear her heart booming with fear. Presently, she heard the door close and the footsteps go back down the stairs. She suspected she had had a lucky escape.

*

Some time later, Laura, resplendent in the pink Jackie O suit, walked to the church down Great Screming's main street, which a watery and fitful sun was doing its best to illuminate. She passed crowds of curious locals all waving paper flags with the Creake crest on them.

'Three daisies rampant on a field of gules,' Tartan Trousers had explained. Laura hadn't quite liked to ask what gules were. Possibly they had been served pickled for breakfast, alongside a pile of fried brains and braised lung.

Still, it was all good material, and here she was in St Jude's, ready to take notes on the most central event of all. 'Bride or grum?' the ushers at the entrance had asked her, and Laura had plumped for grum. Harry had been here for Rupert, after all. And perhaps he might yet turn up late, as people did at weddings in novels. What sort of a novel was this, Laura wondered. Mystery? Comedy? Crime? Farce? All four at once, it seemed to her.

Even standing on her tiptoes in the nude high heels Vlad had chosen, she could see very little over the fascinators in front of her. Just what was so fascinating about fascinators – inconsequential wisps of feathers in red and cerise pink? The men were bareheaded at least, their top hats on the pews beside them, but they were all so ridiculously tall that she couldn't see past them either. For some reason they were all wearing comedy waistcoats; Laura had spotted – and covertly shot on her smartphone – ducks, pizza, the Manhattan skyline, Smarties and baked beans.

The altar was not visible from where Laura stood, only the large cross suspended above it, to which a mild-looking Jesus in a beautifully ironed loincloth was nailed.

The organist was playing a voluntary which sounded like an ultra slow version of 'The Teddy Bears' Picnic'. As a new tune started, one of the fascinators in front nudged a balloon-patterned waistcoat. 'Listen! It's "The Wheels on the Bus"! Soph's favourite!'

The order of service had a white tassel on the fold and a photo of Sophy and Rupert on the front. Sophy's shoulders rose plumply from an unflattering green gown and Rupert looked hot – in the warm sense – in black tie. But they looked happy, Laura thought. Inside were the hymns and a touching little paragraph in which Sophy described how the couple had met 'on the singles table at a wedding. I knew Poop was the one when he told me his Ferrari had rolled into the river during the service. It was just the kind of thing that would happen to me, even though I don't actually drive. His handbrake failed.'

They might not be the brightest, Laura reflected, but they were evidently harmless. She remembered what Harry had said about Rupert and wished them all the best.

'The Wheels on the Bus' now gave way to something more baroque and ornamental, although it could easily have been the theme from *EastEnders*. Whatever it was, Rupert was coming down the aisle to it. He looked pale and tense, perhaps unsurprisingly given that he had last been seen on the floor of the Great Hall, rowing and bawling 'Four-and-Twenty Virgins'.

At his side was Sebastian Hunter, his strange blue eyes switching about the church, as if looking for something. As they landed on her, and lingered, Laura felt a strong repulsion. The groom and best man passed on.

The minutes dragged by. When would the ancestral carriage turn up? Laura could not wait to see the famous Creake tiara. Not to mention whatever Irina had done to the dress. If, indeed, it had been Irina she had seen.

The whispering in the pews had become a low murmuring which grew steadily louder and sounded concerned. Laura caught Sophy's name. There was a sharp exclamation from the front, where presumably the parents were, and a little scream.

Laura tapped the man next to her on his morning-suited arm. 'What's going on?'

Above the frosted swirls on his cupcake-patterned waistcoat, her neighbour looked agitated. 'They're saying shit's disappeared.'

Chapter Thirty-One

After milling about in the nave for a while, emitting exclamations and expletives most out of place in a house of prayer, the guests started to leave St Jude's. A hysterical Lolita Sturmdrang, clinging weeping to her husband, clattered past Laura in her Louboutins, a lifetime's careful manoeuvring wiped out in an instant.

As the guests streamed back to the castle, the locals stopped waving their flags and demanded to know 'if they hog roast be going ahead as planned'.

A clearly stunned Rupert was being led along between a fried-egg waistcoat and another covered in cocktail sausages. There was, Laura noted, no sign of Sebastian Hunter. She walked along behind a group of bridesmaids. They wore dresses with tight black rubber skirts and bodices like padded white straitjackets. Irina, clearly, was, after all, the designer in charge of rebooting the wedding dress. The straitjacket was presumably what remained of Picasso.

Lucy, one of the bridesmaids, could not explain the bride's disappearance. She had last seen Sophy making a final trip to the loo. She had never come back.

Laura, of course, could explain Sophy's disappearance all too well. Had she not been wearing a fabulous diamond tiara? And were not both Sebastian Hunter and Irina on the premises? As the last guest re-entered Creake Castle's ancient walls, a forbidding sound ensued. A hideous, clanking and grating echoed round the gun-hung hall. People looked at each other fearfully.

'What the hell's that?' someone shouted. 'Is it the monster?'

'Yes,' shouted someone else. 'He always pops in when a Creake bride disappears.'

Screams of horror greeted this. 'Actually, I've just made that up,' confessed the second someone, submitting to a series of angry thumps.

But the clanking and grating continued, even louder than before. People clutched each other. Lady Clara Strumpett collapsed in a dead faint.

'It's the drawbridge!' the man in tartan trousers shrieked excitedly. 'Of course it is! Creakes under threat always raise it. It last went up the night before the Brexit vote as a precaution against rampaging Remainers.'

Laura scurried back up to her room. Harry must be told about the latest developments with all speed. She raced along the murder-weapons corridor, catching her foot in a hole in the carpet as she went and knocking something ancient, black and iron out of an alcove. She picked it up, thinking she had seen objects like this in history books. Round, mask-like, with a heavy inward protrusion at tongue level. A scold's bridle? Surely not!

She replaced the hideous object and hurried on. All the doors were shut, including the one at the end where last night she had seen Irina. She slowed down and approached it cautiously. No sound seemed to be coming from behind it. She edged closer and put her ear to the door.

The wood against her face suddenly disappeared and Laura found herself tipping through space. The door had opened. Lying on the floor, her eyes met the pointed tip of a platformed black stiletto-heeled boot. She looked up. Irina looked down, the Pushamoff nostrils flaring so violently, Laura almost felt the ripple of wind.

Irina's thickly mascaraed eyes glittered almost as much as the object she held in her hands. Something large and round that danced with light even in the shadows of the passage. A tiara. A huge tiara. They had got it, after all.

Laura scrambled to her feet as best she could in the restricting skirt, but before she could say or do anything, something hard and heavy from behind now crashed down on her skull. She collapsed like a rag doll to the ground.

She came round in complete darkness. Her head ached, just as it had that morning, and at first she thought she was back in her room. But this feeling was no hangover and this place was, if anything, even darker, as if light had never entered it at all. The floor here was made not of wood but stone. Wet stone. Laura could feel the damp seeping up into her skirt. The air was clammy and cold. Like the air in a dungeon, Laura thought.

'It is the air in a dungeon,' said a clear female voice some distance away.

Laura realised she had spoken aloud. At the same time she became aware of something tight gripping her wrists.

She shook her arms; whatever was holding them clanked dully against the wall. Chains. Manacles. This was unbelievable. This couldn't be true.

'It is true,' said the female voice. 'They've done the same to me.'

'Who's me?' Laura asked, although she felt that she could guess.

'Well, strictly speaking, I'm Lady Sophia Hermintrude Annunziata Ethelfrid Gladys Creake. But you can call me Sophy.'

Their stories tallied miserably. Sophy had been coming out of the loo when something had hit her from behind. She had come round to find herself, as she put it, chained up in the deepest dungeon in the most ancient castle in the whole of Merrie England.

'Not very merry,' Laura remarked, wishing that she had followed her instincts and returned to Paris a few days ago. Curse Mimi and her cruising. A sob rose in her throat at the possibility that she might never see her grandmother again.

'Don't cry,' chided Sophy. 'You'll only set me off, and what good will that do us?'

Laura had to agree. 'My grandmother always says that crying is self-indulgent.'

'She's spot on. What else does your grandmother say?'

Laura considered. It seemed almost comical, given their situation, to discuss Mimi's miscellany of Parisian beauty secrets and life tips. But Sophy seemed fascinated.

Across the darkness, Laura called out what she could remember. The effort calmed her rioting mind.

'Nothing ages like glitter eyeshadow! Pale lipstick looks like a heart attack.'

'Good job you can't see my wedding make-up,' groaned Sophy.

Laura forced back the sob produced by thoughts of her grandmother's flat, Montmartre neighbourhood and cooking. The memories renewed her determination to survive. She would escape, she would see Mimi again. Even if, at the moment, she could not see how. She tried to imagine what her father would have done in her situation, but this was a severe scrape by anyone's reckoning.

Did anyone know they were here? Damn Harry Scott. It was all his fault. If she ever saw him again, Laura vowed darkly, she would... Well, what would she do? Nothing seemed quite bad enough. The least he could do was come and rescue her, but that looked unlikely. Sending messages was a tricky business when you were manacled to the wall. She was on her own and would have to make the best of it.

'Come on!' Sophy urged. 'More grandmotherly wisdom, please.'

Laura forced her thoughts along another line. 'Message T-shirts are out. And flip-flops, and leather suits.'

'But I like to wear all three together!'

Laura laughed. Sophy had an unexpectedly quick wit and an even more unexpected courage. She liked her very much; if they ever escaped from here, perhaps they could be friends. Correction, Laura told herself sternly. *When* they escaped. 'Go to bed with your jewellery on but your make-up off,' she instructed.

'Well, I won't be going to bed with my tiara on, that's for sure. Are you sure Irina and Sebastian Hunter took it?'

'Definitely.'

Sophy sighed. 'Poop's always been putty in that man's hands. I never wanted him anywhere near the wedding. Gives me the creeps. Still, he'll be miles away now. With the family heirloom.'

'Do you mind?' Laura asked. Sophy's tone was hard to read.

'God, no. He's welcome to it. It weighs a ton, looks hideous and gives you migraine. What I really care about is not seeing Poop.' She paused, and Laura heard the ragged sound of a sob. 'He's the only person I've ever met who's loved me for myself. He doesn't care about my title, the castle or anything.'

'You'll see him again,' Laura said robustly. 'And when you do, remember this. Never match your bag to your shoes!'

'Or get Irina Pushamoff to design your dress.' Sophy sighed. 'I did wonder about her when I saw her holding her scissors upside down.'

'They must have bribed your first designer to get it wrong,' Laura mused.

'Actually, the Picasso woman was the second designer. The first one was even more stupid. When I told her I wanted to look like a Sargent, she made a toile like a policewoman's uniform.'

Laura was still laughing as an almighty commotion suddenly split the darkness. A distant booming on what sounded like a very big, thick door. The air was filled with shouts, bangs, crashing and the tearing sound of splintering wood. Someone was coming in. Many people. Heavy boots crunched against stone. Chained to the wall, Laura felt her mirth go beyond the uncontrollable into the hysterical.

A familiar figure loomed in the searching beams of torches. Bright light bounced off a black leather jacket. 'What's so funny?' Harry asked

Laura narrowed her eyes. 'What took you so long?'

Chapter Thirty-Two

Six weeks later

I t was out! It was there! Laura paused by the shelf in the Heathrow WHSmith. The latest issue of *Society*, glossy cover shining in the striplights.

She grabbed it. She did not even look at the model, coy in her pearl-trimmed bustier and powder-blue furs. She had eyes only for the main headline, which dominated the cover in huge red capitals.

'HEIST AT THE HIPSTER WEDDING: Dicing with Death and Diamonds on the Trail of the Bridal Bling Ring, by Laura Lake'.

'The Bridal Bling Ring' was the name the press had given the jewel gang, once their identities had hit the headlines.

'Oi,' said the shop assistant waiting to help people navigate the self-service checkouts. 'You can't walk out without paying for it.'

Laura grinned and retraced her steps. Her hands were shaking too much to push the screen buttons, so the assistant did it for her.

Outside, she ripped the magazine open. Subscription offers and clothes catalogues fell out and spiralled across the pavement.

There it was, just as it had been on Carinthia's flat plan; just as it had been on the proofs.

Eight pages about her adventures with Amy Bender, Mary-Bliss Skinner and Lady Sophy Creake. Eight pages that no one but her could have written, even though Clemency had been present at some of it. Because only Laura had, in her phone, all the notes, anecdotes, quotes and photographs necessary to make what Carinthia, with tears in her eyes, had declared a feature almost as dramatic, shocking, funny, original, surprising and amazing as the seminal investigation that had kicked off her own career: 'Complete Blackballs: Behind the Scenes at Private Members' Clubs'. On the strength of 'Heist at the Hipster Wedding', Carinthia's nominations for Most Influential Publication of the Century were already in. She had submitted them herself.

Laura was skimming feverishly through the text, devouring every detail of the captions and pictures. But the best bit of all was yet to come.

She turned to the magazine's front, to the masthead, and her own name below that of Carinthia's. It replaced the recently sacked Clemency's: 'FEATURES EDITOR: Laura Lake'.

Features editor! Sitter upon the yellow sofa! Exonerated

of any suggestion that she had stolen from the fashion cupboard by the new directors of the department, Raisy and Daisy. While behind-the-scenes diplomatic efforts had eventually secured Hazza and Jazzy's freedom, neither had returned to their post. Hazza had developed Stockholm Syndrome and married a North Korean general, while Jazzy was now working with Nepalese artisans on a range of yak-skin wedding dresses, although her efforts to persuade *Society* to feature them had so far come to naught.

'FEATURES EDITOR: Laura Lake'. She could not take her eyes off it. The only sadness was that her father, who might have been proud, was not alive to see it, and her mother, who was, could not have cared less. Laura had not even bothered to tell her.

She had been too absorbed to notice the approach of the tousle-haired young man in the leather jacket, even though she could normally sense him from miles away and the mere sight of him made her shiver with delight.

'It's in then?' said Harry.

Laura nodded, her heart suddenly too full to speak.

Harry waved his copy of the *Standard*. There were four photographs on the front page. Sebastian Hunter, Clara Strumpett, Irina Pushamoff and Clemency Makepeace. 'HIPSTER HEIST BLING RING BANGED UP'.

Clemency had not been jailed, as it happened. Her involvement, the court had decided, was accidental. A case of wrong place, wrong time and certainly wrong man. While following the case, as she had done over the last few weeks, Laura had been shocked at how truly ghastly Lord Sebastian Hunter was. There seemed few areas of crime, exploitation and depravity into which his bitten blue-painted fingers had not poked.

The very least of it was that he had not been a lord.

His adoptive parents ran a caravan park near Ipswich and had not seen their son for years. 'Always had delusions of grandeur though,' his mother was quoted as saying.

Clara Strumpett actually was a lady, but what interested the court more was the fact that she was a fence. Her DJ-ing business was a front; she had kept stolen diamonds in her headphones and handed them over in the darkness as the music played. The press loved this. 'The Girl with the Golden Ears'.

It sounded like one of the films Caspar was shortly to star in. There was an article about him in the *Standard* too, Laura saw, turning the page. He was pictured in evening dress with Merlot D'Vyne, the model-socialite-actress who was playing his Bond Girl, climbing out of a gondola at the Venice Film Festival.

There was a familiar face in the gossip column too. 'South'n Comfort' was the somewhat predictable title to a piece about Lulu's upcoming marriage. South'n Fried had proposed by means of a cross-stitched sampler during a weekend at a crochet festival and Lulu had accepted with a string of bunting. The couple's crafting interests were now out in the open and, far from costing the rapper his fans, seemed to have made him even more popular and had had a widely beneficial effect. Hobbies had replaced homicide in some of the capital's most strife-torn areas and shootings had fallen dramatically – 'From Drive-By to Dip-Dye' as one headline put it. A beaming Lulu, pictured with her beau at the opening of London's latest nightspot, Gruntbox, was refusing to give details of her wedding dress. 'Is secret, hmm?'

But that Irina would not be making it was no secret. Head of a crime empire stretching halfway round the world, Irina Pushamoff had been on the Secret Service's radar for some time. But the Creake tiara had proved a bridge – or rather drawbridge – too far. Once that was up, Irina and her colleagues had been sitting ducks.

'It was a brilliant idea,' Laura had congratulated Harry, soon after the dust had settled.

He'd looked suitably abashed and modest. 'It was all I could do from where I was,' he explained. 'Rupert was very helpful when I called to explain it was the only way to get his wife back as well as her tiara.'

'But where were you?' Laura pressed. 'And why did you just go away and leave me to it?'

An expression of what could have been guilt fleetingly crossed Harry's face. 'I can't tell you the first, as the investigation's still ongoing, and what you don't know can't harm you. As for the second, I knew the jewel story was in good hands.'

'You mean you left me to work it all out?' Laura was unsure whether to be angry or flattered.

His eyes held hers in a look which seemed to combine approval with something else. 'And you did, didn't you? While keeping me very well briefed, I have to say. I always knew exactly where you were. Anyone would think you were a professional.'

Laura stared at the floor, a crimson tide of pride and embarrassment rising up her neck. 'You didn't know where we were when we were in the dungeon.'

'No, but Irina and Sebastian did. They were more than helpful.' Harry paused. 'After a little persuasion.'

This had sent Laura's thoughts flying to the flails and thumbscrews on the corridor walls. She did not enquire, however. She and Sophy had been rescued, which was what mattered.

As Harry had burst through the door, commandos at his back, Laura had never been as happy to see anyone in her life. She still felt that way now, which was something of an inconvenience as Harry was about to leave for New York, where he would be working on a story which, again, he refused to enlarge on. 'But if I need your help, I'll let you know. We make a good team.' He smiled, lifting a lock of her long brown hair with a gesture that was almost tender.

They did too, Laura thought, and in more ways than one. They had made a good team only last night on the floor-level mattress at Laura's recently acquired flat in east London, not far from the Victorian lavatory where her adventures had begun.

The apartment had made Harry laugh. It was above Gorblimey Trousers, a self-conscious pie-and-mash cafe run by a pair of gay ex-Google executives. Among Laura's neighbours were an old Etonian scyther and a life coach whose life seemed to be in permanent meltdown.

But Laura loved it. After living in a magazine fashion cupboard and what had felt at times like the inside of a designer shopping bag, a place of her own was sheer joy. It was tiny but all she needed.

It was bright and clean, the kitchen was well equipped and, as it was at the top of the building, she had a view over the City skyline, which reminded her a bit of Montmartre but more of New York, where Harry was going and where she hoped to visit as much as work allowed. And who knew: perhaps work might even send her there.

The prospect of separation was not alarming; on the contrary, distance, according to Mimi, was the key to a good relationship. They both had things to do, ambitions to fulfil, work to get on with, even if, in Harry's case, some of it was as clear as mud. But was a bit of mystery necessarily a bad thing? Laura did not have to ask Mimi for the answer to that.

Nor did she fear losing sight of him. They were going to far too many weddings together for that. First up was the rerun of Sophy and Rupert's at a register office in north London and with neither an ancestral carriage nor tiara in sight, as Sophy, with unmistakable satisfaction, had told Laura when asking her and Harry to be the sole witnesses.

Lulu too had stated her intention to have a fuss-free marriage. 'My dress will be simple, hmm?' she was quoted as saying in the diary story. Reading it at her features editor's desk, Laura had smiled, thinking of the enormous, elaborate wedding invitation recently hand-delivered by the ever imperturbable Vlad and currently occupying most of the mantelpiece of her new flat. It was to be a simple little event in the unfussy south of France lasting a simple three days and taking over an entire luxury hotel. Lulu was reverting to type.

Laura just hoped it would go without incident.

But she knew that was unlikely.

A letter from the publisher

We hope you enjoyed this book. We are an independent
publisher dedicated to discovering brilliant books,
new authors and great storytelling. Please join us at
www.headofzeus.com and become part of our
community of book-lovers.

We will keep you up to date with our latest books, author
blogs, special previews, tempting offers, chances to win
signed editions and much more.

If you have any questions, feedback or just want to say hi,
please drop us a line on hello@headofzeus.com

@HoZ_Books

HeadofZeusBooks

www.headofzeus.com

HEAD of ZEUS

The story starts here